MARS

HIGH SCHOOL

BOOK 1: THE OLYMPIANS

Daniel -- THANK YOU for all
you do for our Robinson Rams!
As the lead for the science dept, I
thought it well fitting to share
this little adventure, and the
homage for R. H. S. in its
pages. Wishing you well!

Keep Looking Up! J. Sandrock

J. SANDROCK

MARS HIGH SCHOOL BOOK 1: THE OLYMPIANS

Copyright © 2024 by Mariner Valley Publishing

ISBN 978-1-963019-01-8 (hardcover)   ISBN 978-1-963019-02-5 (paperback)
ISBN 978-1-963019-03-2 (Kindle e-book)   ISBN 978-1-963019-04-9 (audio book)

Cover Design & Artwork: *Alexa Eliza*, via 'fiverr.com'
Chapter Artwork and 'Seven Cities' Map: *J. Sandrock*

Sign up for the **Mars High School** series newsletter: www.marshighschool.com

To correspond by mail with the author: J. Sandrock
c/o Mariner Valley Publishing
P.O. Box 136
Sandy, UT 84091

MARS
HIGH SCHOOL

BOOK 1: THE OLYMPIANS

J. SANDROCK

MARINER VALLEY

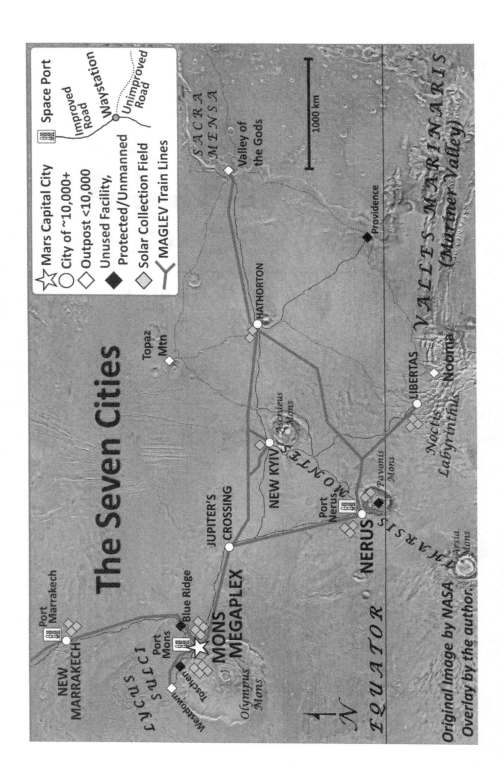

The Seven Cities

Legend:
- ☆ Mars Capital City
- ○ City of ~10,000+
- ◇ Outpost <10,000
- ◆ Unused Facility, Protected/Unmanned
- ◇ Solar Collection Field
- ⌥ MAGLEV Train Lines
- 🏢 Space Port
- — Improved Road
- ○ Waystation
- ⋯ Unimproved Road

Locations:

Port Marrakech · NEW MARRAKECH · LYCUS SULCI · Port Mons · Blue Ridge · Toschen · Westdown · Olympus Mons · MONS MEGAPLEX · JUPITER'S CROSSING · NEW KYIV · Ascraeus Mons · Port Nerus · Pavonis Mons · NERUS · Arsia Mons · THARSIS · MONTES · EQUATOR · Topaz Mtn · HATHORTON · SACRA MENSA · Valley of the Gods · Providence · LIBERTAS · Noctis Labyrinthus · Nooma · VALLIS MARINARIS (Mariner Valley)

1000 km

N

Original Image by NASA
Overlay by the author.

CONTENTS

to all Granger Lancers
past, present, and future,
this story is respectfully dedicated

Introduction

Regarding Mars

Whether you're an expert on Mars, or you're not . . . humor me, take in a few thoughts about the red planet before we begin our story.

Mars takes your breath away--literally. You take your air with you or you die; it's that simple. The surface atmosphere is nearly all carbon dioxide, CO_2, but there just isn't enough of all the other gases to make a real atmosphere. Mars has less than 1% of Earth's pressure (for comparison, the pressure atop Mount Everest hovers around one third, 33%, of Earth's sea level pressure; even the toughest Everest climbers risk their lives with every ascent — they carry O_2 canisters by the armload).

Mars will give you cancer, guaranteed, unless you take active steps to shield yourself from the sun's radiation and the cosmic rays pouring down from space. High radiation can rip DNA apart or cause mutations — cancer being the most common. Only time will tell how those gentler mutations in the first animals and plants on Mars lead to dramatic differences in later generations. The solution is simple: live underground. Magma tubes have already been identified on Mars by the dozen; collapsed 'skylights,' windows into these tubes, prove they exist. Logically, these tubes are likely to connect to empty magma chambers just like the ones we know exist on Earth, deep under volcanoes. Up on Mars' surface, lead-glass shielded domes may provide some protection, allowing greenhouses to work, but living underground is the easiest solution.

Mars gives you wings—its gravity is just 38% of Earth's. Someone who weighs 180 pounds on Earth would weigh less than 70 on Mars. If you can dunk a basketball on Earth (10.0-foot rim), you could manage a 25-foot dunker on Mars, easily. Walking looks more like bounding—you get used to it. I suggest being careful going through low doorways, or you'll have a nice bruise for your trouble. Yet don't be fooled, Mars gravity is still continuous acceleration. Don't try to Spider-Man your way off a 15-story Martian skyscraper and stick the hero landing—you'll be as dead as you would be on Earth. You'll just have some more time to think about it on the way down.

Mars boasts five of the ten tallest mountains in the Solar System. Olympus Mons, the tallest on all worlds, is about three Mount Everests stacked up—if Olympus Mons were here on Earth, its peak would be a quarter of the way up to the vacuum of space. The Mountain, as we will come to know Olympus Mons in our story, would cover more than half of France, or all of Poland, or the entire state of Arizona. It's just huge.

Mars has the largest valley we will ever explore as well—Valles Marineris is four times as deep as the United States' Grand Canyon, and six times as wide. This 'Mariner Valley' would stretch from New York to Los Angeles, or from Dublin, Ireland to the Egyptian pyramids. With slot canyons and side valleys too numerous to count, Mariner Valley and the Noctis Labyrinthus will be a playground for extreme sports, mile-high roller coasters, pressurized-tent camping, and motorcycle or side-by-side off roading. Please confirm your emergency locator beacons are working before you ride down into the Night Labyrinth.

Mars is a place where science sets the measurements—like it or not, distances will be in meters and kilometers—not feet, not miles. Sorry to those (like me) who still drive in miles per hour or humble brag about standing nearly six feet tall. One meter is doorknob height, just hold on to that. Someone two meters tall is ridiculously tall—those folks, I look up to. The ceiling above you is probably about three meters. A thousand of those meters, one kilometer, is just a bit more than half a mile. And before you give science too much pushback, grab yourself a 2-liter Diet Coke—adapting to the metric system isn't as hard as it seems.

Mars is a place of weather extremes—it may seem a cold, lifeless desert, but even the driest deserts have their intense events. Those living in Persia or the Middle East may occasionally hear a meteorologist predict an 80% chance of *dirt* in the forecast. So yes, Earth's dust storms are intense . . . but again, Mars smirks and says "hold my beverage." Dust storms on Mars can last a year—imagine going a year not seeing the sun.

On Mars, one standard year is 687 days, just under two Earth years. This means more months fill up that year, roughly 24 months of 28 days each. The seasons last longer as well (yes, Mars has four seasons too). Because Mars orbits in more of a stretched ellipse than Earth's near-circular orbit, Autumn lasts 142 days, and Spring lasts 194 days. Summer and Winter fall in between those extremes.

On Mars, your age is a different number. There, an eight-year-old can get a driver's license. A ten-year-old is grown up enough to legally drink adult beverages or vote in Martian city council elections. At eleven years old—you've graduated college, or you might have earned that first promotion. At thirteen, those nice auto insurance discounts for your rover kick in. That crusty old science teacher you loved (or hated) is probably twenty-five. Thirty-five is aged on Mars. Martians will count themselves lucky if they see their fiftieth birthday. Because of the strange calendar, Martians will also celebrate everyone's half-birthday, wishing each other, fittingly, 'Happy Berfday.' Every year, Martians will celebrate two Christmases (the first is Krampus), and two Halloweens (the first is spelled Samhain but is pronounced 'Sah-win'). And with all the other extra holidays they will have—it's a sweet deal. The five-day work week and two-day weekend are still a thing.

3

Mars is a place where one second is still one second, one minute is one minute, and one hour is one hour. Yet each day is . . . slightly stretched. Have you ever wished you could just have an extra half hour of sleep every night? Wish granted! One Martian day (a complete rotation on its axis) is 24 hours and 37 minutes. For the sake of continuity, our watches and computers will keep the same time, hour by hour, but with an extra 37-ish minutes added each night. This extra chunk of sleep comes automatically just after midnight, the same way our calendars include a Leap Day in February every four years. Since one day on Mars feels stretched, someone once suggested we call those extra 37 minutes each night 'the stretch.' It's not the worst idea.

Mars is not just a walk down to the local convenience store. At the planets' best orbital positions, it takes five months to cruise through space, coasting to Mars from Earth. Pack a good book for the flight, and please ensure your seat backs and tray-tables are up in their fully-locked position. Just kidding—you'll have your own small sleeping room for the trip.

If you doubt spaceflight will ever be as safe as flying aboard a passenger airliner or driving an SUV cross-country, consider this: the first airlines to carry passengers had many times more mishaps that we hear about today. That safety record improved over time, working through all the flaws and risks of launching into the wild blue yonder. Now the world's aircraft mishap rate is basically zero; between ten and twenty million people board their flights daily without a second thought. As the years go by, see for yourself—spaceflight will be even safer, and will get to that zero-mishap rate in a fraction of the time it took the airlines. Human error and other mishaps may pop up now and then, but your children will live in a time they are free to take a vacation to the moon and it's as commonplace as booking a trip on Expedia or Travelocity. Pack a sweater.

Mars will soon be humanity's second home, (third, if we build a moon base before getting to Mars). We will immediately start castle-building against Mars' harsh conditions; we will re-learn interior design and minimalist decorating will be all the rage. We will raise massive greenhouses to grow our food; we will tap into Mars groundwater to create our lakes, streams, and indoor forests. We will live inside huge caverns, and in the thousand years that follow, terraform the entire red planet — that's progress.

Heroes will rise, make their marks, and be in our flowing cups freshly remembered. Human nature will be our worst companion on the journey, yet we will strive. We will make it every bit the home we have now — maybe better.

So grab a Mars Bar, if you can find one, and let's roll.

J. Sandrock
May 2024

Chapter Twenty-Two

Curiously . . . Not an Earthquake

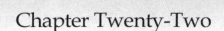

O ther students might have been fooled, but Andie wasn't. Not for one second. She brushed a few auburn-red flyaways and focused on the challenge.

The planet science teacher, one Mr. Steinheiser by name, repeated his claim. "There was never an ocean here on Mars, right? Just look out the window my friends — see for yourself, those dry desert plains below . . . the Lycus mountains. All dry. No rivers. Not one single lake. Our world has always been an empty, airless desert, and always will be. Am I right?"

He was pulling a classic bait-and-switch, which Andie had seen him do last semester in Astronomy 1. She watched intently, smoothed her favorite purple shirt, the one with black-white-yellow stripes down the sleeves. She looked around the room, but would not be the first to speak.

Stein, as students called him, squinted hazel eyes in the sunlight and waited for a response.

Across the room, Carlos spoke. "Yo, just because it isn't there now, doesn't mean the ocean was never there," he said, clearly pleased with his own brilliance.

Stein crossed the room toward him. "That's good logic. Do you have any facts to support that? Or give me an example of what you mean?"

Carlos shrugged. Again, a gap in the conversation. The silence bothered. "Anyone?"

Andie's elbow partner spoke up. "Mars used to have a lot more surface water than it does now—I mean, everybody knows that."

"Okay . . . but 'everybody' can be wildly mistaken. The people on Earth a thousand years ago were certain, absolutely certain, that all the planets, and the sun and their moon, revolved around the Earth—everybody knew they were standing still at the center of the Universe."

"Earth people are stupid," Carlos muttered. The boy next to Carlos high-fived him.

Andie furrowed her brow. A few other students looked at Carlos.

Stein ignored the jab and turned to the class. "My point is, we need evidence to go from 'everybody knows' to truly understanding reality. So, who has a solid example for me?" The teacher walked the room, looking around among two dozen faces. Again, long silence.

"The volcano," Andie blurted out. "That's an example." She gripped a speckled black granite sample tightly. "And Earthlings are brilliant—they built the original twin cities."

Carlos shot back. "Yeah, well, we built the other five."

Andie ignored him and looked up at Stein. He nodded to her. "Go on, Andie, you were making a point."

"Okay. This granite formed from the magma of Olympus Mons, like a billion years ago or something," Andie said. "So the volcano had to be active for this sample to even form. Being extinct now doesn't mean O-Mons never erupted. Same for oceans—just because the water has been displaced over time, doesn't mean they were never here."

"Nicely reasoned," Stein said. "So, the Mountain left us hints and clues to its past, just like with the absent rivers and oceans." He turned to address the rest of the class. "The planet speaks. We just need to listen." He paused, letting the idea sink in. "And can someone else tell me how Andie's mineral specimen became the smooth shape it is now?" He reached out, and Andie placed the egg-shaped rock in his hand. He stepped and held it up.

Carlos was still glaring. Andie looked past him and caught the eye of her best friend Aiyana, who was staring daggers at Carlos. Aiyana smiled at Andie, giving her an air fist-bump from across the room. Andie smiled back.

Stein persisted. "So? Who can tell me how a rock becomes well-rounded?"

Raven-haired Sitara, her lineage from northern India, spoke up from the back row, center. "Oooo. I know, it used to be more . . . rougher, with angled edges, but it got eroded, is that correct?" She pulled her long braid over one shoulder and held up her own specimen, a smooth, black basalt.

"Very good, Sitara. Erosion is the answer. Now, how was your sample, or Andie's sample, eroded? What did the actual eroding?"

Sitara leaned forward, reading from the class notes on her screen. "Stream action, rivers, with sediment in the water, takes angular rocks and makes them well-rounded."

Stein nodded. "Yes. Like taking this class—you become well-rounded."

Aiyana looked away from Carlos and asked Stein, "so we're sure there used to be rivers on Mars? Like, up here on the surface?"

He nodded. "The proof is irrefutable—not only were there rivers, but many of them flowed into a vast sea covering the whole northern hemisphere. In fact, whenever we finish melting the polar ice caps, there will be enough to cover Mars in a dozen meters of water."

He crossed the room to the door and held his hand at doorknob height for emphasis.

"See that? That's one meter. Imagine, twelve of these, way up past the top of Mr. Kranich's class above us. If our school was down on the plains when all the ice melts, we'd all be deep underwater."

"Good thing we're way up here on a mountain ledge, then," Aiyana added.

"True," Stein smiled.

"So what about the rain? And clouds? Were those real?" Andie asked him.

"As we all know, here in the city, rainfall is a once-in-a-lifetime event if you're very lucky. But I assure you, the surface of our world once had weather patterns like cold fronts, warm fronts, even thunderstorms."

Sitara spoke up again. "Have you ever felt the rain, Mister Stein?"

"No . . . though I came really close when I was a junior in high school. I must have been . . . seven years old? Seven and a half, maybe? I barely missed it—that was around Samhain holiday I think." He shook off the memory and refocused. "Anyway, twenty minutes until the bell. Quickly, let's review, what did you get out of today?"

From over by the windows, another student spoke up.

"Gneiss rocks have stripes," Andie's elbow partner said, one elbow propped up on the windowsill. She held a beautiful black and white, tiger-striped rock in her other hand, similar in shape to Andie's sample.

"Good pronunciation. Yes. But even Ares could tell you they have stripes," the teacher nodded at the orange tabby snoozing in the back. Several students glanced at the cat, who went on snoozing in his little bed at the teacher's desk.

"Give me more gneiss detail. What kind of rock is it, and why is it striped?" the teacher prompted.

"Um . . . I don't know, it's the way they formed?" the girl struggled.

From just behind Andie, a boy named Marcus came to the rescue.

"Uh . . . they are metamorphic, and . . . minerals separate under a lot of pressure." Marcus said, voice low.

Andie casually glanced over her shoulder, catching Marcus' eye. In the afternoon sun, Andie's red hair glowed like fire and accentuated her pale-with-freckles look. Marcus looked at her and his cheeks flushed. The teacher addressed Marcus.

"Yes." Stein said. "Tremendous pressure. The kind of pressure that . . ."

Stein stopped, gripping the nearest student station.

Ares the tabby cat opened his eyes wide and stood up quickly on all fours. The cat hissed, crouching down on his haunches, looking wildly around.

"What is that?" a student near the door asked. While the rest of the class looked down or at each other's faces, Andie looked up at a hanging ceiling display of the Solar System. The planets were swinging slightly. The window shades rattled in their fittings, barely audible. A low hum lasted just a few seconds, then stopped.

The planet models swung gently for a few more seconds, then stopped as well.

Stein let go his grip on the desk and looked out the windows. "A tremor. But it feels like it's over now. Friends, be ready to dive under your stations in case we get any more."

Students looked around. Andie turned to look at Ares, who was now also staring up at the planets hanging there, then the cat made eye contact with Andie. Stein walked to the door, checking the door's status display.

"Mister Stein, are we all right?" Aiyana asked.

"I . . . think so? The door didn't seal itself, so the tremor must have been . . . mild. Who felt it? I mean physically felt the shaking, please put up a hand."

Half the students raised their hands. Stein scanned the room, counting. "So, pretty mild — maybe Mercalli level two," he concluded. "Okay, let's do something, let's gather data — I want all of you to grab your tablets, ping a family member not here at school, and ask if they felt anything. Ready go."

Stein grabbed his own tablet and saw he had a ping already waiting for him. He tapped it and read the attached message as students tapped out quick messages of their own.

Ares the tabby cat settled into a laying-down posture, eyes still wide. After sending her own note to her father, Andie looked back up at Ares again. The cat's tail twitched.

A few minutes ticked by. The first responses started coming in as Stein spoke. "Friends, will you please swipe a simple 'yes' or 'no' up to the main screen? Also, if your family member is in a building 5 stories tall or taller, please underline your response."

Within another moment, fifteen responses filled the big screen, slowly orbiting in a word cloud. Then the replies were eighteen, then twenty. Nine out of the twenty replies showed 'yes,' with seven of the 'yes' replies coming from tall buildings in the city.

"Okay, so definitely a city-wide tremor. See how the higher you are in a building, the more likely you are to feel even a little tremble? That's good data . . . but, now we're short on time." He glanced up at the clock, which showed 3:07. "Thank you all for your help in our data-gathering. Okay, three minutes left and you're off to your weekend," the teacher said. "Reminds me, I haven't assigned your homework yet."

Groans from around the room, but several eyed the teacher intently.

From the front row, center, a taller student nudged his buddy. "Stein never gives real homework on a weekend — watch."

From the front corner, Stein said, "your homework, and I want every one of you to do this . . . find and bring with you Monday a mineral sample, a rock, that you found somewhere."

"Just bring a rock?" Carlos asked.

"Exactly. But please don't bring mother's jewelry, or something from Earth. Collect your sample out in our Mons-Plex city cavern, out in nature. Could be from one of the forests, or the mountaintop greenhouses, up at the Overlook . . . wherever. Just a sample you collect. We'll look at them

Monday to hypothesize what they are and how they formed. And yes, it's graded."

A few more groans.

"You've got this." The teacher asserted. "Friends, nearly all of us have lived our entire lives here in this city; I'm certain you've picked up a rock at some point. It's not like I'm asking you to go to Earth and back." He smiled. "Any questions?"

Of course, there were none. It remained a major foul to ask a question if the bell was about to ring.

Stein strode to the door, ready to open it. A few students made quick notes in their tablets then stowed them away. Silence . . . and finally, the ending bell. The students stood as a group and started shuffling toward the door.

"Remember who you are, guys. You're Olympians. See you all Monday." The teacher smiled. "And remember, Spirit Week is coming up! Nerus High School, and all the rest will be here."

Aiyana crossed the room against the flow of students, toward where the cat relaxed. Both girls paused next to Stein's desk. Ares had closed his eyes.

"Ready?" Aiyana asked.

"Yeah, Aiya, almost," Andie trailed off. "Just need to say goodbye to my fellow ginger here."

Andie stroked Ares behind the ears, and he murmured his little cat 'mrrrw?' in appreciation of her scratches.

Andie set down her backpack and let Ares have a solid back rub, all up and down his back with both hands. The cat stretched out both front paws and pushed back appreciatively.

"We're having tilapia tonight, Ares," Andie said. "Wish I could give you some."

The cat looked up at Andie and made an intense amount of eye contact.

Andie paused and looked at the cat.

"What? I'm serious. My dad's tilapia is amazing." Andie said. The cat licked his lips once and rubbed his cheek against Andie's arm. She resumed scratches.

"You're obsessed with this cat," Aiyana muttered, flipping her tight black curls back over her shoulder.

"Well, he is amazing," Andie said simply.

Aiyana adjusted her Tartarus concert tee-shirt over her athletic, curvy frame and picked up her bag. She smiled at the cat, white teeth contrasting nicely with her darker skin.

From nearby, Marcus tapped his glasses into place and fiddled with his backpack. "Bye, Mr. Steinheiser," he said as he walked. Near the door, Marcus glanced back at Andie, making eye contact, and almost walked into the door frame.

"See ya bud." Stein said as they boy left. He returned to his teacher's desk, and passed by the girls to take his seat. He squinted up at the sunlight and dimmed the windows.

Ares looked back at Stein with a 'what gives?' expression, as the light dimmed. Stein didn't see the cat's look as he focused on a new 'ping' from his tablet.

One other student, Reillee, who had stayed quiet the entire class, hummed a tune as he stowed his tablet it in its special pocket. He stood and faced Andie and Aiyana. "You guys wanna meet up in ACSA later?"

"Can't, I have chores," Aiyana said.

"On a Friday night?" Reillee asked, eyebrows raised.

"Yes. My folks . . . well, they're . . ."

"Never satisfied." Andie finished for Aiyana, who nodded.

"That's putting it nicely," Aiyana said, shaking her head.

Andie spoke up. "I'll join you at Sugar House in a while; what about Sitara?" she said, absently scratching Ares behind the ears.

"I think she went off to find Ric; I bet they'll be there too," Reillee said, shouldering his pack and waving a little goodbye.

"Sounds great," Andie said with a grin, watching him go. Reillee crossed the room, humming his little tune, and vanished through the doorway.

"Come on, let's go," Aiyana said.

"Yeah, okay." Andie shook off whatever she was thinking. "Make us proud, you little punk," Andie said to the cat, adding, "lead the Rat Force on to victory." She smoothed the fur down his back.

"Bye Mister Stein," Andie said, turning to leave.

"You ladies have an excellent weekend." Stein smiled, then looked back down at his screen, focusing hard and tapping away as if on some desperate mission. Aiyana said nothing, giving Stein a little wave as she turned to go.

The girls shouldered their bags. Backpacks were still common, though textbooks had never been used here on Mars. Even now, the year 2354 by Earth's counting, packs were still useful in other ways. Behind Stein's seat, a retro-style satchel hung on a peg next to his faded denim jacket and an authentic fedora hat, shipped all the way from Earth.

As the girls walked away, Ares watched them go until they disappeared around the corner. Heading down the science hallway toward the commons, the girls passed under a bright sky-blue ceiling and animated green projections on the walls—to Andie, it felt arboreal, tropical, from some faraway island on Earth maybe. "I swear, I can almost hear the surf," she said.

They walked past Mrs. Farnsworth's biology and Mr. MacIntosh's botany, and a dozen steps later, Dr. Kumar's college-level AP chemistry. Andie spoke up. "Hey, did you catch the latest photos from Prox-B?"

"Who hasn't? It's all over my feeds, pretty max."

"Right? I mean, continents and oceans? Cray-zee."

"Wish I could be where there are continents and oceans," Aiyana said.

"But no advanced intelligence," Andie said, regret in her voice.

"How can they be so sure?"

"Darkness on the night side, apart from a few volcanoes," Andie replied, as if it was obvious. "Civilization means lights at night. Still, they can colonize."

They walked into the Hub, a round common area thirty meters across, with five branching hallways like spokes on some great academic wheel. Each hall glowed with its own sign — Languages, Sciences, Maths, Arts & Trades, and Electives. They walked on, passing the Black Box, perpetually filled with tomorrow's great thespians. A few steps later, they looked in the doorway of the student union, 'S.U.' as it was called, where students hung out, often. Seeing very few chairs or couches occupied, they walked away toward the school exit.

The last areas they passed included the cafeteria, a long side hall leading to the school sports arenas and courts, applied science labs, and the main office. Andie scanned through the science lab windows to see if anyone was inside. Aiyana gave the labs no notice, focusing ahead on the exit.

Six pressure safety doors, each as wide as a person, resembled faucets gushing students and faculty out into the tunnel beyond. Here, the walls and ceilings were all dark stone and cement pillars — breathtakingly utilitarian. Occasionally, fresh urban art appeared on the walls and was just as quickly removed. Social media kept up with the artists' work just as fast as the administrators scrubbed it off.

The girls soon found themselves in a crowd near the 'Mons High School' light-rail train station. A shiny, silver three-car tram hummed on its rails, ready to depart. Its red tail-lamps glowed and bright yellow words "Mons-Plex City Express" scrolled across the displays. The tram was filled with hundreds of students heading to the city.

"Train or scooters?" Aiyana prompted.

"Could we go through ACSA on the way home?" Andie asked.

"Scooters it is." Aiyana replied, and the two walked toward the charging stations against the tunnel wall.

Here, hundreds of scooters stood in mute chrome anticipation. Dozens of other students and a few teachers were in the act of grabbing their scooters for a fun ride down the tunnel into the heart of the Mountain.

No one really called their home, Olympus Mons, a volcano. 'The Mountain' had more . . . click to it, and the name had stuck. To the million people living here, even the tallest volcano in the entire solar system, three times the height of Mount Everest, was still . . . just a mountain.

The silver tram rang its departure chime. The doors sealed and the train pulled slowly away from the school's station, even as another arrived on a parallel track.

The girls grabbed their scooters at random and got ready to mount up. Here, like everywhere across the city, bright green grass, plants, and waist-high shrubs grew in manicured gardens. Shelves of living green stepped up the tunnel walls — they had been strategically placed everywhere.

With one foot on her scooter, Andie reached out to a Boston Fern frond at chest level, fingertips supporting the buds gently. "I love the green," she said, flipping the scooter's power on and walking it around a meter-tall Weeping Fig.

"Green keeps the dream alive," Aiyana agreed, switching her own power on.

"You sound like a MERF commercial," Andie said.

The three red taillights of the tram were far ahead, silently slipping away down the long, bright tunnel.

"Shall we try and catch it?" Andie asked.

As her answer, Aiyana pushed off with her standing foot while twisting the right handgrip, the throttle. She shot away, curly black hair catching the wind. Andie followed, close behind. The scooters practically steered themselves into the proper lanes, and the slight breeze tousled their hair as they were whisked onward. Aiyana called out a *whoop!* and a couple holding hands stepped out of the way as the two shot past.

A balding man walking a small, fuzzy dog jumped aside and reeled in his companion.

"Hooligans," the man shouted after them. Both teens grinned fiendishly, zipping away from the man who had foolishly walked his dog into active scooter lanes.

They nearly caught up to the back end of the train when they reached the place where two wide tunnels crossed each other. A digital, scrolling display in bright letters flashed:

ACSA CROSSROADS
ATHLETIC CENTERS & SOCIAL ARBORETUM >>>
<<< HORIZON VIEW SALON 300M

Leaning into a right turn, and twisting the throttle tighter, the two careened down the right-side tunnel. Just ahead was ACSA, by far the most popular teenage and college hangout zone, in its own huge side cavern. The tram, however, continued straight on ahead toward the heart of the Mons-MegaPlex city. Along with its load of passengers, it vanished from view.

As she finished the tight turn, Aiyana nearly clipped her handlebars on the corner of a SAFE survival pod but managed to swerve around it at the last instant. The handlebars wobbled slightly, but the scooter auto-corrected before it could become a death-wobble wipeout.

SAFE pods, the dive bunkers used for practice in case of natural disasters, seemed to be everywhere—no matter where someone stood in ACSA or in the city itself, a SAFE pod was always nearby.

Moments later, the girls shot out of the tunnel and into the ACSA cavern itself. As living spaces go, ACSA was not the largest, but it was tremendous, nonetheless. Scooter lanes branched left, right, or continued straight. Aiyana and Andie steered neatly down the right-side path, past a sign labeled "East Woods," the third largest forest on Mars.

Aiyana let Andie take the lead, and they slowed to enjoy the forest, with its several thousand trees. The path weaved left and right, occasionally crossing small bridges over running streams, with a few dozen campsites and picnic areas sprinkled along the path. Andie grinned as she looked all around, enjoying the fresh air and pine aroma in the air. The thick tall trees cast a gloom on the forest floor, blocking out much of the bright artificial light that covered the cavern ceiling above. Birds chittered from high branches and chipmunks scurried up their trees at the approach of scooters and the occasional hikers.

After another ten minutes of weaving along the forest path, they left the tree line and rode the path around the back of the Mountain's sole indoor futbol arena and then, past one of three smaller bullseye-handball arenas.

Leaving the big athletic venues behind, they rode into the Teehan Recreation Zone with its many attractions and restaurants. Having left nature behind, the girls now coasted slowly among nightclubs, arcades, and a variety of fast-food spots.

Andie halted outside the classic Golf N' Stuff attraction, and Aiyana rolled up next to her. "Do you have time for centrifuge bowling?" Andie asked. "Just one game? I'm trying to beat 150."

"I… maybe, but I felt my tablet buzz a minute ago. . ." Aiyana replied, checking her tablet. "Yep, it's my folks asking when I'll get started on cleaning the kitchen and living room. I'll have to whoop up on you some other time." She managed a little smile.

Andie set the kickstand down and stepped over to give Aiyana a huge hug. "You always were a better bowler. I'll ping you later. Love ya chica."

"Love ya back." Aiyana let the hug go and took a breath before whisking herself away. Andie watched her go. Aiyana rode on through

ACSA toward a different tunnel—the back door to the city, so to speak. Her chosen path, the West Access Tunnel, was a much smaller tunnel than the others but it also connected to the city itself.

Glancing back up at the flashing, rotating Golf N'Stuff billboard, Andie imagined all the attractions the builders had copied from its twin back in Norwalk, California, U.S.A., Earth, with a high-ceiling trampoline park, putt-putt golf, arcade games, laser tag, and of course, the latest (and greatest) centrifuge bowling alley.

Groups of students zipped past Andie, in twos and threes, on to whatever fun they felt like chasing. Andie hugged her arms around her own shoulders and sighed deeply. She put up the scooter's kick-stand; maybe she'd ride a bit longer, through the West Woods before meeting up with Reillee and the others at Sugar House Coffee. Maybe Ric would be there—maybe he had felt the tremors too.

Shaking off her thoughts, she turned her scooter back toward the trees and the west half of the 6-km forest path. Andie twisted the right handgrip gently, starting off slowly then reaching a fast-walking speed. Passing the first cluster of trees, she saw the pathway was nearly empty of people. She coasted past a smaller SAFE pod and found herself cruising through a thick cluster, a copse of mature pines.

Her handlebars shuddered. Andie looked down, confused. The computer tried to compensate but the shuddering grew more intense. Andie tried to bring her ride to a quick stop, squeezing the brake lever but the nose wheel jackknifed, and she tumbled over the handlebars to the ground. Instinctively, she threw her hands out in front of her, and skinned both palms on the rough pavement. Her hands stung. . . and tingled at the same time. She could feel the ground . . . vibrating.

Something crashed onto the pavement just a few meters away and shattered into smaller chunks. A rock. A rock? Andie stared at where it had fallen. Then another dropped further away, shattering on impact like the first. A low hum filled the forest, barely audible. The branches of the pine trees all around trembled, and the ground shook. She looked up. This was no small tremor. This was a full-on Marsquake.

Chapter Twenty-One

Enough Adventure for One Day

Another rock, small as her fist, struck the scooter's digital display and cracked the plexiglass. The scooter's screen, which showed speed (0 kph), battery status (90%) and the time (3:42 p.m.) flickered and went dark. The tingling sensation in the ground against her hands and knees grew stronger. She looked down, then up again, quickly scrambling to her feet.

The ground still trembled, feeling more intense.

Andie stumbled forward a step, almost tripped, and caught better footing with the next step. She spread her arms wide for balance and took another step. The hum grew to a steady rumble.

The trees made a strange hissing sound and shed dust from their branches, starting near the tops. She looked up at the rock cavern ceiling, casting her gaze wildly around to watch for falling rock.

Though she had stumbled, confused at first, the city's seismic sensors had no doubt in their electronic minds something big had just occurred.

Bllaaaaaaaaoom. Decompression alarms blasted a warbling tone from all directions, in a deafening cacophony. Every tunnel and corridor across every cavern sounded the same alarm. The shaking intensified. Andie was knocked off her feet again, this time bruising her right knee badly. She shakily tried to stand. The alarm continued to warble on. More rocks crashed down around her, making her flinch.

* * *

Three kilometers away, in the heart of the Mons-Plex city business district, the 15-story Mars Emergent Response Force headquarters—MERF HQ—towered over all the other skyscrapers. In a corner office with a commanding view, the MERF Deputy Director stood with his back to the view while he updated the big boss. Bruce Jackson, a tall, rounding man with a receding hairline, spoke clearly in a friendly western drawl as he prepared to leave his office. The display on his desk showed 3:36 p.m.

"Mister Director, all the members of the Mons-Plex city council will tune in for our SITREP in 15 minutes' time. Those minor tremors we felt prompted the Grand Council leaders of Nerus, New Marrakech, and even Dr. Holm of Nooma Outpost to join the conference call as observers." He paused to listen. "Yes sir, and Dr. Holm can weigh in if they need a top geologist's perspective on these tremors."

He nodded as he listened on the line, while simultaneously pulling on his suit jacket. He murmured "Mmm hmm," while slipping his tablet inside a laptop shoulder bag. He picked up a folder containing the latest city status updates.

"Yes sir, and while the tremors appear to be subsiding, they haven't ceased yet. Therein lies our concern." As he listened, he put his desk terminal to sleep. "Absolutely. I'll be down to the EOC in five minutes, and we can run that call. Jackson out."

The first tremors, half an hour ago, had set everyone in MERF HQ on alert. The Director, a thin, aged man named Victor Dunne, was already down in the Emergency Operations Center, nicknamed EOC, which was a heavily secured bunker three stories underground.

Shouldering his bag, he gave the city view barely a glance as he crossed the room, exited, and pulled his office doors closed behind him. He paused briefly at the secretary's station, where his gray-haired, stern office assistant Claire kept the place in tip-top shape. He thanked her for all she had done, she wished him a fine weekend though he was leaving earlier than normal, to head down to the command center. Her display showed 3:41 p.m.

He crossed the lobby and was reaching for the executive suite's glass double doors when a red light lit up and the doors sealed themselves shut.

He tugged the locked doors, rattling them in their fittings, but they would not budge. He was on the verge of reaching for the hand-ident pad on the wall when the furniture started rattling for the second time this afternoon. He felt the tremors in his feet first, and Claire gripped the raised counter in front of her. The waiting area's comfy chairs rattled even louder on the smooth simulated marble, and the sound quickly became deafening. Claire stood, still gripping the counter, her face fearful. She glanced over at the Director's side of the shared space, where the other executive assistant, a man named Grayson, had slipped out of his wheeled chair and was trying to stand. Then Claire screamed as the building rocked sideways.

Amplified as the shockwaves were up on the fifteenth floor, the building swayed, nay, lurched. More screams erupted up and down the hallway, from men and women alike. Desks, bookshelves of carefully curated memorabilia, and even the comfortable seats in the waiting area shifted two meters sideways across the floor, then back, in the opposite direction even further. Furniture pieces thumped up against the walls, loudly spilling their contents. Occasionally came the sound of glass shattering, though the windows held. A loud crash resounded from down the hall, followed by a thump and a yelp of pain. More shouts of surprise, and a few obscenities.

A chair slid across to Jackson, who still gripped the door handles, and thudded into his legs. He doubled over, gripping the doors for dear life. He looked up at swaying lamps and swinging pictures, then saw some fall off the walls. His satchel slipped from his shoulder, and he watched his papers and tablet spill across the floor, right before being run over by another comfy chair sliding in the opposite direction.

He lost his grip on the door handles and fell, hard. Claire had disappeared behind her desk, gripping one of the desk's legs from underneath while the building flopped back and forth.

* * *

In ACSA's West Woods, Andie could see people among the trees, wobbling about comically — stumbling, clinging to each other, sometimes falling. Most shambled away in other directions. A couple stood close by, casting around frantically, the panic plain on their faces. Rocks crashed around at a regular rate, adding new impact tremors to the ground.

Andie remembered the SAFE pod a few dozen paces back. She looked at the couple, still frozen in place. "Over here! There's a safe pod this way," she shouted, then waved a hand in a beckoning gesture. That's when she noticed the blood trickling down her palms.

"Ugh," Andie said, wiping her hands on her black trousers. "Come on," she yelled at the couple. They started to stagger toward her. She turned and headed for the pod herself, leaving the scooter toppled on the side of the path.

From ahead, a pleasant, beckoning tone bumm-bu-bumm-bu-bumm-bu-bumm came through the trees — that would be the pod. She could also see a bright green light through some tree branches. There it was, just twenty meters away.

More bits of rock crashed nearby, one cleanly snapping a branch off a tree behind her. The deafening klaxon continued from every direction.

Finally, as Andie came within direct sight of the pod, the shaking slowed and stopped. A crumbling, and occasionally a crashing sound, echoed around the cavern. She reached the door of the pod, which stood wide open in a fine, welcoming way. The green light glowed, and the two-beat beckoning sound continued, just audible beneath the klaxon alarm. After a few more seconds, the alarm went quiet. The echo reverberated around the ACSA cavern.

Andie ducked down into the pod's doorway. The pod's door began to slowly close on its own. Eyes wide, Andie shouted "No!" and stepped into the path of the closing door. It paused, then opened back up to full-open.

"Obstruction detected," a gentle female computer voice said. "Please remove obstruction so the door can close," it asked politely.

"You can kiss my skinny white…" then Andie saw the couple hobbling frantically toward her. They rounded some trees and staggered closer.

"Come on, you've got this. Over here!" Andie shouted. As they neared the pod, Andie could see the man was holding a hand up to his forehead above one eye, blood running down his face and into his shirt. His lady companion supported him and guided him. As he staggered drunkenly, she helped steer him.

"Please remove obstruction so the door can close," the pod politely asked again.

Andie politely ignored it.

At long last, the couple reached the doorway, and Andie stood aside for them to step into the bunker. One last low, rumbling echo reverberated through the ACSA cavern with weird acoustics, like a ball bouncing down a drain.

Andie popped her head out one last time, casting a wild glance in every direction, then stepped down inside the pod to let the door close. It sealed itself with a 'ptchsss' hissing sound. A comforting tone and soft green light signaled they were safe and sound, for the moment.

"Aargh," the man grunted as he sat heavily on one of the low concrete benches, still clutching his forehead, still bleeding. His lady companion sat down next to him, tearing away a piece of her shirt. "Thanks for holding the door," the woman said to Andie with a nod, still breathing heavily. Andie nodded back and let out a breath she hadn't realized she was holding.

"Can I help?" Andie asked.

The lady pressed the cloth to the injury and spoke without looking up at Andie. "I'm Nurse Soliel, from the Haven, but I'll let you know if we need help. Good, it looks like it missed your eye, babe," then she glanced Andie's way. "Do you have water by chance?"

"Umm, yes, I do." Andie pulled a half-full water bottle from the side pouch of her pack. The nurse accepted it gratefully. She continued talking to him intermittently as she cleaned his wound and kept pressure. He murmured something up at her in soft tones.

Andie slid down the bench a bit to give them space. Aiya! Andie thought suddenly, grabbing her tablet out of her pack. She hit the power button, tapping the screen repeatedly, as if that might make it wake up faster.

The display came up, but there was no signal—zero rings of signal strength in the upper corner.

Then a voice sounded through the cavern and inside the pod's speakers.

"Attention in the area, attention in the area. Mons-Plex is experiencing a major seismic event. This is not a drill. Remain in your SAFE pod or vehicle until given the all-clear. I say again, Mons-Plex has experienced a major seismic event. Remain in your SAFE pod or vehicle until further notice. MERF, out."

* * *

Jackson stood behind the all-call announcer, a man named Shelton, as he finished the twin announcements. He gave Shelton a confirming shoulder pat and walked away. He walked among the rows of emergency stations in the EOC, all arranged in concentric semi-circles in facing a dozen large screens. All the major divisions in MERF were here: Fire, Medical, Police, Atmospherics, Agricultural, Hydro, Planetary Shuttles, Public Affairs, Meteorology, Logistics, Geology, and the smallest, least-used branch, the military. Jackson glanced at each screen as he passed its station, occasionally telling its rep to swipe their status up to one of the huge flatscreens on the front wall.

They needed answers: how much damage? How numerous were the injuries and how severe? What magnitude was the quake? And the most pressing of all—was the worst over with, or was it yet to come?

* * *

After the announcement, it was quiet in the SAFE pod. Andie willed her lungs to slow to a normal rhythm, drawing in a deep breath through her nose, and exhaling slowly out her mouth. The tablet finally found a connection and Andie pinged Aiyana, at the same time Aiyana's ping came in. Andie pressed the 'open channel' option. Faces filled screens. They smiled in unison.

"Holy Moe, Aiya, are you all right?" Andie blurted out.

"I'm good, but I'm—I'm stuck in a pod, inside west tunnel." She spoke quickly, nervously.

Andie could see Aiyana's eyes were wide, looking around frantically. She wore a look that bordered on panic. "Oh, that's..."

"I can't deal with these tight spaces," Aiyana finished for her.

"Oooh, I know . . . but, but think how safe you really are. Um, remember in Chuumock's class, the structures unit? A perfectly circular tunnel bore is the strongest against cave-ins, so there's no worries there." Andie said.

"Uh huh," Aiyana murmured, eyes flickering from Andie to something off-screen and back.

Andie kept talking. "And you know that no one has died in a decompression event since before we were born, right? The cavern seals are strong and flexible."

"Now *you* sound like a MERF commercial," Aiyana breathed, starting to slow her breathing a little.

"Plus, safe pods are even tougher than skimmers or trams . . . and those are basically indestructible."

"Yeah . . . that's true." Aiyana was now breathing a bit more normally.

"So pull yourself out of the dark space, and put that tablet to good use. Um . . . design a next-gen motorcycle-skimmer frame and submit it to Mr. Chuumock for extra cred in welding. Or send it to the Harley people, they'd pay you ten thousand creds."

"Yeah right," Aiyana said, now chuckling.

"Okay, for real, here's what you should do: find the perfect luxury apartment in Shackleton City for after you're a rich and famous skimmer race driver. Don't think I don't notice those live feeds from Luna, open on your tab all the time," Andie smiled.

"I don't watch—" then she sighed—Andie knew her too well. "Okay, yeah, I do." They both smiled together. "All right. I'll do it. I'll find the perfect spot."

"Find something with a view of Earth and let me see the virtual tour later, okay? So, I need to reach out to my dad; he pinged me twice since we started talking. Any word from your folks yet?"

"Nope." Aiyana said simply.

"Well . . . find an apartment. And wait for me at the end of the West Tunnel, I'll catch up with you as soon as we get the all-clear."

"Aye aye, Ellis Ellis," Aiyana said, visibly more relaxed now.

"That's *Andie* Ellis to you, miss. There's no proof Ellis Ellis even existed. He's just a myth."

"Yeah, well . . . thank you anyway, lady." Aiyana said smiling, her shoulders relaxing.

Andie grimaced, lost in thought, then with a little head shake, smiled and waved to the camera. Aiyana waved back and closed the connection.

Andie opened a vid-link to her dad. It took a moment to connect, but then she could see his face on the screen. Her dad, marine biologist Shaw Ellis, smiled broadly with his bushy red beard and receding hairline all mussed and wet, with a scuba dive mask parked up on his forehead.

"Thank the gods. Are you all right, kiddo?"

"I'm fine, Dad, just a few scrapes and a banged-up knee. These will heal pretty quickly," Andie said, holding up her scraped palms to the camera. "But what about you, are you all right?"

"I'm fine," he smiled, breathing a sigh of relief. "Glad you're safe."

"Dad . . . Are. You. All. Right?"

"Yes. Why so intense?"

"Um, your mask. Didn't you tell me that only someone in distress does that with their dive mask?" To which Shaw reached up, feeling the mask, then quickly slipped it down around his neck, under his chin. "Ya got me, kiddo. Dessert of your choice after dinner."

Andie smiled. "Ooh, that reminds me, how are all your little swimming fishy buddies?"

"Funny story—I was ten meters under, not much vis, when the first rock hit the surface and sank to the lake bed next to me. Scared the holy bajeebies out of me—thought one of the giant catfish was about to . . . but no, it's just a rock. So life in the lake seems okay. Some pretty good sloshing around the shoreline, but that's it, I think."

"That's good. Can you see the herd from where you are?"

Her dad looked off-camera briefly, squinting around. "Nooo . . . I don't think . . . nope, not a horse in sight. They must have all bolted for the trees."

Andie nodded appreciatively. "I remember when you took me for a horseback ride just after we landed on Mars."

"I remember it scared the heck out of you."

"Well, horses make those huge bounding leaps in low gravity—I was only nine Earth years old, dad!"

"Yeah. Good times. Hey listen, kiddo, I need to lose this wetsuit and go inspect the lake storehouses and the docks. That means I won't be home until late, probably."

"Okay, dad. Stay safe."

"That's my line."

They closed the connection, both still smiling.

Andie set the tablet down, just now noticing that her knee was starting to throb with pain. Ow. Her palms, still oozing a few drops of blood, also started burning. She winced and flexed her fingers. The nurse lady was watching her.

"I'm guessing those hurt?" the lady said from a few meters away, pointing at Andie's hands. "It just means your adrenaline surge is wearing off. Try to ignore it until we're out of here."

Andie nodded.

* * *

The minutes stretched into a half hour. The injured man lay horizontally, his head resting in Nurse Soliel's lap. He had settled down now, breathing normally and sipping at the last of Andie's water. The lady had opened a wrist-chrono newsfeed and distracted her man with news updates. He ignored the news and looked up at her.

"My Zuzu, you're . . . so beautiful," he murmured, barely loud enough for Andie to hear.

"Yeah," the lady replied, "and you took a pretty good whack to the head. I'll be curious how much of this you remember later, babe." She stroked his brow soothingly.

Andie spoke. "What's on the news nets? Any insight into the quake?"

Nurse Soliel muted her device. "They think the epicenter is close, just a few clicks west and maybe forty clicks deep. Then, more of the same: Sit tight. Don't suit up."

Andie glanced at a cabinet at the far end of the pod, labeled:

S.A.F.E. POD (ACSA-310-2)
EXO-SUITS (40) HERE
- ORIGIN SYSTEMS, LTD. -

"Gotcha." Andie nodded, then stood to stretch her legs, hunching slightly under the low ceiling. She sat back down and shifted her aching rump, now in outright pain against the hard concrete bench. She felt something odd about the seat behind her back.

Andie furrowed her brow, reached around behind, and pulled free a green woven wrist band from where it was stuck in the bench gaps. The bracelet had clearly been here a very long time. Not only was it encrusted with dust, but it lacked a button. In place of a button, a small, hundreds-years-old metal disc held the wristband together. A coin, a real coin! These had never been used on Mars, even in the first colonies. A souvenir of home from one of the original builders, maybe? Even with a hole drilled through it, this was treasure.

The weave suggested a MERF-military background; the pair-cord, tightly woven. Without a second thought, she slipped it on her wrist and turned it a bit, eyes flashing. "Why do they even call it pair-cord?" Andie murmured to herself. "Makes no sense."

She glanced up and noticed the lady was watching intently. She drew breath to speak, but a chime cut her off—a voice spoke over all devices, speakers, and the bunker intercom:

"Attention in the area, attention in the area. Thank you for your patience as MERF Engineers ensure the integrity of ACSA and the Mons-Plex. Minor damage in several exo-corridors and airlocks has been patched, and integrity is verified. This was a 5.7-magnitude seismic event. The epicenter was four kilometers west of the city and forty-one kilometers deep. Anyone with serious injuries, please report to your nearest medical center immediately. If you are immobile for any reason, please ping MERF-Medical and a rescue skimmer will get to you as quickly as possible. You may now resume your activities. Details will be on all news nets this evening at 6:00, and again during the stretch. I say again . . . "

* * *

Bruce Jackson waited for Shelton to finish repeating the announcement. Then Jackson cleared his throat and spoke briskly through the command center's internal speakers. "All EOC controllers, your attention please." All activity in the room stopped.

"The Grand Council vid-conference will start in ten minutes. That's how much time you have . . . to get your status boards updated. Expect the Grand Council to ask you direct questions. Give them direct answers. Don't sugar-coat and don't speculate . . . unless you're directed to do so. Reach out to all your contacts, get us the details, and add them to your part of the briefing."

He paused, before adding, "Track'em, stack'em, and rack'em. Move."

The EOC burst into renewed action. Screen statuses were updated, important calls made. Bruce Jackson sat, rubbing his bruised shoulder.

* * *

As the announcer-voice finished repeating the information, the three citizens of pod ACSA-310-2 stood. The man swayed unsteadily but managed without fainting. The doors hissed open. Again, a pleasant chime.

"Laters," Andie said, "I hope he feels better."

"Thanks again, for getting us in safely, seriously . . . and for the last of your water." She handed Andie her bottle. "That was a small, good thing."

Andie nodded back. "Get that man something with carbs, like a slice of cake, or even a fresh-baked dinner roll. I think he's earned it."

Nurse Soliel nodded, and the two adults hobbled away toward the nearest ACSA clinic. Andie walked back to the cluster of pines to retrieve what was left of her scooter.

She found it quickly, limping now that the pain in her right knee was throbbing full force. She flipped the power switch and tapped the screen, which lit up a mess of random lines and pixels. Fine cracks spider-webbed their way across the shiny surface. The left-turn blinker was on.

She stood on the footboard with her good leg and ignoring the pain in her palms, gently twisted the handgrip. The scooter pulled forward immediately — it still worked. Raising her aching right leg and resting it gingerly behind the left for balance, she wheeled her scooter around, back toward West Tunnel, toward Aiyana, waiting at the far end.

The closer she got to ACSA-west, the more people seemed to be coming and going. Those without scooters were jogging, bounding along in great low-gravity leaps. Scooter traffic surged in all directions, into and out of the West Tunnel. Andie noticed the left turn signal still flashing, but no amount of tapping the screen or flipping the switch changed that.

Andie shrugged and kept riding, throttling the scooter up as she left the nightclubs and restaurants behind. The scooter picked up speed — accelerating to the fastest Andie had ever ridden. The road ahead split into two levels, the upper level for walkers, the lower level for scooters.

Ahead, a familiar sign shone brightly:

^ Up ^
PEDESTRIANS: RIGHT RAMP

SCOOTERS: CENTER LANES
v DOWN v

WEST TUNNEL SPEED LIMIT 15 KPH
(ENFORCED)

As she approached the ramps, she steered left, diving down underneath the elevated walkway. Scooter riders nearby automatically slowed as they entered the tunnel. She readied her grip for the tunnel's speed governor to take over and slow her scooter to 15, basically the running speed an Olympic sprinter on Earth could maintain.

But Andie's scooter did not slow down. All the others around her slowed, but Andie shot onward and started passing others one by one. She yelped, dodged a lady cruising in the left lane, and eased up the throttle. Only then did her scooter slow — so the controls still functioned normally. The governor, however, was as broken as the display.

"Hm, that's interesting," she said to no one in particular. She glanced back at a few annoyed faces, and then she looked forward, evaluating the spacing of other scooters ahead. Andie crinkled up her nose, smiled a devilish smile, and twisted the handle wide open.

Screaming fast, whipping past other riders, Andie saw the occasional glow of colored lights on the ceiling high above, along the elevated walkway. In her mind's eye, she imagined each glow and the historical marker it illuminated — each, a famous achievement in humanity's early exploration of Mars.

Having memorized them all years ago, Andie called them out by name as she zipped under each light. "Mariners! Vikings! Pathfinder! Odyssey! Express! Spirit & Opportunity! Rosetta! InSight! Observers! Orbiters! Hope! Tianwen! Percy & Gennie! MMX! NeMO! Braille!" She grinned widely as she weaved traffic and shouted some more.

After the earliest mech explorers, she passed under the next group—the first astronaut missions to blaze the first trails on Mars. "Survey One and Two! Way-forgers! Founders Vision! VOSS! Olympus Prime!"

Ahead, full sim-daylight of the city glowed brightly—the proverbial light at the end of the tunnel. Andie imagined The Builders themselves, in force with heavy machinery, boring their way into the side of the Mountain to turn this vast, empty magma chamber into the first true Martian city, the capital city, the Mons-MegaPlex.

And she shot right past Aiyana.

"Hey!" shouted Aiyana, standing off to the side. "Andie!"

Andie squeezed the brake hard, and the scooter shuddered to a stop.

"What the flip-flop was that, girl?" Aiyana asked when Andie finally wheeled around and joined her. "You screamed right past me."

"I think the governor on this thing is out—I just took West Tunnel at forty, I think—can you believe it?" Andie, eyes wide, was grinning like an idiot.

Aiyana just stared at her.

"Oh, sorry. The display is broken, see?"

Aiyana looked. "So you think the governor got whacked out too."

Andie nodded, then looked at the perplexed and annoyed faces emerging on scooters from the West Tunnel. She smiled sweetly to them all, waving. "Man, I've been wanting to do that."

"I'm jealous . . . all it took was a 5.7 Marsquake," Aiyana said, finally smiling.

"Right? And speaking of scooters, where's yours?"

"Ah, some punk grabbed it, took off before I could get out — prolly a walker from the upper level," she answered, and took a deep breath.

"You can ride my busted one with me," Andie suggested.

"Sounds good. What's this?" She tapped Andie's new bracelet. Andie told her. Aiyana's eyes went wide when she saw the coin.

"Wow. And, um, are you limping?"

Andie shared her misadventure in the forest, the quake, and getting inside the ACSA pod. As Andie finished telling the story, Aiyana, simply said again, "wow."

"Yeah. So... home?"

"Ugh. Unfortunately, yes."

"You know, we could say you were helping save your friend, who was barely hanging on by a thread . . ." Andie suggested, rubbing her knee.

Aiyana squinted sideways at Andie. "Okay, but just for a bit." Aiyana's adoptive parents still hadn't messaged her, or even pinged her, to see if she was all right.

"Okay, let's ride perimeter loop," Andie said, looking up across the sky-lighting ceiling that towered over the largest inhabited cavern in the entire Solar System.

"But not at forty."

With Aiyana gripping her shoulders for balance, Andie gunned the small, powerful engine and they rocketed away, grinning like fools.

Chapter Twenty

The Ends and Means

The cavern where a million people lived was, predictably, vast. No. Vast did not come close. From one end of the great hollow magma chamber, the opposite end was too far away to see; the sloping walls simply vanished up to the simulated sky dome, a kilometer above.

"Whoa, are you seeing this?" Andie breathed, slowing near a gap in the pine trees, stopping so they could admire the sunset.

The two girls stepped off the scooter and stared up, awestruck.

The CityGlow™ System, a brilliant artificial sky across the cavern ceiling, had dimmed from the bright tan of full Martian daylight into a fiery red sunset. Most evenings, the 'sky' here matched the authentic azure blue sunset Mars was famous for, but tonight the programmers had selected a fiery red, with purples, oranges, and a blaze of gold glinting off the edges of simulated clouds.

"Wow," Aiyana breathed, "an Earth sunset. My mom would have really liked this, I think." She sat down on a flat-topped boulder.

"Do you think about her often?" Andie asked, leaning the scooter against the back of the flat rock and sitting beside her.

"No, but sometimes I talk to her, when I'm having a rough day," Aiyana said, flipping tight raven curls back over her shoulder. Aiyana was mostly Navajo, the Diné, with a generous splash of African beauty in her genes.

Andie nodded. "You told me her name once — Lauryn, was it?"

"Lauryna," Aiyana said, speaking to the sunset. "Lauryna Laughingwater." Aiyana's Diné features were striking, and when she smiled, she glowed with inner and outer beauty. Her curvy frame was strong and fit, from years of unending chores and her own fitness routine, sometimes including a jog along the perimeter path encircling the city.

"Laur-ee-na. Got it. Her story — your story, Aiya — is amazing. I still say you should write a screenplay about it all someday. She was a hero."

"She only stowed away to escape."

"No, I mean making the Hohmann crossing in microgravity while carrying you inside her," Andie said. "The docs said it wasn't possible, right? I mean, I was eight Earth years old when I flew here aboard the *Dorothy Vaughan* and that was stressful enough, with my dad. Which Starship was your mother on?"

"SN-261, the *Carnelian*."

"I can't imagine. It's . . . a marathon, even without being with child."

"She was escaping a monster," Aiyana said, looking intense. Then she turned to Andie. "She didn't even know she was pregnant. The radiation alone should have . . ." Aiyana trailed off.

"Yeah," Andie said. "So . . . what are your superpowers?" she asked.

"My what?"

"You know — you got irradiated in the womb during the crossing. Your superpowers. Like, what color am I thinking right now?"

Aiyana punched her shoulder and smiled.

"Ow." Andie rubber her hurt shoulder.

Andie alone knew Aiyana's story. Lauryna had given premature birth to Aiyana Laughingwater in one of the Mars Arrival Center clinics just weeks after Carnelian landed. The stress of growing a baby during five months of microgravity should have killed them both, but by some miracle, her mother carried Aiyana nearly to term. The strain left small blood clots traveling Lauryna's system long before the Starship made its final approach. The g-forces of re-entry and landing, tolerable to any healthy adult or child, over-stressed Lauryna's body. MERF medical met the ship and immediately put Lauryna into an induced coma and bloodstream filter, to let the fetus grow as much as possible before attempting birth.

After a few weeks, Lauryna's vital signs took a turn for the worse. The unborn baby was at 32 weeks—MERF surgeons performed an emergency cesarean section delivery and brought Lauryna out of her induced sleep so she could meet her daughter.

Weak with fatigue and hazy from the painkillers, she held the baby. Lauryna named her 'eternal blossom,' Aiyana, in the culture of the Diné.

These were the final gifts of Lauryna to her baby girl before an unnoticed blood clot lodged in her brain and closed her eyes forever.

Aiyana was a miracle baby, but no one had wanted her at that time— she was not expected to live long. Plus, an orphaned Earthling, among good Martian people . . . who wanted that? She had been assigned to a family who grudgingly took her in.

Andie shook her arm, bringing Aiyana out of dark thoughts.

"Hey, want to grab your usual?" Andie asked.

"Uh, what?"

"Mango smoothie, ya goof," Andie said, gesturing toward a drink store front, just down one of the paved radial roads. Aiyana cocked her head sideways, noticing a mime, standing near the store, going about his strange silent business.

"Uh, sure," Aiyana replied. "But then I really need to—" but Andie cut her off.

"Wait, did you see that?" Andie blurted out, pointing down the perimeter path toward the tree line.

"See what? It's just an old rockslide."

"No, I saw something. Looked like an animal . . . zipped across the path. There." Andie pointed, standing up and limping forward as she tightened both backpack straps.

"I . . . don't see anything," Aiyana replied. They walked on together.

As they got closer, a flash of black fur darted from one rock to the next, away from the trail. A moment later, it bounded up a side gully, strewn with huge boulders and a dense cluster of tall, full pine trees.

"Oh," Aiyana said. "It's just a cat. I mean, right?"

"I think so . . . maybe he needs help?" Andie said brightly.

"Uh huh. Okay, crazy cat lady, let's just go see if some rando feral cat needs help."

"Glad we agree," Andie replied. Still limping a little, she rounded a few boulders, heading up the gully. Aiyana rolled her eyes but followed. The two left the paved trail behind.

"I think he must have gone into those trees?" Aiyana said. Andie agreed, nodding. They walked on a few more minutes. As they walked up a gentle slope, Andie glanced back to get her bearings.

The path was still visible between trees and boulders, but just barely. Aiyana occasionally rested a hand on a tree trunk, looking around for movement. Birds twittered from the branches above.

"I don't see anything," Aiyana said.

"Yeah, I don't think anyone has been up here in a while," Andie responded. This side ravine was wide enough for a rover to drive up into it, but rockslides and clusters of trees had mostly filled the gap ahead.

"Do you think this was the original perimeter path? Look there, see? It's like the edge of the original route, under the dirt," Andie said.

"Mm, that's great. And what exactly is your deal with this furball?"

"Don't panic," Andie said. "Just making new friends." She looked ahead at a partial rockslide and dense cluster of trees.

Now more than a hundred meters from the paved pathway, they entered the cluster of trees. Sprawling branches dimmed the light from above — the area here stayed in deep shadow. Close ahead, the walls of the cavern climbed straight up to the cavern ceiling, far above.

"Whoa, look at this," Andie said, walking around the back of a much taller boulder that leaned sideways against the cavern walls. "There's a gap, like a cave, and it keeps going." The walls of the entrance fell into shadow. The girls carefully circled the tall boulder and stood in the cave opening.

Andie grabbed the tablet from her pack and pulled out the stylus. She flipped it around backward and clicked on the penlight at the end. Aiyana did the same. They shined their lights inside.

There was no sign of the cat, no footsteps, no meow. Just . . . stillness. They peered in, but their feeble lights showed nothing inside.

"This cave is perfectly hidden," Andie said. "I wonder if anyone even knows it's here?"

Hesitating, the two reached their lights further in. The walls were smooth-carved, and the floor was flat, wide enough for several people to walk abreast. And still, not a sound.

On impulse, Andie bent and picked up a rounded granite rock. She hurled it inside, like skipping a stone across Silver Lake. The rock echoed back in clacks and clunks until it hit something metallic. The ringing sound echoed briefly before the tunnel fell silent.

"Ooo did you hear that? Let's go in, check it out," Andie said, eyebrows raised and looking hopeful.

"No way, I've seen this movie — it's the one where two girls go into a creepy cave and they're never seen again."

"Let's go in," Andie repeated.

"Let's come back with floodlights . . . and a tank," Aiyana said.

Andie turned and looked at Aiyana. "What the heck are you gonna do with a tank?"

Then without listening for her to answer, Andie glanced up. "Whoa, check this." Andie shined her light across the tunnel's ceiling. A spray-painted message in blue letters proclaimed:

GHOSTS OF
LAKE MICHIGAN

TRESPASSERS BEWARE

"What's a 'Lake Mitch-igan'?" Aiyana asked.

"Let's find out later," Andie said. "C'mon."

"But . . . booby traps."

"Boo—what? You've seen too many movies."

"Yeah, but . . . doesn't this give off a 'Raiders of the Lost City' vibe?" Aiyana asked, still panning the pen light around.

"That movie is like ten years old."

"And it's my favorite Harrison Holo," Aiyana said, tipping an imaginary fedora, "Trust me . . ."

"Exactly, it's just a holo. Now pull up your big girl pants, and let's see where this thing goes." Andie stepped inside.

"Rude," came the reply. Aiyana hesitated.

"We'll bring better lighting next time," Andie said, squinting and taking a few more careful steps forward. "Hey look, the tunnel curves to the right, that's why we can't see the end."

"Ugh, fine," Aiyana said, suppressing a shiver. She reached out, free hand resting on Andie's shoulder.

They walked in together, each step slow and measured. Eyes and pen lights scanned all around. Aiyana glanced back as they walked further. After a few moments, the entryway light was lost in the darkness. Spooky.

Another twenty meters, along the curving tunnel, they found a large, well-rounded room. They panned lights around, noticing some furniture off to the left, and fine dust covering everything.

When she looked to the right, Andie jumped. Two red LED lights winked back at them from the darkness. Aiyana jumped back too, involuntarily dragging Andie with her.

They recovered and walked closer, pen lights revealing a metal surface, with the twin red lights. It looked to be an airlock door or some kind of pressure door—a very old one.

"A portal?" Aiyana said, genuine wonder in her voice. The two walked closer to the door and examined it closely. "I don't see any controls," she added, noticing their voices echoed around the chamber.

"Me neither. And no window. I wonder where it leads," Andie murmured, lowering her voice as she spoke. The surface seemed to be porcelain-covered . . . steel? Pretty tough stuff, very different from more modern composite materials.

"Look over here," Aiyana said, looking left of the portal. She reached out to the handle of a large, boxy Exo-Suit locker, set right into the stone wall. She twisted the shiny metal handle and pulled it open. Empty. Not one single suit, just dust. Her toe nudged the sandstone rock Andie had thrown, disturbing a layer of fine dust on the floor.

"Mmm," Andie said, shining a light back at their own dust-footprints on the smooth white tile floor. "No one's been here for a long time."

Further left, along the curving wall, Andie approached the furniture. Three cots held dusty sleeping bags and a few random personal effects. "The prior owners of this hideout, no doubt," she murmured.

"Bet they were teenage boys, judging by this mess," Aiyana suggested.

She picked up a chocolate wrapper, one didn't recognize. "Mars bar? Someone seriously made a 'Mars' bar? That's not very original."

She set the wrapper back down and her toe nudged a plastic dinner plate. The light showed a round rock and an older music player sitting there, the kind of music pod long since replaced by newer models as tech trends evolved.

"So, maybe these teenage boys were the 'ghosts' . . . I mean, you think?"

"Probably."

"We need to come back with a broom and some motion-lights, get it cleaned up. We need to figure this place out."

"Yes, and we also need to get going before someone spots your scooter and comes poking around."

"Ooo, good point. Hmm . . ." Andie panned her light around the walls, looking for something. Low on the wall, to the right of the portal with its three red lights, she found what she was after. "All right—now we're talking. See, there's a power socket in the wall, here next to the portal."

"So?"

"For charging my scooter. With the governor knocked out, I'm keeping that thing, Aiya. I'm freaking keeping that—it's like Krampus came early." She grinned.

Aiyana nodded agreement. "Let's get going."

"Right." Then Andie paused. She looked up at the door. "Hang on. Were there two red lights on the door when we came in, or three?"

"Ummmm . . . Two, I think?"

"Yeah, weird. Now there's three." The original two blinked on and off, as before, and the third stayed steady. Andie looked closely for a moment, then shrugged.

"Do you think we should tell anyone about this place? Bring them in on it?" Aiyana asked.

"Like who?"

"I was thinking Ric, and maybe Reillee."

"Hmm. Four of us, it has balance. But can they keep a secret? I don't know . . . we'll have to think about it before we tell anyone."

After one last brief look around, they walked together back toward the dim light of the cave entrance.

After they exited the curving tunnel and passed around the entryway boulder, the portal's twin lights kept blinking. The third light, the steady one, turned off.

* * *

Twenty minutes later, Andie reached the apartment where she lived with her dad, standing before the smiling digital face of their AI entry, nicknamed Marvin.

"Good evening, and welcome home!" it said brightly. By the end of its greeting, the door had scanned Andie's facial features, weighed her and all her carried items, compared the weight against start-of-day data, and scanned her pheromone-hormone signature, a person's aroma that projects subtly forward, directly in front of a person, every minute of their lives, $24\frac{1}{2}$-7-687.

Satisfied this was in fact Andie Ellis, the door hummed happily open. She stepped in and gracefully hopped over the apartment's founder's stone, a flat, 1-meter wide engraved brass disc, mounted flat into the floor just inside the doorway. The disc's engravings had been worn down by a hundred standard Martian years of feet shuffling across it, but some detail was still visible.

"Hello Hugo," she said to the founder's stone.

The stone, an inanimate metal disc welded into the floor, did not respond.

Andie smirked at the face on the lower left quarter of the disc. Each dwelling and office across the city had its own founder's stone, and no two were the same. Andie's had the following features: the upper left corner showed the Mars Historical Preservation Society logo; the upper-right was a relief map of Valles Marineris, the Mariner Valleys; the lower right showed an early rover, probably Curiosity or Perseverance, and the lower left quarter bore the likeness of maybe one of the Builders, whose name had been lost over generations as the original engraving had worn away. Andie simply called him 'Hugo.' She liked the name.

A ring of words encircled the disc, deep-carved and still legible. The upper half was the motto of humanity's triumphs on Mars: *Ex Martis Ad Astra* — Latin for 'From Mars to the Stars.' The lower half was a numerical designation of their radial city location. In the case of the Ellis apartment, this was South-Southwest, 3.2 km from the Mons-Plex city center, Level 3, walkway 7, door 117. The engraving read: *SSW 32-3-7-117*, which coincidentally served as their home address. She and her father had moved in when they arrived from Earth, a bit more than four standard Martian years ago.

Andie hung her backpack on a peg by the door and said to the stone, "Hugo, guess what?

Again, Hugo did not reply.

"I've got a secret . . . ha ha ha ha haaa ha," Andie sang in a sing-song voice.

Hugo sat unimpressed. Every Founder's Day holiday, the historians and City Council members speechified about how each dwelling's stone was a necessary reminder of the original Founders, the Builders, and a shared vision of achieving great things together. Andie just thought it was a cool cultural piece.

"Dad? Are you home?" Andie called out, kicking off shoes onto a little shoe rack. She noticed her dad's favorite steel-toed work boots were already there.

"Kitchen, kiddo!" came his voice from the next room. Andie realized she could smell a delicious fish fry aroma wafting in. She strode into the kitchen, giving him a hug from behind.

"Oh, hey," he said, wrapping a free arm around his daughter. With his free hand, he sipped a glass of amber liquid on ice, probably his *Skye City's Finest*, whatever that meant.

"That smells amazing. Is it tilapia? Or did you switch to catfish?" Andie asked, plopping down on a chair at their small kitchen table.

"Tilapia. Lemon-pepper with cayenne and blackened, so it's just crispy at the edges. Plus . . . " he reached to open the microzap cooker, where steam billowed out. "A lightly-seasoned broccoli and lemon rice."

"Sounds wonderful, I'm starving."

"I think it's ready," her dad said, stepping sideways to pull the fish tray out of the oven, then setting it next to two plates. Andie scooped out broccoli and rice in liberal helpings. Shaw checked the fish for the right level of edge-crispiness and slid a fillet onto each plate. A third fillet was left on the baking sheet for seconds.

Andie set the two plates down on their small table. Shaw filled glasses with ice water.

They sat and clinked water glasses together. Andie grinned. Everything was set, and they dug in with gusto.

"Mm, this is so good, Dad."

"Yeah, it came out all right. Did you know that the original tilapias brought in from Earth were smaller than our Mars breed?

"Really? How odd."

"Mm hmm, apparently something to do with different radiation levels here mutated the DNA of the fish in such a way that made them grow larger in just a few generations. Then MERF exported the mutated breed back to Earth for an huge profit."

"And it took over Earth's oceans, wiping out everything including the sharks, right?" Andie scooped at the lemon rice and ate enthusiastically.

"Ha! That could be a movie," Shaw joked, "but it may have had other effects too—tilapia schools sometimes behave in ways that seem a little too smart, beyond pure animal instinct. But that's just an educated guess."

They finished their plates, chatting about simple things. Finishing up, Andie's dad stood and went to the back for something, and Andie made to clear the last fillet away.

The door chimed. She crossed to the door and looked at the door's camera feed. No one there. Strange . . . she shrugged and turned away.

Then the door chimed again. "Okay, am I being punked?" Andie opened the door. She looked left and right. No one there.

"Mew," said an orange tabby cat, sitting at her feet. Andie practically jumped out of her skin.

"A-Ares?" was all Andie could say.

"Mew," the cat said simply.

"Uhh . . . won't you . . . come in?"

Ares didn't mind if he did, thank you very much. He sniffed the Founder's Stone as he crossed it, then walked to the center of the room, turned around and sat looking up at Andie with an expectant look.

"Um, what are you doing here? And while I'm asking useless questions, how did you even find here?"

The cat said nothing. He licked his lips.

"You're hungry?" Andie asked. Ares *nodded*.

"Uhhh . . ."

Ares just looked up at Andie.

"Oh right, I mentioned in class we were having tilapia tonight. Hang on, you can understand me?"

Before Ares could respond, her dad appeared in the doorway. "My kiddo, is everything all right?"

"Um, yeah Dad, everything's fine—look who came to visit . . . it's my science classroom cat. Meet Ares."

"The cat rang the doorbell?"

Andie shrugged. "Can I feed him?"

"Well, that last fillet was either going down the chute, or it's tomorrow's leftovers, so . . . sure, I guess?" He looked at the cat for another few seconds. Ares stared back. Unnerved, Shaw turned away. "I've got a few more things to type up about the quake, so I'll be in the back." Andie heard his office door close.

The cat looked at the girl.

"Okay, mister, I'll feed you, but you gotta give me some answers."

"Mew," Ares said simply.

Andie shook her head and walked to the kitchen, keeping an eye on the cat. Ares followed, close at her heels. She cut up the last fillet into bite-sized morsels and set her plate down for him.

Ares dug in. He had the plate cleared in under a minute. Andie cleaned up the dishes and set the steam-washer to sterilize them. She beckoned Ares to follow her to her room. With a single "mew," the cat complied.

They entered Andie's room, Ares standing in the middle of the floor and looking around. Andie closed the door. Ares then stared pointedly at a hamster habitat with mild interest, where the furry brown occupant had just stirred.

"Rr-mew?" said Ares.

"That's Chucklehead—I mean, his name's Charlie Brown." Andie looked at the brown hamster, checked that the HamsterHab door was secure, then sat on her bed and looked down at Ares. "Just don't eat him, all right? He's not a rat."

"Mew," said Ares.

"Does 'Mew' mean yes?"

"Mew," the cat repeated.

"Okay, question—how did you ring the doorbell?

"Mrr-mew, mwrrrrr, mrrrr, mew-rrrr" the cat warbled through several kitty sounds.

"Hang on, that meant nothing to me. Um . . . can you show me?"

Ares squinted his eyes. Then he crossed to the door and leapt up to touch the wall next to her bedroom doorknob.

"Okay."

Ares walked back to the edge of the bed, and leaned up on his hind legs, resting both front paws up against the quilt cover. He looked sideways at Andie.

"Oh, you want up? Sure, feel free." The cat leapt up lightly onto Andie's bed then sat on his haunches, locking eyes with her.

"So . . . where do we start? Hm, if 'mew' means yes, how do you tell me no?"

Ares thought about it, then squinted at her.

"Okay, you convey a 'no' nonverbally with your eyes."

"Mew," said Ares.

"I think I understand. Ooo, here's a good one, how would you tell me that you're hungry?"

"Mrrrr..Meeeew?"

"Okay, so that's 'I'm hungry.' Can you say it for me again?" The cat repeated himself.

Andie reached over, grabbed her tablet, and started making notes.

"We have to keep going, you teaching me . . . cattese, shall we call it?"

Ares paused before replying--he looked at the human, considering. At length, he simply said "mew."

"Okay then. Can I tell Aiya about this? She's the girl from Stein's planetary science class. She's my best friend, and we can trust her."

"Mew," mewed Ares, without hesitation.

"Can we tell anyone else?" Ares squinted his eyes.

"Okay, just Aiya for the time being. Give me just a minute here."

Andie paused the note-taking and tapped open a texting window to connect with Aiyana. She messaged back immediately.

>>> Aiya, RU free to msg

>>> Ya, sure
>>> We can vid tho if U like

>>> Don't want dad to overhear
so let's stick to DMs

>>> No worries
>>> What's up

>>> I want to bring Ric in
and maybe Reillee too
>>> You know, about the tunnel

>>> Yeah I thought about that
>>> They can both keep a secret

>>> Cool, thanks for going along
>>> There's something else

>>> Ares is here
>>> Like, right here
@ my apartment

>>> Oookay
>>> Did you kidnap him from
school or something

>>> No, he just showed up
>>> And here's the freaky bit
>>> He understands everything I say
>>> Like every. Single. Word.

>>>Wait wut

>>> I mean it, I'm sitting here
having a full-on convo w/him

>>> This is weird
>>> So he's some kind of super cat

>>> You're telling me
>>> And yes, supercat

>>> Ric is taking Farnsworth's
AP Bio, right
>>> I bet he will have a clue

>>> Again, this is weird
>>>Let's def ask Ric

>>> Cool. Sugar House @8?
>>> Even if Ric arrives late

>>> Yeah, he's more like a noon

>>> Still. Can you do 8

>>> Yeah, I'll knock out my
tomorrow chores tonight

>>> Cool, thanks Aiya

>>> Wait
>>> For now, let's not tell anyone
about Ares, but showing Ric and
Reillee the tunnel is okay

>>> Um, who would believe me
>>> Don't worry
>>> But make sure Ares is there
I gotta see this for myself

>>> Coolio see you tmro morning

Andie closed the link. She looked at Ares. "Have you ever heard of the 'Ghosts of Lake Mitch-igan?'"

The cat made no response—no mew, no squinted eyes. He just looked at her as if waiting for her to elaborate.

She ran a quick interwebs search using inclusive terms +*Ghosts* +*of* +*Lake* +*Michigan*. The results were mostly shipwreck sites and fresh water marine archaeology, plus a broader reference to someone named Edmund Fitzgerald. She tapped open a shipwreck video, which was unhelpful about the cave, but she learned how to pronounce 'Michigan' correctly.

Andie looked back at Ares — she would have to convince Ares that Ric could be trusted as well. Ric would have some idea how Ares the Supercat became the way he was. He might also have ideas on the mystery portal inside the secret round room.

Ric would know.

Chapter Nineteen

Only the Lonely

Ric sat bolt upright in his bed for the fifth — or was it sixth?–time. He gasped for air, lungs heaving. Covered in sweat, his body trembled. He cast his eyes around in the dark and up at the ceiling.

It took just seconds for him to realize where he was and that everything was okay. But the dream had been so darned real. Again. He exhaled deeply and twisted the blinds on his bedroom window. It was still nearly pitch-black outside his window, but the twinkling lights of the cavern ceiling far above showed him the cavern remained intact. The ceiling had not caved in.

From his corner bedroom window, he looked down across the intersection to his favorite shop, a music and gaming store. The LED "Open" sign was turned off, and a simple night light illuminated the front door. Wiping some of the sweat from his brow, he checked the time. The blue digits showed 4:43 a.m.

Ric grabbed his handy phone from its charging pad and set it next to him on the bed. He sat for a moment, staring straight ahead into darkness of his room. He dialed up the brightness of the device and eased out of bed. He pulled on his favorite pair of black denim jeans and wiggled into a Deep Blue concert T-shirt. He slipped into socks and his go-to, the black buckled boots.

Using the light of his phone, he found his tablet, pocketed it in its oversized cargo-pants pocket, along with his pocket money cards. He left the room quietly, passing by his aunt and uncle's room, and then his sister's room. In the kitchen, he hand-wrote a digital note on the fridge touchscreen, so they would know he was all right. He started to explain about his dreams, then wiped it and started over. He settled on "All's well, just needed some air. Back around lunch. – Ric."

With that, he crossed to the founder's stone, muted the door's voice, and the door hissed quietly open and shut behind him. With only a gentle scrape of his boots on the stairs, he walked down four flights and exited his apartment complex.

Goosebumps rose on his arms, and he rubbed them for warmth. Ric paused to look up at the 'stars.' He was never up at this hour, and it all felt and looked strange, like he had entered another dream. A black and empty cavern ceiling would have seemed . . . ominous, so the 'starlight' reassured him the cavern ceiling was there, protecting them all. A large patch in the stars was dark ahead of him—he squinted up, wondering. Maybe a part of the cavern's sky lights had shorted out?

He made his way past his music/game shop, called 'Got Game?' and turned down an alleyway toward the main avenues. He crossed a smaller street and had nearly reached South Avenue Main, one of the eight cardinal-direction plaza-streets that all converged in the city center.

Passing under a broken streetlamp . . . the little hairs on the back of his neck stood up. He had heard a shuffle behind him—he was not alone. Just as he started turning, an arm wrapped around his neck, and he felt something sharp poking the center of his back. He grunted in resistance, but the arm gripping him under his chin was very strong.

A low voice hissed in his ear.

"Hey kid, your pocket cash—drop it on da street."

Ric stood frozen; his head twitched.

"No, don't turn around, don't even think . . . just drop it in da street."

A chill ran up his spine from the knife-point. Taking a breath, he spoke softly. "I . . . mmm. Okay, you need it more than I do? Take it. After the night I've had . . . just take it."

He carefully reached into his pocket, grabbed out a red-silver pocket money card and let it fall at his feet.

A different man spoke up, approaching from a few meters away. "Oi, this had better bei legit, or ye'll 'have yerself some rage ta contend weth," the second man said, his speech a rough Cockney, or was it more Scottish?

Footsteps told Ric the other man was right behind him. The first still had an arm locked around his neck. Ric's chest heaved with heavy breathing.

Ric glanced down just enough to see a hand snatch the card off the pavement. He noticed the man's hand tattoos . . . skeletal finger bones had been inked on just two of his fingers, the pointer finger and middle finger.

"Hey. Dat one's prolly a fake, Daemon, got a tracker on it," the voice in his ear said. "I seen those before."

"Dinna sey ma name, bloody edjit," the other muttered tersely.

Ric spoke, his voice trembling. "No, sir, that's the real one. Those fake cards, I carry one of those too, but you're holding the real deal. Look . . . "

Ric slipped the other card, an all-silver one, from his other pocket and let it drop on the street. "There's the fake."

Again, the tattoo-fingered hand scooped the card up off the ground where it landed.

Ric spoke up again. "Don't use the silver one—my uncle makes me carry it ever since I got jumped years ago. It's bugged. The one I gave you at first . . . about 80 creds, that's all I have to my name. Just take it, I really don't care anymore."

"What's yer game here, eh?" the Scottish man asked, thumping Ric in the back, but not hard enough to make him stumble. The muscular arm held him tight.

"I . . . nightmares . . . I died in my dreams like five times. There's nothing you can do my brain hasn't already done to me, all right? So . . . just take it. Just don't make this night worse than it already is for me, all right?" He emphasized the last two words, on the verge of anger, or tears.

The restraining arm released him. The point in his back withdrew.

For the moment, it was quiet.

Ric waited.

"Are we cool? Can I turn around now?" Ric asked.

No response. He stood there another moment.

Ric risked a glance over his shoulder; the street was empty. Ric turned. His shoulders slumped, his eyes welled up. Tears ran down one cheek, then the other. He closed his eyes, his head lolled back as he stood in the street. He looked up at the cavern's stars, and . . . they weren't there any more. Another nightmare?

No, this was happening. Then he felt moisture hit his forehead. Wait, that wasn't a tear—that drop didn't come from his eyes. Another landed on his cheek.

He reached up and brushed his forehead.

A water drop on his fingertips glinted under a distant street lamp.

Another drop. Another, and another.

His mouth fell open, and he looked back up. The rain fell into his eyes, on his face, his shoulders, with a light spatter on the street and rooftops around him, the noise picking up and growing louder. A light drizzle fell upon him and the immediate neighborhood.

He gaped, now in a huge smile, heaving breaths, as his tears ran out of his eyes in steady stream, blended with tears shed by the sky above. He choked up, sobbing, and did not care if anyone saw. But there was no one else here, not a soul. Ric closed his eyes and held his arms up to the rain.

Then the drizzle eased . . . and it stopped.

After another long moment, Ric opened his eyes. He stayed rooted, unsure. Many moments passed before he hugged his arms around himself, feeling his wet clothes already starting to dry. The small patchy cloud above him started to dissipate. He hugged himself tighter.

He turned and walked in ACSA's general direction, heading for Sugar House Coffee. Threading back alleys and walkways, the darkness swallowed him up.

* * *

Saturday 'dawned' as the CityGlow™ lighting warmed up a sunrise.

Andie stretched and bounded out of bed grinning. She hastily dressed in a simple black pullover and jeans, hugged her dad goodbye as he sipped his morning cup, shouted out a greeting to Hugo, and left the apartment. She retrieved her beautifully flawed scooter from its most recent hiding place and headed for the ACSA West Tunnel.

Cruising smoothly down onto the lower level and through the tunnel, she kept her speed under control to avoid attracting attention. After a brisk ten-minute ride, she coasted her scooter gradually to a stop and stashed it around the back of "Golf 'n Stuff," hoping no one would grab it. Doubtful — hardly anyone was out and about at this early hour.

Then, walking past the attraction's main entrance, 'closed' sign still displayed, she headed for Sugar House Coffee, a favorite among early risers. She noticed her favorite table was occupied — Ric was already in his usual spot. But he never showed up this early. Like ever.

"Ohai . . . Ric?" She called as she approached the table. "You're here."

"Hi Andie," Ric called back, standing to give her a warm embrace. Ric, with olive skin, jet-black hair, and a magnetic smile, was forever a gentle soul. He earned fast friendship among everyone he met. But as he held the hug, Andie could tell something was off—maybe he would confide in her what was the matter.

Ric said, "you want breakfast? I was just about to order . . . something," letting the hug go and resuming his seat. He grabbed a digital placard menu, its food and drink animations glowing and beckoning.

"I'm starving. What are the specials?" Andie asked, a little too happily.

"I didn't look yet. I may just do a café mocha and see how my stomach handles it."

"Are you all right?"

"I didn't sleep, like . . . at all. The quake . . . I couldn't stop dreaming about it. Why does my brain just run in circles sometimes?"

"Oh. I see . . . what was your dream?" she asked, concern on her face.

"The city cavern ceiling, falling in. Everything was shaking. All the air rushed out this huge black hole in the top. Shattering glass as all the windows blasted open. I kept waking up . . . gasping for air."

"How awful."

The digital menu Ric was holding timed out and went to sleep. Neither teen noticed.

Ric blinked and shook his head.

"Yeah, it got so bad I just gave up on sleep, threw on some clothes, and came here. And then, . . . " his voice trailed off. "I just feel shredded."

"Wow." Andie breathed, and they both held eye contact for a moment. He smiled, his eyes red with exhaustion. She nodded, making up her mind. "Okay, let me order for you." Andie reached out and woke up the tablet. "When my stomach feels yukky, I always order India chai, mild-sweet, with light milk."

"That . . . sounds pretty good, actually." He rubbed his eyes.

Andie nodded and started putting in her own order as well. They both sat quietly for a moment, the sounds of the kitchen softly playing in the background. Neither one was pressed about the silence. Ric put his face in his hands and rested.

Ten minutes later, Aiyana arrived, just as the chai was set down at the pick-up counter, alongside Andie's cup of Earl Grey, with a touch of lemon and sweetener. Andie was returning to the table with the two mugs just as Aiyana approached.

"Heya Ric . . ." Aiyana said by way of greeting, then adding, "You look wiped. Are you all right?"

"Really rough night."

"Well, we have something that will cheer you up. We discovered . . ."

"A-hem, shh," Andie shushed her discreetly, seeing a new face walking into the coffee shop.

Ric's bestie Sitara walked in and trotted over to hug him from behind in the booth. Her bracelets jangled and she shook him as she hugged him, nearly choking him. His eyes went wide, then he relaxed in her embrace, reaching up to hold her arms. He smiled and breathed a contented sigh.

"You feel any better?" Sitara asked, still embracing him from behind and looking at him from the side.

"Much better, you're here. Plus, I hear chai cures everything," Ric said, looking sideways at her.

"That is an absolute certainty," Sitara said. Her gentle Indian accent was pure music.

Ric smiled. "Um, sorry, Aiya, what was it you discovered?" he asked.

Aiyana's eyes opened wide, looking at Andie. They had not discussed including Sitara in their secret. Andie fumbled at another idea. "Um . . . while we were stuck in that safe pod yesterday, we both kind of discovered . . . Earth people in history talk way too much."

"Uh . . . what?" Ric asked, confused.

Sitara released Ric and walked over to a drink dispenser.

Andie continued. "Yeah, I was watching this old World War 2 documentary . . . you know, for Earth History class? Some old British guy rambled on about how we shall fight in the streets and on the fields and among the hills and in the seas and on the shores and in the forests, across the skies, and . . . on and on. It's like he wanted to leave no spot . . . unfought for."

Aiyana snorted and shook her head. "Why do you take that class?"

"I just hope I can go back someday, that's all," Andie replied.

"You're an Earthling?" Ric asked, finally cracking a smile. He sipped at his steaming chai. "Mmm, this is good," he said, lifting the mug in appreciation at Andie.

Andie punched his arm across the table. "Yes, it is good. And this Earthling is tough enough to handle you, Mister Pureblood Martian."

Sitara swiped a card to pay and returned to the table with a Campa-Limon soda.

Sitara eased into the booth beside Ric. Ric crinkled his nose, grinning at his friends, and exhaled a breath he had not realized he had been holding. The happy moment settled in.

Aiyana turned to Andie. "Okay, if you could go back to Earth, other than being crushed by oppressive gravity, what would you do?"

"Mm, I'd want to stand out under the open sky. No Exo-Suit."

Sitara shook her head vigorously, her Hindu lilt stronger. "I think that standing under so much open sky would freak me out proper—like I would fall right off the planet into space." She made a grimace of fear.

"I'd stand outside until it rains." Andie continued. "I was eight Earth years old when I left, and I only have the dimmest memories of rain. So, I'd have to land somewhere where it rains often. I wouldn't want to wait long, to feel that again."

Sitara spoke up again. "Mm, did you guys hear there's a rumor going around that it was raining somewhere in the city last night?"

"No way?" Andie leaned back, shocked. "Ric, did you hear that?"

"Mmmm," Ric murmured, sipping chai. He looked down into the cup.

"I'm with you," Aiyana said. "I'd love to feel that. Complete magic."

Ric cleared his throat. "Anyone seen Reillee yet?" he asked, taking another sip.

"He's on a hike up to the Overlook with his family," Sitara said, "he texted me last night about it. Speaking of which, you, mister, need a diversion," Sitara focused on him, and sipped more soda. "It's written all over your face. I'm thinking of the Gardens, no arguments," then she turned to Andie and Aiyana. "Will you join us?"

"Actually, we already made plans," Aiyana said. "Next time?"

"Very well, next time it shall be."

Ric and Sitara finished off the last dregs of their drinks and stood to exchange hugs with Andie and Aiyana. They left together. The two girls sat back down, now facing each other in the booth.

"Before we head out, just let me grab some food to take along, there's no knowing how long we'll be at it today." Without reading, Andie rapid-tapped on the menu an order for a veggie breakfast burrito. Then she upped the amount to two and tapped payment using a pocket money card slipped from the back of her tablet.

"Looks like bringing in Ric will have to wait."

"Gives us more time to get the space cleaned up. Um, can we pick up that broom and some thousand-hour LEDs on the way?" Andie asked.

"Don't forget a charging cable for your busted-up scooter."

"Don't hate my ride," Andie said.

Aiyana stuck her tongue out through dazzling white teeth. More customers trickled in the doors for their morning cup. The girls' food order arrived at the service counter a few minutes later and Andie retrieved the food. She slid one of the burritos across the table.

Aiyana smiled. "Okay, let's get going then," slipping her burrito into a takeaway bag. "Thanks for this."

"Psh, it's just a thing. So where can we find what we need?"

"I'm thinking R-three, or maybe the Radio Shack. Let's do it."

Picking up their gear was uneventful. They hit the Reduce-Reuse-Recycle store, R-three for short, right as it opened. Andie found a handful of thousand-hour LED lights and sprung for the motion sensor feature, so they could be set to turn on automatically with any motion in the room. They were cheap recycled lights, so the girls settled on five to start. They found a cheap, simple canister duster-sweeper and a wash rag with a bucket. Andie visited the power section and picked out a medium-load cable to charge her scooter.

With their little hoard divided between the two, they left the store with small carrying bags attached to the handlebars. This time, Aiyana had her own ride.

Andie took the lead, driving up the wide avenue that led Northwest away from the city center through Green Acres, where the fancy people lived. After taking a few side roads and alleys, they reached the edge of civilization, where a collection of two- and three-story apartments-above-restaurants had been built. Here, a sandwich-shoppe bodega and the rest of the Green Acres businesses thinned out at the city's edge.

They joined the perimeter path and carefully rode toward the sharp bend where the gully and their hidden cave awaited them. Scanning both directions of the perimeter track before stepping off the trail and heading up the ravine, they led their scooters over bare rock to avoid leaving any tracks. Glancing back, their passage seemed obscure enough.

At the cave mouth, they parked their scooters just inside the entryway boulder, well hidden from outside.

Bearing their shopping burdens, they walked in, and Andie held up one of the new LED lights to see better. "These are so much better than those wimpy stylus lights."

"Yeah, it's not as creepy now." Aiyana set a second lamp down in middle of the bare white tile and clicked it on. The entire space was bathed in a soft glow. Andie stuck two more to the ceiling in strategic points, to brighten the room even better, then linked them all to her handy phone app via Redtooth. She clicked them on and off, then tested the dimmer settings and cycled through different colors. As she fiddled with the lights, a flash of reflection next to the portal caught her eye. There was something metal stuck to the wall they hadn't seen before.

"Aiya, check this out."

They both read the shiny brass plaque:

**HEAVENLY DAUGHTER AND MOTHER, MIGHTY THEIR BOND
THEY FEARED, BOTH DREADED THAT ONE DAY ERE LONG**

**THEY DESTROY EACH OTHER BY THEIR INHERENT NATURE
AND TRAGIC IT WAS, OH, PRESSED IN TOGETHER:**

**ONE BROKEN, DESTROYED, DROPPING HER RING
ONE MOURNED FIERY TEARS, SORROWS TO SING**

**AN ORPHAN REMAINS, EVER SINCE, PUSHED AWAY
SHE DRIFTS, MORE DISTANT, DAY AFTER DAY.**

"If you like that, you're gonna love this. These 'ghosts,' whoever they were, left another message."

Aiyana led Andie over to a spot on the wall above the three cots. Aiyana shined another light directly on it, and Andie read in silence. The letters were tall, as was the symbol next to them. In mediocre urban art stood a meter-tall, bright red "A" with a circle around it.

Under the symbol, a phrase had been spray-painted:

**NO GOVT WILL EVER
SET U FREE**

Here and there were other random personal tags neither could make out. Andie pulled the on the right away from the wall and saw yet more words. In bright blue, even less skilled:

Only the lone one will open the gate.

A small part of the blue letters had been sprayed over in orange paint, leaving the final message to read "Only the lone*ly* will open the gate" but its final artist had done a poor job of it.

"Wow. That's . . . a whole lot, all at once," Andie murmured.

"These dudes were . . . not all right in the head," Aiyana said. "At least one of them, their agent orange maybe, had lost hope."

"How can you tell?" Andie asked.

"Broken knows its own," Aiyana said, pursing her lips and reading the spray one more time. Andie kept her face toward the wall, but her eyes were on Aiyana.

"Shall we have our breakfast first, then get started?"

"Yeah, sure," Aiyana said, turning away to find place to sit.

In the hour that followed, they chowed down on breakfast burritos, commenting occasionally on little details they noticed, listening to the echo of their own voices, and shared a few wild guesses on what the room was for and where the portal might lead. They debated, then agreed on, the five lights' final positions and set them to turn on any time the sensors detected motion in the round room. Andie rolled her boss-level scooter into the room and plugged it in, hoping its nearly dead power cells would recharge successfully.

Out of respect for the original ghosts, neither teen sat down on the old cots. Plus, their sprayed words were strange. A simple sifting through their meager belongings, though, seemed appropriate, to try to find out who they were. No meaningful personal objects were left behind to suggest who they were. They found a multi-tool, with the blade still sharp, and were sad to find the music pod was dead, unable to be recharged.

They shook all the dust from the derelict sleeping bags, to tidy the bunk beds area as well before setting the auto-vacuum loose to clean it all up off the floor.

"We need some more chairs, or cots maybe, of our own," Aiyana said, coughing away some of the dust from a sleeping bag as she shook it.

"Hammock for me, I'll ask for a loan from my dad, and pay it off working at Silver Lake. Do you need help with funding yours?"

"Oh, dang, I forgot to tell you with everything going so crazy—they hired me to be a barista at the Mons MagLev Station coffee shop."

"No kidding? That's great!"

"Yeah, they offered me this afternoon for registration and training if I want to get a jump on the other new people," Aiyana said. "Sorry to leave you alone the rest of the day."

"We're all set here. Plus, I won't be alone if Ares shows up."

"Ares again?"

"Yeah, I was hoping he might join us today."

"How's the cat going to find this place?"

"I told him where it was last night," Andie replied.

Aiyana looked at Andie. "Oh, well in that case . . ." Aiyana rolled her eyes. "For the smartest one in the room, you can be a real knucklehead, you know that?"

Andie sighed. "If he shows up, then would you believe me about how smart he is?"

"Sure. Take a photo, ha ha. And no 'shopping it." Aiyana smirked.

"You're a doubter."

When the time came for Aiyana to leave for training, she left Andie with a huge hug. "Finding this place is . . . pretty cool. I love it."

"Yeah," Andie replied, grinning widely.

Aiyana left with a little wave.

Andie dragged one of the ghosts' folding chairs over by the portal and took a long hard look at the riddle. Presumably, this riddle held the key to opening the portal, but how? There was no keyhole, no button, no controls, no microphone . . . not even an old-style keyboard.

So, Andie sat and analyzed, using her tablet to do searches (how was there any usable Wi-Fi signal under all these tons of rock and cement? It made no sense, but there it was, four circles strong, in fact one of the fastest connections she could remember ever having. Just another mystery about the place.

The day rolled into mid-afternoon, when even Andie had to leave to grab some quality time with her dad for a picnic near the Silver Lake forest. Plus, She was looking forward to seeing the herd again, maybe coax a horse over to her with a carrot or an apple.

* * *

Sunday; Andie spent a few mid-day hours alone in the round room, just brainstorming about the portal and its passcodes. Ultimately two things didn't happen: Ares never showed up, and Andie remained stumped as to how the portal might accept the heavenly daughter and her mother's names, even if she could discover the correct answers. By afternoon, she had had enough and decided to ride the entire 32-km perimeter path in a single ride. She unplugged her scooter and rolled toward the exit.

As an afterthought before leaving, Andie crossed the room to the old cots and crouched to pick up the strange rock. She looked closely at a strange crystal-purple stripe running across the middle.

Pocketing the specimen, she turned to leave. Planetary science homework: complete.

The motion-sensor lights winked out after a few moments of inactivity, except one Andie had set to permanent low brightness, shining softly down on the Portal.

Three red LEDs, glowing in the gloom, became two as the middle one shut itself off.

Chapter Eighteen

Thing 1 and Thing 2

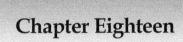

"**N**o way, Andie, is that the rock from the—"

"Shhhh," Andie said. "Yes, it is. Can you think of a better way of finding out where it might have come from? Stein might have some insight into . . . you know, that place."

"Where what might have come from?" Sitara asked, smoothly sneaking up behind the girls and smiling her bright smile.

"Uh . . . where the . . . uh, quake came from!" Andie said, slipping the rock out of sight.

"From the mantle, it appears," Sitara said without hesitation.

"That, uh, deep? I thought it was only 40 clicks down," Andie replied, now more interested.

"It was earlier tremors way down in the mantle that triggered the stronger quake, that 5.7," Sitara explained. "That's what my father says."

"That's fascinating," Andie said.

"Yeah, thrilling. Whups, flat tire," Aiyana said, bending down to tie up a shoelace.

"Okay, I'll see you in class then," Sitara smiled again and walked off.

"So . . ." Aiyana said, finishing up with her shoe. "What if Stein asks you where it came from?"

"I'll . . . uh, say I found it in a rock pile by the perimeter path. I mean, it's sorta true."

"Mm hmm. . ." Aiyana said, one hand on her hip. "Let's just see how that goes."

The girls rounded the corner and entered room F-105. It was the last class of the day; the wall clock showed 1:38.

Aiyana went straight to her seat, and Andie made a quick pass by the teacher's station to scratch Ares' back before going two desks forward to her own station. Most students were already seated, logging in. Andie set her mineral sample, purple stripe glittering, into the tray between her and her elbow partner, whose sample looked to be a gem-quality quartz about the size of a thumb.

"Ooo, that's so pretty," Andie's partner Faith said, seeing Andie's rock.

Before Andie could respond, the starting bell sounded, and Stein closed the door. He gave all his students a moment to settle down and log in. Murmured conversations around the room continued.

The front wall viewscreen showed a flying view through the beautiful Valles Marineris, the 'Valley of the Mariners,' complete with its collapsed side canyons, a few riverbeds, and rare arêtes, standing up like knife edges along the landscape.

Stein walked to the front of the classroom and voice-commanded the windows to dim the sunlight down to one quarter. Ares opened his eyes, squinting at Stein in annoyance.

The teacher took his usual spot, forward off to the side. He smiled and waited for conversations to fade. As the seconds passed, students began to look up.

"Good afternoon. I hope you are well," the teacher intoned, his smile genuine. "Friends, before we jump into today's topic, those who remembered to bring a mineral sample today, please set it carefully in your station's sample tray."

Many students reached into bags or satchels to draw out some rock or crystal, placing it on the tray between them and their elbow partners. Quite a few were reddish sandstone or various black-and-white igneous rocks the Mountain was famous for.

Stein strolled down the left side of the room to the back, observing the rocks that had appeared, occasionally picking one up. He did so without comment, until he was coming back up the right side. At Andie and Faith's station, he stopped. He picked up Andie's sample, looking closely at the purple stripe.

"Where did you get this?" Stein asked right away. "I mean, where did you . . . find this?"

"Just . . . some place near the perimeter track," Andie replied.

Stein focused on Andie. She flushed slightly but willed herself not to look away.

"It's interesting," he said. "See the inclusions in and around this violet stripe? That tight line of color is unique, almost like an amethyst geode got crushed flat after it formed." Stein's voice trailed off, his thoughts far away.

Andie tried to keep a straight face.

"I'd be curious to know where it came from. I mean, maybe there are some more."

"I don't think so, it was different from all the granite rocks nearby. Looked interesting."

Stein paused, making eye contact, and then set it back in the tray. "Indeed it is. Will you see me after class, please?" Andie nodded, caught off guard. Stein strode back to the front of the room glancing at the other stations, but not stopping.

He cleared his throat and continued. "Also, ladies and gents, before we analyze your rock specimens, I want to announce two very special things coming up over the next several weeks."

Behind him, the animation faded into a calendar, with the next three weeks displayed. The headline read "Homecoming: Spirit Week."

"The first thing, as you can see, is Spirit Week. To get us warmed up, this coming Friday there's an exhibition match — Bullseye-Handball against Nerus. But just before that practice match, we're having an exciting celebrity lecture, if you care to show up a bit early. Now, during the final Spirit Week itself, there's not just athletics — some of you are very plugged in to our academic competition, the one we all know as Knowledge Bowl." His eyes flicked to Andie, whom he knew to be on Mons High School's top K-Bowl team.

"But take a closer look at the end of that last week, my friends — you may notice we have homecoming party with the big dance, our annual *Titan's Rage*."

"There were like eight hundred kids last year," Carlos said. A few murmured conversations bubbled up in the back and across the room.

"We may see more this year," Stein said. "I heard a rumor they revived the *Helios*."

The room fell silent.

"Wicked," someone whispered from the back. A few nods around the room followed. Several students smiled. Low-gravity dances, and all the crazy ideas that prom committees had tried out over the decades, made the Titan's Rage a big deal.

The bottom half of the slide faded to a map of all human settlements, mainly the seven cities of Mars.

"You can see that athletes and K-Bowl competitors arrive on their MagLev trains the beginning of that third week, and they're coming from all over — there's Nerus High, Robinson High, New Skye's Portree High, Hathorton High, The Kyiv Lyceum, and Uintah High. And get this: Nooma

Outpost is sending students this year. So, our guests will be staying in the ACSA student hostels and — " again, he was cut off by Carlos.

"Those rooms are like broom closets," Carlos said.

Stein wasn't pressed at being interrupted. "Right? They are tiny. But, all those students, easily three or four hundred headed our way, will be joining us in class that third week, so be ready for everything to feel . . . a bit crowded."

Murmurs around the room sprang up; Stein gave them the time to process the news.

"So get to asking somebody, if you want a date for Titan's Rage." Andie's eyes flicked back to where Marcus sat, involuntarily. Aiyana glanced back Andie's direction and gave a knowing nod to Andie. Andie's eyes went wide. She felt her cheeks blush as red as her hair.

At the mention of 'asking somebody,' conversations sprung up again simultaneously around the room. Stein simply let them play out. The best thing about Stein — he did not insist on silence or that they revere him as the 'sage on the stage.' Here, students were seen. They were valued, respected, and always given their space, their time.

Only when Sitara raised her hand did Stein call for quiet so he could hear her question.

"At the celebrity lecture, Mister Steinheiser, who's to be presenting?" she asked. Students listened in, wanting to know more about this coming Friday's scrimmage against Nerus and the unusual lecture before it.

"I hear several experts were asked — but it was Dr. Jan Holm, who you may know as the Nooma Outpost Research Facility director, who will be our keynote speaker that night." Stein had the viewscreen jump ahead to a different slide, displaying an image of the Olympians' main auditorium alongside a picture of a wizened researcher. Stein imagined that probably wouldn't mean much to most students, but he pressed on.

"If you attend his lecture that Friday before the match, you will have your mind blown. Plus, I'll give you some extra credit if you like that idea. Also, I've learned that a handful of students currently on final approach from Earth aboard *Lucky Seven* and her sister starships might be there — so it's going to be quite an evening."

"I heard Lucky Seven almost blew up last week," a short girl named Aeryn said from the far side of the room. "Like, an explosion in space or something." The room quieted for Stein's comment on this.

"I heard the same — that ship must live up to its name though, because she and her whole flotilla are arriving, perfectly intact, day after tomorrow. They must be keeping the details . . . hush-hush," Stein responded.

Though all starships had nicknames, Lucky Seven was Starship SN-700, the one that enjoyed a reputation for good fortune. Many passengers making the Hohmann Transfer crossing from Earth to Mars (or back) hoped to fly aboard Lucky Seven. Andie spoke up, snapping the room out of its lull in conversation.

"Is Lucky Seven landing here? Like, Port Mons?"

"Let me see . . ." Stein lifted his tablet and tapped a few links. "No, it looks like they're landing at Port Nerus." Andie nodded — a look of disappointment barely noticeable.

"What other questions does anyone have?"

"The Geo-thingy — will the speaker talk about the quake?" came a voice near the window.

Stein nodded to the girl. "That's my guess, Dezi. Olympus Mons is not extinct after all, but just dormant for . . . fifty-odd million years? That's huge. But what woke it up? What does MERF know, and what are they doing about it? These are questions I'd love to have answers to."

Dezi nodded her agreement.

Marcus raised his hand. "Mister Steinheiser, what's the second thing? You said there were two things," he asked.

"Ah yes, thank you. See that Friday in two weeks?" Stein clicked back

75

to the full calendar. "Thing number two I wanted to tell you about is our next field trip."

More conversations started up, and Stein raised his hands for quiet.

"We're making a group hike up to the overlook, and this trip is only being offered to this Geology class and the five Astronomy classes. I'll have more details by the end of this week — we'll see how many of you commit to going."

"It's just a hike up to the overlook? I went there last month with my family," a brunette teen named Lesly said from the middle of the room.

Stein nodded. "I know many of you have been up there before. So, tell you what . . . I'll kick in pizza, and we might even get to have a special presentation of the Universe. Also, you'll need to find yourself a hiking partner for that evening. There's no limit on this trip, and no cost, but those who wish to go must sign up at least a full week in advance and have found a partner."

Several more conversations bubbled up from around the room as students discussed what this could mean, who was interested in going.

Andie raised her hand. Stein called for quiet. "What does 'presentation of the Universe' mean?" asked Andie. Even in the dimmed afternoon sun, her red hair caught the light, glowing almost orange.

"I'm saving the details for a surprise, but don't let anybody tell you science trips are boring." he said, with a wink and a sideways grin.

"Probably the Tyson Planetarium after we get back," Carlos muttered.

Stein smirked, gave a half-sideways tilt of his head, and let the boy's comment stand.

"You'll find the details of the meeting time and place, as well as parent permission forms, on our class web site. Now, if you have any other questions, please just catch me after class."

He clapped his hands together and held them together. "Okay, now, let's change gears, catch the weather report, and dive into today's activities."

Some students grabbed out their tablets, and others tapped their tabletop touch screens awake and logged in. The classroom lights stayed low as Stein brought up the daily forecast.

Chief Meteorologist Jaelyn Ackerman, wearing a pleasant gray-blue business suit and letting her long straight black hair trail down her back, smiled at the camera.

"Well, friends, it's going to be continuing pleasant conditions in the city despite Friday's quake excitement; the environmental controls are holding steady, and our city sunsets this weekend have been absolutely gorgeous. Just look at this photo sent to us by Bree Townsend of Green Acres, isn't that something?" The backdrop behind Jaelyn showed Friday night's fiery sunset. "But here's the shocker—this past Saturday morning, if you can believe it, we have reports of a light drizzle an hour or so before sunrise—just incredible. Chances of another drizzle remain minuscule, but don't lose hope, folks, it just might happen to you!"

Jaelyn turned to a western hemisphere map of Mars. "Across the deserts, the dust storm forecast is clear overall—chances for a surprise dust event remain under 10%, so our solar fields are soaking up energy under optimal conditions—but be careful if you're vacationing down in the Night Labyrinth—dust sweeping off the high plains above could bring you limited visibility in those slot canyons. So be sure your beacons are on and working before you head into any isolated areas." The slide switched to an animated orbital model of Mars, with fuzzy patches behind Mars in its orbital path.

"As for space weather, solar output has been normal to low, so no extraordinary radiation measures are needed. Micro-meteorite activity is also at a low as the planet is in between those comet tail debris fields. So take that shuttle ride up to Phobos, folks, all launch windows are in the clear. And you can fire up your Harleys and Hondas because it's going to be excellent dune skimmer riding weather for several weeks. Now let's look at our ten-day outlook across the seven cities . . ."

Jaelyn continued to describe ideal conditions and fair weather across Mars, with only minimal concerns or cautions. Clearly, she loved her job.

The weather ended, and Stein launched the group into the day's activity, a digital observation sheet for students to enter their observations and measurements of the specimens they had brought to class. It was graded, so students got down to business.

Using a comprehensive specimens guide, students looked through eye loupes, the small magnifying glass jewelers use, to examine their samples. They noted colors, inclusions, structures, and a dozen other details. Partner-pairs worked for forty-five minutes before submitting their work.

In the last part of class, Stein reached into a drawer and brought out a handful of miniature seismic detectors. He passed them out around the room for students to take readings.

More than one asked if the continual low-level vibrations were aftershocks from Friday's Marsquake, or just someone walking down the hallway. Rather than giving them his own suspicions, he had students type in their own educated guesses, their own hypotheses — even he couldn't be certain what was making the devices twitch every so often.

Eventually, the ending bell rang. Nearly all stood and filed out. Andie dutifully stayed, approaching Stein's desk, standing next to Ares.

"Andie. Thanks for staying. You have your sample?"

Anticipating this, she handed the purple-striped rock to her teacher.

He took it quietly and examined it closely from all angles, nodding as he did so.

"Well . . . it's unique," he said, as he peered through his own eye loupe. "The only other time I've seen a mineral like this was probably eight years ago. My own science teachers were baffled as well — it was part of the reason I got into geology in the first place."

"Did you or your former teachers find out where your own sample came from?"

Stein shook his head. "It's just . . . one of those mysteries, I'm afraid." He looked into Andie's eyes. "I'm curious about exactly where you got it."

Andie didn't like where this conversation was going.

"You seem to know something more, Mr. Steinheiser, can you shed some light?"

Stein's turn to turn a little red in the cheeks. He handed the specimen back to Andie.

"Um, no, I don't, uh . . . it's just a lot like the one I saw long ago, that's all." He smiled, regaining his composure. "And I wanted to say thank you, for bringing it in—geologists love a good challenge," he said.

"So, some things remain a mystery," Andie said.

"Some things will never be explained to our satisfaction, yes." Stein nodded. "Too often we're stuck with only knowing part of the story, and the most interesting things stay . . . hidden." There was no edge in his voice, no accusation—he spoke gently, thoughtfully.

Holding eye contact for just a second longer, Andie nodded, gave him a small smile, pocketed the rock, and turned away. Aiyana stood waiting at the door.

Ares watched Andie go from his little bed. Stein stared ahead for a long moment, lost in thought before refocusing back on his work.

Joining the last surge of students exiting the school, the girls decided that Tuesday would be the day to bring Ric and Reillee in on their little secret. That left them one more day to plan out how they would give it the proper spectacle their hideout deserved, but mostly to one-up the boys. After that, they would try to get the stubborn portal open.

They grabbed their scooters, cut through ACSA as they went, and a few minutes after exiting the West Tunnel, arrived at their bend in the perimeter path. Checking both directions for walkers or riders, and finding the coast clear, they stepped off the path and sneaked away among the trees and boulders.

With scooters parked just inside, the motion-lights glowed to life, and Aiyana flopped down into one of their newly installed hammocks. Andie dragged a chair over to the portal and considered the riddle. Aiyana swiped through images and vid-clips on social media.

"We should call this place *the Pocket*," Aiyana mused. Andie looked at her, as she explained. "You know, because it's like a pocket cave, off to the side of the main city cavern."

"It's more of a carved access tunnel, but sure, I like it. The Pocket."

At that moment, who should wander into the room but a fuzzy orange-tan tabby cat.

"Ares!" Andie jumped up to go greet the cat.

The acoustics, amplifying Andie's voice, reverberated all around. The cat freaked. He shot back out the tunnel at warp factor seven.

"Um, what just happened?" Aiyana asked.

"His startle-reflex, I think? Prolly freaked him out by calling his name so loud." Andie stood to go after the cat--maybe coax him back inside.

She was gone for more than five minutes. Aiyana looked up over the top of her tablet every so often until she saw Andie walk back in.

"I found him, talked him down."

"Is he all right?" Ares trotted lightly at Andie's heels.

"Ask him yourself," Andie said.

"Um, Ares . . . are you all right?"

"Mew," Ares mewed, glancing around the round room at his echoed meow.

"Mew means yes," Andie explained.

"I . . . dayum." Aiyana seemed at a loss for words.

Andie went over to the portal. "Ares, maybe you can help me—I'm trying to get this door open. We call it the portal. See this brass plaque here? We think these words are a clue of how we get the door to open, but we just can't find any way to enter any information, even if we figure out the right passwords." Andie lifted Ares so he could look at the shiny surface. He looked at the brass, seeing his reflection, and looked back around at Andie.

"Oh, I didn't even think—do you read?"

Ares squinted back at Andie. She set him down.

"Gotcha. Sorry."

From the hammock, Aiyana said, "See? Normal cat; he didn't answer you that time."

"He understands me perfectly—he says 'no' by squinting his eyes. A lot of his communication is nonverbal."

"You're serious?"

"Mm hmm," Andie said. She sat down in the chair and picked up her tablet. Ares jumped up on her lap.

"Okay, let me read it to you."

She read out the entire riddle to the cat, feeling slightly silly.

Aiyana had vanished back into her tablet. "Hey, did you see your network connection is, like, really screaming fast?"

"No, Ares and I are working on this mystery here," Andie said.

"Because I'm watching a feed from the Boca Chica Starbase, back on Earth, as they roll out some new version of Starship, and the resolution is crystal. Wait . . . this can't be right. Andie?" Aiyana said.

"Hmm?"

"Check your signal strength."

"Whoa. Five rings. What's the green center dot mean?"

"That's what I'm looking at, I've never seen the center light up before. It feels even faster than fiber optics at home. But I'm not complaining."

The cat stared at the portal. Andie noticed him staring. She lifted one eyebrow.

"Ares, do you think it's the portal?"

Ares looked at Andie, curiously, but said nothing.

"You know, the portal . . . like it's somehow making our tablets and phones connect better."

"Mew," Ares said. To this, Andie shifted the cat off her lap and stood.

"Aiya, let's run a little experiment. Sleep your tablet, and I will too."

"Um, okay."

Andie looked at the portal lights. Two lights blinked on and off, a third one glowed steadily.

"Hm. No change. Okay, let's get all our devices outside the . . . pocket, and see if there's any difference. Aiya, could you carry them down the tunnel to the entrance?"

"Sure, but don't break our amazing network speeds in here." Aiyana stood. She stacked up two tablets and two handy phones and walked away. Andie watched the portal closely.

After a few seconds, the third light winked out, leaving just the two others blinking as usual.

"You can come back," Andie called down the tunnel.

A few seconds after Aiyana returned, light number three started blinking again, on and off. "Look, see?" Andie pointed at the light.

"Okay, so somehow the portal itself is giving us a faster wireless connection than direct-connect fiber optics at home? That makes no sense."

"I know, weird." Andie took her devices back, and Aiyana laid back down in the hammock. "At least we found the third blinky light and our network speed are . . . connected."

Aiyana's nose was back in her feeds, watching a live feed from inside the hydro-expeditionary base under the ice of Europa. People came and went, some in submersible suits, others wearing standard rocket crew ship suits. She scrolled on.

Andie brought up an image of the portal's riddle and opened a new search window. She opened a search string where she searched names from folklore first, those names that bridged ancient religion with modern-day Astronomy.

Andie considered the planets first. With the notable exception of the Greek god Ouranos, all eight planets had Roman names. She scratched Ares, who was up on her lap again. She shared her musings with the cat.

"If only Bode had stuck with Roman gods when he named the newly-discovered seventh planet. It might have been called Caelus [see-loos], make sense? That's the father of Saturn. Instead, Bode gave us everybody's favorite planet to mispronounce, Uranus."

"That's quite the star talk you've got going there," Aiyana said without looking up.

"What? He's a good audience." Andie looked at the cat. "See, the one the Greeks called 'Ouranos' was the god of the heavens. The Romans called him Caelus, which is where we get our word 'celestial.' So . . . when someone talks about a celestial place, it's a recycled idea that originally referred to Zeus' grandfather, Caelus."

Ares just looked at her. She stopped scratching his ears. "What? I actually pay attention in Stein's Astro class, whereas you, Mister Fuzzball, sleep through it."

Ares murmured a low "Mrrrrew," and hopped down.

"What's up?"

The cat rubbed her leg once with his shoulder, trotted off down the tunnel, and left.

"Was it something I said?" Andie called after Ares. He did not return.

She shrugged and resumed her search. Quite a few other heavenly objects, including dwarf planets and comets, were also named for beings of mythology across many cultures. Most stars were still known by the original names given by the earliest Persian astronomers. Andie put all that knowledge to good, yet fruitless, use right now. She read the first line of the riddle again.

Were Earth and Venus ever considered mother and daughter? Nope.

She found no link there, and certainly no 'orphan' drifting away, like an asteroid or something. Maybe that first couplet intended a more generic use of the word 'mother' or 'daughter' in the same way vessels, even starships, were always referred to in the feminine. She expanded her search to all deities, including the classically male ones, just in case.

Zeus' illegitimate son Dionysus, Andie found fascinating—in one telling, the child had been raised among river nymphs to hide him from Zeus' wife Hera, who had vowed to find and kill the child. In other tellings, the boy had been left by Hermes with a caretaker who raised him as a girl, thereby saving his life. Eventually Hera found the child and he had to go to the underworld, Hades' domain, to save his mother. Ancient Greek gods clearly had little or no boundaries in their actions.

On a side tab, Andie opened a notes section to compile all the valid possibilities. She researched and wrote with a digital stylus anything or anyone possible. She focused on what might be 'drifting away.' If she could find the orphan, whoever that was, she would find the heavenly daughter and her mother. She kept at it.

What about the Romulus and Remus? Twin brothers, not sisters.

What about variants of the same heavenly object, like Luna and Demeter? Or should she cross cultural bounds and link ideas over time? Luna, Artemis, Diana, Demeter? She expanded the list to include binary stars, rocking the traditional Persian spellings.

Drifting away also happened at the galactic scale, given the ever-accelerating expansion of the Universe . . . but galaxies seemed too big to be 'celestial daughter and mother.' Besides, galaxies like Andromeda were falling faster and faster *towards* Milky Way, not drifting away. Andie rejected galaxies outright. The answer had to be individual objects within, or near to, the Solar System. Within a half hour, she had a list more than a hundred word-pairs long.

She looked up at the plaque. The riddle was frustrating enough to make her want to chuck the whole thing, but helpful enough to give a glimmer of hope, keep her guessing. It was maddening.

She knew she could use more help, and hoped that Ric and Reillee might be the key to unlocking the next step. Tuesday was only a few hours away. Tuesday, they would keep at it until the Portal stood open.

Even Ares might be able to help — if he would just show up and stick around.

Chapter Seventeen

That Darned Cat

Tuesday, after school. As the four rounded the huge boulder, Ric was the first to speak. "What . . . is this?" Ric's open-mouthed grin made Andie grin right back at him.

"Go inside, see for yourself," Andie said. Not needing to be asked twice, Ric walked on ahead into the dark mouth of the tunnel. Gritting his teeth, Reillee followed.

Ric's head nearly brushed the ceiling, so he ran his hands across the 'Ghosts of Lake Michigan' warning words as he passed under them. In the darkness, he hadn't noticed the writings. Aiyana and Andie watched carefully. Aiyana shrugged and ran her hand smoothly along the ceiling above, imitating Ric.

"You guys, this is epic," Reillee said. "Your very own secret side tunnel."

"You ain't seen nothin yet," Aiyana murmured, almost in a whisper. Reillee looked back at her, doubt on his face. She nodded encouragingly. He had almost caught up with Ric as they reached the round room. The motion-sensor lights blazed to life. Ric squinted, then gaped as he looked around the room.

"It's bigger on the inside?" Ric said.

He winced at his own loud voice as the sound reverberated back from around the room.

"Ooo, I wonder if there's a sound center in the room," Reillee added as an afterthought. "The acoustics are trippy." As he made for the center of the room, he looked over to the right, at the portal. "What are those three red lights? Hey, is that a door? Is it an airlock?"

"We don't know, and maybe, and no clue," Andie replied. "It doesn't want to open."

Ric took an interest as well, and both boys crossed to look at it more closely. "So, there's no latch, handle, or controls . . . no hand ident plates, no viewscreen, no keyhole . . .?" Ric asked the obvious question. "So, no hint how it works?"

"Look to your left—the octet on the wall plaque," Andie said.

"The octet?" Aiyana asked Andie.

Andie nodded. "We have to call it something."

Ric read the octet over Reillee's shoulder, and murmured, "so it's probably meant to be opened gently, so no brute force . . ."

". . . or explosives," Reillee said, shaking his head in disappointment.

"Because if that's an airlock door, blasting it open is a singularly bad idea," Ric said.

"And here's our biggest clue, my dude: that Exo-Suit locker."

"Right? We're thinking the ghosts got through," Aiyana said.

"Ghosts?" the boys both said together.

"Jinx, buy me Campa-Cola," Reillee said.

Ric shook his head and looked at the girls. They explained the warnings they had found at the tunnel entrance. Aiyana pointed at the three vacant sleeping-cots.

"Well, that makes sense," Ric responded. "I mean, they aren't here anymore. Plus, look at the way they left things—like they didn't need to tidy up. So whatever secret the portal hides, they got through and . . . moved on."

"Or there isn't anything there," said Aiyana, still lounging in her hammock. "Maybe it's a broom closet or some practical joke from among the builders."

"Long way to go for a practical joke," Reillee said.

"I'm betting it's a big deal." Andie joined the boys at the plaque. "The portal looks old tech, but legit enough—just look how big it is. Big enough for even Ric to go through in a full Exo-Suit."

"Who were these . . . ghosts, anyway?"

"No clue. None of my Interwebs searches, no matter how cleverly I try to word them, turns up anything close to an answer. I figured out where Lake Michigan is, though." Andie sighed heavily and walked away.

"I still think they just made it up. Threw a dart at a map or something," Aiyana said, fluffing a pillow.

"So what's the story with those cots?" Reillee asked, walking over to check them out.

"We've sort of left them undisturbed. There are chocolate wrappers, a dead early-model music pod, and some other stuff . . . we think they were probably teenagers like us."

The room was quiet for a moment. Ric looked at Reillee, who nodded.

"So it's ours then," Reillee said.

"That means it needs some serious castle-building," Ric said.

"My thoughts exactly," Reillee agreed. They pulled two folding chairs from behind the three cots. They chatted together over Ric's tablet, occasionally looking up, around the room, and pointing occasionally, debating then adding ideas to a list.

While the boys plotted taking over the planet, or whatever, Andie kept at the riddle, examining the octet plaque from all angles. There was something subtle that she was missing, she just knew it. The plaque? She wiggled at it, tried to swing it upwards in case it had a hidden hinge. She twisted its frame in case it was on a vertical hinge. Nothing.

HEAVENLY DAUGHTER AND MOTHER, MIGHTY THEIR BOND
THEY FEARED, BOTH DREADED THAT ONE DAY ERE LONG

THEY DESTROY EACH OTHER BY THEIR INHERENT NATURE
AND TRAGIC IT WAS, OH, PRESSED IN TOGETHER:

ONE BROKEN, DESTROYED, DROPPING HER RING
ONE MOURNED FIERY TEARS, SORROWS TO SING

AN ORPHAN REMAINS, EVER SINCE, PUSHED AWAY
SHE DRIFTS, MORE DISTANT, DAY AFTER DAY.

"Grrrr…" Andie growled, then slammed her small fist against the steel door, hoping it might budge. Aiyana flinched at the loud noise. Andie looked around for something to ice her hand. The boys returned back to their plotting.

* * *

Wednesday morning, and a few new pieces of furniture had appeared, including a plug-in portable beverage cooler, specifically one with an ice maker. Also in place, a small set of portable speakers and a short shelving unit to set them on. These items had been very carefully sneaked into the Pocket during the night.

After school, Reillee surprised Andie with a small, folding tray-table, since she seemed to have deep-dived into researching every kind of portal the builders or architects of early Mars ever used. Her tablet sat atop the table and she kept at it. Andie ran carefully worded searches for any others that might have been built this way. So far zippo—there was nothing remotely similar, not in its style or by using passwords. It seemed the information had either been expunged from the records or forgotten over the last hundred standard years.

* * *

Thursday. By evening, the round room boasted still more upgrades — three more chairs, a 2-level metal bunk bed with mismatched foam mattresses, and one banged-up, second-hand automated floor vacuum to keep the white tile floors free of dust. Most of these items were clearly hand-me-downs from the Reduce/Reuse/Recycle place, cleverly found and even more cleverly sneaked in by the boys.

* * *

Friday, around sunrise, the group gathered in the pocket before classes — Fridays had a delayed start, so they had informally agreed to meet here and head to school as a group. The surprise this morning: someone had sneaked in an oversized red Afghan carpet, easily four meters long and three wide, and left it spread out across the center of the room. The thing was *huge*.

The problem was, neither of the boys would admit to bringing it in . . . to say nothing of how it had been brought in unnoticed.

The boys played the most convincing act of innocence and confusion, even pointing fingers at each other when challenged by the girls. Ric even went through the theatrics of suggesting Andie had brought it in and was playing coy, all with a straight face. Eventually everyone let it drop — their new magic carpet dampened out most of the sound reverberation — they could almost hold a normal conversation now.

This also prompted them to start kicking off their shoes, like they were at home in their own living rooms. Aiyana let out a long, contented sigh, seeming relaxed for the first time in weeks.

Flopped out in the lower bunk, Ric spoke up to Andie, in the bunk above. "I bet you were right—they figured it out. The Ghosts of Lake Michigan, I mean. Like, they totally got out of here."

"What makes you sure?" Andie said, peeking down from the top bunk.

"Well . . . they're clearly not here anymore and took their valuable things with them. Maybe they left the Mountain? I mean, that's a legit Exo-Suit locker there, correct?"

"A lot of good that is," Aiyana said from a hammock. "Someone emptied it out."

"Proof I'm right, Aiya," Ric said. "They put on their suits and stepped through to Shangri-la." He grinned.

Aiyana grinned back, chuckling. "You're hopeless."

Ric responded immediately. "Hopeful—we'll get through, and then we'll finally be freeeeeeeee."

"Like those guys?" Aiyana thumbed over her shoulder at the wall across the room, toward the words "NO GOVT WILL EVER SET U FREE."

Whoever had engraved the octet, like these other urban artists, the 'Ghosts,' left no clear answer of what their words might have meant. Maybe nothing.

Andie hopped down to read the octet again, murmuring a random phrase aloud every so often. She reached up and brushed at the dust that still wasn't on the plaque, and noticed one of the letters shifted, just slightly.

The letter shifted.

"Holy crap!" Andie burst out.

Andie pushed on the starting letter "O" in the fifth line of the octet, the brass central circle inside the first letter. It wiggled just a bit, but then caught, refusing to budge any further.

By then, the others were already crossing the room, converging on

Andie and the portal.

"What?" "What is it?" Questions came quickly. "Find something?"

"It moved. This letter right here . . . the 'O' . . . it moved when I pushed. But then . . . nothing happened."

Each teen reached up, pushing on the letter.

Even more nothing happened.

"Okay, read it again," Ric said.

Andie murmured through the entire octet, stopping at the words 'oh: pressed in together.'

She pushed both letters "O" simultaneously.

Something clicked.

A small panel dropped open under the plaque—an antiquated QWERTY keyboard. Above the letters, two text fields lit up.

Blue cursors blinked in both blanks, as if eager for someone to type something after a decades-long sleep. Four teenage faces, eyes wide, stared in silence.

Andie beamed, smiling ear to ear.

"Oh my," Aiyana finally murmured. Andie licked her lips in anticipation, checking the time—they had thirty minutes before delayed-start Friday classes would begin. Time enough to try a few ideas.

"Let's see if we can get this thing open." With that, Andie entered what she believed to be the most likely candidate. In the first blank, she entered the brightest of the Seven Sisters, and what seemed to be the next most likely. In the first blank: *Alcyone*. In the second, *Electra*.

Everyone held their breath.

Squinting sideways, Andie poised her finger above the 'Enter' key. Reillee grabbed both of Ric's shoulders, and Aiyana rested a hand on Andie's forearm.

"Moment of truth," Andie said, and clicked Enter. The device gave an error sound, a ***beep-beep***. Then both blanks cleared, the twin blue cursors blinking as before.

"Hm," someone said.

In the next ten minutes, the keyboard had been used for dozens of attempts, idea after idea. All rejected. Andie hammered in entry after entry, all resulting in the annoying 'beep-beep' reject tone.

Maia. Merope.   *Beep-beep.*

Taygeta. Celaeno. *Beep-beep.*

Atlas. Pleione.   *Beep-beep.*

Earth. Mars.   *Beep-beep.*

Caelus. Neptunus. *Beep-beep.*

Selene. Artemis.   *Beep-beep.*

Luna. Hecate.   *Beep-beep.*

Andie gave her hands a rest and squinted at the display. "You mock me, sir?" she said to the access control panel. Reillee spoke up.

"Ok . . . 'heavenly daughter and mother' could be objects in space, like constellations . . . or, or early planet names, even before the Greek names were assigned," Reillee suggested. "My history teacher says the first gods humanity ever worshiped were actually the planets as they crossed the night sky—like they were heavenly beings going about their business."

"Or could they be people who did great things before they died? Like they have already passed on, and they're in 'heaven' now?" Ric asked. "Two people in history, like a mentor and a padawan . . . Marie Curie and Irène Joliot-Curie . . . or Annie Jump Cannon and Cecilia Payne. . . Katherine Goble and Mary Jackson."

"Okay, but . . . the orphan? What about the orphan drifting away?" Ric asked, sitting up.

"Hm. The Voyagers are drifting away, they're somewhere in the Kuiper Belt still, aren't they?" Reillee offered.

"Yes, but that's two orphans. The octet only mentions one orphan," Andie said. "Plus, the Voyagers are clipping along at fifty thousand clicks an hour. That's screaming fast, not drifting away."

The teens took a few moments, each lost in thought.

Andie kept entering ideas, and the keyboard kept rejecting them. It was almost time to head out for school; Aiyana walked over to stand by Andie. Andie glanced at her briefly, then focused back on the riddle.

"How's it going?" Aiyana asked.

"I've got like twenty ideas all swirling around, but I'm not sure how many chances we get before this thing locks us out."

"Dee, it's probably an old maintenance shed . . . it's not a bank vault," Aiyana said.

"That's another concern — what if it's alarmed or . . . or, if fiddling with his thing brings MERF down here to investigate?"

Aiyana looked back at her.

"I mean, this is our space, we're the keepers of the secret. I don't want to ruin all that." Andie sighed. "Maybe we should just let mysteries be mysteries. There are some things we may never discover."

"Babe, it's a door. It's not like death or demons or *Tartarus* is lurking on the other side," Aiyana said, smiling.

"Tartarus rocks," Reillee said from across the room. Ric high-fived him. They had both seen Tartarus in concert earlier that year.

"Maybe some doors weren't meant to be opened." Andie looked into Aiyana's eyes.

"Maybe. But see this?" She rested a hand on the keyboard. "It was meant to be opened. You'll figure it out. I believe in you." Aiyana paused before adding, "you need to get outta your own head."

Aiyana gave Andie a side hug as they both looked back up at the display, twin blue cursors blinking, patiently waiting for them to try again. Behind them, the boys stood and shouldered their packs.

With great reluctance, the girls pulled themselves away from the portal. Andie clicked the keypad shut, brushing her hand softly across the brass.

She was the last to leave the Pocket.

* * *

After school, the friends headed straight back to try some more. By now, as they walked in, all four had adopted the habit of brushing a hand over the 'trespassers beware' warning while passing under it. The room lights flipped on as usual.

Ric kicked off his shoes, grabbed a Campa-Cola from the cooler, and lounged in the lower bunk. Andie hopped up into the top bunk and fluffed a pillow to relax after a long day. Reillee put in some ear buds and started head-nodding to a righteous beat.

In her hammock, Aiyana cued up the series *Roads of Mars*, the "Waystations" episode, which featured the old Mons-Nerus Highway. Though it was only three-quarters the length of Earth's old 'Route 66,' it shared some striking similarities: overnight rest stops, quirky attractions, roadside food stores, and perhaps the most important for wheeled travel on Mars: vehicle maintenance and MERF rescue stations.

Half an hour passed. Something caught Ric's eye over the top of his tablet; he looked up.

There seemed to be a tabby cat walking into the room, looking for all the world like he owned the place. Ares arrived at the middle of the huge Afghan carpet, looking tiny. He looked from teenager to teenager in turn.

"Um, guys? How is it our, um, science cat is in the room with us?"

Andie looked up. "Oh, I invited Ares to join us," she said casually.

"How does he even know where here is?" Ric asked.

"Um, I told him, duh." Andie rolled her eyes and looked back down at her tablet.

Ric leaned out to look up at Andie. "You're so weird," he said at length.

Andie didn't hesitate. "You have no ide—"

"Shh!" Ric whispered. "You hear that?" he whispered. They all strained to listen. Nothing. Then, the slight crunch of gravel, from the end of the entry tunnel.

"Quick, the lights," Aiyana whispered.

Andie clicked them all off using her app. A second later, Reillee switched his tablet off, plunging the pocket into near-total darkness.

The crunch of gravel stopped. Silence dragged out; their eyes eventually adjusted. The three red LED lights gave only the faintest hint of where anything in the room was. In his socks, Ric carefully stood, crouching slightly in the dark. The pen-light in his hand was off, but ready for action. He took a few steps across the soft Afghan carpet.

Ares, curious about whatever all the humans were looking at, could see perfectly fine through the darkness. He trotted away, toward the entrance. Andie saw his movement.

"Hey, ssst..." Andie reached out to stop Ares from walking away, by trying to speak up without actually speaking up.

Ric eased along quietly behind the cat, down the tunnel. The crunching sound came again, this time more faint. Whoever was there was trying very hard to be stealthy. Ric could see a silhouette walking along the side of the tunnel ahead, running a slender hand along the wall. Then he heard bracelets jangling slightly. Bracelets that sounded familiar . . .

"Who's there?" Ric bellowed.

The shocked girl screamed, dropped her bag, and sprinted back toward the entrance.

The cat bounded back toward Andie. The girl slipped on the loose gravel and executed a perfect wipeout, coming to a sliding stop sprawled out on her back.

Andie turned the lights on.

"Uh . . . Sitara?"

"Oh . . . Ric?" Sitara clutched her chest, breathing heavily as Ric walked over and looked down at her, grinning.

She looked up at him. "What in heaven's name are you doing, you bloody Kho-taa?" She took his offered hand and sat up. "I swear . . . *tere baap ko us raat chup chaap so Jaana chahiye tha!*" She muttered as she stood, dusting off a hurt hip and wiping grit from her palm.

A shocked silence followed. Ric helped brush some dust off her back. "How did you even find this place?"

"I followed that darned cat, he led me straight here."

Reillee shook his head. "And . . . what did you just call Ric? A bloody um, what?"

"Kho-" Sitara began.

"She called me a bloody donkey," Ric answered. Sitara nodded. Ric added, "believe me, she has called me much worse."

"And what was that other thing you said to him?" Reillee asked.

Sitara smiled sweetly. "Much worse."

She blinked long, beautiful eyelashes at Ric, then glared.

Chapter Sixteen

Went Not by the Wayside

The proverbial cat was out of the bag, now that Sitara had found the Pocket. The four gave her a brief tour, and she found the whole thing 'delightful.' But she was still 'extremely cross' with Ric.

He drew her out of her dark mood. "So, you just followed Ares here?"

Looking comically small in the center of the carpet, the cat looked up. With an innocent 'who, me?' expression on his fuzzy little face, he began to preen himself, starting with the right shoulder. Cats have no shame.

"I was late leaving school today, Ric, so I thought I might surprise you at your house, and he was there on your doorstep, just waiting. When I went to pet him, he moved away from me a few steps, and then looked back at me, to follow him. He could not have been more clear about it."

"Ares, you can't lead anyone else here, all right?" Upon hearing his name from Andie, he paused his bath and looked over at her. "Okay?"

"Mew," he said. Then followed a few more kitty noises. "Rr-mew mrrr-mrrrw?"

"What was all that about?" Ric asked.

"Um, who knows?" Andie said, turning back to the Portal keypad. Without looking up, she added, "so, are you guys going to that keynote lecture tonight?"

"I thought we had that exhibition match against Nerus? They sent their varsity and JV teams weeks before homecoming," Reillee said, looking from Andie to Ric.

"The bullseye match? Count me in, my dude." He fist-bumped Reillee.

Andie leveled a stare at both boys. "Come on, there's more to life than bullseye handball, you know."

"Yeah, there's Tartarus."

"And *Deep Blue* . . . and Bruce Guthro."

"And Bruce Guthro. That man makes me want to sneak aboard a random MagLev and see where the hobo train takes me," Reillee said.

"Focus, boys." Sitara asserted. "Let's see if we can learn a few things about the quake. My father has said some pretty wild things, and I for one would like to know that the worst is behind us."

"Ugh, fine, let's go do something nerdy before smash mouth handball."

"In that case, we better scat," Andie said, "Dr. Holm is on in just a half hour or so."

Aiyana gathered her things. "We should avoid being seen as we leave."

As they all carefully made their way out, the conversation wandered from *bullseye* to the quake and back again. They took special care not to be observed walking toward the perimeter path.

Ares strutted, caring not one bit if he was being observed.

* * *

Even back-to-back with the evening's handball scrimmage against Nerus High School, a famous scientist should have drawn only a small crowd of a few hundred students. But upon entering the 1500-seat ACSA arena, they found it well more than half-filled. Quite a few alumni, many adults, and both teams' cheer squads were already co-mingled with the student crowd.

The handball players themselves were absent, warming up on a nearby practice court, probably.

Andie glanced around for Ares, who had vanished again.

"There's some decent seats over there," Ric said, using his advantage of height to see over the crowd. The others followed, with Andie bringing up the rear.

"What's with this crowd?" Aiyana asked, as they squeezed past a couple on the aisle, and found seats high in the center section.

"Maybe people are interested in the quake?" Andie suggested.

"Well, our nerdy science teacher is enjoying himself," Aiyana replied, pointing down front. Stein was there, exchanging a hug with a dark-haired woman in a navy-blue rocket pilot's flight suit. "Is that Stein's wife?"

"I don't think so, isn't his wife an attorney? The lady down there looks like a pilot . . . plus, she looks a little young for him."

"He's not that old, is he?" Aiyana said. Stein shook hands with a couple other pilots and flight engineers, then they took their seats down front. "Wow, there's a bunch of kids from Nerus," she murmured, noticing a cluster of maroon and silver across the crowd.

The friends looked around the arena, people-watching. Here and there, small groups of Robinson High's blue and gold were also mixed in.

Andie noticed someone walking in, toward the empty seats beside her—a boy she didn't recognize, with a few others in tow. He was handsome, with brownish-blond hair and a gentle expression. He smiled at Andie, and gesturing, said, "Are you holding these seats?"

"Um, no, be my guest," Andie said, noticing a faint bruise on his forehead. His wavy hair did not quite cover the bruise. He nodded his thanks to her.

She gestured at his forehead as he sat. "What happened there?"

"I'm a klutz . . . and they even warned us about doorways before we made landfall."

"You just got here from Earth? Or Luna?" Andie was suddenly very interested—this boy had a story to share.

"Yes. Earth. I'm still trying to get the hang of things. Like doorways," he said. "I'm Trace." He said, leaning over to offer a handshake. Andie briefly shook his hand.

"Andie, with an i-e," she replied. "What ship were you on?"

Trace looked down at his feet. "Uh, Lucky Seven," he replied, barely above a whisper.

Andie turned toward him in her seat. "Are you serious? Wh-what happened on the flight? All we've heard are rumors about some explosion or UFOs or micro-meteors or something."

"I heard the same thing," Trace replied. "Someone in one of the other ships saw something, I guess?"

"So . . . no idea what it was?"

"Um, I didn't actually see any . . . explosion; a Starship's windows are all forward, up on the dorsal side. Hard to see behind."

Andie squinted, considering. "Hmmm. Yeah. I only have dim memories of my own crossing—"

A voice over the loudspeakers interrupted her.

"Ahem, may I have your attention please?" resounded through the arena. A tall, fit man in a blue suit and dark tie stood at a lectern, waiting for conversations to settle. When the room fell silent, he continued.

"Good evening. I'm Principal Chojnacki, and I'm pleased to see so many Olympians from our own Mons High School, and of course our visiting team, the Nerus High Legionnaires!"

A round of applause and cheers filled the space. The principal waited for quiet, smiling and nodding up at the crowd.

"Now, before we begin tonight's preliminary match, we have a special treat for you, a guest speaker who has agreed to join us on short notice all the way from Mariner Valley's *Nooma Research Station*. It is my honor now to introduce to you Mars' pre-eminent geologist, author of more than a dozen books and host of the podcast *MarsRocks*. Ladies and gentlemen, please join me in giving a big welcome to Dr. Jan Holm."

Polite applause greeted the short, grey-haired man in his classic olive-drab tweed suit. He crossed the arena floor and shook hands enthusiastically with Principal Chojnacki, who then stepped down into the front row next to Stein and took a seat. The applause faded.

Dr. Holm held a cordless microphone and tapped his black-framed glasses back into place on his nose. He smiled up into the lights and the faces in the crowd. A hush fell. He spoke in a gentle English accent.

"What a kind welcome, thank you ever so much."

From his pocket, he drew out a clicker. The huge flatscreens of the four-panel jumbotron showed a high-definition view of the planet from orbit. Mariner Valley stretched away to the right, the three Tharsis Montes peaks, the triplets as they were known, stepped their way across the equator, and massive Olympus Mons dominated the left side of the image.

"I had prepared a discussion of how Mars' two tectonic plates moved along their transform boundary to form that famous valley, but I've shelved it for another time."

The image dove down toward the ground smoothly, traveling across the valley, zoomed past the triplets, and twisted sideways to the right until the horizon leveled itself out. Olympus Mons appeared to be flying toward the viewer at an impossibly high speed.

"Let's talk about the Mountain awaking from its slumber instead, shall we?" His words were met with more than a few nods from the audience.

The image dove right into the ground and straight down through layers to the mantle, beneath which the core of Mars still 'sloshed around.'

102

Dr. Holm took less than fifteen minutes to walk the audience through the structure and rock strata, showing layers upon layers right up to the rock layer that was the foundation of the capital city. He shared several possibilities explaining how the recent quakes were triggered and finished by focusing on an unexpected culprit—humanity itself. He kept his ideas brief and entertaining enough to hold everyone's attention.

He concluded his thoughts with a creative flourish about the god of war not having surrendered yet—the next move in Mars' battle plan would be 'quite impossible to predict.'

"The God of War may just be starting his campaign; the next twenty years may be . . . interesting, to say the least. I encourage all of you to pay close attention, and never stop being curious. In fact, your ideas may shape the fortunes of us all. Thank you for your kind attention."

A polite round of applause followed his cryptic final comment, and he opened the floor to questions.

Several audience members descended the steps to an audience microphone standing in the aisleway. A slender gentleman in a charcoal suit jacket was first, speaking in a slight German accent.

"Dr. Holm, thanks for taking my question. I'm Dr. Müller, a new arrival here on Mars, an anthropologist by trade. I wanted to ask you if there is any truth to the rumor that some underground engine left by an ancient civilization might be triggering all these smaller tremors? They seem to have a pattern, when analyzed over time."

Dr. Holm smiled broadly, "You mean, 'What if it's aliens?' What if aliens are making the ground shake?"

"No sir, I don't think there's such a thing as aliens on Mars. But what about the Jovis Petroglyphs? Aren't they worth looking into? Some ancient race of hyper-advanced humans perhaps?"

"Come on, that's been well-debunked," Dr. Holm answered. "That was a couple kids playing with paint they found in a shed fifteen standard years ago."

"Yes sir, but they claim they painted over ze strange lines, ticks, und circles . . . they claimed some original language was already there. Something, or someone, left those marks on the chamber walls long before modern humans arrived on ze planet."

"There's nothing to support what those boys claimed, and they are long since grown up. I bet we couldn't even find the cave they painted under Jupiter's Crossing if we tried . . . besides, on Mars, technically we're the aliens. We're the ones poking and prodding—carving and destabilizing. All right then, who's next?"

The German man nodded his thanks and stepped aside for the next one in line—a student, by the look of her. The girl angled the microphone slightly downward and spoke confidently.

"Dr. Holm, I'm Laura Piper from Robinson High. I wanted to ask you about what you said in your comments, about how humanity could be triggering these quakes. Could we really have such an impact on the Mountain? I mean, how many are we on Mars . . . two million? Two and a half at the most? I can't imagine that we really make that big a difference. Could we?"

"Well, it's certainly possible. And since we know Mars' mantle and core are still sloshing about, just the right pressure in the right place could affect geological change. Ever thought about how much a thousand buildings weigh? Or ten thousand buildings? All concentrated in one location, and in the case of Mons, with a million people crowded inside? Just add it all up. Plus, the mass of all the water we've pumped into Silver Lake, and all the air we breathe there, filling that entire complex, where before there was only vacuum."

He paused for effect. "Even the air has mass, and therefore weight. And it does all add up."

"I'm sorry, sir, I don't follow. How could one point on the city's foundation layer . . . destabilize an entire Mountain?"

"Your critical-thinking mind is keen, dear girl, never let it go by the wayside. To answer your question, consider this: think of the plateau as a balanced surface, sitting neatly on the layer beneath it. Where the magma came up billions of years ago in the center of the volcano, that's the pivot point. I'll use my arm as a rudimentary example." He held up his arm, bent at the elbow, horizontal in front of him.

"So here at my fingertips . . . that's where the city is located, and way over here at my elbow, that's the opposite side of the Mountain. With me so far?"

The girl nodded.

"Okay. So we've been filling up this empty part, here at my fingertips with people and buildings, and water and air for more than a hundred standard years. With even just a small amount of weight added, what direction would you expect my hand to move?"

"Um, down?"

"Correct, Miss Piper, correct. And when my hand out here sinks down, what's happening way over there at my elbow?"

"I guess it's rising up?"

"Yes, not nearly as much as I'm dramatizing here, but yes. Even a slight lifting of the pressure here at my elbow can destabilize what's underneath . . . to the point of collapse, or releasing pressures beneath, if the change is enough. Then something under here crumbles away, and all those lovely seismic ripples, the P-waves, the S-waves, the L-waves, oh my. Those quake shockwaves trigger movement all through the Mountain, and beneath it . . . and then we all get to make new friends in our nearest SAFE pods."

A chuckle rippled around the room.

"So you see, that's my point. We can't rule out human action directly affecting the Mountain, no matter how few or many we may be. Even the grandest storms announce themselves with a simple breeze. We should just make our mark on Mars in a careful, balanced way."

"Thank you," Laura said, stepping aside and returning to her seat.

"My pleasure. And who's next? Yes sir, what's on your mind this evening?"

The next man introduced himself and asked his question—something about drilling down to the epicenters to relieve the pressure, or some such.

'Q and A' went on for another ten minutes. Then Dr. Chojnacki led a final round of applause for their honored guest and announced that the bullseye-handball exhibition match would begin in fifteen minutes.

Andie found her mind wandering to what insights this boy seated next to her might have on the quakes, given he had just arrived the week prior. But before she could strike up a new conversation, he excused himself to join his fellow Legionnaires over in the visiting team's cheering section.

As the game start clock ticked down to zero, the arena filled up nearly to its full capacity.

The match began with raucous cheering, the crowds of students shouting their support until their voices gave out. A hard-fought contest ended with the Legionnaires edging out the Olympians, 89-83.

As the crowd stood to head out, Andie searched briefly for Trace and his friends, but they were lost in the sea of humanity. She knew they would soon travel home to Nerus. Maybe they might return for the Homecoming gathering, two weeks away?

The weekend passed. The school week that followed slipped by, one day after the next, and Andie forgot about her fellow Earthling named Trace. There were new things to get excited about, and Friday night's field trip up to the Mons-Plex Overlook topped the list.

Chapter Fifteen

Through the Eye of the Needle

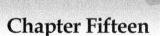

"**L**adies and gents, we are out of time!" Stein called out to the classroom. Students packed up their things and got ready to leave for another weekend.

The day had started with a lively spirit assembly welcoming two early arrivals--visiting student groups from Uintah High and New Skye's Portree High.

They immersed themselves into the Olympians' classes and after lunch, students from New Kyiv's *Lyceum* arrived and mingled into their assigned classes as well. The groups from Nerus, Robinson, and the others weren't expected until the following week for Homecoming.

"Reminder—for all those going on the field trip hike tonight, we meet at *The Needle* archway at 5 pm; please don't be late! Any questions about that field trip, please see me after." Stein opened the door as the Friday afternoon ending bell rang.

Andie waited for Aiyana to join her at the cat. Before they met up, Stein was already speaking to Ares.

"Okay, mister, you can't do your disappearing-reappearing act this time around. We'll spend some quality time together tomorrow, I promise. But tonight, I need you to stay here. I hope that makes sense."

"Mew," Ares said simply.

Stein looked up at Andie. "I can never tell with this guy. I hope he doesn't do something crazy like follow us up the tunnel trail."

Andie bit her lip. "Uh, yeah," she said. "And . . . why's that a problem?"

"Because we're g—" Stein stopped himself. "It just wouldn't be safe."

Andie nodded, not following his logic. She scratched Ares under his chin, and he closed his eyes to lean into her attentions like always.

Aiyana watched from a few feet away. "Ready to roll, chica? ACSA for dinner, then our cool field trip?"

"Yes. So you don't have to go home right away then?"

"Excused from my chores tonight, thanks to Mister Stein and his field trip," Aiyana said.

"Wait. Chores on a Friday night?" Stein asked.

Aiyana said nothing.

"Sorry, not my business," the teacher conceded, managing a smile.

"It's okay, chores aren't a problem. I've gotten used to it. It's just . . . my folks can be a little . . . intense, sometimes," Aiyana said. Stein nodded.

Aiyana turned to Andie. "Let's go."

Andie crouched next to Ares, face to face with the cat. She whispered, "we won't be in the pocket tonight, but maybe tomorrow, okay?"

Ares murmured a 'mww.' Maybe that meant yes? It was hard to understand him when he mumbled. She scratched his ears one last time and stood. The two girls said goodbye to their teacher and left.

Ares watched them go like always.

* * *

The smallest exit from the Mons-Plex city cavern itself was not officially named *Eye of the Needle,* like a small city gate from ancient Earth, but many called it that anyway. The pathway snaked up an extinct lava tube, a capillary, just wide enough for a few people to walk side by side.

Many simply called the hike the Needle. As it wound up and into the stone cliff face like a curvy bit of string, the path twisted back on itself as it made its way up to a broad natural shelf overlooking the city.

Five p.m. approached. Twenty-eight students gathered around Stein and fellow science teachers Dr. Aditya Kumar, Bill Shackleton, and Brooke Farnsworth. Principal Chojnacki joined them—he often participated in excursions like this one.

Stein clapped his hands three times and called for attention using the outdoor voice all teachers seemed to possess. "Ladies and gents, please gather around. We are hiking up tonight for a special presentation of the Universe. Geology students, please watch for changes in the rock walls, see if you can name the igneous layers we will be passing through. Astronomy students . . . um, enjoy the rocks as well." He paused. The last few side conversations calmed down.

"Now, please pay very close attention, this is your safety briefing. Mrs. Farnsworth will cover all safety aspects of the hike, and answer your questions, so please give her your undivided."

Brooke Farnsworth, short spitfire of a biology teacher with reddish pixie-cut hair and an engaging smile, stepped forward and likewise spoke loudly for all to hear.

"All right, everyone, listen up! We are going up some steep terrain inside the caves and tunnels of this hike called the Needle. If you have never been up this trail before, or if you want to make sure not to get lost . . . please open the MonsMap app on your devices. In fact, everyone please open them up while I talk about a few things."

Some students consulted tablets; others tapped on their handy phones.

"As we reach the steeper parts, it's best to always walk with your shoe treads flat to the ground—this minimizes the chance of you slipping or spraining an ankle. The more contact and traction you have with the gravel along the trail, less chance you'll fall flat on your . . . the less chance you'll fall down." A few chuckles.

"Trust me when I say you are not going to want to reach the top exhausted or with a twisted ankle. We have something very special in mind. Plus, you may have heard there's food. This is true, and we thank Principal Chojnacki for picking up the bill. So those who rush the hike and get winded or injured or lost before reaching the top . . . you will forfeit your food to someone else."

She had a way of putting good behavior in the students' best interests.

"So please, be careful, take your time, and . . . Stick. With. Your. Partner . . . at all times. If you do not have a partner, please stand over here with Mister Steinheiser and we will make sure no one is flying solo. All right, now no one gets to race ahead of me and Principal Chojnacki, and please don't wander down any side tunnels; you might get lost and miss out on the best part. If you lose signal or your app gets bugged, just follow the white stripe on the floor, it leads all the way to the top. Are there any questions?"

No questions.

"All right. As you walk past Mister Steinheiser here, swipe your device, your wrist chrono or your handy phone, so we can make sure the number of students heading up and the number returning later are equal. In science, we hate it when numbers don't balance—that leads to us having to do paperwork. So please don't test us on this," she smiled. Many smiled back. Mrs. Farnsworth was also many students' favorite among all their teachers.

"Final thing, please grab a power protein bar and a water bottle as you are accounted for. Yes, everyone is expected to take these. All right, off we go." Brooke Farnsworth strode forward, joining the principal as the first partner pair to be accounted for. They walked to the needle's archway, water bottle and ration power bar tucked away.

Students queued up.

A student named Zach approached the entryway with his partner Faith. "Hey, Mr. S., we're heading up for a several-hour hike, right? Back here by midnight, latest?"

"That's the notion," Stein said, glancing sideways at his colleague Bill Shackleton, a wry grin on his face.

"Then why the extra food and water?" Faith asked. "Isn't there already food up at the top?"

"That, my friends, is a surprise that I think you'll truly enjoy."

The boy shrugged and nodded slightly. He and Faith swiped their wrist chronos, grabbed water and a bar, and vanished through the archway.

Andie and Aiyana ended up smack in the middle of the group. As they were about to enter the archway, Andie grabbed her partner's arm. "Aiya, look," and pointed vaguely toward a pile of rocks off to one side of the tunnel entrance.

A little fuzzy orange face vanished behind the rocks. The girls looked at each other. They stepped out of line to have a talk with Ares.

"You can come out, you little furball," Aiyana said.

"She didn't mean that. But yes, you have to come out, Ares," Andie added. After a moment, Ares walked around and sat a few feet away, looking up at the girls.

"You can't come with us," Andie said.

"Rr-mew," Ares said with an interested expression. Or was that concern? Andie couldn't be sure.

"Look, Stein said you can't come along on this one, and no, I don't know why. You know he trusts you as a tough little . . . guy, no matter what. But you need to stay here, here at ground level."

"Rrrrr," Ares meowed. He squinted his eyes at Andie.

"No." Andie was adamant. "You can't come." Then she thought for a moment. "Look, what if we guarantee that we'll take you . . . wherever Stein is taking us . . . as soon as we can? Let me at least find out why you can't come, then we'll go together."

Ares' eyes went wide, but then squinted again.

"I promise."

The cat mumbled something. He turned to walk away, toward the nearest buildings, mumbling and burbling in his little kitty language all the way.

Andie shook her head, and smiled, suppressing the urge to laugh out loud. Stein called out from the entrance, where he and the other teacher stood. All the other students had gone in.

"Time to roll, ladies, if you want to be included."

Andie and Aiyana collected their water and power bar, and each scanned a device they carried on their person—Andie, her watch, and Aiyana, a handy phone from her back pocket. From the archway entrance, Andie glanced back for a quick look around. The cat was gone.

Stein accounted for all 33 souls on the school's group hike, and texted that total, as well as all transponder search codes for every participant to the other teachers and the principal.

He stowed his tablet in a thigh pocket and closed the food and water storage boxes. Time to hike.

Before them stood a carved archway in the rock face. The entryway could have been carved in a smooth curve, but a creative engineer among the builders had shaped it to resemble an old-world castle stone entrance. It looked like one block of stone was set upon another, with gaps left for the cement joints. It even had a mock keystone at the top of the arch.

Aiyana stepped through the archway, but something caught Andie's eye. She looked down.

"Mister Stein, what's that? Is that a year?" Andie pointed at the base of the carvings, where the neatly machine-engraved initials M.K.S. stood out clearly, with 2132 beneath.

"Oh my. So, it's 2354 on Earth right now, and that would put it at . . . more than two hundred twenty Earth years ago. That's, hang on . . . 118 of our standard years ago. This archway is . . ."

"Ancient," Andie finished for him.

"Well, in Mars terms, I suppose." Stein shook his head, marveling at it. Bill Shackleton looked on as well, saying nothing—the builders had done truly special things.

Andie brushed her fingertips across the inscription, wondering who M.K.S. might have been. Then she stepped through the entryway and joined her partner for the hike up the needle. The tan-and-speckled walls closed in around them, gently curving left, and sloping upward. Stein and Shackleton followed closely.

"Mister Stein, what did they do with the builders' bodies when they passed on? Like, where would M-K-S be buried now?" Andie asked, briefly walking backwards with a hand on Aiyana's shoulder.

"We don't really know," Stein admitted. "It's a lost part of history. I've heard some suggest they're buried along one of the old driving routes between the original twin cities—like maybe somewhere out there is a massive cemetery, but no one has been able to find it."

"How *did* people used to drive across Mars?" Aiyana asked. "Like, in side-by-side skimmers or rovers or something?"

Mr. Shackleton spoke up. "Oh yes, before the MagLev tracks were recently laid down, a whole road network connected all seven cities—trains have only been running for about thirty standard or so." Aiyana nodded to his reply.

The tunnels widened. One could not quite reach out to touch both side walls of the tunnel, but it was close.

"The color in the stone layers here is so dramatic," Mr. Shackleton observed, his deep voice echoing off the walls and high ceiling above.

"There's something . . . medieval about it." Bill Shackleton was a huge history buff, and always seemed to interpret situations through the eyes of humanity's past. Stein liked his colleague.

Well-concealed power lines connected thousands of lamps, mostly yellow, along the main trail and side trails as they walked. The single, fading white stripe kept everyone on course.

The tunnel straightened out, while the roof overhead yawned much taller, tapering naturally several stories overhead to a long line of darkness. Some of the lights glowing upward were in other colors: oranges, violets, greens, and blues. The girls before them had opened the gap, hiking at a faster pace, and were just reaching the first of the SAFE pods along their hiking trail.

"Can you imagine being in here if the power failed? What a nightmare." Bill said.

"Mmm, I had a cousin who was in the Shotwell Breezeway when they did that blackout drill last year. Remember that?" Stein asked.

Bill nodded. "I'll never forget it—my oldest was stuck in the Big 'Vater, on his way down from the greenhouses. Freaked him out." He shook his head at the memory.

They reached the first SAFE pod, stepping over the doorway and starting their march through its center.

Bending his head slightly, Bill asked, "How many of these are there, along the hike?"

"My map app shows . . . six, including this one," Stein responded.

The needle's path up through the living rock prevented the typical placement of SAFE pods alongside the trails, so the hiking path simply went *through* them. In an engineering *tour de force*, these larger dive bunkers had been designed with pressure doors on both ends.

The six bunkers had been placed at regular intervals, each protecting a part of the climb up to the trail's highest point, the city Overlook.

Over the course of forty-five minutes, the group transited all six bunkers, and hikers had passed among cleverly backlit magma stalactites and stalagmites along the route.

With small, side tunnel outcrops and occasional alcoves near the summit, here were plenty of places to be alone — poets, introverts, and the odd crazy-in-love couple enjoyed the labyrinth of spaces to find solace.

The overlook itself was a broad balcony-like structure just under the city cavern's ceiling, where hikers could take in the grandest views of the entire Mons-Plex below, from Green Acres in the West to Silver Lake, the grand forest, and the MagLev *Terminus* train station, to the East.

Off to the side of the overlook, a short stretch of the tunnel met an external airlock, leading out to the Martian surface. Not often used, it connected with a plateau and dust-blown roads where outdoor vehicles had gone about their business for a century or more.

A handful of students lingered to take a few pictures of the blue, simulated sunset, matching the real sunset outside. The stragglers headed eventually found the short tunnel's domed gathering area. Here, partner pairs reached the top of their hike — everyone had arrived.

"Where's the food?" someone in the back asked.

"Patience," Mrs. Farnsworth replied.

On the opposite wall, set between several Exo-Suit lockers, was the inner door of the airlock, an aluminum composite door with a sign in glowing aqua-colored letters reading:

INNER DOOR
EXIT

The inner door stood wide open. Andie and a few others peered curiously inside. The airlock could fit six or eight people, and at the far end, another door with its sign in bright amber-orange letters read:

EXIT
OUTER DOOR

Stein and the other teachers did a quick nose count. 33 people, good to go. Mrs. Farnsworth crossed to the center of the room.

"Will everyone please isolate yourselves with your partner? We want no solos, no lone wolf activity please." She said, her voice pleasant, with a hollow reverb effect in the domed chamber.

Students complied, standing in pairs.

Stein stepped to the closest Exo-Suit locker, opened it, and pulled out a long rack of brand-new suits. He grabbed one off a hook and tossed its ten-kilo heft to a nearby student.

"Everyone, suit up please," Stein said with a fiendish grin.

"Wh-what?" several students said in unison.

"It's a star party, friends. We've been in touch with all your parents directly, and they have given their consent for you to share this little adventure. No one will be forced to go outside."

He let that sink in.

"We're really going outside? Like . . . outside, outside?" a student from the back called out.

"We are. Given the excellent safety record of these Exo-Suits, and the plateau out there with its safety guardrails, it is very safe. All we require is that you take your own safety seriously, so we all can have a positive, memorable experience."

A bold few stepped forward to grab their suits, stepping aside for the others who followed. Other teachers helped pass out suits from multiple lockers and encouraged students to don their suits, no need to wait.

Andie passed a suit to Aiyana, then held her own, undoing the chest piece to climb in. She wiggled a shoe into one pantleg, and found it was a snug fit, but not uncomfortable. Both legs in, she shimmied the suit over her back, and helped Aiyana with her arms. Then she saw the look on Aiyana's face — she had turned pale.

"I hate these things," she said simply.

"I know, Aiya, but we can't back out now. Plus, have you ever been outside?" Andie asked, while slipping the green pair-cord woven bracelet off her wrist and into one of the suit's pockets.

"Does riding the MagLev to New Marrakech count?"

"No. Now let's do this, we've all practiced how to wear these before."

After most were suited up, helmets still open, Brooke Farnsworth spoke again. "Full safety checks, please, everyone . . . each of you need to have two people check off your air pressure and suit power: your partner plus one teacher." Rustling sounds and small beeps filled the room as students started pushing buttons on their suit wrist-controls. The strange little twang of suits powering up filled the room, echoing all around — it was almost comical.

"Sealing your helmet is not necessary until your air tanks and power cells have been checked. Once you and your partner are both checked off, please stand by the door. Once everyone is set, we will seal our helmets, link our radios, and then, head outside in groups of six."

Sealing up and suit power/air checks took ten minutes. Once everyone was in the green, they found that only two suits out of thirty-three needed fresh power cells, easily swapped out from the lockers. The group stood ready for radio checks and helmets.

Stein stood up on a large flat rock by the door, where everyone could see him.

"I know you all know this, but please humor me and pay close attention." He held up his left wrist. "Everyone see this first button, right here on your wrist? That's your private channel with your partner. To link with your partner, hold the button down for a full five seconds right next to your partner while he or she does the same. Once you've done this, your personal channel will remain on the entire time you are wearing the suit. Please communicate often, and never lose sight of your partner, not even for a minute. Everyone got that?"

A silent chorus of nods around the room. Again, he held his left hand high for all to see.

"If you press both your radio buttons for two seconds, you will be on our common all-call channel, and everyone in the entire group can hear you. After we get outside, I ask you to leave that common channel for emergencies only, or to interact with the whole group; teachers will be using that channel to make announcements. So please don't step on a teacher's all-call unless you are having a no-kidding emergency or answering a teacher's question to the whole group."

More nods around the room. "If you lose reception, first thing to check is your radio antenna, this black stubby, bendy thing behind your helmet. Make sure it is twisted all the way in."

Then Mrs. Farnsworth spoke up again.

"Also, please do suit cross-checks with your partner, every ten minutes at least. You'll be checking comms, power, and pressure. Any problems at all, both you and your partner return immediately to the airlock door, step inside, and perform a rapid re-press of the airlock, that big red button inside. If you understand what I just said, please give me a big thumbs up."

Brooke and the other teachers waited until all hands in the room showed thumbs up.

"All right, helmets closed first, connect your partner-radio second, and then we'll line up to head outside."

With radio checks complete a few moments later, Stein herded Dr. Kumar, Mrs. Farnsworth, and Principal Chojnacki in with the first student pair, and sealed the inner door. He pressed the red glowing De-Pressurize button, and once the display showed ATM 0.0, swung the silver door-lever upwards, and heaved the outer door open.

Back inside, the crowd of waiting students pressed in, craning to watch the inner/outer door procedure.

Andie and Aiyana looked at each other through perfectly clear, rounded face plates.

"Isn't this exciting?" Andie asked, grinning widely.

"Fantastic." She shook her head inside the helmet, then scratched at her nose using the small brush mounted inside the helmet for that purpose.

As one group after the next stepped through, the numbers in the room dwindled. Finally, Andie and Aiyana had their turn, along with a couple other stragglers. Andie stepped over the doorway and ducked her head instinctively. Aiyana followed. The inner door closed. Stein looked at each of their wrist displays in turn, checking suit pressure.

Andie grinned with excitement. Aiyana gritted her teeth back, resisting the urge to rip the helmet back open again.

The outer door swung open and Stein led the way.

The girls followed, up to the outer door threshold, seeing long shadows stretching out before them.

Stein held out a welcoming arm, inviting the last of his students to join in the brilliant, fiery blue Martian sunset.

Chapter Fourteen

The Night Sky

S tudents flipped down their sun visors so they could watch the sunset without squinting.

The sky colors deepened, and Andie and Aiyana walked over to the edge guardrails, where a drop-off plunged down among boulders into the gloom of a deep ravine.

The slope of the Mountain rose up and up behind them to the actual summit, several kilometers above and behind them. Dusty roads led away in both directions, branching up and down the side of the Mountain, twisting through valleys and canyons. The broad plateau here was wide enough to park a hundred cargo rovers — the 'pickup trucks' still used occasionally by MERF and private companies. For now, the plateau was empty of vehicles.

The sun slipped below the horizon and the first few pinpoints of light began to appear above them.

Stein pressed both all-call buttons. "Friends, as we await full darkness, you'll see planets become visible, followed by stars with the highest apparent-magnitude then the dimmer stars to follow. See that bright dot just above the horizon, to the right of where the sun set? Would someone care to tell me what that is?"

"Is it Earth?" One student answered, taking the chance to use the all-call feature.

"Yes it is—well done," responded Stein. "Now, we know all about Mars' two moons, but let's talk briefly about Earth's moon, Luna. Where do you think it came from?

"It formed with the Earth? Or . . . was it captured like Neptune grabbed Triton?" one student asked.

"Good thoughts, but neither of those is correct. Other ideas . . . ?"

"It grew out of the Earth, a blob that was tossed aside as it cooled?"

"You're getting warmer . . . " Stein said. He loved seeing them struggle with an educated guess, for that was where true learning took place. Those who played it safe, never risking being wrong . . . Stein encouraged them to be brave—take a chance. Those who took a stab at it, took a little risk . . . these would be tomorrow's leaders, inventors, creators, and explorers.

"Did it explode?" one student asked.

"It was born in violence. So yes," Stein said. "What we know from humanity's first visit to Luna is that the moon is mostly silicates, light materials, and lacks real abundance of heavier elements or heavy metals."

Some students watched him, others were glued watching the faraway Earth as he talked.

"This suggests that an early planet, maybe one as big as our own Mars, called Theia, crashed into the young Earth, or violently grazed it at least. The debris kicked up from that giant impact was significant, leaving a rocky ring around the young Earth, similar to the icy rings of Saturn. But all that debris started to clump together right away under normal gravity.

"Now, I know you might have heard this before—Gaia, Theia, and the moon left behind from that violent, creative event. But there's still one problem. None of that explains why the near side of the moon, the one facing Earth, with its huge dark 'seas' of cooled lava fields . . . could be so radically different from the far side, the one no Earthling can see unless they fly around the back in a Lunar Starship.

"So why is the material on the far side of the moon so much lighter than the denser lava field formations on the side facing Earth?"

He stared around, to see if any looked like they might venture a guess. No faces betrayed this hope, but all intently listened as they looked at Stein or watched the distant Earth.

"What you probably haven't heard before is that the ring of debris around the young Earth didn't form just one moon . . . it formed at least two, at first. Picture this: one huge, rounded chunk, the larger one, was in the lead as they both raced around the planet in a fraction of the time. The larger one, slightly more massive, had a bit more gravity. It pulled on the trailing moon, the smaller one, tugging it closer and closer . . . until it caught up, and the two gently merged together."

He paused. More students turned to look at the pale blue dot, visualizing what he was describing.

"That merger heated up the surfaces of both again, and the larger of the two poured out some of its magma insides, forming those huge lava lakes, the dark mare that Earth sees every night. The opposite side, made of much lighter materials, made the moon grow larger as a sphere, sure, but made the overall end-product . . . lop-sided in its center of mass. The heavier part eventually faced the Earth permanently, that's what we call a tidal lock, and the less massive, less 'heavy' side faces away from the Earth, forever."

He paused, letting it sink in.

"See it in your mind, friends. For while we will see many incredible things tonight, that may be one of the most unexpected stories we can tell. Remember Gaia, her daughter Theia, and of course Luna, drifting away a centimeter every year as she orbits the Earth."

Andie's eyes went wide; she grabbed Aiyana's arm. But before she could say anything, Stein was on the radio again.

"All right, I've rambled on enough, please wander out a bit, staying with your partner, and if you haven't already, helmet trim-lights on, please. See if you can spot familiar constellations, planets, and even galaxies, like the one in Andromeda. Prepare to have your minds blown. Go, explore."

Andie let go of Aiyana's arm but said nothing about what she had just figured out. What if her suspicion was wrong? She kept silent.

Student pairs dispersed across the plateau. Occasionally a student would mistakenly speak in an all-call by accident, but eventually they all got the hang of it.

In the moments that followed, darkness covered the area and more stars came out. Stein watched the partner pairs to ensure they were sticking together. Whenever necessary, other teachers nudged students back together. Stein flipped a small switch on the plateau's railing, switching on a low-light glow that showed the boundary edge of the safe area.

The teachers had another surprise in store – in a nearby tech shed against the Mountain flank, they produced two wide-bore reflecting telescopes and began assembling them in the low gravity.

Once calibrated and oriented, hand-held controls panned the scopes from point to point, peering at different parts of the night sky. Students gathered in small groups and began queuing up. Andie approached the one Stein was orienting and asked, "What are you looking for?"

"I have . . . found . . . a Subaru."

"Excuse me?" Andie asked.

"It's what the Japanese call this open cluster of blue giant stars. It's very special in their culture, take a peek." Stein stepped back, letting Andie approach the eyepiece lens.

"See if you can tell me its other designation," he encouraged her.

Andie squinted through her glasses, careful not to jostle the scope. "Oh, that's . . . um, Pleiades. The Seven Sisters."

"Very good." Stein said, smiling in pride at his most brilliant student.

Aiyana stood nearby. "So it's . . . Subaru, like the vehicle maker?" Aiyana asked.

"Exactly. You know the oval symbol, with the little diamonds in it?"

Andie looked once more at the glittering blue giant stars. "Oh wow . . . yeah, I guess I can see it now." She stepped aside to let Aiyana and others in line have a look.

Through three telescopes, students saw the Galilean moons of mighty Jupiter: Io, Europa, Ganymede, and Callisto. They saw the delicate and beautiful rings of Saturn with its huge moon, Titan.

Then Sitara approached Stein with her partner, asking about the constellations. "Mister Stein, I was wondering, why some stars appear so much brighter, even if they are much smaller," she said.

"It's all about distance: the difference between absolute magnitude and apparent magnitude." Stein thought for a moment. "Hm, how can I explain this, even if it's not all the stars we can see? Okay, imagine I hold a small LED, a candle, right up to your face. It would seem pretty bright, right?"

Sitara nodded inside her helmet. Andie and Aiyana, hearing Stein's voice on the all-call, rejoined Sitara and several others to listen in.

"That's its apparent magnitude, which in this case is very luminous, being right in your face, but it is still just a dim little candle. Now, suppose I carry that candle up to the top of one of the *Sulci* mountains far over there, on a nice, clear night. You might still see it, but barely. And if I turned on one of ACSA's futbol-stadium floodlights on that same faraway mountain, I ask you: which is objectively brighter, the candle or the floodlight?"

"The floodlight, obviously."

"Good. That's absolute magnitude. Now, pretend I'm standing a dozen paces away, on the rim of this drop-off with my candle held high, but I leave that floodlight on, a hundred clicks away on a mountaintop. That floodlight might appear dimmer, and the candle close by might appear brighter. Absolute magnitude, apparent magnitude."

"I see . . . " Sitara said.

Aiyana spoke up. "But you said not all were like that."

Stein looked at her. "Yes, I did. Let's take a look at . . . hm, I wonder, is he up yet?" Stein scanned around, turning away from the sunset's direction. "Yes, good."

Stein slipped a simple green laser pointer out of a pen-pocket on his arm. He pointed the green beam of light toward a group of stars.

"Right there . . . see the curve of these three stars? That's the lion's head, basically his mane."

Sitara nodded, adding "I see it, so cooool. So that's Leo."

Stein continued. "Correct. And see the bright one where his head meets his body? That's not a star."

"Wait, what?" Aiyana asked. "How can it not be a star?"

"Because it's two stars. They just orbit each other so closely, to our eyes, they merge—together they look like one. Those were among the earliest binary stars discovered. So that's why they seem brighter—our eyes can't separate the two from each other—they merge into one brighter star to us."

He paused. Students visualized two stars in a tight orbit. Then Aiyana turned back to Stein. "Can I borrow your pointer? I'd like to show the others."

"You can keep it, I have more in the classroom," Stein said with a smile.

Then, seeing the hopeful look on Sitara's face, he quietly handed her a green laser pointer as well. Sitara smiled, accepted the device, and strode purposefully away with her partner. The wonders of the Universe opened up to them all.

* * *

Another half hour went by, and hunger overtook curiosity and wonder. Stein and a couple volunteers positioned a self-extracting geodesic dome on one side of the airlock door, a dome that could accommodate fifty Exo-Suited occupants. Perfect for fitting twenty-eight hungry teenagers, their teachers, and their food.

With hardly any manual work needed, rod-and-piston joints self-extracted the dome until it stood up, reaching two stories tall at the top and easily ten meters across.

The genius of the design was it held its hemispherical shape whether pressurized or not, so as long as all the occupants had functioning Exo-Suits, it required no airlock. After the last rod clicked into place, Stein nodded to Brooke. She pressed both 'all-call' buttons and spoke to the group.

"Ladies, gentlemen, allow me to interrupt your gazing and invite you to join us inside for a bite to eat, and you can also replenish your compact-80 air canisters. No, this is not optional, I must insist you take on a fresh tank, and try the Little Caesars X-Treme, or some other tasty choice." She looked over at Stein, who was fiddling with the entry control panel, and continued.

"The dome will be illuminated shortly . . . ah, there it is. Please enter in through the orange-lit archway at the same time as your partner please, so no one is left behind. Plus, and this next part is very important: Please DO NOT, I repeat DO NOT, open your faceplates just because you stepped inside. Once you are inside, immediately do double high-fives with your partner, and hold them up, both hands please. So it should look like this, thank you Mister Stein, and hold this pose, face to face, until we are all in and say it's okay to open helmets. Let's have no decompressions here tonight."

"All right, let's go. Everyone inside the dome please, and immediate high-tens with your partner."

The group filed inside, and Stein let a couple of his faculty mates walk in ahead of the others, mostly to carefully monitor students entering, and slap away any hands reaching up to faceplates or helmets. Nearly as important, they kept a close watch on the orange Little Caesar's cube-cases, to ensure no one opened pressurized food containers before the dome was pressurized.

Tonight would be no EPDs, explosive pizza decompressions, either.

As partner pairs (plus one trio) held up high-tens with each other, a few giggles passed through the common channel. Stein and his partner were the last to enter the dome, after he made one final call in case any had not yet stepped inside. Helmet counts confirmed: all present and accounted for, 33 under the dome.

The dome seal was a relatively simple process: pull shut and seal its single door, then fill the air from the large canisters at the doorway.

Everyone's wrist displays showed the atmospheric pressure in the dome rising. Students watched their wrists and giggled at the novelty of holding hands together up in the air. Eventually, every wrist display showed ATM 1.0, and Stein swept his helmet open with a flair. Since he could be heard throughout the domed room now, he invited students to stop holding hands and open their helmet visors at their leisure.

Faculty members and their one administrator opened the pressure-sealed box-cases with the pizzas inside. Having allowed for a larger group, they set out the first six pizzas. Students and educators alike chowed down on Little Caesar's with gusto. Hot and steaming on a Friday night, each slice was as delicious as they could want, given the lack of an authentic Mars-brick oven.

Principal Chojnacki approached Stein, remarking as he looked around the domed space, "this may be the best showing we've ever had at a stargazing event."

"That's because Astronomy is amazing." Stein beamed.

"And it had absolutely nothing to do with free pizza," Brooke winked as she drifted past, slice of pepperoni in hand.

"Hey, it isn't the free . . . ok, it's the pizza. But good times, right?"

Stein let the moment ride out, then checked his chrono for the time. Students ate, chatted, laughed, and ate some more. They mingled and ate under the dome for 15 minutes, and their bellies were, for the most part, full. Time for one last bit of stargazing.

When students were mostly finished, Stein announced two minutes until sealing up suits to head back out. The time came, all suits were re-sealed and re-checked. Everyone confirmed fresh air tanks and pizza cubes were sealed up tight. After a final confirmation, Stein de-pressurized the dome and opened the door back outside.

Telescope scans of the sky continued. Over in another part of the sky, viewers were treated to the Hercules Supercluster, more than half a million stars visible in one view. Others glimpsed the strange blue glow of the Ring Nebula, the twin circles of the Whirlpool Galaxy, the near-edge-on view of vibrant Sombrero Galaxy, and the dramatic filaments of the Crab Nebula.

Stein checked his own pressure and the digital readout showed 19,100 kPa. Well in the green for another 45 minutes at least. His tank was good, and his air filter-scrubber looked good. Time for an all-call suit check — Stein pushed both lit buttons.

"Your attention please? Everyone please check your air supply . . . also please visually check your partner's . . . and speak up if you or your buddy are under 15,000 kPa." In unison, nearly everyone glanced down at their wrist displays. Stein waited for a response, but there was none. Stein continued.

"Good. And it's time for another great moment--if you'll permit me, please look to the West, right where the sun had set. In another moment, you might see a bright star rising off the horizon and crossing the sky. That's the MOSS, our very own Mars Orbital Space Station. In under three minutes, it crosses the entire sky and sets in the East."

Many looked West and a few low "ooooh" murmurs were heard

in helmet earphones as a bright dot lifted above the horizon. When the MOSS reached about three-quarters of its trek across the night sky, a bright rectangle flash shined down, then just as quickly, it vanished.

"Wow." Several simultaneous voices.

"Yo, what were those – like, its solar panels?" Carlos asked.

"I think so, yes?" said Brooke. "It caught the sun's light at just the right angle. Incredible."

"You know they're as big as six tennis courts?" Sitara added.

A few seconds later, a bright light off to the North drew everyone's gaze. A planetary shuttle rocket blasted off from Port Mons, its blinding nozzle expelling a blaze of glory. It quickly disappeared over the horizon to the North in a graceful, curving arc of light.

Shaking his head in wonder, Stein turned back to the dome. Double-checking that neither people nor refuse had been left inside, Stein activated the process to collapse the structure at its swing-arms. A moment later, the dome was stowed away in its large standing crate.

Some students drifted back to the airlock in their partner pairs, with teachers helping them pass through smoothly. Soon only a dozen stargazers remained outside.

Since hugs were ill-advised in Exo-Suits, high fives and shoulder bumps sufficed—they would be talking about the event for days. The last cluster of students and a couple teachers lined up for long-exposure group photos – first huddled together, smiling for the camera, and then staring up at the sky in random directions. They captured a good moment.

The teachers began packing up the two telescopes for storage. A few last fist-bumps, and the group was near to calling it quits for the night.

Then . . . someone pointed out into the darkness. "What is that!?"

Several students looked. Most took in a simultaneous gasp. A couple instinctively gripped the arm of the nearest person, and others simply held their breath.

The headlights of a side-by-side skimmer had slipped below the roadway across the ravine — falling, tumbling in slow motion like a skydiver into darkness below. In the weak gravity, they fell for what seemed a long time before the first impact.

With the first impact, the lights twisted and blinked, on and off, down, down, down — tumbling until they were swallowed up by the abyss of pitch blackness below.

Automated Emergency Alerts blasted out into every Exo-Suit. Now everybody was staring in the same direction, gawking in shock at where the lights had vanished.

The deafening tone skipped a few beats, then cut out completely.

Every stargazer stood frozen in place, staring across a pitch black, utterly silent ravine.

The stars, worlds, and moons looked down in anticipation.

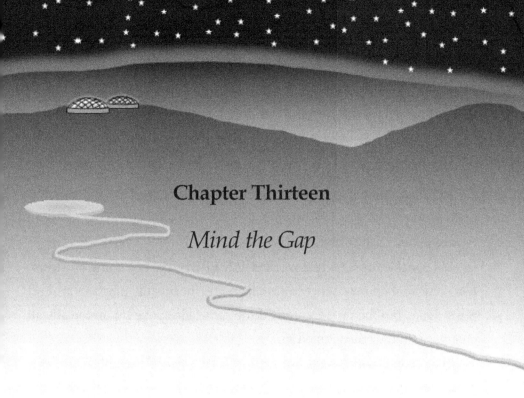

Chapter Thirteen

Mind the Gap

The spell was broken—eight burst into action while just a few stood back, confused. Most started making long bounds heading down the nearby road, the one that skirted the ridgeline toward where the skimmer had run off the edge.

Principal Chojnacki looked at the small group huddled together and hastily blurted out, "I'll get hold of MERF Rescue!" He began tapping at his wrist display to make the call.

"Okay!" Brooke Farnsworth responded, also rushing toward the curving roadway along the mountain slope.

"Wait!" Stein all-called on the open channel. This brought everyone up short. "Everyone please stop for just a moment."

"Fresh O-two tanks please, everyone, that crash is not close by." He turned to the dome-locker, which still had a dozen air tanks in it. "Oh, and everyone please make sure your suits are set to ping your location every two minutes."

Stein doled out fresh tanks and each partner pair assisted each another with opening the back suit shell casing, un-screwing the partially used tanks, and inserting full tanks.

Within moments, eight Mons High Olympians bounded away in long, leaping steps, along the ridgeline road, barely wide enough to accommodate two lanes, in the direction they had last seen headlights.

Within ten minutes, the group stood huddled above where the skimmer had gone over the side. Below was inky blackness—no sign of the wreck or its occupants. Just inky black in all directions.

Bill Shackleton, who had worked at MERF before becoming a teacher, had some limited experience in search and rescue, mainly practices around Silver Lake, but the process seemed the same. He spoke up on the all-call channel, and the others tuned in.

"For search and rescue, we form a search line. All eight of us here, please line up along the edge, and very carefully ease yourself down the hillside, taking extra care not to lose your footing or fall into some crevasse. We want to save those passengers, not create more victims. First partner pair, you are on the far left, then the next two, and so on, down the line.

Students and faculty paired up with whoever they seemed closest to. Andie was second from the farthest-right position. Aiyana was the farthest-right member of the search party, on the extreme end.

Suit helmet lights had been turned up to maximum and the group had managed to scrounge four bright hand-held lights—anything to make the search easier.

Mr. Shackleton's voice came over the open channel again—calm, self-assured. "Please stay within eyesight of your partner, try to keep the search line even, and mind the gap that might open up as the line moves downslope—we don't want to go around the vehicle and miss it. They might not have much time—we can be methodical while still avoiding reckless risk. We don't need any heroes."

Stein and Shackleton each teamed up with a student, lining up somewhere in the middle of the search line, and Brooke Farnsworth remained paired up with the principal on the far left end of the search line.

Andie and Aiyana re-linked their private channel and did a quick radio check. As a group, the impromptu search team eased over the edge of the road onto a downward slope. At first, it seemed to be easy going.

After five more minutes, the group started to fan out with the curve of the downward slope, and the grade became steeper. Nothing approaching vertical, but steep enough to force them to be deliberate as they went. Pebbles and small rocks rolled away under every careful step.

The left end of the search line naturally swept further left, and the right swept further right, so much that opposite ends of the search line could no longer see each other's lights among the boulders and ridges.

Andie checked in with her partner. "Are you all right, Aiya?"

She was breathing heavily and answered "I'm good. Any sign of a vehicle yet?"

"Nothing down or ahead of us, or even off to the left. Maybe we should sweep right?"

"Yeah . . . sounds good," again, the response with labored breathing. Aiyana could feel sweat forming on her brow with the exertion of the search. The two continued downslope, and seeing they were halfway to where it bottomed out below, Aiyana stopped a moment to catch her breath.

"How ya doing?" Andie asked.

"I'm . . . okay. I just haven't done anything like this in a suit before. And my feelings toward my suit have not changed."

"I know what you mean. My legs ache." Andie swept the hand flashlight around.

Aside from each other, they saw no other lights, though they occasionally caught bits of search party conversation over the radio. Their headlamps shined about a dozen meters then were swallowed up in the gloom. The night wrapped around them like a cold, dark blanket.

The boulders took on a looming, ominous quality.

Aiyana started up again, rounding a boulder twice her height, with Andie going around the other way. With one gloved hand in contact with the boulder, and while trying to peer around to keep eyes on Andie, she briefly neglected to look down as she stepped.

She lost her footing.

Sliding down a steeper drop, her suit back hit hard against the rocks behind her. She slid a few meters further, setting smaller rocks tumbling. She grabbed at a rock jutting up and stopped her fall, but a helmet-sized rock was falling towards her too quickly to dodge. She turned her helmet away, taking its impact on her back. A jarring crunch rippled through her suit. She held on to the rock for dear life. The rocks around her stopped tumbling.

Finding a flat spot to perch upon, she scrambled to her feet, quickly checking her wrist for suit integrity. *ATM 1.0*. No leaks. Whew.

She stood, hands trembling, and exhaled a sigh of relief.

"That was scary," she said, looking around. "Andie?"

No response.

She felt around for better footing, and hugged onto a rocky outcrop to steady her as she stepped. Her helmet light fell on something among the rocks at her feet—a short, black, flexible stick--her suit's radio antenna, the one that stands up right behind the hard shell of her helmet and visor.

Aiyana reached up behind her shoulder, and found that it had, in fact, broken clean off. In her hand, the threads of the antenna itself were missing, so it couldn't simply be screwed back in.

"Andie? Can you hear me?"

Silence.

"Hello? Can anyone hear me? Anyone on this channel, please, respond?"

More silence. She stabbed both buttons down, knowing that if any broadcast got out, someone, anyone, would hear her.

"Hel-loooo..." No response.

"Anybody?" Nothing.

"Hooo boy." Aiyana said, casting around in all directions, looking for her partner's lights, any lights at all. The darkness closed in around her. There was no going back to look for Andie, the way behind her was too steep. Going down slope was out of the question.

Left with one option, she pressed ahead around spindly outcrops and jumbled boulders, neither climbing nor descending the slope. Each rocky pinnacle and boulder looked more ominous than the last.

Some looked as though they had faces passing over them as she turned; they leered, they mocked.

"Andie?"

No reply. Aiyana reached a point where there were no good directions to go. No path forward. If she stayed trapped here, she would die. Then, alone in the dark, lingering to search for her partner, Andie might die too. Aiyana squeezed her eyes shut, waiting for the rising panic to fade. It did not fade. She opened her eyes and looked sideways. The boulders around her leaned down toward her. Her suit pressed down on her, all over her body.

She crouched down and covered her face plate, her gloved hands over her helmet.

"Lauryna . . . ? Mom . . .?" she spoke, barely a whisper.

"Please . . ."

All was quiet.

Between her gloved fingers, she risked a glance up the slope, and could clearly see the blanket of stars, and a dark, straight line below which no stars shined—the road! The dark line of the road was still there, above her, maybe seventy-five meters up at most. She raised her head to look around and saw a possible way to climb back up. "I can keep searching from up there, right?" she whispered. "Andie probably already headed back to bring help."

She took a single step up-slope, walking away from whoever was in the wrecked side-by-side. But she would be safe, right?

Bright in the lights of her helmet, she saw her own boot take that single step. She stopped.

"What am I doing?" she said softly.

"What am I doing?" a little louder.

"What am I doing!" now, practically shouting. "Pull it together Aiya!" She took a deep breath and through gritted teeth, yelled her primal scream—somewhere deep in her mind, she realized that rising anger was stronger than fear in this moment. Anger, she could control. Panic—not as much. So, she got angry.

She did the next logical thing—yelled at herself some more. "Those people could be injured, maybe dying, and you're gonna punk out like a little chicken? Brass up! Brass up and keep going."

"He-hello?" came a voice over the radio, very faint.

Aiyana jolted, snapping her head up inside the helmet.

There had been a hello. She had most definitely heard a hello. She looked wildly in many directions at once to see if there was any clue where the hello had come from. Nope, just darkness.

On the verge of turning and climbing away, she spotted a tiny pinpoint of light, very faint. It shined weakly from further ahead, the same distance below the road as where she stood. The small light held perfectly still.

"Now Andie, how did you get ahead of me?" Aiyana asked in a soft tone, wondering if anything she said was transmitting at all. "Okay, regroup and form a plan? I'm coming." Silence, no, a tiny bit of intermittent static over the earphones. A bit of static, but no voice.

"Okay, don't be weird with me now," Aiyana said. "I see your light, so if you jump out and scare me, I'll kill you. No one'll find the body."

She was calming down—fear, conquered by her anger, was now . . . curiosity about the strange, stationary light. She carefully checked her footing as she made her way. The radio stayed quiet for the moment.

She made progress, glad for not being alone in the pitch darkness. "Hellooo?" the weak transmission repeated in her ear, much more clearly this time.

Finally. Here, in front of her, shining out from between two points of rock, was the small light she had seen. The corner of a vehicle came into view--a tiny LED beam of light sneaked out from where its cover-casing had cracked, but the other running lights on the vehicle were covered, blocking any other light from escaping.

On a small, flat part of the slope, she stepped right up to a four-wheeled rover, bright red, flipped over on its roof.

The headlights and taillights of the vehicle had all been shattered, bits of glass scattered everywhere. The glass chips reflected her headlamps as she carefully rounded the vehicle. Inside, a small dome light was on. Some of the glass canopy, on which the vehicle now rested, showed spiderwebs and long, wandering cracks. And then there was . . . movement inside.

She leaned down and bent under the front of the vehicle, and saw two teenage faces looking back at her. They had fallen out of their seats— natural, considering the vehicle was upside down. The two rested directly on the glass canopy windshield, one teen cradling the other.

Neither was wearing an ExoSuit, but both were moving, breathing.

The teenage boy cradled the girl, and he was sitting inside, topless, as he held her close in his arms.

"Um," Aiyana muttered. "Why aren't you wearing a shirt?"

The boy gave no sign that he had heard her. He just squinted into her bright headlamps. She crouched down to look inside and got her first glimpse of the girl—pretty, blonde. Her face was white as a sheet and her whole body was shaking. Aiyana recognized this condition from her middle school health class. This girl was in shock.

Aiyana spoke again, making eye contact with the boy. "Can you tell me your names? I'm Aiya."

The boy saw her lips moving, but he pointed at his own ear and shook his head.

"I can't hear you," came weakly over the radio.

Aiyana nodded, leaning over to the vehicle. She pressed her helmet hard up against the glassite vehicle windshield, and shouted as loudly as she could. "I can hear you over the radio, but I think your receiver is broken. Or maybe my suit radio is broken. Do you have Exo-Suits in there?"

The boy inside nodded. Then he spoke. "But Shawna . . . she's pretty banged up. See her head?"

Aiyana nodded. She looked closer, seeing the girl was wearing a second shirt. That explained the topless boy at least. He had been trying to warm her up, stabilize her, but an extra shirt would make little difference. It must be getting cold inside the busted-up skimmer — scary cold.

Shawna looked up through the glass at Aiyana. She spoke in a voice clear enough, asking, "I can't remember the last four hours, is that normal?"

She shrugged and shouted back through the helmet-canopy contact. "I'm not a doctor, but that doesn't sound normal to me. But you're both alive, that's, like, really lucky, wreck like that."

Shawna's shaking intensified. She reached up and held a free hand at the bruise on her head. Aiyana shouted again. "Can you move her?"

The boy's voice came over the radio again. "I better not, she might have hurt her back, and . . . well, look at her leg."

Aiyana looked downward. Oh.

She could see — Shawna's leg wasn't . . . quite . . . right. Just below the knee, it was bending sideways at an odd angle, but Aiyana couldn't see any blood. There's some good news — she wouldn't bleed out.

"Okay." Aiyana shouted again. "Help is on the way. My principal called MERF, and they should be here any . . . " and right on cue, she caught the flash of lights in her peripheral vision. She turned her head to see a long line of flashing blue-and-yellow lights on vehicles above, making their way toward them from where they had been stargazing.

Aiyana pointed up, showing the unfortunate couple that help was on the way.

She could see, clearly enough along the curving edge of the road above, two police vehicles, two ambulances, and one hook-and-ladder treaded rescue truck, basically a long red fire department tank with a compressed foam gun on the top and boxes of gear attached to the sides.

She could see them, clear as day . . . right as they blasted on by at top speed and kept on driving. They hadn't seen the wrecked speeder at all.

"Oh dammit . . . " Aiyana muttered.

She leaned back against the vehicle. "I have to go up and get their attention, tell them where we are. I need you all to sit tight, help will be here very soon."

"Okay," the boy said, with a serious, focused look on his face.

Aiyana took one step toward the steep rocky slope, then stopped. "Umm, what if I can't find you, when I make that eighty-meter climb back up to the road?" she muttered to herself.

Then Aiyana remembered her teacher was a science super-nerd. And science super-nerds at star parties loan out green laser pointers.

She pulled the pointer from its pocket and wedged it into a crack in the housing of the vehicle and tried to aim it right at the lip of the road above, so she would at least have a green dot to zero in on. She touched her helmet to the windshield one last time.

"I'm sticking this laser pointer to the side of your vehicle. If no one comes within five minutes, it means we can't find you in the dark. I want you to gently rock the vehicle if you can, which will make the green dot move. Maybe we'll find you that way."

"Okay, I will," said the boy, with the same focused look on his face.

She stepped a few steps to the side, to avoid raining down rocks and pebbles on the vehicle. She started the climb. With adrenaline coursing through her system, she climbed the fastest, safest route she could find, headlamps shining directly in front of her.

Though she worked out and toned her body routinely, never skipping leg day, she reached the road completely out of breath, heaving in and out in ragged, deep breaths.

"Over here!" she shouted as loud as she could.

No response from the MERF convoy — the vehicles had collected along the slope where the search had begun in the first place. They clearly could not hear her.

"They're here. O-ver-heeeere!" Aiyana shouted, voice cracking with the effort. She jumped up and down, pointing her headlamps wildly around to grab their attention.

She cursed, knowing again . . . anger would give her strength, prevent her from giving up.

She felt a fresh surge coursing through her blood as she jumped up and down, screaming in futility. As she jumped around, she took to alternately blocking and shining helmet lamps.

From a kilometer down the road, one MERF police officer happened to glance in her direction. He tapped his partner;s arm and pointed.

"Hey, Jonesey? There's some dude doing the funky chicken in the road. . . should we check this out?"

Five minutes later, all vehicles had been repositioned above the correct spot. Oversized flood lamps, attached to the hook-and-ladder truck, blasted a wash of bright light down the steep slope. The flipped over red skimmer became immediately visible among the rocks.

On either end of the five parked vehicles, the police cruisers took up sentry posts, with the two Ambulances each a step closer to the center of the action, where the red truck stood.

Though the vehicle was clearly visible in the flood lamps, Aiyana could clearly see on one corner of the vehicle, a green laser dot winking up at her.

The team leader approached Aiyana and looked her in the face, talking to her. Aiyana reached in her pocket, pulled out her broken antenna, and tapped it on her own shoulder. The team leader understood immediately. He grabbed Aiyana firmly by both shoulders and pulled her in, pressing his helmet directly against hers.

"Can you hear me?

Aiyana nodded, saying 'Yes sir, I can."

"Okay, tell me what you know."

"Uh, okay. Two teens are in the crashed skimmer, a bubble side-by-side model with a small airlock extension, and the outer glassite is cracked pretty good. Inner layer is still okay, I think? Her leg is broken, but not bleeding . . . oh, and she has a bruise on her head and can't remember the last four hours. She is white as a sheet and shaking. The boy seems fine—a little too calm, in fact. I'm guessing their air lock might still work."

The team leader nodded.

"Thank you, we'll take it from here." He let her lean back away and gave her a big thumbs-up and a wink. Aiyana nodded back, exhaling the breath she did not realize she had been holding.

Andie finally appeared. She grabbed Aiyana by both shoulders and immediately started yelling at her, but all in complete silence. Aiyana held up her broken antenna and saw the dawning awareness on Andie's face— her tears flowed in a steady stream down her cheeks, but whatever fears she had been fighting, they melted away at seeing Aiyana. She smiled and grabbed Aiyana by the helmet for a long moment.

Stein and the others arrived, immediately enthralled with what the MERF teams were doing.

The high-angle rescue was a wonder to behold. Three MERF rescue technicians unspooled two long metal cables, which dropped down over the edge of the road. As the cables disappeared over the edge, so did three highly trained veterans. Within ten minutes, the boy came up first, walking up the slope with his rescuer and wearing an ExoSuit of his own. He was firmly gripped around the waist by one of the MERF technicians, who had clipped them both in and used the retracting cable to pull them, walking straight up the steep slope.

Stein accompanied the boy as he was escorted into the back of the left-side ambulance, and followed him inside. Aiyana stepped inside as well; the door swung shut behind them.

The pressure lock cycled until it showed as backlit in bright aqua, and ATM 1.0 appeared on both the door display and three suits' wrist displays.

A MERF technician in a plain blue jumpsuit opened the cab section door of the vehicle, stepped in, and immediately began evaluating the boy. A small array of medical diagnostic instruments checked his vitals, looked for stress indicators within his bloodstream to indicate internal injury or broken bones. She attached a lead to his wrist, his temple, and something else to his neck. She looked over the boy, read his vitals without needing him to take off his suit, and asked him a series of canned questions. Stein sat down opposite the boy, and when the MERF medical technician was finished, he had a few questions of his own.

"What's your name?"

"Brendan."

"Brendan, did you call your folks yet? They must be worried sick."

Brendan shrugged. "My own handy phone got busted up, so we couldn't call . . ."

Aiyana leaned in. "Here, you can use mine." She popped the device off its arm band and handed it over. "You could call Shawna's family too." Brendan nodded and linked the device to his own suit, and with its antenna intact, was able to make both calls. Outside, the high-angle rescue continued to unfold.

Calls to his parents and his girlfriend's parents complete, the technician disappeared back through the vehicle's control cabin door. She pulled the door shut and sealed it.

"Shall we head back out?" Stein asked.

Aiyana spoke up. "Ooo, hey, Brendan, before we go, did you happen to grab that green laser?"

"Oh deuces, I'm sorry — must still be down there. It happened so fast."

"It's cool, I'll get it in the morning when there's light." Aiyana smiled.

After all three suits were re-sealed and checked, Stein cycled the air and opened the ambulance back door. None of them needed the ambulance ride, so they exited the vehicle.

A full forty-five minutes later, the cables began a slow wind-up, reeling in their burden below, centimeter by centimeter. Standing as close to the ledge as they safely could, Stein, Aiyana, Andie, and the others watched as a bundled burden, held perfectly level, was walked up the side with slow, graceful precision among shifting cobbles and small rocks.

Three MERF veterans, shoulder to shoulder, gripped handholds on a body-board, where Shawna had been firmly strapped down. Confident, muscled strength kept her board perfectly level as the two truck cables attached to her board were slowly reeled in.

They brought Shawna carefully up over the lip of the cliff side. The spectators finally got a closer look — she had been wrapped and bound up tight to the body board, cocooned in shiny wrap and foam layers like a big burrito, with snug straps securing her ankles, hips, chest, and forehead to the body-board, preventing even the slightest jostle.

The three veterans let the cable reel in until it was next to the fire truck, then they settled Shawna the Burrito Girl down with a feather touch.

Once she was stationary, the three veterans stepped aside without a word. Four suited medical crew took their places to perform the classic 'one-two-three-lift' maneuver. They carried her to the second ambulance, easing her board gently down onto what looked like a diving board sticking out the back. It looked like the ambulance van had its tongue stuck out.

The tongue of the ambulance retracted, consuming the girl into the vehicle. Stein turned to Brendan. "She's still going to be scared. Bound like a mummy, all banged up from the crash . . . you need to get over there and climb in the Evac Unit with her."

"Will they let me do that?"

"Don't ask, just climb inside."

"Ignore the technicians, focus on her. Reach for her hand; let her see your face. Let her hear your voice, talk her through the whole ride to the hospital. I don't think they'll object." Again, the serious, focused look came over Brendan's face. "Okay . . . okay. I'll do it."

He made eye contact with Aiyana and turned away. He made his way to the other vehicle and climbed in. A MERF rescue tech pulled the door shut behind him and a moment later, the ambulance pulled away and headed back toward the city.

Aiyana, Andie, Stein, Bill Shackleton, and the other members of Impromptu Astro Search Party Extraordinaire walked back up the road, eventually arriving at the airlock, some chatting, and others strolling in quiet contemplation. Aiyana took her time in forced silence to reflect.

Through the airlock, they stowed their ExoSuits in lockers, swapping out partially used air canisters with new, full ones as a courtesy to the next people. Andie retrieved her green bracelet from the Exo-Suit pocket.

As Aiyana hung up her own Exo-Suit, Stein reached over and yanked its "Maintenance" red tag open, so the next routine check by MERF's tech squad would inspect and repair the radio before it could be used again.

"I'm proud of you, Aiya," Stein said, looking intently at Aiyana. "This moment belongs to you. 'A' for the day."

She smiled back at him. "Thanks. I was so scared."

"I bet. Oh, one more thing—I know you want to head back down tomorrow to search for your green pointer—but I don't want you going alone. It's still an accident site and even in daytime, there's danger. Either let me go in your place, or take a partner, and use some good safety lines going down the slope."

"Okay," Aiyana said, thinking it over.

Sitara stepped forward. "Well, you got one thing quite right, Mr. Steinheiser," she said, Exo-Suit flopped over her shoulder.

"What's that?"

"It's been a very memorable experience."

"Don't let anyone tell you star parties are boring," Stein said, grinning.

Sitara grinned back, hung up the suit, and walked away with Ric as the last of the star party crew headed back down toward the city.

Half an hour later, the city tram eased to a stop in Aiyana's neighborhood. Andie embraced her in a lingering goodbye hug.

"Please don't ever scare me like that again?"

"I was scared enough for us both," Aiyana said, letting the hug go.

"See you tomorrow." The tram doors closed and they both waved goodbye.

Andie sat down and messaged her dad she'd be running very late because of the incident, and that everything was all right and she was safe back inside the city.

She made a beeline for the Pocket. Her next task could not be put off another minute. The 'heavenly daughter and her mother' had waited far too long for their names to be declared.

* * *

During the midnight Stretch and again during the morning broadcast, a news team described the evening's drama in a 30-second spot.

The anchor gave a brief intro: "Authorities say the teens were driving way too fast for conditions on the winding road up near The Needle's mountainside overlook, careening more than sixty meters downslope into the ravine below. Thanks to a group of high school stargazers, MERF high-angle rescue teams were able to find the teens before any decompression or injury complications set in."

The broadcast jumped to footage of the rescue in progress, Shawna being loaded up into the ambulance, with the MERF on-scene captain's voiceover.

"It would have taken us a lot longer to find them, if the students hadn't alerted us to the exact location," the MERF team leader said. "We're grateful for their help."

Then it jumped back to the news anchor. "Both teens were taken to Mons Central where their injuries were treated; both are expected to make a full recovery. Stay with us."

* * *

Hands trembling, Andie entered in the first code: T-H-E-I-A. Then, she entered the second code: G-A-I-A.

She looked down at Ares, who stared back up, eyes wide open.

Andie pressed ENTER.

The blue entry blanks turned dark. A hiss of trace gases escaped around its entire seal.

Under its own power, the door slowly opened.

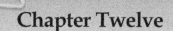

Chapter Twelve

Of Course, Another Way In

" I can't believe we're doing this. Do we really need to do this?"
They stepped into the star party's airlock access room from the
night before.

"Hey, this was all your idea," Andie said, stifling a big yawn. She
reached for a fresh suit.

"Mew," Ares mewed, his nose nudging his little cat Exo-Suit after
Andie set it down.

"It was my idea, wasn't it. Are you okay?"

"I only got a couple hours' sleep. Mmm, but yeah, I'm okay. Energy bar
and chai to the rescue."

Aiyana nodded, then brushed her hand over the red-tagged suit, still
hanging where Stein had pulled the tab just seven or eight hours before. She
pulled out a different suit, a fresh one. While Andie slipped into her own
new Exo-Suit, she stuck her woven green bracelet into one of its pockets.

They needed to get a jump on anyone else who felt like visiting the
crash site. "Besides, I want to find that laser-pointer, it's like a badge of

honor now." Aiyana put on a determined look.

"You really think you need that thing to prove how brave you were?"

"I wasn't . . . yes, I . . . is that hard to understand?"

Andie nodded. "I bet you'd like a closer look at wrecked skimmer too."

"Yeah, I've never heard of a wrecked skimmer; they take a brutal beating and just . . . keep on going."

"If I didn't know better, I'd say you're obsessed with fast rides."

"Maybe it can be salvaged," Aiyana said, hope in her voice.

"And maybe it wants a new owner?" Andie said with a flourish of the hand, raising her eyebrows comically.

"A girl can dream. And what was that you mentioned as we passed through the last SAFE pod? Something about the Pocket?"

"Yes, but later, it can wait until after we find your laser pointer. Then I can show you."

"You could just tell me."

Andie didn't reply.

Before hiking up, Andie used the last of her pocket money to rent the cat Exo-Suit from an automated supply locker, the ones that are open 24½-7. Buying one was out of the question—they were just too expensive. She carried the 2-kilo suit up the hike, Ares gracefully trotting alongside. A promise had been made, and Ares stuck to Andie like glue, stubbornly refusing to let her wiggle out of bringing him along.

The cat's suit also had its own emergency transponder beacon and radio transmitter. Given last night's technical difficulties, they both agreed having Ares along and not needing him was better than needing him and not having him. When they had reached the inner door, the cat had climbed right into the pet Exo-Suit without a fuss.

"Have you done this before?" Andie asked Ares.

"Mew."

Andie interpreted. "Mew means yes."

"Uh huh."

"We've got 2½ or 3 hours of air in each tank. In Ares' suit, he has slightly more, according to the rental waiver I had to read. I also grabbed three of my dad's 'compact-40' air tanks as a backup, so in case we're down there a long time . . ."

"Why do you think they call the big ones 'compact-80s'?" Aiyana asked, reading the label on the top of her tank.

"I asked my dad once. He told me it's a carry-over from scuba diving back on Earth. He said it's like carrying 80 cubic feet of compressed air on your back. Or something."

"Oh. Is that a lot?"

"Not sure . . . all I know is our rebreather CO_2 filters stretch one hour of air into, like, three hours, if we don't exert ourselves. Plus, we have these," patting the three smaller backup tanks. Fully suited up now, she flipped her helmet faceplate down and powered up the suit. Aiyana did the same, and almost in perfect harmony, they clasped their left hands together to sync the private radio.

Then they both added Ares' radio to the channel. The cat's suit had two smaller tanks in pouches along his back. The smaller compact-40 backups could work for Ares as well, though their bulk would make walking awkward for the cat.

Both girls had brought compact, powerful safety cable-reels clipped to their suit belts for rappelling down to the wreck, along with the standard short knife and a multi-tool every suit came with. Andie had picked up an old digital camera from the Reduce-Reuse-Recycle store as well as a short cable-leash to tether Ares as needed.

Final suit checks looked good for the humans and their chatterbox kitty.

As they opened the inner door, Ares leapt lightly into the airlock and stood waiting by the outer door. Aiyana closed the inner door and Andie tapped the controls to purge the air. A loud hissing faded down to silence.

Andie tapped the camera awake to examine it, checking power and memory. She knew Aiyana would want images of the wrecked speeder, and the beat-up old camera was cheap. The camera's memory was not impressive, several terabytes only, but it was enough to record in hi-res for 24½ hours straight, if needed. She clipped it to the chest piece of her Exo-Suit and started the recording.

Leading them back to the spot where Aiyana had done her attention-scream-dance the night before, she looked over the edge down the rocky slope and the ravine, and . . . no vehicle. Just rocks, broken glass glinting in the sunlight, and more rocks.

"Wha—?" Andie said.

"Whoa, it's already been pulled up," Aiyana said, pointing at deep scrapes and red-paint gouges in the dust and rocks on the edge of the road. In just a few short hours of darkness, the accident clean-up crews had finished their work and left.

"Wow, those guys move fast," Andie mused, looking up and down the road. The spot looked very different in full daylight. Ares just stood at the edge and looked down.

"Come on, I wanna find that pointer."

Aiyana leaned her weight against a tall, standing boulder at the edge of the road, and heaved. Satisfied it would not budge, she looped the adjustable cable around it, and double-clipped the device to the center of her belt. She cinched the coil lock down and snugged the cable tight against the boulder—there would be no slipping off the edge today, please.

She checked that the flex-cable could feed out freely without being caught on anything, and reset the cable length display to 0.0 m. Now they could both monitor how much line was playing out, and how much they both had remaining before reaching the end of the 50-m tether.

Andie did the same, on the other side of the boulder, pulling partially in the other direction. She reset her cable display as well, and attached a carabiner end clip of the 2-m tether to the back of the cat's suit, and secured the other end onto her belt. Andie lifted up the cat by the leash, watching him slowly turn in front of her. The cat was not happy; he kept eye contact with Andie during the entire rotation. She dangled Ares over the edge until the cat's feet gently touched down on the slope. No kitties slipping off the rim today either, please.

The girls examined each other's safety brake clips, which would lock down if the cable fed through it too quickly, like the brakes on early-model elevators. A stop like that would give them a jolt, but at least no one would go tumbling down into the deep ravine below.

They looked at each other and acknowledged, ready to go. It would be more of a steep walk than true rappelling, but they would take no foolish risks. Time to descend.

Looking past the cat, who was now straining to walk head-first down the slope, Andie turned a simple lever on the cable, like an old-fashioned twisting 'Chuck' key, to feed out the cable. The device began to run cable through the gears at a slow, steady rate. Andie started her own descent, sucking in a deep breath that was audible over the channel. As the cable played out, the cable display climbed.

While both girls remained facing upward, Ares pulled at his leash below Andie, walking down the slope face-first at a leisurely pace.

"Look, Ares is going Ozzy-style," Aiyana said, looking down at the cat.

"Why do they call going head first 'Ozzy-style?'"

"Not a clue."

Occasionally Ares had to crawl over a small ridge or boulder that let him hang for a few seconds, followed by a slope that allowed him to walk once more. The cat was rappelling.

The monotone voice in their helmets began calling out cable length.

"Ten . . . meters."

Andie checked her descent rate and made sure the two were close, and that no lines would get tangled up.

"Twenty . . . meters."

They continued, carefully stepping, and occasionally hopping, around some rocky outcrop.

"Thirty . . . meters."

At thirty-five meters, both girls turned their dials back, to slow the rate of play in the cable.

They had arrived. At 38m, Andie flipped off the chuck key.

The mechanism reeling out the cable abruptly stopped, and Andie noticed Ares was already standing on all fours. They stood comfortably on the flat rocky shelf where the skimmer had wrecked.

Andie kept Ares on the 2m lead, still attached by carabiner to her belt. The cat looked over the edge curiously but took no dangerous actions.

Among the shattered plastic, polymer fragments, and bits of metal here and there, both girls searched for the laser pointer; no sign of it. They shifted small rocks aside, to find wherever it might have fallen, and even Ares joined in the search. Nothing. Looking sideways along the slope, Aiyana saw pieces of an older, in-line skimmer wreck, a desert motorcycle, judging by a dust-covered front wheel fender wedged between two rocks.

"This is not a good road for vehicles," Aiyana mused, pointing.

"Mew," Ares said back.

They kept looking for the laser pointer. Ares nosed around looking for whatever cats found interesting. On the verge of giving up, a flash of reflected sunlight caught Aiyana's eye, nearly buried in the dust at her boot.

She reached down and brushed aside some dust and small pebbles, finding a shiny, oval piece of chrome, nearly buried. Tapping the dust free, she recognized it as a chromed hood ornament from the skimmer, broken off during the fall. Turning it over to see the front, the six diamonds of the Pleiades glittered in the sunlight.

Subaru.

"Huh." Aiyana said aloud to no one in particular.

"What? Whoa." Andie said, at a momentary loss for words. "Uh, forget laser pointers; that's your badge of honor, babe," Andie said at length. Aiyana nodded, not saying anything.

She brushed the last of the dust free and slipped the oval into a thigh pouch. She zipped it shut, and then looked up at the wispy clouds rapidly crossing a tan sky. Light years away, beyond the skies, the Seven Sisters shined brightly. She could see them clearly in her mind.

"All righty then. Shall we head back?" She turned back toward the rock face, reaching for the chuck mechanism to reel the cable in. Andie turned too but couldn't quite turn all the way around — Ares was tugging on her as he crouched near the edge of the next drop-off.

Curiosity got the better of Andie too, and she peered carefully over the edge where the cat had been looking. Just below them, three or four meters at most, was another flat space, a balcony. It looked . . . human-made: a smooth surface with sharp corners and a straight edge. Gripping her anchor cable tightly with one gloved hand, she leaned further over the edge, trying get a better look.

Along the straight edge, the glow of white tile showed through a coating of red dust.

"Look, there's white tile among the rocks down there; it looks smooth, like a terrace or something."

Aiyana leaned over, though not as far.

Andie spoke up again. "We still have at least another dozen meters or so on these belt spools, and hours of air in our tanks . . . shall we?"

"Um, no thank you very much. That's a straight drop."

Andie made an almost comical face toward Aiyana, a smiling, mouth gaping open happy face as she twisted the Chuck key gently and lowered herself down over the ledge. With her free hand, she gently lifted Ares over the side and let him free-hang behind her.

"Andie!"

"Come on. Live a little."

"Definitely prefer it to dying a little," Aiyana muttered.

Andie's torso, arms, and smiling helmeted face slowly disappeared over the edge.

Aiyana looked up the slope, checked the spool numbers, and with great reluctance, followed Andie over the edge.

Andie was below her, standing on the flat ledge, which had the definite feel of a balcony, cut right into the side of the Mountain. Andie stepped back from the edge as Aiyana lit softly next to her.

"And what have we here?" Andie asked no one in particular. Standing before it now, they looked over a squared-off frame over an airlock outer door — a very old one, all white carbon-fiber and more of the white tile. The door itself had a small half-moon window.

"Look, there used to be a road to this door . . . I guess?" Aiyana pointed where the flat balcony led away, widening then ending abruptly at a crumbling edge.

Andie brushed dust off the half-moon window, then peered inside.

"I can see an inner door, it's closed. Nothing else to see."

Aiyana checked her air supply — 28,300 kPa of breathable air remaining, according to the wrist display; enough for two hours more of light exertion. Andie gripped the door's D-ring handle; Aiyana held Andie's shoulder for safety. She gave the handle a twist. A mild fissing of trace pressure escaped the edges of the doorway. A puff of dust whooshed over their boots.

Andie pushed the door open, and Ares peeked inside. Both girls un-clipped their cable boxes and stuck the devices in a rock jutting out by the entryway. Taking a deep breath, Andie stepped into the airlock first, Ares at her heels. Aiyana followed.

Inside the outer door, Andie reached down and un-clipped Ares' leash, coiling the cable in several loops then pinning it to her own belt.

"Looking good, there, Indy," Aiyana said.

"Huh?" Andie asked. "Oh, my bullwhip. Now all I need is one of those hats."

"A fedora?" Aiyana said.

"Yeah, that." Andie examined the inner door. There were no warning lights on, but the inner door seemed stuck. She struggled to lift the silver arm with all her strength, growling a little with the effort . . . and nothing.

"Gggrrrr...." Andie grunted, then released the handle. "No power, it won't move."

Then both girls heard a "mr-reow," over the radio.

"What?" Andie said, giving up on her exertions and looking back at the cat. Ares was sitting back at the outer door, one paw on the open threshold of the outer door.

"I think he's saying close the outer door, maybe? But there's no way there's full pressure inside. I mean, right?"

The cat refused to budge. Aiyana shrugged and reached out to pull the outer door shut. Ares stepped back, and the door closed without a sound.

Andie turned back to the inner door and braced both feet for another Herculean effort. Gripping the silver arm with both gloved hands and flexing her fingers in as tight a grip as she could manage . . . Andie wrenched the arm, letting out a mighty grunt.

The lever flipped up like it weighed nothing, and Andie whacked herself in the helmet with both hands, spilling her on the ground next to the cat. She turned her head inside the helmet, looking face-to-face with Ares. Ares looked back.

Aiyana began laughing, unsuccessfully tried to stop, then laughed even louder.

Face as red as the planet she were poking around in, Andie stood, shook her head, and pushed the inner door open. They stepped through. After Ares had followed, Aiyana closed the inner door.

"Atmo?"

"Nah, it's a vacuum." Both wrist displays showed ATM 0.01.

The light coming in through the small outer airlock window was just enough to see the room before them. They both turned on helmet lights.

"What's with all the white tile?"

"I dunno, it doesn't make much sense."

Ares, eyes adjusting to the lower light faster than human eyes could, had stepped away deeper into the room, the gloom beyond, leaving little kitty suit paw prints in the red dust. Andie noticed his absence and called Ares back so she could turn on the cat's little suit lights.

The three looked around, panning their lights here and there. A tunnel as large as the room led away into complete darkness.

The place seemed long abandoned, forgotten. "What is this place even for?" Aiyana whispered, awestruck.

The tiled room held a few other surprises. Against the right wall, several older two-wheel skimmers stood parked in a row. One, two . . . five total, in various states of repair, banged up and slightly discolored: three white, one aqua blue, and the last, a bright canary yellow. These resembled traditional dune-skimmers, but instead of the normal twin tank treads, they had actual wheels. Black, rubber wheels. Weird.

"I think I'm in love," Aiyana said, walking right over to the first and stabbing a few controls with a gloved hand. Nothing lit up on the first one.

Undaunted, she walked to the next skimmer in the line. The panel lit up when she pushed the power button. "It works!" She looked back down the yawning tunnel, considering options and brushing dust from the skimmer's display. The power meter read 80% in green numbers. She thumped the front tire with her gloved hand.

"Check this . . . 80% and in the green."

"But how? This thing has sat here for fifty standard years? Or longer?"

"Small-canister fusion core, maybe?"

"Maybe." The skimmer trembled at idle, shedding dust as if eager to run. Aiyana brushed off the logo, an H-D with a stylized skull between the letters. She grinned fiendishly.

Ares hopped up on the back seat of the bike, and Aiyana snorted with a big smile. "You wanna get this thing moving as much as I do?" Then she swung a leg right over the cat and mounted the bike, easing it forward off its under-kickstand. The front tire settled down to make contact with the ground. Andie frowned from a few meters away.

"Oh no . . . no no no no no . . ." Andie muttered, noticing Aiyana straddling her new ride, Ares perched behind her.

"Whadda ya say, Andie?"

"I . . . don't ride."

"It's a piece of cake—just ride behind me . . . look, there's a cargo strap you can pull over your lap to keep you on it." Ares hopped down, then leapt back up in front of Aiyana and parked booted paws up on the handlebars.

"Come ooooon . . . think of how much more we can explore down that tunnel before we start to run low on air."

"Solid point." She looked down at her usable air meter on her wrist display. 27,500 kPa; enough usable air for roughly a couple hours, given they no longer needed to walk these tunnels. "All right, but no matter what we find or don't find, we need to start heading back at the first sign of trouble, or whenever usable air drops below 60 percent. Agreed?"

Aiyana drew breath to answer, but Ares beat her to it.

"Mew," said the cat, who crouched down, looking over the handlebars.

"Mew means yes," Aiyana said. Andie sneered.

Andie straddled the vehicle, pulled the lap strap over her thighs, clicked it, and located the quick-release button. She checked the camera, which was still recording, though while she was riding back-seat, all the lens would see was the back of Aiyana's suit.

"Ready?"

"Ready."

"Mew."

Aiyana pulled the bike out of its parking spot, awkwardly wobbling and almost hitting the opposite wall.

"I got this . . ." as she stepped the bike backward and turned the nose wheel toward the tunnel. She adjusted the rear-view mirrors and after fiddling with a few other controls, found the slider button for the headlights and turned it up to maximum brightness, high beam.

"Ooo, that's better," Andie said, looking over her shoulder. Aiyana looked down at the controls. The heads-up display had a compass—they were pointed West-Southwest.

Aiyana started off slow, then finding a proper balance, eased the speed up to twenty-five, almost thirty clicks an hour, faster than any Olympic athlete could sprint. She checked the speed gauge then swerved slightly to dodge a fallen rock.

"You know, this thing can go twice this fast," Aiyana said as they whipped down the tunnel.

"Yeah, how 'bout no," Andie said in her ear. Aiyana smiled widely in her helmet.

The skimmer rode smoothly, with only the smallest occasional bumps. Andie's hands reassuringly gripped her shoulders as they pressed on ahead. She could hear Aiyana's breathing over the radio—she was having the time of her life.

"This ride was prolly meant for two workers, maybe shift workers, who worked these tunnels back when they were being carved, right?" The tunnel was round-ish, but not a perfectly smooth bore. It seemed flat enough for a smooth ride.

"Maybe . . . did you notice those splotches of spray sealant in the tunnel cracks every so often? Almost like these spaces were once pressurized." Andie paused. "But what for? There's no one down here."

They drove on ahead, powerful headlights piercing the darkness and revealing an alcove ahead, carved into the side of the tunnel. Aiyana slowed to a stop.

"I don't see anything too interesting," Andie murmured, "broken-down drills and tunnel equipment." As an afterthought, Andie patted the Compact-40 air cylinders she had thought to pack, tucked neatly into her ExoSuit legging pockets, above the boots. They accelerated back up and powered onward, down the tunnel.

Just a moment later, they rode right into a larger space—the skimmer headlights and the motorcycle's under-glow did their job illuminating all around. Aiyana brought the skimmer to a halt and switched it off.

"Check it out, it's like ACSA Crossroads in here."

"Yeah, how many tunnels do you count? Five?

"One, two three, yep, five. That big one on the right looks interesting, I can see something on the floor inside."

"Oh really? Yeah, I see it too now. Whoa, dig the archway." Even the cat looked up at it, then hopped down from his perch.

A broad carved archway, a true rarity among the builders, led into an even larger room. A cavernous room. Andie dismounted. She checked the camera attached below her helmet, confirmed it was still recording, and did a slow turn in place, capturing the five tunnels. As she turned, she paused to glance down each direction, then ended with the largest, the archway. She leaned back so her helmet lights would illuminate it better. Across the top of the archway, block letters had been very carefully machine-carved directly into the living rock:

QUI ULTIMUM SACRIFICIUM
ANIMOS SUOS LIBERAT VAGARI AETHER
EX MARTIS AD ASTRA

"My Latin sucks . . . ultimate . . . sacrifice, okay . . . is that animals? Or movement? And 'liberat' sounds like liberty, maybe freedom? Aether, ether, what the ancient ones called 'space' or the Cosmos . . . vagari, could that be . . .hm."

"Maybe viagi, like a voyage?" Aiyana suggested. Andie nodded, reaching up to rub her chin in thought, then when it bumped her helmet, she held it still and blushed again inside the helmet. She quickly dropped the gloved hand and noticed Ares. The cat stared back.

"Okay . . . I think it's about making the ultimate sacrifice, being free to voyage through the Cosmos. And of course, we know that last line, from Mars to the stars. The Founder's Stone thing," Andie summed up.

"Do you think this was where those words were first carved? To commemorate the dead?"

"Mew," said Ares.

"Okay, let's check it out." The two girls and their cat entered the place together, stepping cautiously, reverently inside.

No footsteps had disturbed these dusty floors in a very long time. In perfectly aligned rows upon rows . . . bodies laid to rest. Thousands of them.

The dead, laid here, each in their final resting place—ten thousand people, maybe more? The sound of silence here was . . . ominous. Each body lay flat on a carved stone—no, these were poured cement rectangles. Each had a simple plastic sarcophagus shell set down over the body.

Andie leaned down next to the first one she came to. The plastic was frosted, opaque, up to shoulder level, but the face inside was visible through clear plexi-plastic casings. The woman lying here was dressed in simple off-white daily wear with light blue highlights, and had been done up in funerary makeup, brown hair with gray streaks . . . and she looked like she was sleeping. A brass plaque, engraved and mounted near her head, bore the following:

SALLY MAY PETERSON
2103 - 2181

Examining another slab, Aiyana spoke up. "Holy Moe . . . Andie, these must be the founders . . . or, the builders. I mean, right? Look at the dates!"

Andie was too stunned to speak, she merely nodded. Earth dates! The dates on this sarcophagus suggested the woman had been interred here more than a hundred standard years ago—two hundred Earth years ago, easily nine or ten generations.

She peered deeper into the chamber. The room stretched out to the left and right, easily as big as a full football field. Or bigger? Their lights did not reach the farthest walls.

"Look, none are higher, or lower, than the others--all equal."

"Yeah. And some have stones set on their face-shields. There's one with a necklace draped over it, and a cross."

"You mean a rosary?"

"Yeah, that."

Here and there, small white or black stones had been placed carefully at the head of a sarcophagus, along with the occasional rosary, Muslim Misbaha beads, or some other artifact, lovingly draped across the plastic covering, now also covered in dust.

Aiyana wandered on ahead, directly toward the far wall. She raised her helmet lamps up to another inscription, carved in standard English. She read the words aloud:

WE HONOR OUR BELOVED DEPARTED
IN PEACE THEY REST, FOREVER FREE
UNTIL THE MOUNTAIN CLAIMS THEM

"That last bit is strange," Andie murmured. She brushed a gloved hand over one of the plastic covers nearby, stirring up some dust. A wrinkled, gaunt man's face lay within, eyes closed and mouth hanging slightly open. The burial case did not appear pressurized, so no decomposition had taken place, no decay. This could just as easily be someone's great-grandpa, thin with age, sleeping on a slab. The carved plate read:

BOLIVAR ESPERANZA
2094 - 2151

From several slabs off to the left, Ares jolted, mewing abruptly, and staring straight up. Andie noticed the cat's strange behavior and walked over. Ares stood stock-still, staring up above one grave slab in particular . . . specifically, at a fixed spot above it. He didn't move a muscle or twitch so much as a whisker. Andie frowned and walked closer.

Then Ares turned, dashing away in large, graceful bounds, back out the door toward their skimmer. He stopped and turned back to watch from the doorway.

"What, Ares? What? What did you see?" Andie called after the cat, seeing his lights standing still under the archway. The cat said nothing. She walked to the name plate where Ares had been staring upward.

Her blood ran cold.

ELIAS ELLIS
2089 - 2137

Chapter Eleven

The Dead End

"Whoa," Andie finally murmured, exhaling. She was too stunned to even take a picture, though the camera must still be recording. "Aiiiiiyaa?"

Aiyana tore her gaze away from the wall carvings and ran over. Headlamps danced wildly in the darkness as she made it to Andie. "Are you all right?"

"No," Andie said, pointing down at a deceased man under his plastic shell, with a jovial face, almost smiling under an auburn-reddish beard. Aiyana read the engraving.

"Oh sh…"

"Yeah," Andie said, crouching down to look closer.

"So he was real," Aiyana whispered. "But not Ellis Ellis. Elias Ellis. Or Eli Ellis, maybe?"

Andie nodded. "I wonder if he had family, I mean, it's possible we're related, right?" They both scanned the body carefully. "I have so many questions right now."

"Mm, look for a wedding ring," Aiyana suggested.

"Brilliant," Andie replied.

There was nothing on his left hand, but on his right, Andie could just see a dark line through the plastic covering. She lifted the edge of the plastic to peek under.

"Wait, don't do that," Aiyana protested.

"Do what? I see something on his other hand. Whoa, I think it's a ring drive." The ring drive on the body's thin fingers was like an old-school thumb-drive, but worn rather than carried.

In a moment of deep-seated intuition even Andie herself didn't understand, she slipped the ring drive off the corpse's finger, and put it into her Exo-Suit suit pocket. She had to know more about who he was, and if any of his stories was true. They both stood still, looking down.

A glint of silver around his neck caught one of the headlamps. "Maybe I should look at his necklace too?"

"I think we've done enough tomb raiding for one day," Aiyana protested. "Leave him be."

Andie stared down for another moment at Elias' final resting place, shaking her head.

The cat meowed from the doorway, and the girls, still in a daze, flinched at the sound of the cat's meow. Reluctantly, they turned away. Andie shook her head in disbelief and rested a hand on the pocket where the mysterious ring drive was tucked safely away.

With one last glance around, the girls headed back to the entry door, matching their own prior footprints in the dust. And they noticed it — Ares was nowhere to be seen.

They exited the crypt chamber and scanned around.

"There, his little footprints," Andie said, pointing down the middle of the three tunnels they hadn't explored yet. After another dozen meters, the tunnel dipped sharply downward, at a steeper angle now, but still manageable without slipping. The cat prints continued onward.

"Ares, where are you?" Aiyana asked the darkness, seeing a soft glow of the cat's suit somewhere far ahead. The cat did not answer.

After a few more minutes, the tunnel leveled out in a smaller, rough-rounded room. Ares stood in the middle of the room, facing another airlock door, opposite the way they had come in. Andie recognized this one from her recent research in the Pocket, exploring early airlock designs. This one had to be the oldest she had ever laid eyes on—like something straight out of Earth's earliest space missions. Even stranger, it had been painted a bright blue. Weird.

Aiyana glanced up. "Look at the ridges in the ceiling here—probably this was originally a natural lava tube. Then . . . they just . . . closed it off with this blue door?"

"To hold in the air pressure for everything above maybe," Andie said.

"Mr-reow," the cat said back, still looking ahead, at the door, through his little kitty faceplate.

Thankfully, the blue door here also had a small window set into it, another half-moon shape, about a hand's-width tall. This was set roughly at an Exo-Suit's faceplate height above the floor, perfect for peeking through. So they both did, taking turns.

Aiyana leaned her head side to side, allowing some of his suit's light to pan around in the space beyond. "I don't see a second door, do you?"

"No, just this one door. That might be a problem."

"What problem? Let's just open it," Aiyana said. "It's Mars-standard 0.01 ATM here, see?" She held up her wrist for Andie to see. Andie also noted Aiyana's air meter showed 79% remaining.

"Yeeesss, but what if some of the atmo from layers way back behind us comes rushing down through the space we're in here? Or something worse? This is not a secure airlock."

"I—" Aiyana started to respond.

"Mr-reow," Ares muttered again across the shared channel.

"What?" Andie asked.

The cat repeated his demand.

"Don't tell me he needs a litter box?" Aiyana said.

Ares squinted at her.

"Mr-reow," Ares muttered again, looking at Andie, then up at the door.

"Oh. You want a peek?" Andie shrugged. "Okie-fine."

She picked the cat up and held his face up to the window for a moment.

"Seen enough?" She asked.

"Mew," the cat replied.

Ares wriggled out of Andie's grasp then sat in place, resting a booted paw up against the door. He sat still as a statue, not moving his paw, looking up at the girls.

"Look, I want to go in too, but that's an insane risk. It doesn't have a second door inside. We don't know what's there, or if it will suck us both down inside, and leave us unable to get back."

The cat looked up, paw still in place.

"No, we can't," Andie persisted, it's probably nothing but more rocks, and a perfect opportunity for us to get lost."

"We won't get lost—our suits are auto mapping every direction and the distance we go," Aiyana reminded her.

"Don't encourage him," Andie replied.

The cat looked up and blinked, his paw still in place.

"I want to know too, but it's not our place. We need a proper survey team to map all this."

The cat looked up, paw still against the door.

"No."

The cat still hadn't moved a muscle.

"Ugh, all right," Andie said, walking over behind the cat, who stood back up on all fours now, easing back from the door to let it open.

"Stubborn little punk."

Aiyana watched the exchange, slightly bemused. Andie walked over and brushed some dust off the words printed on the door. She nodded, understanding how to open it now.

"Strange . . . it swings inward, toward us. Probably in a decompression event, it would automatically slam shut and keep the pressure on this side of the door safe. Then, the upper caverns and city above us would be okay . . . Cleverrrr . . . ."

Andie let the word hang in the air as she peered one last time through the window. "I'll probably have to give it an insane yank to get it open, it's designed to keep our tunnel pressurized, and the space beyond may be a perfect vacuum. Shall we be crazy daring?"

She gripped the handle, expecting that when he swung it down, probably nothing would happen. The hinges were on this side of the door, meaning she would have to pull the door inward. She'd be fighting against escaping pressure from above and behind them, like trying to pull a champagne cork . . . from inside the bottle.

Without the proper equipment, she didn't give it much of a chance.

She swung the handle . . .

And promptly got knocked on her rear end, because the pressure on the other side of the door turned out to be higher — much higher.

The door swung open violently, shoving both girls backward, and sliding Ares across the room.

"Whoa."

"Rrrrr . . . " Ares murmured, sliding in the wind but managing to keep his feet.

The door swung open and stayed open as the strange wind whistled up through the doorway, strong at first, but then dwindling to a slower breeze. Eventually the air pushing against their suits could not be felt at all. Wrist displays spiked at *ATM 0.21* but quickly dropped to *ATM 0.02*.

Both girls checked each other over, then they hefted Ares—no damage they could see. The cat wriggled to be put down, then walked forward, stepping through the open door. He paused at a pile of small cobbles and fist-sized rocks that had accumulated inside the doorway.

They nudged their way through the rubble and stepped through. The cat merely bounded gracefully across the tops of the larger rocks until he was clear of the pile. Andie turned back to close the door behind them. With Aiyana's help, the two managed to pull the door back closed, sliding the handle into its 'sealed' position.

"At least it will be easy to open from this side."

Ares squinted into the black tunnel ahead.

Andie turned her suit's headlamps up to maximum brightness and adjusted the cat's suit lamp settings as well. Aiyana did the same.

The tunnel on this side of the blue door was natural, not carved at all by machines. The floor had bumpy ridges, and the ceiling showed rivulets and frozen drips where some magma flow millions of years earlier had run through the tube then drained away to the deeper magma chambers of Olympus Mons.

They continued on with Ares close by, carefully stepping over ridges and rough floor, occasionally stubbing a booted toe—but not enough to cause pain or compromise a suit.

The tunnel curved down, right, down, and left, no branches, no change in its diameter. Ares walked slightly faster, a few paces ahead of them. After another few minutes, he let out a low kitty growl and stopped.

"Rrrrrrr . . ." the cat's low growl lasted a few seconds before trailing off.

They had found another round room, but here, the floor simply dropped away.

"Careful, there's a drop off," Aiyana put out a hand to stop Andie from walking right over the edge.

"Thanks," Andie whispered. Ares peered down over the edge.

"Look over there, like ten meters away, the wall curves side to side." The opposite wall also curved up to a rounded dome above, perfectly smooth.

"Why on Mars would someone cut a round room like this?"

"I . . . don't think this was the builders. They would probably have smoothed out the tunnels behind us, these rough magma tubes."

"Okay, then who?"

Andie shrugged. "Wow. Look, it's a complete sphere." The curving walls above, below, and on both sides had no flat surfaces, no sharp edges or angles, and no exit. Everything curved so perfectly in their helmet lamps that it was tricky to look at. Andie swayed a bit and Aiyana kept a hand on her shoulder.

"So . . . weird round room."

"Mr-reow."

"What's that he said?" Aiyana asked, looking down at Ares.

"That's the sound he makes when he wants me to do something. It's like . . . his call to action."

"Mew," Ares confirmed.

"Um, no thanks. We fall in there, we'd get stuck. So, nothing else to do here but go back, see?"

"Sadly, that sounds right. But something's bothering me. We're standing in a natural magma tube here, right?"

"I guess, yeah."

"So where is the rest of the tunnel? Magma tubes don't just . . . end. So this one just ends in this, what did you call it? Weird round room? It makes no sense--it should continue, straight across, right over there."

Aiyana looked down at the cat, who had just crouched.

"No, don't you even think abou—"

And the cat leaped over the edge. Andie grabbed at him but caught nothing but vacuum.

"Ares!" both girls yelled simultaneously.

The cat's suit lights slid down the smooth wall below their feet, leveling out several seconds later and coming to a stop at the bottom of the bowl. He stood and turned around, making strange turns here and there, like he was looking for something. After several seconds, the girls heard the cat's voice over the radio.

"Mr-reow?"

"Ugh, you little punk."

"Kitty, there's no way for us to get you back up. Why'd you do that?"

"Mr-reow."

"Ooo, what about your cable? Why not use that?"

"Oh yeah, that's a thought. But . . ."

"But? Oh. One of us has to go down and get him."

"One of us? You're the fitness nut, Aiya," Andie said. "You're the only one strong enough to pull a person back up." Aiyana shrugged. That much was true.

Sighing, Andie unclipped one end of the cable from her hip and let it dangle over the side. The loose carabiner did not reach even halfway to where Ares was nosing around on the floor — he was far out of reach. The cat acted oblivious to their actions and found something he had become intently focused on, down on the floor in front of him.

"Mm, I could slide down, and toss him up to you?"

"But then you'd be stuck down there."

"I could run in wider and wider circles until I was high enough for you to grab me."

"You watch too many social media vids."

Andie shook her head. "Okay. There has got to be a way all three of us make it out of here. Let's inventory: what do we have?"

"We need our suit hoses and all to stay alive, and I didn't exactly pack my spelunking kit, did you? Even a SAFE pod has supplies we could . . ."

Andie's eyes flew wide. "My bracelet! I put it in my pocket, just like on Star Party night."

"Your bracelet? Wha—"

"The one I found during the big quake in the ACSA safe pod—it's like my good luck charm, but it catches inside my Exo-Suit gloves, so I've just stuck it in a pocket whenever I'm suited up."

"What good will a bracelet do?"

"Watch and see. It's pair-cord."

"Oh, cool. I never understood what 'pair-cord' means," Aiyana said.

Andie fumbled for the short emergency blade tucked into every Exo-Suit belt. "Yeah, weird name, isn't it? There are like twenty strands inside, not two. Here we go."

She had the bracelet in one hand and the suit's short blade in the other. Very carefully, she slipped the sharp edge up under the coin, the 'button' that held the woven bracelet closed. With a simple slice, the cord parted and the coin fell free. Andie grabbed at it, but it slipped over the side and down into the sphere room. Ares saw its movement, tried to pounce on it, but it rolled past him and vanished.

"Oh no!"

"What?"

"The coin fell down there."

"Hm. Look for it when you go get Ares?"

"Yeah, that might work." She picked at the cut ends, awkwardly unraveling the cord with her gloves. The cord eventually stretched out to an impressive three meters, floor to ceiling height in an average home.

"Urg, it's hard to tie knots with these gloves on." Andie said through gritted teeth.

"Here, let me try. I sometimes need to patch up my clothes, if you can believe that." Andie handed her the end, holding the other end for safety.

After a few more minutes, Aiyana had looped a secure knot onto the carabiner clip at one end of the metal tether. The other end clip, Aiyana slipped onto her own belt. Andie held the other end of the tether cable in her grip and sat down, legs dangling over the side.

"Careful not to bang your suit or your tank on the ledge."

"Fair point," Andie replied, looking down toward Ares. She took a deep cleansing breath and turned sideways while pushing slightly with her hands. She cleared the edge and slid cleanly down the side. When the cord pulled tight, the loose end slipped out of her hand and flopped on the curving side wall behind her. The momentum of her slide carried her down into the center of the bowl. Ares jumped out of Andie's way as she slid to a stop.

"Yikes! Almost yanked me over the side," Aiyana said, one hand still gripping a rocky ridge in the tunnel wall.

Andie stood and checked her suit, glancing at her wrist display and patting down her helmet and back, to see if anything had been broken or pried loose. It seemed okay. The pair-cord tether dangled nearby, within easy reach.

"You look good from up here," Aiyana said.

"Yeah, my suit seems fine . . . huh, even the camera is still recording," she said.

Andie looked down at Ares, then searched around for her coin. No sign. Just the shimmer of her headlamps in the shiny black floor. The cat was fixated downward as well, and Andie pointed her helmet lights his way.

"There are small gaps in the floor here—it's not perfectly smooth after all." She shined her headlamps over the cracks, trying to see if the coin might still be stuck inside one. No such luck.

"What is it? What do you see?"

"Uh . . . I can't tell?"

"What? Is it like holes in the floor?"

"No, it's two thingys . . . pointed thingys—chevrons. Then a line of cuts in the stone underneath. It almost looks like . . . writing."

She bent to point her camera down at the floor so it would record the strange cuts in the rock.

"The chevrons point directly that way, opposite from where you are." Andie looked at where the chevrons pointed and saw nothing but more of the smooth black wall, curving up and out of sight above. The strange lines, deeply shadowed, contrasted clearly in her lamplight:

"I'll show you on the camera later. It's freaky."

"Weird. Did you find your coin?"

Andie cast around again, searching the floor. "No. It's gone. Dang it."

"Well, let's get you out of there."

"You don't need to ask me twice; this place gives me the creeps."

Andie scooped up a protesting Ares, wriggling in her arms as she crossed to the side where the thin rope's end still dangled. She stretched her arm out to reach, gripped it, and wrapped the end around her hand three times for security to avoid slipping.

"Okay, do you have a good grip up there?'

"Almost . . . okay, just don't give me any hard jolts, my grip on these rough walls isn't the greatest."

"I'll try," Andie said, stepping up the curving incline, then wrapping the rope an extra wrap around a gloved hand. The other hand still held Ares, who had stopped wriggling and was craning to look down at the floor over Andie's shoulder.

As Andie got to the steepest part, she couldn't go any further with just one hand. Without warning him, she heaved Ares up over the edge. He barely cleared the edge and landed sprawling. The thin rope of the pair-cord cut painfully into her gloved hand, and she was reminded of the scrape and scabbed-over cuts from ACSA during the big quake. Then she felt wetness slick her palm inside the glove. Great.

But with Ares up and safe, Andie now had both free hands to scramble higher, and she lunged with her left hand to grab the other clipped end of the metal leash.

From the top, Aiyana did one mighty biceps curl with her right hand. "Urrrrgyeaahh!" she grunted until she saw a gloved hand slap up and over the edge. "Grab . . . my . . . boot," she grunted as Andie fumbled to get a grip on her booted foot. With more grunts and strain, Andie's torso and one leg lifted up, over the lip and finally, she rolled over into the tunnel.

Both girls breathed heavily for a moment. "We need . . . to slow . . . our breathing," Andie panted.

"Yeah . . ." Aiyana replied, taking one cleansing breath and slowly letting it out.

Another moment passed. Andie stood and helped Aiyana to her feet. Then Andie clipped a carabiner to Ares, and the other end to her suit, in case he got any other bright ideas.

The two stood looking back down into the round room for a moment. Then they turned away and started back up the magma tube.

"I'm sad you lost your coin."

"Me too," Andie said. Then, as an afterthought, she said, "maybe the great Vulcan took it as an offering?"

Aiyana chuckled. "Maybe. We did make it out of there in one piece."

As they walked, Andie checked her displays. She was down to 65% air remaining. Almost time to be heading back. They arrived at the single blue pressure door, eased it open, and closed it behind them. Several moments later, they were back in the junction room where the five tunnels met.

"Hm, we have just enough air to look down one more tunnel before we absolutely have to head back. Ares looked at the left-side tunnel, one leading slightly upward. Andie felt the tug at her waist, the cat still being leashed to her.

"He wants to go this way, it would seem."

"Up is better than down at this point. Shall we take the H-D?"

"The what? Oh, the skimmer. Sure, that's smart. Let me just do something first."

Andie popped open the back seat, finding a small cargo container underneath. She slipped the compact-40 tanks out of their bag and stowed them under the seat. Then she snapped the seat back shut. The two saddled back up, and Ares had his little suited paws on the handlebars like before. Andie clicked the lap strap across and into place. "All set back here."

Aiyana hit a few switches and twisted the right handle. They found themselves in a gentle tunnel, riding up and curving to the North on the display, and eventually around to the Northeast. They passed by more alcoves with random equipment, long abandoned. The tunnel widened to double its size, and the walls looked machine-carved. Not perfectly smoothed like the sphere room, but clearly cut by the builders. An alcove appeared ahead.

More small and medium-sized vehicles were parked here and there in new alcoves, including a tank-looking vehicle, treads and all, but much smaller than the hook-and-ladder behemoth from last night's star party.

Slowing to look it over, Aiyana tapped her wrist and Andie slapped her shoulder in confirmation. She gunned the engine again, shooting onward down the tunnel.

"Whoa, there's a light ahead," Aiyana said.

"Wait, what? How is that possible?"

"I'm not imagining it, look."

As they neared the distant glow, finally within range of headlights, the small point of light resolved itself to be yet another airlock door, this one much newer than the early model doorways behind them.

They dismounted and took turns peeking through. A lone LED-bulb glowed inside the airlock, shining weakly through the window.

"We should look inside, then definitely head back." Wrist displays showed 57% and 59%. This door, having power of its own, showed the space beyond to be pressurized. Andie pressed the right sequence on the outer door to get it to evacuate the air inside so they could open the door.

As they closed the first door and began to add the proper pressure inside, a brighter light flipped on ahead of them, on the other side of the second door. One airlock cycle later, they stepped through the inner door and looked around. Aiyana closed the door behind them and re-sealed it.

They gazed around a well-lit, pressurized, large, curving tunnel. Looking back at the airlock they had just transited, Andie pointed. The door had a huge red "X" on it, a simple symbol of danger, and sometimes of radiation. A sign stuck above the window read:

AUTHORIZED PERSONNEL ONLY
NO ADMITTANCE / DOOR ALARMED
(VACUUM BEYOND)

Aiyana scanned around the edges. No data wires, no alarm, just a simple power line to the door's controls. This door was never intended to be used again, but it certainly was not alarmed.

"Good one," she said, pointing a finger at the sign, and turning away. Ares took a few steps further, and Andie clipped him back on his tether before he could get too far. Then she took a proper look around. She saw several colored stripes along the wall, with arrows interspersed every so often, all pointing from right to left down a long, sloping tunnel that descended away to the left.

"Wait. Is this . . ." Andie started to say. "Noooo, it can't be." She glanced at her wrist to confirm the huge tunnel was at ATM 1.0, proper N_2-O_2 mix. Before Aiyana could object, Andie twisted her faceplate and helmet free, letting it flop backward. She breathed in the air, sniffing it deeply. It smelled slightly metallic with a hint of some other odor she couldn't identify.

"Yep, I know where we are. Well, roughly."

Aiyana twisted open her helmet as well, letting it flop backward.

"And how can you know that? How do you even know what these tunnels are?"

"Because I explored them last night."

Aiyana looked puzzled, then her eyes flew wide open. "You mean . . ."

"Yep, last night, I entered in the proper codes for the Pocket portal."

"But that's . . . um . . . and you didn't tell me?"

"Well, I was going to, before we went down a cable to recover . . . that, remember?" She reached across and patted the pocket where Aiyana had stashed the Subaru vehicle ornament. "Then we got, uh, distracted."

"Hm. Well, let's at least get out of these suits."

"I think we can find our way to the Pocket directly now, if we can just follow the builders' bread crumbs."

They slipped out of the Exo-Suits, shut them down, and Andie freed Ares from his little cat suit.

"We should carry these with us, right?" Aiyana asked.

"I'm actually thinking if we stash them here, just inside the big-X airlock, we could bring back fresh tanks and explore some more later."

"But what if we need them now?"

"Hmm. We could use auto-mapping to find our way back, and we should get a ping from the city above us—take us right to our bat-cave."

"You seem pretty optimistic."

"I am. See those stripes on the walls?" Andie indicated parallel green,

177

red, and purple stripes.

"Mm hmm."

"If we can swim upstream, so to speak, go against the arrows, we might be able to find where the red and purple lines first meet. If we can find that spot, I think I can get us to the Portal."

They set out, walking opposite the direction the arrows pointed.

Ten minutes of determined hiking later, mostly uphill, and with only a couple wrong turns, they found their objective.

"This is it," Andie said. They followed a narrow, unmarked side tunnel, and came to a familiar-looking white porcelain-covered metal portal.

"I can't believe you figured it out," Aiyana breathed, looking at Andie with new-found awe. "And what's with the lens up there?"

"Lens? Where?"

Aiyana pointed so Andie could see. Sure enough, a small black camera lens with a remote antenna was attached right where it could keep an eye on the tunnel, just outside the Pocket.

"Well, as long as there aren't any cameras inside watching us, I have no complaints. Looks like it's just keeping an eye on this tunnel. That feed probably hasn't been looked at in a century."

"Hm. Still, someone is, or was, watching this doorway for a reason."

"Come on, I want to get this ring drive cracked open, see what secrets our friend Ellis Ellis feels like sharing," Andie said brightly.

"I think you mean your great-great-great-great-great-great-great-grandfather."

"Yeah, not saying all that. I think I'll just call him . . . Uncle Eli."

"Uncle Eli it is then."

* * *

By Sunday afternoon, Andie had located an antiquated drive reader that might work for Uncle Eli's ring. She linked the reader pad device to her tablet and set the ring on it. A micro-LED on the ring itself winked on, then off. Nothing else happened.

"Huh." Andie looked over at Ares, who was taking an interest. Ares walked up to ring on its reader pad and looked at it closely. He batted a paw against it lightly. No change.

"Maybe the user needs to wear it?" Ares just looked back at her.

Andie slipped it on her right-hand middle finger, with the LED part pointing down. She rested her hand on the reader pad. No change.

Furrowing her brow, she twisted the ring around, so the light was pointed up. She rested her hand on the pad one more time.

A green LED glowed on the ring. Andie's tablet also lit up; a new file directory window opened but it looked fuzzy, out of focus. Encrypted? No, because a few seconds later a video file icon appeared on top of everything else, in sharp focus. With her left hand, Andie floated the tablet's pointer over the file icon, to see if it might show any metadata.

The floating window showed:

```
Filename: 2607.E.Ellis.Jr
Creator: E.Ellis
Duration: 1:09
Encoding: glendower_biomet_ind(mons.mars.net)
Created: _ _ _ _ _ _ _ _ _ _ / _ _ : _ _
Modified: _ _ _ _ _ _ _ _ _ _ / _ _ : _ _
Accessed:
```

"Weird. Creation and modification dates both scrubbed, and never accessed after being created. Uncle Eli . . . what have you left for your beloved son?"

She held her breath. She clicked play, and upped the volume.

The video filled the screen. A kindly, aged man's face smiled up at her.

Andie did not see any resemblance to her dad or to herself, but she knew this must be the infamous Elias Ellis.

> "My son—you have traveled far. If you are watching this, know that I am gone, but the richness of all we have accomplished in a lifetime of creation and exploration . . . is now yours. I failed you; I know this. But now I entrust to you a legacy that must be fulfilled—for the good of all people in this world. My will is failing, my strength, gone. I implore you, live beyond my mistakes. Find the doors that lead to knowledge, understanding, life enduring, perspective, and unlocking the future. Do this, not for me, but for humanity. I should have followed you, but Mars has bound me. The idea that you have returned . . . it gives me hope. My son, hope is a good thing, perhaps the best of things. I hope this finds you. I hope you are well.

The video ended, and the icon minimized itself into a spot on the screen and vanished. Several rows of file directories snapped into sharp focus, with dozens of sub-directories each.

Andie let out the breath she had been holding. Ares looked at her with wide eyes.

Through the afternoon and into the night, Andie explored his research and tried to follow his designs. The man was a DaVinci—artist, inventor, and sculptor, but what he sculpted was next-gen designs for humanity's success on Mars. The Great Elon had given humanity its original vision as a multi-planetary species, sure, but Elias Ellis took that vision and ran with it. He became a figure of both legend and controversy before vanishing into obscurity in the two hundred fifty Earth years after his passing.

Uncle Eli led the engineering effort to transform the largest magma chamber ever found into a thriving city of ten thousand—the one that now boasted a million citizens. He took the MagLev concept and forged it into reality, connecting high-speed rail between the Mons-Plex and the city 'near us,' which came to be called Nerus. Over time, his designs led the twin cities to expand to seven, with more predicted in his work. His designs were hailed as the work of a genius, though those who worked closely with him found his obsessions almost maniacal.

By Tuesday night, Andie accessed a hidden folder where that first video message had vanished. She opened Uncle Eli's personal video journals—more letters left for his son. Feeling guilty for intruding, but knowing that Elias, Jr. was also her ancestor, long deceased, she watched them, one after another. The boy's best friend had vanished, apparently, and was assumed dead. Eli, Jr. had blamed his father for his friend's death and left Mars forever with bitterness in his heart. The pain of his son's loss seemed to have broken Elias. He died alone—his work, unfinished. A pile of mysteries filled his life's wake.

By Wednesday night, Andie had summarized what she had learned about the five *Color Portals* commissioned by Uncle Eli. She read her notes:

Portal	Location	Key to Open	Reward	Notes
1. White	The Pocket	Knowledge	Perspective	Theia/Gaia
2. Red	Warrior Way (?)	Leadership	Access	??
3. Orange	Villa Jovis (?)	Honesty	Understanding	??
4. Green	Murdo's Fount (?)	Loyalty	Life Enduring	??
5. Blue	Magma Tube	Courage	The Future	Sphere Rm?

In his video journals, Uncle Eli made one verbal reference to a sixth door, encouraging his son to seek it out after passing through the others. He remained maddeningly unhelpful as to the sixth door's color, location, purpose, key, or the reward it guarded, if it even had one.

By Thursday night, with Ares as her wingman—wing-cat—she had found no better perspective about going through the Pocket's White Door. No new insight into Mars, the city, or her own existence. What perspective? The only perspective she gained was there was a sprawling network of unused, pressurized tunnels beneath them, as broad as the city itself.

Aiyana had been busy working the coffee shop, so Andie plowed on alone, researching in isolation. Ares, though he was certainly good company, did not express any ideas as to what 'perspective' could be found by transiting the white door. He just tagged along for the adventure.

Exploring the tunnels together, she found yet another doorway, no special color, that did not match anything on Uncle Eli's list. This one led directly East. She found this baffling too—the only thing this far East was the outside slopes of Olympus Mons. This door did not even have controls, keyboard, or engraved plaque—the only way to open it seemed to be a digital key card slot for a key she did not have.

Feeling both motivated and frustrated, she rolled into Friday trying to distract herself with all the festivities of Homecoming Week. She had her own varsity competition, Knowledge Bowl, to prepare for.

The sleep she desperately needed . . . did not come easy.

Chapter Ten

Bowl For Olympus

Friday. Andie assumed she would never cross paths with that boy from Earth again, the one from *Lucky Seven*. Yet . . . he had just sat down with the opposing team at the K-Bowl semifinals.

The excited, rolling conversation of the crowd here in the school's small arena filled the space with anticipation of the match, and Andie almost didn't notice him in the excitement. Then Andie saw Aiyana and her other friends in the crowd. She waved briefly then leaned in to chat with her two varsity K-Bowl teammates.

"You guys, check it out, it's the kid from *Lucky Seven* on the other team," she said to her teammates Viola and Yuvi.

"What? So he just got in from Earth . . . and he's already doing Varsity K-Bowl? I don't know if I'm impressed or insulted," Yuvi said, smiling and shaking his head.

"I'm trying to remember what his name is. Thrace? Tryce? Something like that."

Viola spoke in a whisper. "He'll have the Earth topics covered; maybe that's why he got picked? A ringer?"

"Yeah, but is he helping or hurting them? Sure, he'll know his Earth topics, but on the other hand, he'll be clueless on Mars history, geography . . . our celebrities, our holidays," Yuvi said.

Andie shrugged and the three of them got back to their final strategizing for semifinals. Privately, Andie decided she would keep a close eye on . . . she tapped open the competition rosters . . . a close eye on this 'Trace Worthington' person.

Semifinals marked the last surge of events of Mars' Homecoming Week, the last great push leading up to the big Saturday night dance. Of all the sports and celebrated events coming in these final hours, Knowledge Bowl, K-Bowl for short, was Andie's favorite.

Andie qualified for top-tier Varsity with her younger teammate Viola, one-half year behind Andie in school, a sophomore. Viola was a whiz at pop culture, current events, and modern history. Andie's other teammate was the team's veteran player, Yuvraj, 'Yuvi' to his friends. Yuvi was a half-year ahead of Andie, a senior. He was a whiz in geometry, algebra, physics, and musical theory. He also played a mean bass guitar. While some students buckled under pressure, these three teammates thrived.

The judges called for quiet; the first round got under way.

As the conversation in the arena calmed, Andie eyed Trace and his two teammates once more, then glanced at her own two teammates. They looked ready. Yuvi took a deep breath, held it, and let it out slowly. Viola looked composed. Game faces on, they settled in.

The Chief Judge cleared his throat and spoke into the microphone.

"Welcome to Knowledge Bowl, Semifinals round three. In this round, we have our home team, the Mons High School Olympians—"

The arena burst into thunderous applause. The judge let it go for a few seconds, then held his hands up for quiet.

"Facing off against the guest team, the Nerus High School Legionnaires."

A chant of "Le-gion! Le-gion! Le-gion!" Rose up from the visiting school section. Again, the judge held his hands up for quiet.

"Yes, welcome indeed. Competitors: you are reminded that each correct response earns your team one hundred points, while every incorrect response loses fifty points. We will have four standard rounds of five questions each, chosen in turn by your team from a pool of ten pre-set categories. Following the four rounds will be the final round, the barrage of twenty questions, each worth fifty points." This was well-known to all.

"Audience members are reminded to save your applause and cheers for the end of each round, and under no circumstances will you call out answers or help competitors in any way. Heckling or insults will result in you being removed from the competition space—remember, we are opponents, not enemies." His comments prompted a few murmurs, which hushed quickly as he spoke again.

"Per tradition, the visiting team, the Legionnaires, will choose our first category. May the better team win."

Four large screens, hanging above the competitors like a miniature Jumbotron, flashed the ten categories.

Martian Sports	Zombie Fest
Earth Renaissance	Greek Mythology
Rivers	Impressionist Art
Natural Disasters	Equal and Opposite
Lunar Exploration	Begins with 'Last'

After a brief huddle, the Legionnaires chose "Begins with 'Last'" to start the game. The last few whispers in the audience died away completely.

The judge said, "Good luck to all. Hands on your buzzers please, and round one begins with this question: What traditional Catholic blessing is given just prior to death?"

Two buttons slammed down. The computer indicated the Legionnaires were faster.

"The Eucharist," Trace's teammate, a skinny kid named Jeff, spoke into the microphone.

"I'm sorry, that is incorrect. Remember the category."

Andie spoke into the Olympians' microphone. "Last Rites."

"Correct."

"What does a mixologist or restaurant host typically announce when an establishment is about to close for the evening?"

This time the Olympians were faster.

"Last call," Yuvi said.

"Correct." Yuvi grinned broadly and winked at the audience.

"What is one's . . . final opportunity?"

The Legionnaires.

"Last chance," came the response.

"Correct."

"What 'party evening' did golden age pop star Katy Perry sing about?"

Legionnaires buzzed in; Olympians did not.

"Oh, um, Last . . . Friday Night," Trace said into the microphone.

"Correct." A few murmurs around the room.

"Quiet please," the judge advised. Then came the last question.

"For the final question this round: What is one's 'final' option . . . also an indoor skiing attraction near Venusville, in Nerus City?"

The Legionnaires nailed the buzzer hard, but the Olympians were just a hair faster.

"Last Resort," Viola said.

"Correct."

Applause erupted across the competition space.

"The score after the first round stands at Olympians 300, Legionnaires 150." More cheers and encouragement went up. They proceeded to Round two; the Chief Judge called for quiet once more.

The Olympians selected Natural Disasters. The judge paused for the last audience murmurs to die down.

"Round two begins with this question: What fictional threat destroys five of the seven cities in last year's hit film 'Dark Ice?'"

Two buzzers. Legionnaires were faster.

"A comet strike," Trace's teammate Shelli said.

"Correct."

"A planet's changes in its obliquity, inclination, and axial precession cause what?"

Two buzzers. Again, the Legionnaires.

"Milankovitch Cycles," Trace said.

"Be more specific please," the judge said.

"Uh, ice ages."

"Correct."

"What are two names for large-scale tropical cyclones on Earth?"

The Olympians edged out their opponents.

"Hurricanes, and . . . typhoons." Andie said.

"Correct."

"A 1902 eruption on Earth's Island of Martinique was the third deadliest in all of human history. What is the name of that volcano?"

Neither team rang in. The buzzer beeped as time expired.

"The correct answer is . . . Mount Pelée."

"For our last question in Round Two: Which city sank in a 'single day and night of misfortune,' according to Homer?"

Two buzzers. Legionnaires got this one.

"Atlantis," Trace's teammate Jeff said.

"Correct." Cheers and even more applause than before. The Olympians started chanting their school name. Then the judge updated the scores on the board, and announced, "The score after round two stands at Legionnaires

187

450, Olympians 400."

Rounds three and four each left the contest extremely close. At the end of Round three, Rivers, Legionnaires led by 100. By the end of round four, Equal and Opposite, Olympians had cut the Legionnaires' lead to 50 points. The score going into the fifth and final round stood at Legionnaires 950, Olympians 900. The final round, however, was the dreaded *Barrage*.

Barrage round always had exactly 20 questions delivered in a fast, steady stream, with just 5 seconds before the question disappeared and the next one appeared on the screens. Usually requiring a one-word answer, any of each school's three contestants could answer on their competition tablets.

If two or all three teammates from the same team answered, all responses needed to be correct to earn the points. 'Ringing in first' was not part of the final round — the goal: answer as many correctly as possible for a final surge of points — each question was worth 50. Incorrect answers did not incur any penalty during Barrage.

The Olympians used the tactic of each teammate calling 'mine' if they knew the answer. Not only would each of the three teammates have to pay attention to which questions had already been 'claimed,' they had to be certain of their answers.

Andie's role was the *net*: she deliberately paused a full second before claiming any question. Then, if neither Viola nor Yuvi grabbed it, Andie would automatically take a stab at it. Her role as the catch-all net had given their team an edge in some previous matches.

The round began. Questions flashed on screens in rapid-fire succession, and students on each team hastily scribbled answers on competition tablets. Andie was a study in concentration, taking nearly every science question, and a few of her off-topic questions her teammates did not know for certain.

20 QUESTIONS:

1. What was the artist Picasso's given name?
2. Who was Luke's father in Star Wars?
3. What is the largest crater on Mars?
4. Who is widely recognized as the 'Mother of Botany?'
5. What geologist's term describes plants exhaling water?
6. Who is Mars' tallest-ever citizen, standing at 314 cm?
7. Where was gold first discovered on Mars?
8. Who was the first human to set foot on Ganymede?
9. Who invented the sport Bullseye Handball?
10. What is Carbon-14 commonly used to measure?
11. What is Earth's most-watched song contest called?
12. In astronomical units, what is Mars' average distance from the sun?
13. How many centimeters are in kilometer?
14. Which Harvard astronomer discovered the Horsehead Nebula?
15. Which scientific theory explains continental movement?
16. To the nearest million, how many people live on Luna?
17. What is the chemical formula for sucrose?
18. Including Earth, how many space bodies have humans walked on?
19. Where did the U.S. transcontinental railroad finally meet?
20. What is the United States' equivalent of the Moxie Awards?

Within a few short, hair-raising minutes, the round was over, and the final buzzer rang. Scattered applause broke out, then faded. Tabulating scores and double-checking the points totals took the judges a moment. It was close.

"Ladies and gentlemen, we present the correct responses, and team results for the final round. Let me say first that both teams performed admirably well. Now, let's see those correct answers."

The mini-jumbotron glowed with the answers.

Correct Answer	Legionnaires	Olympians
1. Pablo	YES	YES
2. Darth Vader	YES	YES
3. Hellas Basin	YES	YES
4. Janaki Ammal	YES	YES
5. evapotranspiration	NO	YES
6. Jamesyn Ritter	NO	YES
7. Sacra Mensa/Valley of the Gods	YES	YES
8. Marius Gray	NO	YES
9. Jessica Sterns	YES	YES
10. Sample age/radiometric dating	YES	YES
11. Eurovision	YES	NO
12. 1.5 A.U.	YES	YES
13. 100,000	YES	YES
14. Williamina Fleming	NO	YES
15. Plate Tectonic Theory	YES	YES
16. 11 million	YES	YES
17. $C_{12}H_{22}O_{11}$	YES	YES
18. nine	YES	YES
19. Promontory Point/Utah	YES	NO
20. Tony Awards	YES	YES

The judges held off on the final score for one agonizing moment longer. "And our winner is . . ."

"The Olympians!" The cheers erupted at seeing the home team earn the victory. The screens above showed:

FINAL SCORE   Legionnaires: **1750**   Olympians: **1800**

High fives and hugs, with no small amount of disappointment on Trace and his teammates' faces. Their dedicated supporters in the visiting section cheered regardless.

The judge spoke again. "Thank you, K-Bowl enthusiasts, for your attendance and spirit today. As a reminder, our next competition, between Robinson High School and Portree High School, will begin in twenty minutes. The two top-scoring teams out of the eight semifinalists will advance directly to the finals, so please check your K-Bowl app for those updates in an hour or so."

After the round was complete, Trace walked over to where Andie and Aiyana were standing, just offstage.

"Hey, we know each other from Dr. Holm's lecture, remember?

"Yep, I remember. This is Aiya."

"Hi, I'm Trace."

"Hi. So you just got in from Earth? How are you getting settled?" Aiyana asked.

"It's so different, I'm . . . overwhelmed." Trace said, brushing his hair to cover up the fading bruise on his forehead. "Andie, you played an amazing final round."

"Thanks, you weren't half bad at the Earth categories."

"I was going to say the same. How did you do so well? You rocked all the science categories, and a few of the others."

"Yeah, I almost wrote down the formula to glucose before I switched it to sucrose in the nick of time."

"Nicely done," Trace said. They paused, reliving the intensity of the Barrage.

Aiyana spoke up again. "So you came here by *The Thread*? How was your train ride?"

"That train was the most intense thing I've ever been on. It moved at like two hundred miles an hour."

"Two hundred what?"

"Um . . . miles? Oh . . . "

"Yeah, you're not in Kansas anymore, Dodo . . . " Andie smiled.

"That's Toto."

"Toto. You're not in Kansas anymore. Wait, have you been to Kansas? Never mind. Here we're on kilometers, meters, hectares, and liters."

"It's just so strange. Feet and miles are still in use in some places where I came from." Trace mused, feeling like a fish out of water.

"Aren't 'feet' based on some dead English king's foot size?" Aiyana asked, somehow managing to be half-judgey, half-curious.

"Um . . . " Trace was at a loss for words.

Andie spoke up. "And I have no idea how many feet are in a mile — I'm glad they didn't ask that one in K-Bowl."

"They used to teach that, I think it's like five thousand two hundred or something." Trace said, shrugging.

"Isn't base ten easier?" Aiyana asked. Andie elbowed her in the ribs.

"Yes . . . just not what I was raised with, I guess." Trace smirked.

"Hm. Hey, a few of us are going to go watch bullseye; Nooma sent a team, can you believe that? So, Trace, wanna come with?" Aiyana asked him, as two more teenage boys approached, Ric and Reillee.

"Uh . . . sure. I don't know what bullseye is, and, um, where's Nooma?"

Ric and Reillee walked up to join them, jumping in. "Nooma Outpost is perched on the very rim of Mariner Valley — I've always wanted to go. By the way, I'm Ric. And this is Reillee."

"Hey what's up, I'm Trace."

Reillee was at his elbow. "And bullseye is . . . bullseye handball. Um, how do I put this? Small-arena, five-on-five, where the ball is passed from teammate to teammate, like basketball, but without dribbling, and the basket is a high bullseye set in the wall, not a hoop with a backboard. The bullseye rings are the targets at each end of the court. The 'tender' is the only one who can take two steps any time he intercepts a shot on goal, but otherwise, it's catch, stop, pivot, throw to a teammate, or take a shot on the goal. Pass-pass-pass-score, like that."

"There's way more to it than that," Andie said. "It's full-contact, pads and light helmets, where torso-charges and shoulder charges are fair game, but blind charges to a player's back will get you ejected. Checking must be from the side, or from straight-on."

"Sounds like a mash-up of basketball, hockey, and . . . archery," Trace said. "So, what about this target? You said there are rings," Trace inquired.

"Three rings around the bullseye. Touch sensors light up the ring wherever the ball makes contact, and the closer you are to sinking a bullseye, the higher the points. The outer ring is 1, second is 3, inner ring is 5, and sinking a perfect bullseye is 9 points. Nines are tough, the bullseye is barely larger than the ball. The throw's gotta hit perfectly."

"Yeah, sure, I'm interested."

"The arena's in ACSA, we better go if we wanna make it."

"ACSA? Like, where our visitor hostels are? All those restaurants?"

"There's way more than just places to sleep or eat—you'll love it. Best spot in the whole city."

"Sounds cool. I skipped the exhibition match two weeks ago so I could do a little exploring, but it seems I barely scratched the surface." Trace grinned as they walked out of the K-Bowl arena, visibly relaxing for the first time since Andie had seen him.

Ric pinged Sitara, who met them at the ACSA main handball arena.

* * *

Nooma Outpost, the ultimate underdogs, became the darlings of Homecoming week—they became the ones most cheered for, especially by spectators with zero connection. They became the unlikely celebrities among the eight high schools and enjoyed their fifteen minutes of fame. Andy Warhol, it appears, was right . . . even on Mars.

"So there's no soccer or football here?" Trace asked Ric.

"With 'pitched' games like football have one big problem: the fields."

"Yeah," Reillee interjected, "the fields would need to be, like, four times the size they are on Earth for long throws, goal kicks, and so forth."

"Someone built a full field in New Marrakech, one with real grass—but it's really used mainly for track and field events now."

The friends walked past a Mars regulation basketball court. The biggest arenas here, for high school sports, were basketball and of course, Bullseye-Handball.

"Seven-meter rims, can you believe that? Basketball is a crazy sport."

Trace shook his head, adding "Again, that 'meters' thing went right over my head. Zzzzooooomm." He made a slashing motion over his head.

Reillee clapped Trace on the back, adding, "My friend, you have a lot to see and experience in your next few weeks and months getting settled. That's where we come in; best you learn it from the best people."

Reillee grinned and nodded his head, wholeheartedly agreeing with what he himself had just said.

Trace leaned back a bit, his eyes wide. "Uh, yeah, sure?"

"But let us still keep one or two secrets, Reillee . . . " Ric said, eyeing him very pointedly.

"Of course, we still need to keep a few things tucked away in our pockets," Reillee said.

Andie glared at Reillee, then looked back at Trace. "Speaking of secrets, what really happened aboard *Lucky Seven*?" Andie asked.

Trace just looked back at her. "I don't . . ." he trailed off. "I can't really talk about it."

"Come on, we're dying here. All we're hearing is speculation in the news media that some missile got launched at you, and barely missed, or aliens buzzed you or something," Reillee prodded.

"Yeah," Ric said, "there must be something you can tell us. Did you see anything at all?"

"Uhhh . . ." Trace said, then trailed off again. Eventually he shrugged.

Aiyana broke the silence. "Leave him alone, you guys, can't you see he'd tell us if he could?" A few nods around the group.

"Soooo, why don't you join us for dinner and the big dance, Trace?" Andie asked. "You'll even up our numbers. Unless you have other plans?"

"Okay, that sounds all right, unless either of our teams makes the finals. But regardless, I'm not down to talk about *Lucky Seven*," Trace said.

"Oh, someday you'll tell us," Reillee said, grinning ferociously. "Because friends got each other's backs."

They found their seats and settled in to watch the New Kyiv Wizards take on the Portree High Sea Eagles.

Trace smiled. It was good to have friends, at the very least. This Mars thing, overwhelming to him at first, might just work out.

* * *

"Things might just work out, boss," Dr. McAllister said, looking up at Deputy Director Jackson as they both scanned the latest swarm of tremors passing through the Mountain. Jackson looked hard at his chief geologist.

"So what you're telling me is the swarms are decreasing, not increasing," Jackson said.

"Well, I wouldn't say that—they're increasing in frequency, technically, but the epicenters are going deeper and deeper. Almost like the mantle is helping to sort out the layer stresses and crustal shear we've been seeing."

"I don't like it," Jackson replied. "I'd sleep better at night if all those stresses worked themselves out up here on the surface where they could . . . be resolved."

"Up here? They'd shake the seven cities. Trust me, down by the mantle is better."

"Better, huh. Then why are the hairs on the back of my neck still standing up?" Jackson asked.

"The further away these tremor swarms are, the better off we are."

"Dr. McAllister, where does water first begin to boil in a pot?"

The geologist said nothing, then nodded.

Jackson turned away, deep in his own private worries. Something was just not right about the most recent trends; he just couldn't articulate what.

Chapter Nine

Of Olympians And Legionnaires

"Son of a monkey smack!" Trace said in frustration, reading the K-Bowl app halfway through the game. The teams that had made the final round had just been posted.

"Son of a . . . what?" Aiyana asked.

Trace did not answer.

Taking his cue, Andie tapped open the notification and then she too murmured an expletive. Despite an impressive performance, neither team had made the finals.

"Grr, so close!" Andie muttered, scanning the list of competitors.

Aiyana peeked over her shoulder. "Yeah, well, Robinson's a powerhouse—they almost always win or get runner-up, right?"

"Mmm," Andie muttered. "But check out who's top of the list. I definitely did not see that one coming."

Then Andie opened a chat window to message her teammates and see what they wanted to do in preparation for the next round of competition, the school-year-ending championships.

Trace was still looking over the final results:

FINAL STANDINGS	SCORE
1. New Kyiv Wizards	2100
2. Robinson Rams	1950
3. Mons Olympians	1800
4. Nerus Legionnaires	1750
5. Portree Sea Eagles	1600
6. Uintah Warriors	1450
7. Nooma Explorers	1400
8. Hathorton Raptors	1400

"Well, gives us more time to get ready for tonight," Aiyana prompted, nudging Andie. She *sleeped* her tablet and looked at Aiyana. After a deep breath, she nodded, forcing a smile.

"Okay. I could use the distraction." They all enjoyed the rest of the match, thinking about a fancy dinner and the dance, the *Titan's Rage*.

* * *

Five friends, their number now grown to six, met on the front steps of a fancy Green Acres restaurant called *Valentino's*. Since none of them had any romantic interest in calling the evening a date, they simply went as a group to let the adventure unfold.

Sitara had on a bright purple sari; the form-hugging bodice was cut in traditional Indian fashion, her midriff showing above the snug dress that fell to her ankles. The shoulder shawl was a shimmering silver cascade that fell elegantly across her chest. She donned glittering silver strappy 2-inch heels and wore her long raven braid up in a twisted high flair. She had chosen a purple and silver teardrop bindi for her forehead; the overall effect was stunning.

Reillee must have been thinking something similar, because he had chosen a royal purple, popped-collar shirt paired with a classy black sport jacket with violet pin stripes. He completed the look with a narrow black silk tie with iridescent threads sewn in. When it caught the light just right, it flashed different colors.

Ric and Trace had collaborated to visit a local tux rental shop—Trace had nothing fancy of his own to wear, yet. The two rented similar, classy rigs that paired a bowtie and tuxedo studs instead of buttons down the front, with matching cuff links. Ric opted for a black collared shirt and off-white pearl studs, and Trace had gone the opposite way, a white shirt with shiny black studs.

Andie wore a classy, above-the-knee, sleeveless dress in deep green, with glittering sequins in a splash across the chest and down her back, paired with matching green velvet heels. Her hair up, with tight red ringlets down the right temple, and the right touch of makeup turned the slender, nerdy student into a knockout.

Aiyana looked equally striking, having found a jet-black velvet, sheath dress that went to her ankles and a thigh-high slit up the left leg, a deep scoop neck and a halter top to accent her fit, curvy frame. Her hair was half up, half down, in its usual tight curls. She had gone bold with her makeup, white fluorescent eyeliner, three glowing white dots on her cheeks, and four thin white lines down her chin as an homage to her Diné heritage.

The girls exchanged hugs, detailed compliments, and smiles. The boys, fist-bumps, but not a word spoken—just that knowing nod men do.

Once they all had arrived, they swept inside and were seated at a table in a back corner. Gents held the chairs for the ladies, and they took in the fancy ambiance with its views of a tree-lined park across the street. Light jazz flowed smoothly through the place like a forest stream.

Their server, a polite gentleman named Trent, welcomed the group and set down ice waters all around. Ric asked him for the unending salad for the entire table to start. The man nodded and slipped away to give them time to contemplate the menu.

"Do you think they'll do the drop tonight?" Ric asked, lifting his ice water glass and taking a gulp.

"Oh, I sure hope so, that would be a-mazing." Sitara said, grinning excitedly, leaning forward to tap a glowing green dot next to her water. The menu popped open, embedded in the glass. She swiped through to look at appetizers and drinks.

Reillee nodded his agreement, tapping his own menu open.

Trace smoothed his tux jacket, and said, "Wait, you want them to drop something? That sounds . . . ominous."

Sitara responded. "Oh no, it's not what you think, it's when they bring out this—"

"Hold on, let him discover it for himself," Reillee interjected. "Remember your first time?"

Sitara nodded. "Oh yes, I remember it well. It was . . . righteous."

Trace hunkered back in his seat, a strange little smile on his face, watching them drink their waters. "Can I at least get a little hint?"

"Sure," Andie said. "You don't have anything like it back on Earth. I guarantee it."

"Sounds . . . topper," Trace said.

"Wait, what?" Ric asked.

"As in T-Man Tawpdawg? Hip-hop artist? Topper?"

Sitara shrugged.

"Never mind. It's like maxed-out. Sounds pretty max."

"That one, we do have."

"Heh, okay."

The conversation lagged while they placed their orders, most ordering some variant of pasta or an entrée that seemed the least messy. The server brought out a delicious-looking bowl of romaine tossed with carrots and tomatoes and a side carafe of light vinaigrette. Aiyana reached for it and started the bowl making its rounds.

"Can you guys help me understand something?" Trace asked.

They listened as they served up the salad and passed it around.

"You have two Christmases every year, and two Halloweens?"

Reillee shook his head. "Well, not exactly. Little Halloween is called Samhain, and the regular one is still Halloween, but they're 340 days apart. All that matters is both have ghosts, ghouls, and trick-or-treating."

"My favorite part of both is the haunted houses," Sitara added. "My little brother Sundoo really wants to do the Tilting Tower this time. I think she's old enough."

"So you spell it Sam-hain, but it's pronounced Sah-win?" Trace asked.

"Exactly. It's a Celtic tradition, a harvest thing," Andie said, a note of pride in her voice. "So . . . for Samhain, a lot of people ride up to the mountaintop greenhouses, way up, above the city, to help with a big harvest. Oooo, and sometimes there's even a corn maze. But on Halloween, it's completely ghosts & goblins and candy."

Trace nodded, "Sounds really cool. And there's two Christmases? Two Christmas Eves, two Christmas mornings? Two Christmas dinners?"

Aiyana spoke up. "You're close . . . Krampus is the first one, it happens technically at the end of Spring."

"I love that one." Sitara jumped in. "For that one, it's tradition for each person in the family to draw randomly and give just one gift to one other person. It also involves pranks and practical jokes because the original Krampus was kind of the opposite of Saint Nick—a troublemaker, a trickster."

Ric jumped back in. "Oh, and the Christmas dinner thing? Always at home for Christmas, I think it's like that on Earth, and everything shuts down. But the Krampus-nacht dinner? Always in public—everyone goes out to eat. Kids try to spot Krampus lurking in the alleys or the . . . shadows

... the back alleys ...."

He lost his train of thought for a moment.

The others waited, watching Ric.

He shook his head, rousing himself. "Anyway, kids try to see him coming so they can warn their families where the trickster is lurking."

"Sounds dark for Christmas. You all have the most . . . unexpected traditions."

"It's not as bad as it seems," Aiyana continued. "Most fairy tales originally had pretty dark endings, didn't they? But they were re-written to make them more G-rated . . . mm, wasn't the Ice Queen actually hanged at the end of the original fairy tale, after she froze the whole kingdom?"

"I'm just saying it's hard to follow." Trace frowned.

Andie leveled a stare at him. "Just let it go. And enough of that 'you all' stuff, Trace. You're one of us now, Martian citizen, my brother."

"Yeah, embrace it," Sitara said with a smile. "You're one of us."

Reillee nodded, humming some tune that had nothing to do with the light jazz dribbling out of the restaurant speakers. He was seeing the drop in his mind, something he had only seen once before.

The rest of dinner went smoothly, the six enjoying their Italian fare. The sim-chicken parm was as close to the original thing back on Earth as he could have asked for, and Trace said as much.

Pleasantly filled up, the group skipped desserts and split the bill. Dinner was just the evening's opening scene; the main event was yet to come.

* * *

It was 9:30 by the time they walked into their ACSA dance venue. With students from all the visiting schools blending in, and nearly all Olympians attending, the hall was packed with dancing and mingling students. An extremely popular entertainer, *DJ Ser*, had been hired to spin, and she

202

wasted no time getting the party off to a high-energy, respectable vibe.

The six friends walked in through a blacklight-infused entry corridor; different parts of their attire flashed and shimmered. Reillee particularly loved the way his tie caught the light.

They entered the main hall, a high-ceilinged sporting venue with long black drapes infused with a rainbow of patterned LED lights across their surfaces, going all the way up into darkness. The curtains themselves pulsed with light in long lines and cris-crossing patterns. Tables had been set out at the far end, and one set of bleachers left open for students to relax or enjoy their refreshments. More students poured in by the minute.

From nearby on the floor, a group of Nerus Legionnaires noticed Trace and waved. Trace gave them a peace sign back but didn't walk over. The legionnaires had formed a dance circle, and an athletic couple had jumped into the center, shaking and gyrating to the fast-thumping music.

Sitara was already stepping little dance steps on the side of the action, eager to get out on the floor. Andie gave a solid head nod in time with the music, and Reillee had already started his air drums in perfect sync with the song. Ric scanned the dance floor, and Trace simply looked up and around, open-mouthed as he took in all the lights playing over the walls, ceiling, and floor, with its hundreds of dancers.

Sitara, nudging Trace on the arm, said, "Come on, ya leggo, show us what you've got," she said, using the nickname Olympians reserved for their rivals.

"Oh, I don't dance. So, you got me on this one."

She squinted sideways at Trace, still doing little dance steps that set the shimmering purple fringes and silver shawl sparkling. "We'll get you out there before the night is over," she said confidently.

Sitara grabbed Andie and Aiyana by the hand and dragged them both away to dance a sped-up remake of *The New Romantics*.

The guys held back, waiting for their set. The evening rolled on.

Halfway through the dance, the DJ flipped from a mix of fast and slow sets to mostly fast, group dance tunes. Once the floor was filled, and lively, DJ Ser knew the time was right to amp things up. She let the beat die completely, paused a full second, then hit the opening chords of the Tartarus cover of retro-classic 'Jump Around' by *House of Pain.*

When she hit this part of the playlist, the crowd erupted in cheers. The dance floor filled even more.

"Oh yeah." Reillee cried aloud, "this one rocks. Ya coming?" He looked at the others.

"Yeah no," Aiyana said, adding, "but you go enjoy your little man battle."

"Why won't you go?" Reillee asked, wearing a look of mock injury.

"Why not? Um, hello? Skirts & dresses? Less than half a gee?" Aiyana replied.

"Yeah, dude, two-meter vertical leaps and the odd random perv crouching to get a peek?" Andie added. "That's a big fat 'no' from me as well."

"So go run do your little chest bump thing." Aiyana concluded.

"Don't mind if I do," Reillee responded. "Ric?"

"I'm in. I'm gonna reach the rafters tonight. Come on, Trace, let's get our jump on."

"Oh, I'm not much of a dancer," Trace said, looking down.

"Come on, it'll be fun. All you gotta do is . . . jump around." Reillee grabbed him by the shoulder.

Trace shrugged free. "Nah, you guys go ahead. I'm still trying to find my groove."

Reillee nodded at Trace. Ric tugged Reillee by the sport coat. "It's cool, the man will join us if he feels. Let's wreck it."

Reillee looked at the girls and winked as he backed away. He and Ric bounced into the middle of the floor, already getting started.

Pack it up, pack it in, let me begin
I came to win, battle me, that's a sin
I won't ever slack up, punk, ya better back up
Try and play the role and yo, the whole crew'll act up
Get up, stand up, c'mon, throw your hands up
If ya got the feelin', jump up towards the ceilin' . . .

Trace smiled, and noticed most girls were hanging back. A few joined the horde of masculinity on the floor though. Trace saw several boys tear open their fancy collared shirts to reveal bright red tee shirts underneath, with "JUMP AROUND" in big white block letters.

Everyone had their own moves, and Trace found himself nodding to the beat before the main chorus was belted out in all its pride-o'-the-Irish glory. He leaned forward a little more.

As the song ended, the DJ let it fade and die completely.

Conversations settled around the arena. Many returned to their seats.

A hush fell. The lights dimmed to low.

Faintly at first, as if from far away, a soft synth rose up.

The beat resolved itself into the first bars of a house mix of the *Darude* classic 'Sandstorm.' The volume grew; the song started to wind up.

A shrill shriek of excitement and ecstasy rose up from everywhere across the dance hall. The floor was filled with students, boys and girls, within seconds.

Darude's twin synthesizers matched melodies, repeated and echoed each other, intertwined, and rose in crescendo, building up slowly at first, then faster.

By now, the crowd went ballistic, and most of the wallflowers reluctantly shuffled onto the main floor. The group of five surrounded Trace and basically crowd-pressed him to join in.

"This one, you can't miss," Ric shouted in his ear over the pounding beat. Soon they were all pressed in together by the mass of teenagers.

DJ Ser started low, a deep-voiced, breathy rumble into the microphone. She spoke over the music in low, seductive tones.

"Where the light washes down over the red desert . . . "

Then she raised her voice a little louder. The music rose with her.

Trace looked left and right, trying to understand the hysteria gripping the room. Everyone seemed to be looking up. But it was pitch black—nothing up there.

Wait, there was a light up there. And it was glowing brighter.

"What was Apollo's chariot, crossing the sky . . . " DJ Ser intoned.

Trace could feel vibrations, reverberating in his chest.

The light above grew ever more luminescent, and he could see now it was a huge, glowing sphere. The brightest point of light was the core, a white, slow-pulsing heart, beating its energy up to the surface all over the sphere. All eyes were locked.

"From where the light washes down upon us all?" DJ Ser raised her voice to a fevered pitch. The cheers of a thousand teenagers rose up.

DJ Ser's voice peaked.

"Heee-leeeee-ooooooooossss!"

Darude hit the fast-thumping bass beat of the Sandstorm track at the perfect instant.

The room erupted with screams and cheers, all eyes locked on the glowing, blazing sunbeams now blasting out from the sphere above.

Trace gaped in wonder. Sitara grinned and clapped her hands. Andie and Ric and Reillee and Aiyana yelled through their smiles, the spectacle glowing and growing above them.

The huge lighted ball fell toward the crowd below.

The lighted glowing sphere, covered in glyphs that matched the original fabled Sphere of Helios back on Earth . . . fell faster toward the dancing crowd.

At ground zero, directly below the ball, a surge of students leapt up in unison to meet its fall.

The ball struck fifty pairs of outstretched hands and bounced back upward. At the instant of first contact, the internal lighting flashed into a crazy dance of colors, and the central light started thrumming bright-dim, bright-dim in perfect sync with the beat.

As it floated back up toward the scaffolded ceiling, a scintillating twist of colors erupted like a supernova across the surface. More bright beams of colored light shot out from the sphere in every direction, in perfect time with the music.

Trace took a deep breath, put his head down in stern concentration, and edged toward the center of the crowd.

The sphere peaked, and dropped again toward the throng, where another surge of students looked up to meet its fall. Trace took several deep breaths, then crouched, tensing his muscles. He popped his head sideways one time.

The Sphere of Helios was falling faster now right toward center floor. As Andie and Aiyana watched, they both saw several of the more athletic teens, including a couple girls, leap into the air and rise at least a half-torso above the others jumping up around them.

And then there was Trace.

Sitara's jaw dropped. Andie and Aiyana, likewise, gaped. They both knew he was Earth-athletic, but *dayum*.

Trace cleared the rest of the students, with space to spare between his feet and the heads of those around him . . . he blasted up like a champagne cork. When he hit the ball, slightly off-center, he hit the Sphere alone, outstretched arms swinging in a sideways sweep. The impact knocked both him and the sphere sideways, in opposing directions.

The blow Trace landed set the sphere spinning, a crazy glowing world on its axis. The crowd goggled. Before, the Sphere had rolled and bobbed, bouncing up and down, but this was different. A primal scream erupted from a thousand voices.

They had found their new favorite Helios bouncer.

Darude powered on, through the fast first half of the song.

Trace fell toward a different group of students, landing on a group of girls, who scattered and tumbled to get out of his way. He fell hard on a knee and elbow, grunting in pain. Getting back on his feet quickly, he saw a group of teenage boys cheering and coming his direction from multiple paths through the crowd.

"Dude. You rock!"

"Whoa man, low-Mars orbit . . ."

"Yessss. That was maaaaaaxx.."

Other shouts like this one followed, along with a few high fives and more than a few hard claps on the back. The sphere was bounced back up again in another surge, still spinning wildly.

The song hit the slow part in the middle, where synths owned the moment. Then the crash of bass beats in groups of five, boom . . . boom, boom, baa-boom, set the tune winding back up again.

The sphere kept bouncing, this time spinning off the heavy curtains, just below a projection of the glowing words "Sphere of Helios" running up the wall in urban art script, an immense two-story tag. While everyone watched the glowing words and the sphere, Trace slipped away through the crowd to rejoin his new friends. He limped a bit and rubbed his bruised left elbow.

Sitara spoke first. "Holy — Trace, that was incredible."

"Thanks, I was so scared to get up there. I've never really . . . "

"You were worried about messing up?" Reillee asked, adding, "Man. You're gonna make tonight's news during the stretch. I mean, look, it — it's going viral." Reillee held up a vid clip of Trace leaping, full body above the rest of the crowd, and the resulting impact on the Sphere.

The spinning beams of the sphere flashed in the camera and speed-

splashed across the walls. The clip repeated itself.

"That's gonna single-handedly bring *Darude* back," Ric laughed.

Aiyana and Andie checked their own feeds. Sure enough, that clip, and dozens from other angles, were going places, fast.

"Wait until people figure out you're a Nerus student, you'll have more friends than you know what to do with."

"I was just having fun."

"Well, whatever it was, you're officially a disturber of the peace."

"Max," Trace smiled. He got lost in thought for a moment, seeing something far away.

"Hey, you okay?" Andie asked.

"Yeah, just thinking about this . . . girl I met on the crossing, who I get to see in a few days" he answered, shaking his head. His cheeks flushed.

"Yeah, well, tonight she's gonna be thinking about you too," Reillee grinned, fist-bumping Trace. He stayed with his friends on the floor until the end.

As they were, so caught up in the moment, no one noticed when Andie slipped away early.

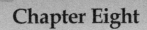

Chapter Eight

Petunias, Potatoes, Or Pasture?

Andie stared up at the ceiling, headache throbbing to the bass beat from the night before. Her ears were ringing. She climbed out of bed at the crack of . . . 8:34 a.m. The soft white noise of a Tibetan singing bowl murmured soothingly in the background from her tablet.

She fed her hamster, shuffled down the hall, raised the bathroom light level to one-third, and reached for a toothbrush. While getting cleaned up, she messaged Aiyana.

>>> Aiya, Can we get
out today

Aiyana's reply took a bit. By then, Andie's long, deep red hair was brushed, teeth sparkled, and she was back in her bedroom, picking out an outfit. Something blue and red. Or purple. Maybe maroon?

>>> Yes, when would you want
to meet? And, um, where at

Andie checked her chrono. After a moment, she tapped her response.

>>> Meet at Big 'Vater
I haven't been up to the
Greenhouses in forever,
does that work

>>> That's a hike but
I love sunshine. Deal
>>> I've got to clean up dishes,
sweep and mop
>>> Give me an hour

>>> You're the best

Andie drank a glass of cold water, hoping the throbbing ache might subside. Then she followed it with a couple dissolvable ibuprofens to make certain it would go away.

"You can do this," Andie told the face in the mirror.

Andie's own face didn't seem convinced.

In a different neighborhood, Aiyana jammed through her chores in record time, making sure that the parts of her work that 'mom' and 'dad' harped on . . . were above criticism. She didn't want anything delaying her meet up with Andie; something in her messaging seemed serious.

Aiyana scrubbed harder at a cooking utensil then set it in the steam cleaner under the countertop. She put a small oatmeal pack, apples & cinnamon, in the MicroZap oven because it was fast. She kept her head down and focused while humming some of the words to a drum circle chant on her ear pods.

Chores complete, Aiyana pinged her folks to let them know and added a note that she would be leaving to meet up with a friend who needed her. Anticipating a challenge, she opened her standard Saturday morning chores list, marking all items 'complete.'

Andie finished getting dressed, easing the maroon diagonal-striped top over her slender frame, and pulled on blue stretchy jeans. She slipped on red socks and soft sneakers, then looked in on her dad, who was at his office terminal typing some work thing about Silver Lake. Pictures of Andie and her dad were pinned up all around his viewscreen. She approached him from behind and cleared her throat.

"Heya sprite," her dad said, looking down to finish a sentence in his report . . . then he turned to smile up at her.

"Hey Dad, whatcha doin'?"

"Planning the next trout spawning season, then it's off to Silver Lake for the day."

"All work and no play . . . um, can I head out to meet up with Aiya?"

"Of course . . . did you eat?"

"I'll grab something at Sugar House maybe."

"Sounds good. And where are your adventures today?"

"The greenhouses — I just want to see something growing. Maybe grab the free French Fries."

"Okies, just stay where I can ping you if something comes up."

Andie smiled. "That's like telling me not to leave the planet, Dad."

"Well . . . don't do that either. Chucklehead would miss you."

"His name is Charlie Brown, Dad. And he's fine, I just gave him some hamster treats."

"Okay . . . well, learn things." It was his usual sign-off.

"Go jump in a lake." It was her usual sign-off.

"Love you, li'l brat," her dad said, reaching out for a brief hug.

"Love you too Dad," Andie said, kissing him on his reddish fuzzy cheek and turning away. She walked down the hall, said goodbye to Hugo and Marvin, then vanished through the doorway. Her dad's keyboard clicks faded behind her.

Aiyana got to the small, wooded rest area near the creatively named Large Elevator before Andie, even though Andie lived closer. She picked a park bench next to one of the tall pine trees at the edge of Green Acres. She could just glimpse Valentino's across a large, manicured park.

Andie made it to the rendezvous a few moments later.

"Good timing, the lift is almost down," Aiyana said by way of greeting.

"Any trouble getting free?" Andie asked, walking right up to Aiyana.

"Not this time." They hugged.

"Ugh, I can't imagine being hounded for perfect cleanliness like that."

"I'll manage." Aiyana shrugged, clearly not wanting to talk about it. "Are you sure you don't want to head over to the Pocket? It's pretty close."

"No, I need something completely different. Plus, those lower tunnels seem to go on forever. Give me someplace warm, someplace bright."

"Then let's get up there." Aiyana stood and slipped a green pine cone in her pocket.

"What's the pine cone for?" Andie asked, suddenly interested.

"It smells nice. Thought I might keep it in my room, on my windowsill until it opens."

"I better grab one too; I'll put it next to my HamsterHab," Andie said, hopping up to pluck a small green one free. "CeeBee always stinks just a little bit."

"It's here," Aiyana said, nodding toward the stone column. They walked around the elevator toward its opening. As they stepped inside, Andie looked up high above, where the column melded into the city's curving walls near the cavern ceiling. She visualized the cylindrical shaft, a conduit leading to the sloping plateau, the very rooftop of Olympus Mons.

Aiyana brought her back to reality. "Sitting or standing?"

"Um, doesn't matter to me."

"Okay, let's sit."

They crossed the standing passengers level to the center circular staircase. Up went to the seating area and down led to the cargo level. They stepped up the stairs together, emerging into rows of movie theater-style folding seats. On the screen, a 30-second safety video played on a loop. They eased into back row seats and made themselves comfortable facing the large curving display.

A pleasant voice invited riders to be seated or hold on to the handrails, as the elevator would depart shortly. In one corner of the display, a digital timer ticked down to departure: 22 . . . 21 . . . 20 . . . 19 . . . 18 . . . and so forth, until the voice intoned,

"The door is closing. The elevator is now departing for the greenhouse level, which will take approximately twenty minutes. Please enjoy your ride."

The front screen flipped away from the safety video to different scenes from the greenhouses above. Sunlight percolated down through an idyllic forest of ten thousand trees, the largest off-Earth forest in the Solar System. It neatly faded to a view of the largest single pollinator garden ever built by humans, with its 17 species of honeybees, bumblebees, and other helpful insects going about their business. The last one showed rows of produce, and people tending their own small plots, each growing . . . whatever they felt like growing. In the background, rows upon rows of potatoes grew in short green shrubs, with rows of corn in their deeper green, towering along the background.

The girls rode up the lift in silence, watching the high-definition greenery on parade, each lost in her own thoughts.

As the 20-minute countdown reached zero, the elevator slowed and shuddered gently to a halt. They descended the curving stairs, passing a few early risers already heading back down to the city as they stepped out of the Big 'Vator.

Ahead, a large breezeway sloped on and up, like those commonly found in airports or spaceports. Someone long ago had nicknamed this passage "Watney Way," and the name had stuck. Now they passed under a large, green-highlighted sign that proclaimed:

THE PATH OF THE BOTANIST
WATNEY WAY
- OVERCOMING THE ODDS -

Moving sidewalks ran both directions, with a pair of two-level SAFE Pod bunkers halfway up. These pods were each capable of seating a hundred or more and they looked like long silver boxcars from some old Earth freight train. Someone had spray-painted a few words on the side, but clean-up had already been started, rendering the words unreadable.

Aiyana broke the silence. "Did you hear? Some of our Martian potatoes . . . were actually crossbred with the last potatoes grown by Mark Watney?"

"Wait, what? You believe that? Dude was a book character, a movie character like two hundred standard years ago," Andie shot back.

"No, that vid was a docu-drama—even the TV series that followed was all about the first colonists. They just re-told the early missions after NASA settled Mars. Made good money too. You didn't know that?"

Andie scrunched her eyebrows. She looked at a loss for where to begin. "Um, no. Watney was a character in a movie in the early 21st. And before you get any other clever ideas, Ares is our science classroom cat, not Watney's actual NASA mission to Mars."

Aiya just looked back at her, grinning, as they giant-stepped onto the next moving sidewalk. "You fall for nothing, do you?"

"Nope, and can we not debate fictitious potatoes for a minute? I'm . . . deep thoughts here."

"Sure, okay," Aiya murmured, leaving Andie to it. They reached the end of the main breezeway's moving sidewalks, where the tunnel branched three ways.

Aiya looked straight ahead, then right, then left, down three equally impressive passageways leading up to the sprawling Top-of-the-Mons rooftop greenhouses.

The left-side sign read:

1. FLOWERS / POLLINATOR GARDENS

The central sign read:

2. VEGETABLES / GRAINS

The right-side sign read:

3. ROOFTOP FOREST / PASTURE ORCHARDS

"So . . . shall we make it flowers," Aiya held out her left hand, "oorrr . . . veggies?" Then she held out her right. "Or the forest?"

"Um . . . what?" Andie asked, uncharacteristically ill-at-ease. Her face was pale.

"Petunias or potatoes, silly? Or the pasture?"

"Uh, right. Let's go with . . . the potatoes."

They walked straight ahead, up the center breezeway.

The two rode another moving walkway, this one shorter, a hundred meters or so. Natural, incoming light met their gaze as they stepped out under a broad, sweeping dome — the plateau slopes of Olympus Mons.

They found an empty patch of green grass a few minutes' walk from the breezeway and flopped down in the sunshine. All around them, rows of vegetables and other produce poked up from the ground in neat, manicured rows.

Andie settled on her back, staring straight up at the glass dome above, the sunlight touching her pale arms and face, warming her torso and her legs.

Aiyana looked at her, propped up on one elbow. "Okay, tell me."

"Okay, but . . ." Andie said, looking at Aiyana's eyes as she flopped on the grass.

"You can tell me anything," Aiyana said.

"I know. So . . . I've held this inside for a long time, until I was totally sure of it."

"Okay . . ."

"I'm non-binary." Andie carefully pronounced out the syllables, looking down as the words came out through gritted teeth.

"Oh," Aiyana said. "So . . . non-binary, like 'they-them' non-binary?"

"Yes," Andie said softly, still looking down.

"Like not all girl or all boy, but something in between? Or both?" Aiya asked, trying to understand. Her face softened from initial confusion into a warm smile.

"Most days, I'm all about my feminine worldview, but once in a while, I'm decidedly feeling masculine," Andie said, still looking down.

"So . . . you're a . . . two-spirit," Aiyana said reverently, as if happening upon something wonderful. Her eyebrows raised, she reached out a hand to touch Andie's arm.

"A what?" Andie looked up at Aiyana, finally holding eye contact.

Aiyana hopped up on her knees to explain. "Omigod, in the traditions of *the people*, you're what they called a 'two-spirit.' Truth, they held a place of great respect among the Diné."

217

"Diné?"

"It means 'the people.' . . . the Navajo people. This is incredible," Aiyana said, eyes flashing with joy.

"I'm glad you're happy." Andie was smiling now.

"No, yes, I'm totally . . . of course I'm happy. Why didn't I know this about you before?" Suddenly there was no containing Aiyana's enthusiasm.

"I mean, I should have noticed ages ago, and asked. You've always been an un-parallel thinker . . . is that a word? Un-parallel? It is now. You're, like, the only one who lives up to Stein's challenge of being the smartest one in the room."

Andie just looked at their friend. Aiyana looked back at Andie.

"Sorry, I kinda hogged the mike there." A little, awkward smile.

"It's all right, I was really hoping you'd be chill about this." A long pause. "Thank you."

"So, you were . . . hoping?" Aiyana asked. "Do you like me . . . like . . . like me?"

"Wait, what? Oh. No, no, I'm into boys. I connect with them so much easier because of this more masculine side I have, entwined with all the feminine stuff. Twine. One big ball of red-and-blue-and-purple twine, that's me."

"So you're not attracted to girls."

"Hm. It's not that I find girls unattractive. You're a total sexy goddess — it's just I'm not attracted to women physically. But I'm sure others who are non-binary . . . they probably are."

Aiyana just looked back at them, a little smile still on her face. At length, she spoke up. "Okay. Okay. See if I understand here. Who you are, who you know and feel you are, deep down inside is one thing . . . and who you are attracted to, that's a separate thing?"

"Yes!" Andie practically jumped up, a victory cry. "She gets it." Andie had a tear in their eye and a huge smile on.

Aiyana's words came tumbling out. "Okay, let's settle down, waitaminute, waitaminute, waitaminute. You gotta help me understand how you keep those two ideas straight . . . sorry . . . organized . . . you know, in your head."

"Welllll . . . the head is a good place to start. Like . . . in my mind, I can see beauty in other girls, and I admire the makeup, hot outfits, cute hair styles, and all that. But my heart doesn't tell me I want to cozy up to a girl for the rest of my days. I'm into dudes." Andie said, then continued.

"But Aiya, our head and heart can both be mistaken—I know this. So I needed time, lots of time for what my Uncle Nikos calls a gut check. Gut instinct helps us sort out the thrills and fears, all those highs and lows. He thinks women don't have the emotional wiring to ever do a gut check, but I disagree with him. A woman can have her intuition and also do a gut check. I think."

"What's the difference?" Aiyana asked.

"Not a clue. Anyways, I'm still not a hundred percent on what is the most authentic me, day to day. It's also like something my dad told me ages ago, when . . . "

Aiyana interrupted. "Wait, does he know you're . . . ? Have you told him yet?"

"No." Andie looked down, then back up at Aiya. "You're the first." Andie was practically looking through their eyebrows, head down but still making eye contact.

"Wow." Aiyana looked at Andie. "Wow, I'm so . . . honored." Aiyana held a hand to her chest in the universal gesture of sincerity.

"Yeah . . . " Andie said, letting out a little chuckle.

"So what did your dad say, the thing that helped, you were saying?"

"Oh right. He thinks sooner or later you've got to make big choices in life, and that we're happiest with those choices if they reflect who we authentically are on the inside."

Aiya nodded. Andie pressed on. "'Throw the switch,' he calls it. He says the mind can only give us what's . . . quantifiable. Um, like . . . like you buying your first desert Harley-Davidson, okay?"

Aiyana nodded. "You know I want one."

"Right, and you know in your mind that such a skimmer can accelerate really super fast, and you know the brand is reliable, has a tight safety record, and the price is right. But that brain-knowledge can only get you so far. What makes you really want that skimmer is the second part of knowing—the heart."

Aiya's eyes glazed a bit.

"Hey, with me so far?" Andie asked, sensing they might be losing their friend to dreaming about a Harley.

"No, yeah, totally with you. But I'll never afford one."

"Sure you will," Andie retorted. "So that's the second part: the heart."

"Okay . . . " Aiya blinked, re-establishing eye contact.

"How do you know if you love the ride until you throw your leg over it and take it for a spin?"

"Sounds amazing." Aiya said.

"See? That's your heart, already in love with the idea of . . . tearing up dust trails in the Night Labyrinth."

"That would be incredible," Aiyana agreed, eyes flashing.

"And yet, you should still hold off. Your facts-knowledge and heart-pulse can both change as you grow into who you authentically are, and what you need to chase after in life. My dad and my uncle both said the final check for you to be truly happy—it's your gut."

"Wait, how's that?"

"Your gut. Like the difference between a crush and enduring, true love. Your gut will tell you, give it time, and you'll know you're chasing something that jives with who you truly are."

"And your gut tells you that you're non-binary."

220

"It does."

"For how long?"

"Since the end of 8th grade."

"Three school years? That's a long time to keep that inside." Aiya mused. Then, she added, "your dad sounds like a pretty cool guy."

"Please. He's a total nerd who's always cracking the stupidest jokes." Andie smiled.

Aiyana smiled back. "You're lucky. My folks . . . never mind. Okay . . . hm. Let me process here. You don't have a 'thing' for me or other girls. Who do you have a 'thing' for?"

Andie didn't hesitate. "Marcus. He's really cute."

"Marcus? Nerdy, glasses, fourth period, Marcus?"

"Yeah. Him." Andie blushed a little.

"That guy like . . . never talks," Aiyana said.

"I've overheard him do a voice chat with his gamer friends in the S.U. . . . or maybe it's his pre-calc study group. I'm not sure, he seems to relate to people through his tablet. Either way, that man has one . . . sexy . . . brain."

"If you say so."

The friends giggled and hugged each other, hanging on for a moment longer than a typical hug. "Love you chica," Aiyana whispered in Andie's ear.

"Love ya back," Andie managed a whisper, choking up.

"Wait, is 'chica' all right?" Aiyana asked, leaning back to look Andie in the eye.

"Ha. Call me dude for all I care, it's non-specific." Andie replied, before letting out a long breath they had been holding.

"Okay, so you're not hung up on labels?"

"I've thought about that. Okay, put it this way — those who know me, I think they deserve to really know me. I can't make anyone call me 'they' or 'them' any more than I can make others change who they authentically are.

221

If someone denies the person who I know I am, deep down, are they really even a decent human being? A friend?"

"And does their opinion even matter?"

Andie nodded. "Not much to me," they said. "So no, labels and pronouns don't matter to me much. To others, pronouns might be very important, because that is them being their authentic selves."

"I can see that."

Then Aiyana smiled widely.

"I see you."

"Thank you, Aiya, you have no idea. Hey, I'm . . . starving, I haven't eaten. Nervous stomach, for some reason," Andie said.

"Okay, no arguments. We're grabbing some free French Fries and going to the Janaki Tree to mark this moment."

"Oooo, I love that. I've been thinking of getting it inked across my back someday."

"French Fries? On your back?" Aiyana said, giggling. "Who gets French Fries tattooed on their back?"

Andie punched Aiyana in the sternum, giggling back.

"Ow."

"Don't make me punch you for real, I'll knock you into orbit," Andie said.

"Ha. You wish. Okay, tattoo the Janaki Tree . . . won't your dad freak out?"

"I don't think so. C'mon, let's walk while we talk." They stood. "Dad waited until he was like eighteen or nineteen standard before getting his first." They walked back toward the ramp.

"No kidding, why so long?" Aiyana asked.

"Something about being absolutely certain it's what he wanted, something that would stand the test of time, or some such."

"What did he end up getting?" Aiyana asked, very interested.

"A Captain America shield on his left upper arm, can you believe that?" They slapped their left arm for emphasis. "It was before we left Earth—we lived in the U.S. back then."

"You're right."

"I'm right?"

"Your dad's a total nerd."

"Yep. Oh, what would you want to get, if you got inked?"

"I think I'd get the sun, just here on my arm. Or, or maybe, a bat. You know I saw one once? Up above the Overlook, there's a small colony hiding out in some ceiling side cave . . . can't imagine what they even eat, there's hardly any bugs in the city."

"That's . . . wow," Andie mused, imagining it.

"And hey, speaking of bats, what are you gonna be for Samhain?" Aiyana asked.

"Let's see . . . in honor of our Celtic ancestors and the harvest . . . I'm thinking I'll wear the tightest, slashed-up jeans I can find, then borrow my dad's vest, coat, and Scottish ascot tie. A mash-up of naughty and respectable."

"You don't have the butt for tight jeans," Aiyana said casually. Andie looked back. "What? It's true," Aiyana persisted.

"Don't rain on my fireworks," Andie retorted. "And there's nothing wrong with my . . . backside." Andie paused, distracted. Then they added, "What about you? Costume."

"Mrs. Jensen collects vintage stuff, and she has one of the early ExoSuits, the orange ones the builders used. I was thinking of borrowing that . . . but without a helmet."

"Like . . . kind of a Founder's Day-Samhain crossover," Andie replied. "That's cool. So, Mrs. Janson, the English teacher?"

"No, Jensen, the one in the counseling office. She's always nice to me when I have to go visit her."

"Cool, cool." Andie nodded, staring off in space, picturing it. Then, they looked back at Aiyana. "So do you want to do neighborhoods this year? Or hit the plazas for goodies?"

"Never too old to celebrate a good harvest, ha ha, but let's pass on the candy. How about we do a nice haunted house then find a party?

"I don't know . . . "

"I could find out which one Marcus is going to . . . " Aiyana let the words trail off.

"Shut up—and don't you dare—I never should have told you about him."

"Then come to a party with me." Aiyana said. "Carlos and his buddies asked me to join them, and I need a wingman. Wing-person."

Andie thumped Aiyana on the arm. Aiyana pretended like Andie had broken bone. "Ow-wa."

"Okay . . . I'll think about it. And I'll have to see if my dad agrees." Andie said.

"Hold on. You're . . . almost nine, right? That's basically adult, babe. Just tell him your plan and let him know when you're coming home. Act like he's already agreed and let him hear it in your voice that you expect his support. It's like some Jedi mind trick thing you can pull on adults."

"You're crazy, I can't trick my own dad."

"Maybe you should."

"Maybe I should."

They reached the common area with its snack counter, sun-soaked benches, small gift shop, and a cluster of short trees. The Martian sky dominated through a spider-webbed geodesic dome.

"Okay, fries or onion rings? Hmm . . . "

"Rings for me, please," Andie said, stepping up to the counter. She recognized the boy behind the counter as having graduated last year from Mons High but couldn't remember his name. His name tag read "Peter."

"Sure thing and for — hey, wait, I know you two . . . you're juniors at the high school now, right?"

"Yes, we sure are, Peter," Andie said.

"My name's actually . . . Bryce. I just wear Peter's tag."

The two just stared at him for a moment, not sure what to say. Andie remembered him now; his name really was Peter.

Peter-Bryce continued. "Tell ya what, I'll give you the Olympians official discount. Today, your food is free," he said proudly, raising his eyebrows and smiling broadly.

"Ha." Aiyana said, "It's always free here, unless they start charging."

"Nope. If we started charging, this place would be overrun. No one values what they can get for free, even if it's as amazing as . . . a-these," he said, brandishing a plate of onion rings, air-fried to perfection. "Enjoy."

He set the steaming plate of onion rings down in front of Andie.

"And what'll it be for you?"

"Fries for me, please. And waters for us both."

"You sure? We have the new Diet Blueberry Habanero Campa-Cola . . ." he said, letting his voice trail off as if he was about to break into song.

"Ew. Yeah-no."

"Don't know what you're missing."

"Have you tried it?"

"Nope. Don't know what I'm missing either." Then Peter the Bryce, Lord of French Fries broke into a whisper. "And let's keep it that way." He winked, smiling again.

The two said their thanks, collected their food, and walked away to fill their cups from a chill-water dispenser.

"That guy was . . . a little too happy."

"Right? That extreme good mood. Drive me crazy if I was around someone that bubbly and upbeat all the time. Like looney tunes."

"For sure."

They sat eating their food, dipping occasionally in fry sauce. It was hot, steaming, delicious. When they had wiped the last of the crumbs away, they stood to stretch and drop their bamboo utensils and plates in the recycler.

They skipped the gift shop and went directly toward the forests and orchards of the Pasture Greenhouse.

This one was different from the other two greenhouses—it boasted real rolling hills. In most places, the farthest one could see in any direction was maybe twenty or thirty meters before the trees blocked out the view. Pathways twisted back and forth through several forested areas.

This greenhouse also had streams running through it, an uncommon thing on Mars. A campground of twenty-five yurts ran along the largest stream and was often booked up months in advance.

"I wonder if there are any pocket caves up here," Aiyana asked, as they came out of the tunnel and into the forest.

"I'd bet there are, somewhere in these woods. We should come back, try to get lost maybe." Andie said, eyes flashing in excitement.

"You're already lost, dude."

"Ha. Well, you know what they say . . . not all those who wander . . . "

"Not all who wander are lost," Aiyana finished for them.

The two entered a glade of tall oaks. Birds sang energetically in the morning sunshine and chipmunks climbed and leapt from tree to tree, making their little chirping sounds. The song of life here always inspired visitors to quiet down, let nature put in a few words.

The winding path continued on.

Autumn was approaching in Greenhouse 3, and just a few of the quaking aspens had begun to turn from green to brilliant yellow. The temperature was only slightly cooler than normal. Chipmunks were hard at work storing up for the artificially induced 'winter.' If they somehow knew by instinct the seasons were under human control, they never showed it. They just did their chipmunk thing.

The birds had a rougher time when the seasons changed — migrating was impossible. Even worse, Mars' weak magnetic fields left the birds clueless as to which direction to fly. In winter, they bedded down in warmer pockets of the massive habitat; they survived all the same.

After another ten minutes of wandering, Andie and Aiyana left the deciduous forest area and entered a dense forest of pine trees, Douglas Fir and Spruce, chosen for their oxygen-producing ability. Here, rocks and boulder-covered hillocks filled the spaces between trees. Among the tall pines, the twitter of birds and chitter of chipmunks was still never far off.

"So . . . how can we commemorate this moment? You shared a deep personal truth, I've just decided to buy my own high-performance dune skimmer someday . . . we should mark the moment," Aiyana said.

"Ooo, I know, let's plant a new tree." Andie said, eyes flashing.

"Um, what's to stop the MERF Aggro people from yanking it out before it's even a sapling?" Aiyana asked.

"Hmm . . . we hide it someplace hard to find, then come back often to add fertilizer, water, and make sure it has sunshine."

"Okay, where are we going to come up with a seed, silly? They aren't just lying around."

They both cast about just to make sure there weren't seeds just lying around. Then they locked eyes, speaking almost in unison.

"Pine cones!"

Both pulled out a pine cone.

"How's yours? Opening up yet?" Andie asked.

"Nope, mine is totally green, and still tightly sealed shut. Smells nice, though."

"Mine looks like it's maybe opening up," Andie said.

"Where?" Aiyana walked closer to have a look.

"Up here, the tip." Andie tried prying the pine cone open, and only partially succeeded. Aiyana grabbed a fallen stick nearby, snapped it in the middle, and made a make-shift chisel. She pried the end open enough for a lone brown seed to fall into Andie's hand.

"Yes . . . good work."

"The double-A tree," Andie proclaimed, holding up the pine seed between thumb and forefinger.

"Like the DoubleTree resort? You're so goofy."

"Wait, I didn't mean it like that. Okay, let's come up with a better name," Andie said.

"Nope, it's the Double-A Tree now, and always will be. Andie and Aiya tree."

"Okay, now comes the real challenge. Find a spot that's well-hidden."

The two left the trail behind, vanishing among the tall trunks. They pressed on deeper, searching out the most secluded spot in the forest.

* * *

Half an hour later, brushing dirt from their hands, the two made their way back out of the pines, toward the center under the vast dome—the wooded heart of Greenhouse #3.

Here, the most famous tree on Mars stood atop a high hill. The teens walked forward slowly, reverently. The Janaki Tree, a Western White Pine, towered above everything else.

"She's taller than her Earthly ancestors, you know," Aiyana said, looking upward.

"Well, lower gravity, right? Some scientist friends of my dad's think she might still grow a little taller."

"Let's find a bench. I just want to feel this moment."

Andie nodded, still looking up. As they walked around the base of the hill toward a row of benches, they paused together to read a large, mounted brass plaque.

THE JANAKI TREE

AGE: 87 STANDARD YEARS
(164 EARTH YEARS)
HEIGHT: 55.3 METERS (181.5 FEET)
ALTITUDE: 24,788M ABOVE MMD
(81,325 FT ABOVE MEAN SEA LEVEL)

VERIFIED BY GUINNESS RECORDS
HIGHEST TREE IN THE SOLAR SYSTEM

The two backed up to a park bench and sat.

"I see you," Aiyana murmured to the tree.

Andie let out a deep, contented sigh.

Hand over her mouth, deep in thought, Aiyana felt something . . . a spark, deep inside. What was that? Was it the heart thing about the future? Or the gut thing about life, that thing Andie had mentioned? She couldn't be certain.

The two friends just sat for a long time, watching, listening, feeling.

Chapter Seven

As The Clock Tower Tolls

A ndie peered sideways at Marcus in class. They hoped for a chance, somehow, to strike up a conversation with him. Stein had given students one final challenge today: a geo-sample identification exercise. He had randomly shuffled all the students to new partners, and Andie just happened to end up by Marcus.

Their given sample looked like granite, but this specimen had more of the pinks and black flecks, so it was likely quartz monzonite. Andie had already studied this type of igneous rock in prep for next week's 'minerals' exam, so this felt like it would be a piece of cake.

Andie let Marcus take a shot at it, looking closely under a large magnifying glass.

"The small crystal bits, embedded in the mostly pink matrix, those are quartz, correct?"

"Yep," they replied, writing down his observations with a digital stylus pen. "And the others?"

"Biotite? Or . . . feldspar? I'll have to look it up, I think. Oh, here's another question, just occurred to me."

"What's that?" Andie asked.

"Are you doing anything for Samhain?" Marcus asked, setting down the magnifier.

Andie was stunned. "Uh . . . I don't have any real plans yet. Nothing set in stone."

"Set in stone, is that a geology pun?" Marcus smiled.

"Uh, sure?" Andie turned a bright shade of pink and got back to jotting down the names of each of the three minerals embedded in the sample's surface. She looked at Marcus.

His words came tumbling out in a hurry. "Well do you wanna go to the Tilting Tower with me?"

Andie just looked back, again stunned. "Uh . . . "

"I—I'm sorry Andie–it just sort of slipped out. I mean, do you wanna . . . It's okay if you don't, I mean . . . " Marcus stuttered, then shut up. He looked like had been smacked in the face with a tablet.

"I'd love to."

"I'm so sorr—wait . . . really?"

Andie just smiled.

"Cool." Marcus replied. "Okay."

"But . . . I want to go through with a group of friends, they've been talking about it, is that all right?"

"Sure, whatever you feel like is good for me," Marcus said, recovering some of his wits. "Like who?"

"Sitara is bringing her little brother Sundeep, and Ric and Sitara are always hanging out. Plus there's Aiya; I think she's joining Carlos and one or two other friends."

"So, a group tour, I'm down. Could be fun, could be." He smiled, clenching his fist so Andie wouldn't see his fingers trembling.

"Right? Then maybe we can find a party after. Get some food, do the whole costume bit. How's that sound?"

A warning timer pinged. Two minutes remained.

"It's . . . it sounds great." Marcus said. Andie smiled.

They quickly finished up their remaining observations and correctly identified the sample as quartz monzonite, justifying their conclusion with proper scientific estimates.

Stein made a few closing comments. The ending bell rang.

"I have to run, get to Earth Studies for a make-up test. Wish me luck!" Andie said, shouldering a backpack.

"Oh right. Remember that Church Hill guy. . . . and Hiller too . . . why were there so many World War II leaders with landscape names?"

Andie laughed out loud, snorting.

"Yikes," Andie said, covering their mouth and turning three shades of red. Andie bolted out the door and down the hall, dodging students and heading for the Elective Hallway. The rest of the school started pouring out the doors.

Marcus just grinned like Krampus had come early, though *Little Christmas* was still a couple months away.

* * *

The evening of Samhain arrived, a Thursday this year.

The streets were filled with trick-or-treaters, adults in masks heading off to costume parties, and the inevitable MERF enforcement patrols ensuring no one took the 'trick' part of 'trick or treat' too far.

Ric, Sitara, and her little brother Sundeep, 'Sundoo' as she called him, left her house together. They walked through neighborhoods toward the last apartment units on a street at the western edge of the city, the college district. At last, they could see their objective, straight ahead of them, up a hill, nearly pressed up against the sloping side of the cavern wall. Aiyana,

Carlos, Andie, and Marcus were there, waiting to meet them.

As the best haunted house in the city, designers had made it up to look like it was leaning precipitously, about to collapse any second, though it was perfectly stable. A large, glowing full-yellow moon floated behind the tower on nearly invisible stilts.

Every so often, a deep gong of a bell sounded out from the top of the leaning tower itself. On the grass near the tower, a crooked hangman's tree stood sentry. Two very realistic-looking vultures perched on a low branch, glowing red eyes watching carefully and blinking occasionally.

A cool breeze flowed through the space, and white mists hugged the ground, with another set of glowing eyes, these yellow, somewhere in the darkness matching the low, murmuring 'who-two' of an owl. The overall effect was chilling.

The seven approached an iron gate, where a long line of teens and young adults on the left waited for standby tickets. On the right, a smaller group gathered at a pre-ticketed podium where two ghost-faced receptionists greeted their guests.

Ric led the way past the longer line, heading directly for the front under a glowing, red-lettered "Reserved" sign that hung crookedly.

Sundeep stared at the house, fixated. Above the entry door, a small group had just entered a door that swung shut with a dull thud, under a sign hanging slightly sideways, with bright, glowing purple letters that warned everyone:

abandon all hope, ye who enter here

"Welcome to the Tower, I'm Tim. Do you have reserved times?" the attendant asked in a bright, cheerful voice, despite his ghostly visage.

233

"Yes, we do." Ric interjected proudly. "It's under Ricardo Molina."

"Let's see . . . yes, here you are. Group of seven?"

Sitara spoke up. "Yes, but we'd like to stagger going in, if it's all right? This is my little brother Sundeep."

"Well, hi Sundeep," Tim the Tower Guy said in a bright happy voice. "How old are you?"

"I'll be six-and-a-half in just two weeks."

"Just a fortnight until your half-birthday?" He smiled broadly; Sundeep nodded enthusiastically. "Well, that's worth celebrating! Welcome to the Tilting Tower." Tim said with genuine enthusiasm.

Tim leaned close Sitara and spoke low, so only she could hear. "We'll adjust the experience settings to a super fun level, just the right adventure for your brother."

"Thank you very much, that means a lot to me." Sitara smiled.

Sundeep was practically hopping in place. "Mister, what's the bell for?" he asked.

Tim crouched down to look the boy in the eye. "You know, they say it's excellent good luck if the Clock Tower tolls right as you're walking in the front door. You'll have good luck all month, maybe longer."

"For real? That's so coooool." Sundeep looked as eager as Sitara had ever seen him.

"You're darn right it's cool. Okay, let's get everyone else checked in." He looked down at names, and alternated looking up, taking a simple roll call for the group. "Do we have . . . Andie? Good. And Marcus? Excellent. Aiyana? Good. And Carlos. You're all here."

Tim continued without pausing.

"Excellent, let me share a few things. First, right up ahead, halfway up the walk, you can group up on that pad off to the right and take a selfie, it puts the moon peeking out from the tower, and please don't forget to tag us," he said, tapping the first three names off the list.

"Also, there's refreshments at the end if you want to buy a snack and a soda."

The door thudded shut again, behind a larger group that had just cleared the main entrance.

"And why don't the first three of you take these cool glowy neck loops—yes, they are yours to keep—and start heading up the walk. Your friends will join you for that selfie in just a moment."

Sundeep looped the glowing green band proudly around his neck, and boldly stepped forward, not waiting to be asked a second time. Ric and Sitara hustled to keep up.

The remaining four friends huddled at the podium.

"Friends, a couple notes before you all head up the walk and join them. We have a few options that your young friend Sundeep wouldn't be able to do. First, intensity: we have Cream Puff, Full Scream, and Black Death. Which one sounds like what you're after?"

"Can you tell us the difference?" Aiyana asked.

"Don't mind if I do. Cream Puff, they stay out of your personal space, you each wear this green glowing neck loop, and they won't touch you or even get close. Jump scares are rare, and nothing is too extreme. Full Scream is our most popular. Jump scares and visuals throughout the haunted house are at full strength, and the actors can tap you on the shoulder, wrist, ankle, or upper back, but never your torso, legs or anywhere on your head."

Tim took a breath. "Black Death is the same as Full Scream, but if one of you gets even slightly separated from the others, you may find yourself pulled through some side door . . . and have to find your way out all on your own, on an entirely different path."

He let the silence draw out.

"Do people ever come back as a solo for that last option?" Marcus asked.

"Happens all the time. We like it when they do that, the house is always hungry." Tim's eyes flashed.

The door thudded from up the walkway again.

The four just blinked, thinking it over.

"Um, I think we want the extreme one," Carlos said, looking at Marcus for confirmation.

Marcus looked at Andie, who shrugged and nodded. He also noticed Aiyana's simple nod.

"Black Death it is," Marcus confirmed.

"Excellent. One of you will need this yellow headlamp, and who wears it is entirely up to you." Tim held out a simple yellow LED light on an elastic band. Carlos grabbed it at once.

"Finally, you can opt for the ultimate thrill: it's called Blackout. Every so often, a Black Death group is randomly selected and plunged into total darkness. All the lights fade down to zero and all you are left with is that tiny yellow headlamp to get you through the rest of the house. It lights up about arm's length in front of you, that's it."

Tim paused again for effect.

"Blackout may happen for your entire walk-through, or for some of it, or none of it; it truly is completely random, chosen by the house itself. What do you say?"

"Uh, sure?" Andie asked, looking at their friends' faces.

"Excellent. Please remember: you are not allowed to touch any of the actors at any time, for any reason. Everybody understand? Okay then," said Tim, "Black Death Blackout. You guys are gonna have a blast."

"Right? This is gonna be wicked," Carlos said, feeling brave.

"If all of you make it out," Tim said.

"Ha ha." Carlos' smile faded a little.

Tim just looked back at Carlos, then he gestured with open palm toward the path, where Ric, Sitara, and Sundoo were waiting at the selfie spot.

"O-Okay, let's do this." Carlos said, trying to sound brave, but not really succeeding.

When they got to the selfie spot, they posed for the picture. Another welcome, ghost-faced attendant stood there, unseen from the entryway down on the street, and saying nothing. How had they not seen her before? Several of their handy phones snapped photos from different angles.

From the bushes nearby, a low growl, then quiet.

Next, a squeal and the unmistakable sound of bone-crunching, that seemed to go on for a while.

The attendant, saying nothing, but using hand motions, pointed at the three wearing the green loops. With an open palm, she gestured for them to proceed up the rest of the front walk and on into the house.

As Sitara, Ric, and Sundoo approached the front door, they stepped up onto the covered front porch, and the door opened with a long, drawn-out creak. With only the slightest hesitation, they stepped through the door, and the bell sounded from the tower above. 'Dong . . . '

"Yesss," the four heard Sundoo exclaim, and then the door swung shut with a resounding thud behind the three others.

All four teens smiled together, watching the house and preparing for their own experience.

Carlos reached out, took Aiyana's hand, and started to step forward.

The attendant mutely stood in their way. She held up her right hand, stopping them all in their tracks.

Carlos looked down at her. "What?" he asked.

Still holding up the halting hand, she then raised her other hand, gesturing off to the side, where an unseen pathway in the darkness was suddenly visible, ghost globes hovering softly on either side.

Like the attendant here, the lights had been strategically placed to be invisible from onlookers back on the street. It was like this path did not exist until this moment.

"Uh, have you guys seen anyone else enter this way?" Carlos asked.

"I wasn't paying attention. Aiya?" Marcus asked.

"Nope," Aiyana said.

They all hesitated.

"Nooowww," the attendant whispered insistently.

The sound of bones crunching, still snapping and splintering, followed them as they turned down the side path and walked in a new direction, and rounded a hedge of tall bushes.

As they made the turn, the frontal view of the house was lost. The sounds of something being chewed on also faded. It suddenly seemed very quiet. Too quiet. Crickets in the distance, maybe, but otherwise nothing.

The four huddled close, walking forward toward what looked to be a side door of the house, sagging on worn and rusted hinges.

Off to the side, the hedges pulled aside to reveal a dark flatscreen with its four sides obscured by shrubbery.

The screen blipped to life. From where they stood, a glowing figure of a dog shimmered in the distance, small and far away, as if down a long tunnel. It turned its head toward the four of them, noticing them for the first time.

Crouching as if to launch itself, the dog sprinted straight at them, still a digital display on the screen.

It ran right up to them until it seemed to be standing just inside the shrubbery frame.

More visible now, the dog was clearly a hound, a massive hound. Inside the screen, it stood probably one and a half meters tall, basically eye to eye with the four teens who now huddled closer together than before.

The hound glowed with a blue-white halo, and did not seem to have any substance or normal color to its body. It stood, for certain it stood, but there was nothing inside the screen for it to stand on, no visible ground. It appeared to be standing in a perfect void of blackness.

It made eye contact with the four teens, lowering its head and emitting a low growl.

Then, the dog threw back its head and howled, a long, loud howl. At the end of its howl, it vanished in an explosion of blue-white pixel dust, and the screen went dark once more.

Then the path lights around them faded away. The darkness left by the dog vanishing now seemed to envelop them all. The bright neon moon above cast strange shadows through the branches of the crooked hangman's tree. One pair of glowing, blinking yellow eyes regarded them from deep in the hedges.

The door opened with a drawn-out creak. A red light shone down, casting the doorway in an eerie crimson glow.

The Tilting Tower had invited them inside.

Bam! A huge crash behind them made them all jump, and they hurriedly ran through the red door. As they clutched each other tightly, the door swung shut behind them.

* * *

Exiting the house, Sundoo looked breathless.

"Hey, little brother, how was that for you?" Sitara asked, tousling his hair playfully.

"It wasn't that bad, and the bell rang for me." That seemed to be the highlight of the evening.

"And how's your candy apple?" her older sister asked.

"Very cinnamon-ey," Sundeep said, nibbling the sticky apple treat.

"Did you see the others at all, inside?" Ric asked.

"No, not once."

"Maybe the house ate them?" suggested Sundeep, taking another bite.

"Then we should go to the front of the house, where it spit them back out because they don't taste very good." Ric ran spider fingers on Sundeep's head for effect.

The boy yelled, "Aiieee, Ric, don't do that. You almost made me drop my apple."

Sitara spoke up, "Oh look, they're over there. They look . . . breathless."

The three walked over to stand with their four friends. All four were, indeed, breathing heavily.

"What was that dog at the beginning all about?" Aiyana asked no one in particular.

She stood wobbly on her feet as the two groups merged.

"Oh, you guys saw a dog? No fair," Sundeep said, pouting a little.

"Trust me, this dog . . . you didn't want to see. He was big and tall and very scary." Andie said.

"You guys really didn't have a dog howl at you when you walked in the door?" Carlos asked.

"No, but there was this really really cool cartoon dragon named Lumpy who kept accidentally lighting his screen on fire, you know, on the inside? We saw him like four times inside, and he was really funny. Did I tell you the bell rang for me?"

"Twice." Sitara rolled her eyes.

"I don't know, but the way that dog ran toward us, and howled, then vanished in a puff of smoke . . . that gave me chills." Aiyana was still trembling a little, hugging her shoulders.

"The part that got me was when they crowded us to the end and dropped us down that slide to the exit, that freaked me proper. I almost peed my pants." Andie exclaimed.

"I don't like falling. Or heights." Marcus looked a little pale by the light of the streetlamps.

"Those pictures they snapped just as the floor slid out from under us? Your face, Marcus. Priceless." Andie was grinning now.

"I know, right? I looked like someone zapped me with a taser or something. I'm just glad none of you bought those pictures, because that . . . is . . . embarrassing." He looked down, shaking his head.

Aiyana and Andie made eye contact behind Marcus' back, grinning. Andie pulled the printed picture just barely showing from a shirt pocket, and then put a single finger to her lips so Sundeep wouldn't give away their secret.

Then before the boy could say anything, Sitara gave him something else to think about.

"So what's the bell mean for you? Remind me again?"

"I'm gonna be lucky. Allllll yeeeeear loooong." Sundeep smiled proudly, taking another bite of his apple.

Bored with the conversation, Carlos noticed his boys hanging out, looking at the group pictures on the screen and he wandered off. He joined in poking fun at people's costumes, and laughing at the horrified expressions captured on the screens where pictures could be purchased.

Aiyana just shrugged and put an arm through Andie's. The remaining six walked away down the street, blending in among the last of the trick-or-treaters knocking doors. It was well past sunset, and they wanted to find a party.

They found several.

* * *

After the last gathering, it was getting late. Early. The last gathering they visited, a party at a fellow Olympian's house, had decent food and a delicious treats table. As it wound down, Andie and Aiyana said their goodbyes to the others and walked home together.

"Okay, it's just us now, so spill. How was it with Carlos in the dark?" Andie asked.

"Eh, nothing I couldn't handle," Aiyana replied.

"Are you going to go out with him again?"

"I don't think so . . . he got a little handsy. Nothing too extreme, but he definitely was taking advantage of the darkness and never once checked in to see if I was okay with it. I had to pull his hands away a couple times."

"Oh my . . . "

"It's like . . . boundaries, dude! Respect the boundaries. Or at least ask where they are . . . yeesh," Aiyana said, and shook her head.

Then she looked at Andie. "Speaking of which, how was it with Marcus?"

"Uh . . . he was . . . a gentleman, asked if he could hold my hand, and let me hang on his arm on occasion. Never put a hand on me, never made it weird."

"Wow, patience and respect? You don't see that every day. Did you kiss him?"

"Just a little peck when we said goodnight."

"He seems like a good guy."

"I like his shyness. Is it weird that I think that's attractive?" Andie asked.

"Totally weird. But it's also you, so go with it . . . who cares what anyone else thinks?"

"Yeah, you're right. Why am I over-analyzing a good thing?"

The two walked on, until they, too, split up to head home, giving hugs good night.

Chapter Six

It Was Just The Calm

The next afternoon, Friday, students flooded out the door — an amped-up enthusiasm filled the air. This was a four-day weekend; many had vacation plans, and no small number of students had plans to race home and be lazy after a long week. Dozens had been pulled out of school by parents at mid-day so families could get a jump on weekend travel across the Seven Cities.

The rush to the train station, or in the case of wealthy travelers, Port Mons spaceport . . . meant that the small resort city of *Libertas* would be surging with tourists and adventure-seekers heading down into the Night Labyrinth. Nerus had just re-opened its 'Last Resort' indoor ski slope and opening night of the Tartarus concert in New Kyiv would prove to be among the hottest tickets for the weekend. Agri-turismo groups headed for New Skye to learn about the low-gravity distillation process, and others to New Marrakech to explore greenhouses and the huge open markets. Those who wanted peace and quiet headed for the Valley of the Gods resorts or a wheeled-vehicle excursion up the Topaz Mountain.

Rather than blasting out of town, Sitara, Ric, Andie, and Aiyana met up in the Student union to grab a bite, and do a bit of plotting on Reillee's behalf. Only a few last-minute details needed to be arranged, because before Reillee had to depart for family time, they were all going to celebrate Reillee's half-birthday. 'Berfday,' it was often called.

Reillee turned eight-and-a-half today, which, in solidarity with Earth, was the common time for a young person to complete driver's ed and test for a skimmer and rover license.

Reillee had shared his excitement with friends in his classes but knew he had a weekend of intense study ahead, to pass that test on first attempt. Tonight was his family party, but his friends had insisted he join them beforehand for another crack at the portal.

He wasn't stupid; he knew they were cooking up some surprise, but he played along without letting on his suspicions.

* * *

Four, anticipating the arrival of the fifth, set up a surprise of sorts. It was Reillee's Berfday, after all. They dimmed all the lights . . . and waited.

At length, he arrived.

The crunch of shoes on gravel . . . Sitara crouched in the dark, seeking a little payback—it was all too familiar.

As he passed under the blue warning words on the ceiling, Reillee reached in his pocket and pulled out some big-bang snaps he had picked up along the way. Bang! Sitara, hiding ahead in the darkness, jumped and screamed at a loud pop at her feet.

"What in all the—" Sitara said, breathless.

"Bwaaaa ha ha ha ha ha ha . . ." Reillee laughed until he had no breath left to laugh.

"You must think I'm completely stoopid," Reillee said, breaking down laughing again. "What did you think of that big bang-snap I tossed at your feet, Sitara?"

Sitara was not impressed, hands on her hips. "Um, you are a complete and utter—never mind." Reillee grinned like a little kid.

Ric, however, who had hidden outside among the shrubs and boulders, had followed Reillee in. He approached him from behind, quiet as shadow.

"Boo!" Ric said, grabbing Reillee with his fingertips in the ribs.

Reillee shrieked, slipping and collapsing to his knees. He nearly deuced his pants.

"Oooooo . . . " Reillee growled, standing back up. He twisted around as he rose, and took a grab at Ric, who danced back out of the way. Ric and Sitara laughed hysterically.

At this point, Andie hit the lights, many of which had been changed to shine in different colors, some flashing, others steady.

"Happy Berfday," several of his friends cheered in unison.

Reillee smiled, rubbed his knee, and joined his closest friends to eat berfday cake, set out on a table away from the Portal. The music on someone's device cranked out some of Reillee's favorite tunes, at a low enough volume so as not to attract attention from outside.

* * *

Jackson reached for the doors of the executive suite to make his exit. At this spot, he remembered with perfect clarity what had happened exactly three Fridays before.

He gripped the handles and paused for a fraction of a second. Nothing happened—the doors swung open gently at his touch. All the furniture stayed put. As he turned, he said his customary goodbye to Claire, giving her a knowing smile and thanking her for all the hard work. He knew that the entire staff had been coming in early, going home late, and pedaling as hard as they could all day, every day, for weeks.

That quake had turned everything sideways. Yet for now, the danger had subsided. Finally . . . looked like this weekend might be something approaching normal. Jackson loosened his favorite blue tie as he stepped into the elevator and smoothed his hair in a barely-kempt comb over.

He still stood tall—slouching was still not in his nature, but he craved a break from burning the candle at both ends. After weeks of non-stop senior staff meetings, planning sessions, multi-department action groups, public appearances . . . he just wanted an evening to himself, and maybe read a contemporary thriller. A quiet meal and a walk through the forest might be in order as well. The elevator pinged as it arrived at the ground floor.

Moments later, he swept out of the skyscraper and onto the street, noting his timing was good—a silver tram had just pulled up to the light rail station labeled 'MERF HQ.'

He noticed a lady nearby, then recognized her as one of the action officers in MERF's Medical Division. He nodded to her but couldn't recall her name. Jackson stepped aside to let her board first. She smiled and thanked him by name, bright white teeth a contrast to her dark skin. Her voice had a pleasant Nigerian lilt.

He followed her up the single step and chose a seat behind his colleague. He set down his briefcase and tried to relax. The front and rear tram doors hissed shut and the vehicle silently pulled away from the station . . .

Then three things happened in perfect unison.

Jackson's wrist chrono buzzed, alive with a glowing red ring, indicating the highest severity of emergency.

The train jolted back to a halt and sealed itself in place.

An automated voice announcement blasted out over all speakers, tablets, and chronos:

"Attention in the area, attention in the area. Mons-Plex is

experiencing a seismic event. This is not a drill. Remain in your SAFE pod or vehicle until given the all-clear. I say again, Mons-Plex is experiencing a seismic event. Remain in your SAFE pod or vehicle until further notice. MERF, out."

Jackson slipped an earpod in one ear.

He grabbed out his tablet and tapped a priority break-through call to MERF's sub-level Emergency Operations Center, the EOC.

The Duty Officer's face came up on the screen immediately. Jackson recognized him, a professional night shift leader named Higgins. Jackson didn't waste time with formalities—he tapped the call to 'secure' and a confirmation tone sounded in his ear.

"Talk to me, Scott."

"Sir, you're not going to believe this. We've got four . . . no five epicenters now, all moving at once. Five. It's . . . it's like the Mountain is . . . wait, that isn't possible."

"Just talk me through it. Tell me what you're seeing," Jackson said.

"It's all over, spread across the entire base layer of the Mountain. Wait, scratch that, these are all much deeper." Higgins paused. "Uh Oh."

"What?"

"Make that six."

"Okay, stay with me . . . what depth is the shallowest?"

"Looks like . . . forty-five clicks deep. All the rest are deeper."

"Do you show the depth of the deepest one?"

"Looks like it's . . . clear down near the top of the mantle. That one is giving bizarre readings, like it's driving all the others."

"What's our confidence level?"

"Stand by . . . okay, confidence is high, sir. Ninety-five percent or better. All instruments are working perfectly, and they all agree. Even the satellites agree, the Mountain is in motion."

"What part?"

"Uh, all of it I think," Higgins replied.

At that moment, noticeable shaking began inside the tram. Riders instinctively grabbed bars and looped hand grips above.

Jackson stood, grabbing his briefcase with a free hand.

On the screen, Higgins shook his head and continued his report.

"The ground radar halo shows magma levels rising . . . damn. Everywhere. It's rising everywhere, sir."

Jackson cut in. "Do you have a fix on the rate? Rising how fast?"

"Stand by . . . "

An agonizing few seconds drew out.

Though he was a patient man, he used the delay to walk forward, passing by his lady colleague and going to front of the tram. His colleague stood up behind him, following close.

Seeing the tall, suited man standing forward of the yellow line, the driver spoke up.

"I'm sorry sir, but you can't get out until it's all over."

"The hell I can't," Jackson said, pressing his palm to the driver's ident plate.

The front door hissed open immediately.

The rear door remained shut, also immediately.

"How the . . . ?" the driver murmured.

Jackson's colleague was close at his back. He noticed he had a shadow.

Pausing in the doorway, he turned back to face her, and opened his mouth to protest.

She interrupted him before he could speak. "Look sir, the door is open. Just let me get in there, do my job." Again, that beautiful Nigerian lilt.

Jackson nodded, and the instant they both cleared the door, it hissed back shut and re-sealed.

As he walked around the front of the bus, Jackson saw a very confused driver press his own palm to the ident plate, but of course nothing happened.

He headed straight back to the headquarters building, his very determined colleague matching him step for step. The vibrations continued, making footing unsure at best. They managed to make progress.

Pedestrians in all directions, up the street and down, were running into buildings or diving into any SAFE Pod they could find. The hiss of doorways sealing themselves and the dull thuds of bunkers closing . . . resounded intermittently up and down the street.

* * *

Far across the city, tucked away down inside The Pocket, five teenagers lolled in bunks and hammocks, listening to stand-up comedy or scrolling social media. Andie munched on a Twinkie. Reillee, as usual, was making up some impromptu rap song, this one about how excellent Friday nights felt and how Twinkies compared with berfday cake. Ares was not in the Pocket, for a change.

Then . . . every tablet, chrono, and earpiece in The Pocket stopped whatever it was playing and sounded out the all-call about the quake. By the end of the first go-through, all five teens had stood, confused.

By the end of the repeat, they could feel the ground trembling.

"Oh, not again . . . " Sitara said, grabbing a bunk for support. Ric grabbed the other end of the bunk where he stood and held tight, knuckles white with strain.

The shaking intensified, knocking over chairs and setting the hammocks swinging. It was hard to stand, the ground was so unsteady. Furniture and objects bounced and clattered loud echoes throughout the round room.

Someone screamed. Then all five were knocked off their feet.

* * *

Stein stood back from Ares' food dish, having just filled it with the cat's favorite, fish-flavored treats. The cat eagerly took his first bite, then stopped and looked wildly around. Stein sat back in his couch, not noticing. He reached for his tablet to make a video call when . . .

The door to his apartment sealed itself shut with an audible hiss. He instinctively looked at the door, then looked toward the sound of a low growl. Ares jumped up on the couch, claws sunk into a cushion, ears laid back. His low kitty growl continued.

The all-call announcement grabbed his attention. As the words poured out of all speakers, he set down his tablet and stood, shakily, to cross the living room toward the door. Then, the room trembled, and Stein could hear the rising, telltale rumble of the quake building up.

A quick jolt in the quake knocked him sideways into a bookshelf. Then all the books spilled on the floor alongside a couple small statuettes, which shattered into tiny fragments.

* * *

Less than three minutes after the quake began, Jackson walked smoothly into the EOC to review the most recent situation reports on the screens before him. He shook his head in silent frustration. Other action officers and station controllers looked up at the cutaway of the Mountain, fear in their eyes, but they maintained composure.

Magma levels everywhere were higher than ever seen before.

Jackson drew a deep breath, punching in a priority call to the Director.

The EOC, which had been a buzz of activity . . . hushed. Everyone listened in to the important phone call, while still focused on their screens.

Jackson described the magma, building deep beneath Olympus Mons, followed by lots of nodding, and more than a few times saying 'yes, sir,' and 'no, we're completely out of options' . . .

Jackson signed off with a final 'I hope so too. Jackson out.' He hung up the phone.

Pausing only a second, he drew in another deep breath, exhaled, and pressed the green button on his Command Center intercom. He angled the slender microphone up and bent slightly to speak into it.

"Emergency controllers, your attention please. Given the rising magma is an unstoppable, direct threat to the city, we have no choice but to begin Total Evacuation Protocol. Before T.E.P. goes into effect, you will each have one minute, that's sixty seconds, to contact your families. Tell them that they should follow the directions they will soon hear in a city-wide broadcast. Then, all outgoing non-secure comms will be disabled. After making your family calls, please run your Omega Checklists and report completion. Move with a purpose, one minute begins now."

Turning off the channel, Jackson turned. Then he bent forward, right into Shift Leader Higgins' personal space, leaning over a keyboard, touch surface, and the man's flat screen displays.

Higgins rolled his seat back and out of the way, to let his boss work. Then he reached for the nearest non-secure phone line to call his wife.

Rushed, hushed conversations filled up the EOC.

Jackson punched the "Emergency Actions" tab on the screen, scrolled down to the last one on the list, then swiped two fingers across the top to bring up an "Authorization Required" prompt. He pressed his other hand to the ident plate next to the keyboard.

A square, flush-mounted panel above the screen popped open. It bore a single gold character, engraved on its surface.

The hinged cover now open, Jackson paused for the clock above him to count up to 60 seconds, then mentally added a few more seconds for final goodbyes among his controllers. He pressed hard on the lone glowing red button inside, keeping it pressed in for a further ten seconds.

Unsecured comm lines switched off. Automated recall notifications went out to all controllers not already in the room, directing them to report immediately. The backdrop lights in the room turned red, and the EOC went into soft lockdown. Three dozen Emergency Action Binders around the room were opened and flipped through, to the checklist no Controller had ever run through, except in practice drills.

Higgins looked up at Jackson. "Sir, I never thought you would be pushing that button in my lifetime."

Jackson sighed. "That makes two of us, my friend. Now . . . please inform me when all stations report completion and tell me the instant that city-wide broadcast is ready to go."

"Yes, sir." He turned to his screen, then looked up and scanned the room. Several dozen small screens around the room now showed views of the city, street intersections, and tunnels not normally monitored.

Other screens showed a seismograph digital scan, with a flat series of flat red lines breaking into wildly flipping peaks and valleys, typical of a major temblor like this one. The moment magnitude monitor twitched upwards to a peak value of 6.5. Then, after dropping to 4.2, it jumped back up to a new high point, 6.7.

The massive shock absorbers under the building were being tested. For now, they did their job well. Higgins' coffee mug barely showed a ripple in the dark surface. He did not give the brew the slightest notice.

He remained focused on the large viewscreens stretched across a curving front wall, clear up to the ceiling. Each now showed a critical area's status and progress, and the center screen showed a simple status update in bold red letters on bright white background:

CITY EVACUATION IN PROGRESS

Status: 0% Evacuated

Recalled personnel, the backup controllers and staff workers, started trickling in through the outer security doors. They received their updates then stayed out of the way for those currently on shift to do their important work. Within one hour, the EOC would be in hard lockdown.

The good people of the MERF EOC collectively rolled up their sleeves to try to save a million people.

* * *

Sealed up in his own apartment, Stein and the cat just looked at each other helplessly, waiting for a lull in the shaking. When it did not subside right away, Stein stumbled over to a wall display cabinet to grab down his favorite drinking vessels, a collection he had curated for years. He gently set them in the kitchen sink on a hand towel for safe keeping. He heard a crash from the back, probably the bathroom mirror or something.

Then several bizarre things happened.

A green light switched on in his apartment's entry way—a light Stein didn't know was there. His attention captured, the next thing he saw was his Founder's Stone *lift open*. It swung slowly up without a sound. He stared in confusion, as a warbling klaxon sound blasted out across the city.

The warbling tone was replaced with a woman's voice, quickly but carefully enunciating every word.

"Attention in the area, attention in the area. All people in the Mons-Plex, please proceed to your nearest Founder's Stone immediately, and use

253

the passageway there to exit the building. This is a complete evacuation of the city. This is not a drill. Keep order and move as quickly as you can. If you have medical training, please help any injured you meet along the way to make their exit. Take nothing with you—leave your possessions behind. Exo-Suits are not, I repeat, not required at this time. This is a complete evacuation of the city. Below your Founder's Stone, follow the painted arrows and lights to staging areas, where ground vehicles and MagLev trains will carry you to safety. Once each vehicle reaches capacity, it will automatically depart, so please fill every seat. Move quickly and help others wherever possible. I say again . . . "

The entire announcement was repeated, word for word, carefully but hastily inflected.

Stein glanced down into the open manhole and ladder that had suddenly appeared at his feet. He grabbed his tablet and saw his bride Tanya was trying to reach him. Faces filled screens. Her hair was disheveled, there was a bruise on her forehead, and blood seeped from her bottom lip.

"Stephen? What do we . . . ?" and words failed her.

"Tia, take the founder's stone, get your partners and all your staff to follow. Convince them. It's all right. When you get to the bottom of the ladder, you'll find some ramps or steps or something. Follow the green lights to an exit vehicle. Whatever kind of vehicle it is, jump in and get it moving. I'll try to find you along the way."

"Is this that tunnels thing you told me about? What you called it—the, the Undercity?" She was frantic but holding it together.

"Yes. Exactly. The one I found behind The Ghosts' Hideout when I was a teenager. We all thought they were just unfinished spaces or . . . or . . . abandoned construction tunnels. Now I see it's a crazy evacuation plan."

She paused, looking slightly off screen as she walked.

"Do you see it? Your founder's stone? Is it open?" Stein asked, holding the tablet in both hands.

"Yes, I can see it, and it's open." She raised her voice a notch. "You guys, this way. Hurry."

She glanced back at the screen. "When will I see you?"

"My honey, I have no idea what happens next." Stein preferred honesty over sugar-coating.

A loud crash on her end caused her to wince and go off screen briefly.

"Just go. I'll be all right, and so will you," he said. "Trust the builders."

"Okay," she said, eyes glistening just a bit.

"I have to go too. Need both hands for the ladder. See you soon love." He said, looking into her eyes.

"Okay," she said, again looking away to the left. She hesitated, searching for words.

The screen went dark, its signal interrupted. The ground was shaking again.

Stein took one step down the ladder, then stopped himself. He tapped a quick link on his tablet and in his display, saw the tunnel feed from the camera he had set up outside the Portal the same night he had dragged in that infernal, huge Afghan carpet. The camera feed seemed to be one big beige blur, with strange fuzzy blobs disrupting the image.

"Go, you guys . . . you got this." He murmured, knowing the students, on the other side of the portal door, inside the round room, couldn't hear him. He climbed a couple more rungs down the escape ladder. Ares lingered above. The cat leapt over the founder's stone above Stein's head and stood near the apartment front door. Stein climbed back up to see what the cat was on about. The cat was pushing his two front paws against the door—he clearly wanted out. Stein clambered back up and pushed on the door, which was no longer sealed.

The door opened easily, and Ares stepped through, then looked back at Stein.

"What? Evacuations are this way." He pointed down.

"Mr-reow" said the cat, taking a step further, again looking back.

"What? You want me to come with you?"

"Mew," Ares said with finality.

Stein looked back down to the screen, where he expected to see the portal door still sealed, or, even better, five students tearing off down the hallway toward the staging areas. But the camera still showed that strange beige blur. Odd . . . why weren't they making a break for it?

Oh. Because the announcement directed evacuation via Founder's Stones, not ancient, forgotten puzzle portals.

The beige blur on the camera feed began to clear. Dust in front of the camera was settling down, and the image refocused. Stein could make out the hallway just outside the white door—now filled with rocks, almost to the ceiling where he had stuck the camera.

He swiped over to another camera view, one he had put up in a tree to keep an eye on the forest entrance to the hideout, hoping to see them racing out toward the nearest buildings.

A dawning horror rose up inside him; the cave entrance was gone, closed off beneath a massive rockslide.

His students had been buried inside. Trapped.

Chapter Five

Fell Things

"N̲ow what?" Aiyana yelled, coughing through all the dust.

"Was the whole forest exit caved in?" Andie asked, covering their mouth with a shirt collar.

"I'm looking . . . it's the boulders outside, they're all collapsed. But there's no way to move those, each prolly weighs a ton," Ric said, gasping and coughing. "It's totally blocked."

"The portal!" Sitara yelled.

Andie quickly entered the THEIA and GAIA codes, and the door began to cycle. It opened a few centimeters, then stopped. The door shuddered, then tried to open a second time. Again, at just a few centimeters, it stopped.

All three red lights winked on and off in rapid succession.

Ric leaned over the others and peeked along the seam of the partially open door.

"There's like, a rock or a bunch of rocks here too, blocking it," he said, still squinting with one eye against the door. "It's closed off too."

Fine beads of sweat formed on Andie's brow, cheeks now a rosy red.

The others stared hard at the door.

Aiyana wiped away a tear, but kept a stern, determined face, staring at the portal. Ric and Sitara had involuntarily held hands, willing the door to open, somehow. Reillee looked to be on the verge of panic, pushing in vain against the slightly-open door.

* * *

In the city streets, chaos reigned. Stein stumbled several times, but still made progress. The shaking ground made his running look ridiculous, as rocks and bits of buildings crumbled and fell all around him. The din of klaxon, buildings being fractured, and of taller structures collapsing wasn't just loud . . . it was deafening. The echoes reverberated throughout the city.

Weaving along streets and back alleys, partially assisted by Ares' innate sense of direction, the unlikely pair made progress.

"I hope we don't make too many wrong turns," Stein called out to the cat as they ran toward the building nearest to the Pocket, as best he could guess. People staggered into and out of buildings all around, and the occasional tram disgorged its passengers to seek out their closest founder's stones. Front doors of public-access buildings stood open, everywhere.

The trembling in the ground faded. It made running easier; Stein and Ares made better progress.

Arriving at a soft serve & smoothie shop as near to The Pocket as he could hope for, Stein let out a deep sigh of relief, finding the store's AI had the door wide open as well. No one was inside. The founder's stone here was, like his own, standing wide open on a hinge and basically inviting him in. He leapt for the ladder and descended. Ares followed.

* * *

Andie wiped dust and sweat from their eyes. They slammed a fist against the metal.

"OPEN." Andie yelled at the stubborn door.

The door shuddered. The gap widened a bit as the door pushed to a hand's width gap from its frame.

"You did it?" Ric cried.

"Um, I didn't do crap." Andie said, stepping back. The sound of rocks and pebbles tumbling over one another came through the door, and it opened a few centimeters more.

After some more sounds of rock shifting, and pebbles scattering on the other side of the portal, the portal swung a bit further open. All five teens took a step back.

The sweaty, rosy face of their science teacher peeked through the gap.

"Hi guys. Where's the kaboom?" He kept pulling at rocks in a jumbled heap on the other side of the portal door. After another minute of furious scrabbling and rock-shifting, the gap was wide enough for Stein to squeeze through.

The teens were still at a loss for words as their teacher stepped in.

"What the—?" Reillee asked. The rest stared, too stunned to react.

Andie peered past Stein into the corridor beyond the portal. A fuzzy little orange face appeared at the bottom of the gap. Andie smiled widely when they saw Ares.

"Our own personal MERF rescue?" Ric asked, a big smile of relief washing over his face. He wiped tears and dust from his cheeks.

Stein grinned back. "You guys totally had this—but I had a camera watching the tunnel there, and when the ceiling collapsed outside, well, I figured you might need a hand," Stein said, now walking past them. They parted to let him pass as he headed to the Exo-Suit locker. The low rumbling continued all around them.

"Mister Stein, how do you even know about—?" Andie's words were drowned out by the rumble growing louder.

"Ghosts!" Stein yelled above the din, managing a grin. "I guess they are real," he said, glancing at Sitara. She coughed and smiled back at him.

The floor rolled beneath their feet. Sleeping cots shifted further from their original places.

Every person in the room bent their knees reflexively, trying to keep their balance.

Stein yanked at the old Exo-Suit locker doors, which only reluctantly parted and swung open.

"Um, sir, that's empty," Sitara said.

"But is it?" Stein asked, wry grin on his face. He reached in and punched the heel of his hand against the back panel, causing it to fall away sideways. Behind the panel, a larger space was revealed, set deep into the wall.

A dozen Exo-Suits, recent models, hung neatly on their hooks.

"Here. Take these." Stein called out, reaching in and tossing the first one he grabbed to the nearest student.

"That's convenient," Reillee observed. Then the trembling stopped.

Stein paused. Dust still choked the air, but it was quiet. He paused, looking back around the room. "No . . . this isn't . . . this isn't over." Teenagers looked around the room, as if the walls might suddenly come crashing in.

"How do you know?" someone over his shoulder asked.

"The aftershocks will be worse this time . . . everything here in the city . . . everything weakened in the first minutes of a quake this extreme will collapse with the next set. Mark my words."

From the door, Ares growled a loud "rowrrrr," and squinted at the people inside, his tan-orange face, comically small in the huge doorway. By now, Stein had finished passing out suits to all five of his students.

Then he tossed his suit over one arm, lowered his head, and crossed the room to where the original ghosts' three sleeping cots stood. Stein stopped at the center one and grabbed at a corner post. With a deft twist of the plastic post-cap, he reached inside and pulled out a small object and slipped it in a vest pocket. Andie watched carefully but couldn't see what he had retrieved.

Ric just stared at Stein as he did this, an almost comical look on his face.

The ground trembled. Just a little tremble. Then a bigger one. A small cracking sound from the ceiling above them. Then a massive crumbling sound from somewhere deep in the walls. Everyone looked up, even the cat from the doorway. Ares hissed a low hiss. Nothing had visibly changed, but that sound . . .

"Time to go!" Stein hollered, and squeezed through the portal door. The cat jumped aside but stayed close, following as he walked. Ric remembered to grab his tablet off the cot, and Andie stuffed a few power bars in their pants cargo pockets and followed.

Nobody hesitated to follow Stein, each bearing his/her/their own burden, a ten-kilo Exo-Suit. The cat fell in with the others, trotting along a few steps behind Stein's heels.

The portal thudded shut behind them. The cat alone stopped to look back at the sound, then ran to catch up to his fleeing humans.

The tunnel curved as it descended, and the portal door was soon lost from view. Everyone focused ahead, breathing deeply from the exertion.

"Where are we . . . going?" Aiyana asked, panting the least of all in the group. She shifted the Exo-Suit from one shoulder to the other.

"Back to the city. The tunnel I came through a few minutes ago leads up to the smoothie sho—" he stopped. The way ahead was completely blocked, mid-tunnel. The dust here was still settling.

"Oh . . . crap," Stein muttered.

"Is there another way out?" Ric asked, his voice trembling.

"Yes," said Andie. "Remember the tunnel leading out?"

"The 'Inner Door' Exit? But that one's sealed, I've never—" then Stein saw Andie's intense stare, a little Mona Lisa smile playing at the corners of their mouth. "You figured it out?"

"We figured it out," Andie said.

"Then . . . wow. Let's go!" Stein said, coughing in the dust.

"It's back that way and left." Andie said, putting on a fresh burst of speed, knowing the adrenaline surges would help everyone make good time.

Stein glanced around for the cat.

"Ares, let's . . . "

The cat sprinted past him, following Andie in the exact correct direction.

" . . . go."

"But green arrow lights go back the other way," Ric said.

"We're not going that way, it's just another cave-in, right before a big intersection," Stein said. "I checked when I was getting my bearings down here, trying to find the right way to you."

"Aren't there other paths around the cave-in? Cross-cutting tunnels?" Andie asked, breathing heavily as they carried the heavy suit.

"Normally, yes, but we're at the very edge of the city, those cross-cutting routes are more frequent near the center. We're isolated to just a few fringe tunnels here. The only way ahead for us is . . . well, outside, thanks to your creativity. I just don't know how we are going to make it work yet."

The group reached the end of this new passageway, where another portal door stood, two red lights glowing. Their trusty tabby cat was already waiting there, looking back as if to say what took you so long? Everyone in the group was now breathing heavily from the exertion.

Above the large, round airlock door, a sign glowed bright aqua-green letters:

INNER DOOR
EXIT

Stein put both hands on the door and squinted through the small window. "I'm glad you've solved this one, because my buddies and I never even found a keyboard — let alone a code to open it."

Aiyana stepped aside, grinning a rare smile. Andie spoke.

"See this stylized logo here on the side? Aiya and I figured this must be Elias Ellis' monogram." She pushed it. A small silver concave surface device flipped open, like a chromed spoon, with a small needle in the midst.

"Ellis? As in . . . Ellis Ellis? Thought he was an urban legend," Stein said.

"He was very real. We found his grave site; his real name was Elias. He was the architect for all these tunnels and sealed them up after they were completed."

"His grave site? It's here?"

"Well, somewhere over there, I think," Andie said, pointing to the left and down through the stone walls.

"Yeah, about a kilometer deeper than here, I think," Aiyana added.

"You ladies are extraordinary," Stein said, marveling.

Andie smiled, then continued, saying, "But no amount of typing opens this one — Elias left two ways of getting the inner door open after they sealed it shut for the final time. The first must be whatever key card fits in there," Andie pointed at a small credit-card slot.

"Yeah, we saw that, but a physical key makes no sense at all. What's the second?"

"Ah yes, the second. He genetically encoded it to himself, so he personally would never need a key, should it become lost. Watch this," Andie said, pressing a palm and gritting their teeth. A small *snikt* sound sounded, drawing a drop of Andie's blood.

"In a way, Eli himself told me," Andie confided. "But we weren't sure until Aiya and I each tried. Apparently, there's still enough of the right DNA markers in my blood for the door to think it's him or his son."

The door made a dull, satisfactory clunk. Andie set down the Exo-Suit, heaved with both arms, and the door swung open on its hinges.

"Andie Ellis." Stein shook his head in wonder.

"But wait . . . you came from Earth as a child, you can't be his descendant, right?" Ric asked. "I mean, on Earth, he wouldn't live very long if he was born here. His internal organs would give out in the heavy gravity. Right?"

"See, that's what I thought too. But then I stumbled on a video letter he left for his son, Eli Jr., pleading with him for forgiveness, and for his return. It appears the two fell out, hard, after the death of his son's best friend. Eli, Jr. left Mars to go live in the early Lunar Colonies. He never returned to Mars and his father died, heartbroken and alone. Generations go by, a little back and forth between Luna and Earth, and my own great grandfather settled in Colorado. Eventually his grandson, my dad, Shaw Ellis takes a job here at Silver Lake, so my dad and I fly here aboard the *Dorothy Vaughan*. So—here we are . . . I mean, what are the odds?"

Stein looked at Andie, nodding, so Andie continued. "Apparently Elias and I still share enough DNA markers to open his biometric locks—when we followed Ares into the burial chamber, it all just sort of rolled out."

"So . . . the cat helped you find your ancestor."

"Mew," said the cat from near Stein's feet.

Stein gaped. "Did he . . . just . . . respond?"

The room was silent for a few seconds.

"He's as smart as any of us, if you can believe it," Andie said.

Aiyana shrugged, nodding. The others stared, bewildered.

"Look, I have no idea how, so don't ask. Shouldn't we be getting out of here?"

"Yes, I think that would be wise. Suits please, and inside, quickly," Stein asserted.

The door swung the rest of the way open, leading to a five-meter square chamber and another portal door beyond that. Above the next door was a similar lighted sign, this time in yellow-orange glowing letters:

EXIT
OUTER DOOR

They all started donning suits as they shuffle-stepped forward. One by one, suits were unzipped and powered on. Everyone was making good progress getting arms and legs in all in the right places.

"Last one through, please close the inner door." Stein said firmly. A moment passed. The door behind them thudded shut.

"How did you know about any of this?" Reillee asked Stein.

"My buddies and I opened the white Portal, but we called it the Gate, about seven standard years ago. We explored the hell outta these tunnels, but most aren't in use, leading nowhere. Well, until today, anyway."

"What's beyond that next door?" Sitara asked, pulling the suit up one leg.

"It looks to be another long tunnel," Andie said, flexing fingers into the gloves and reaching for the zipper. "But there aren't any tiles—just looks like bare rock. Safe guess, this leads us out of the mountain; out before more things collapse."

Sitara peered through the outer-door window, seeing only darkness. "I think that I may be seeing some starlight in the distance? I'm not sure," she said.

Everyone was now zipping up, at least halfway through donning their Exo-Suits.

Stein switched on his wrist tablet control panel. The cat stood very close to Stein's booted feet, just looking from one human to the next and back.

"Can everyone hear me?" Students gave thumbs up or murmured 'yes' in their turn. He flipped the top closed and checked power and pressure.

"So . . . who were the other . . . ghosts?" Aiyana asked, pulling her helmet over her head and zipping up. But Stein didn't hear her, his suit blocking the sound, and her voice, too soft for him to hear. Stein pressed two familiar buttons on his wrist pad.

"Quick roll call . . . and please also tell me if your suit checks are all green." Finishing this set of instructions, Stein stepped over to the side and reached for a pressure case, a black one, similar to those that had held Little Caesars for the star party.

"Ric?" He prompted, selecting a case he thought might work.

"One sec . . . Ok, mine's good," Ric replied in Stein's ear.

Stein pulled the case from its shelf and set it on the ground.

"Um, Andie?"

Stein opened the case.

"All set, Stein," Andie's light voice confirmed.

The cat jumped in the case without hesitating.

"And Sitara?"

"I'm all right here," Sitara replied with a little tremble in her voice.

Stein snapped the lid shut on the case and twisted the pressure seal switch closed.

"Reillee?"

"Good to go," Reillee replied in a much calmer voice than before.

Stein tugged on the case handle, ensuring it wouldn't pop open without the pressure-release button also pressed. He would just have to trust the seal would hold as long as required to keep Ares alive.

"Aiya?"

"I hate these things," Aiyana said, looking at her wrist. "Pressure and power look good." Another sigh. Her own warm breath trapped against her face, and the sweat beading at her forehead always made Aiya breathe faster and feel . . . trapped.

Stein replied, "I'm not a big fan of suits either. Always feel a little too pressed in."

"How do you deal?" Aiyana's breath rasped through the mike. "I mean, there's gotta be some way to talk yourself down."

"For me, I cut in some cool air, drop the suit temp a few degrees below your comfort zone. Gives your mind something else to focus on, and controls those beads of sweat on your brow."

Andie and Aiyana clapped their left hands together, syncing their private channel as they had on star party night. Then Aiyana dropped the temp in her suit. Stein continued.

"Plus, we may have one helluva hike ahead of us. It's at least ten clicks, straight down, to the plains below."

"What happens after that?" Sitara asked.

"Your guess is as good as mine," Stein answered. "But you heard the announcements—they're evacuating the entire city. Maybe someone will stop and give us a ride? First things first, get out of this mountain."

Stein hefted the sealed box-case right up against his helmet, so they were in direct contact. He opened his mouth wide to shout, then paused before saying a word. He muted his radio mike.

"Kitty?" Stein shouted. "Can you hear me?"

A very distant "mew" came back through his faceplate. He hoped that meant yes. He held the case's top handle in his left hand and reached for the door with his right.

"Stein? How did you know? That there would be pressure cases here? For Ares, I mean?" Ric asked.

Stein answered, mouth moving but no sound.

Ric gave a confused head shake and tapped the side of his helmet.

Oh, Stein mouthed, un-muting his mike. "Sorry. Pressure cases. I didn't know, I wasn't sure anything usable would even be here. I was about to stuff Ares in my suit with me," Stein mused, patting his abdomen.

"Would that have worked?" Aiyana asked.

"Probably not. Desperate times." Stein smiled at Aiyana and Ric. He turned back to the outer door. Andie reached out a hand to steady themselves when another jolt passed through the ground.

Stein punched the big red button on the inside of the outer door and swung a large metal arm upward until it locked in place. A clearly audible, long-drawn-out hiss, sound growing fainter by the second, told him the air was being bled from the large room and the door could be opened in a few more seconds. A few intermittent tremors vibrated the ground beneath their feet.

"Okay, lights on, everyone. And let's all please stay on 'all-call' unless you need to have a private convo. Let's roll."

He swung the door open and holding the cat-case ahead of him, Stein led his small crew into the yawning, rough-carved cavern beyond. Waiting for all five students to clear the door, he closed and sealed it. A lone floodlight, activated by their movement, illuminated the area around the door, but not much else. Ahead was dark.

He stepped away from the airlock, walking slightly faster than a stroll.

The wide and tall industrial tunnel led toward a deeper darkness. No, not complete darkness . . . Sitara was right, there were stars, visible far ahead where the tunnel ended. Students followed closely, feeling the crunch of gravel and seeing small puffs of dust where they stepped.

"Just another couple hundred meters, and we should be under open sky," Stein said, voice low.

He tried not to think of Ares, hopefully still breathing fine inside the box. Then he thought of Ares even more. Or his bride, running through gods-knew-what chaos and trying to get a spot on some train or sand crawler.

Or a million other people, all in their own private, panicky hell, running for their lives as the Mountain raged, rested, and raged some more.

Darkness. Helmet spotlights barely illuminated the area just ahead of each of them, though the sounds of everyone breathing on the open channel were oddly reassuring. Everyone huddled closer to someone else. Occasionally, Stein felt the weight shift inside the case as they walked, reminding him the cat was still okay. Good.

"How long do you think Ares can breathe in just the air that's in the box?" Andie asked.

"Long enough to find a place to let him out, I hope. Ten minutes maybe? Fifteen? We're still pretty far up the side of the Mountain, so I'm hoping we can flag down someone in a tracked vehicle, or get to of the MagLev train lines."

The group continued forward, trying to keep a good pace. Darkness, with the distant glow of starlight ahead . . . sounds of people breathing over the radio.

"Oooo, look." Ric spotted them first. Off to the right, he saw parked vehicles and equipment in a huge carved-out alcove at least five stories tall. Here, in an old motor pool of sorts, vehicles, and industrial equipment filled every available space. In the back, tall cargo cranes and drilling diggers were left in neat rows. Cut into the walls were repair stations, machinery, and coiled tubes and hoses hanging on hooks. Here and there, dust-covered dark stains discolored the stone floors.

They walked along the work zone, approaching three driving vehicles parked at the far end, lined up neatly. The first two were tracked vehicles, like old-world tanks but without guns or turrets, and boasting much larger view screens in the front and sides. The dusty windows were all fitted trapezoids and triangles. Ten or maybe a dozen people could squeeze inside if they didn't have any cargo.

The end vehicle looked like an old eight-wheeled exploration rover, painted white with two pairs of giant off-road solid rubber wheels in the front, and two pairs in the back.

Stein set the Ares box down to examine the rover closely. The front of the vehicle was the people section, and the back carried a small cargo space, with a hinge connecting the front to the back, allowing for tight turns. He looked inside the front windows, seeing four seats in the cockpit, and a small airlock to allow entry and egress. The cargo space in the back section still had some kind of rectangle-container loaded and strapped down.

Students walked around the vehicles, not quite believing their luck.

"Will these even still work? They could have been here for a hundred years," someone said on the open channel.

"No, they're not that old, check out these manufacturing plates by the airlocks. Closer to twenty-five standard years old."

"Jeez, twenty-five, that's old."

"Heeey." Stein said.

"Sorry."

Stein shrugged it off, allowing himself a small smile. He picked up the cat case and walked to the rover's entry door. The name Endurance was painted in bold letters below the front windows. "Let's see if any of them power up. Control panels look similar . . . if you're near one of the other vehicles, start pushing buttons."

Ric walked over to the controls on the venerable, treaded tank. He jabbed a few buttons. It started right up, lights coming on inside.

"Old but sturdy, eh, Mr. Stein?"

"You're damn skippy," Stein said back.

Sitara pushed control buttons of the other treaded tank but it stayed dark. A quick check around the back revealed its nuclear power core was pulled out, for whatever reason, when it was parked the final time.

The white wheeled rover vehicle didn't respond right away either, but when Stein brushed off some caked-on dust buildup, he got the control pad to glow a dim red. He pushed what he hoped was the right sequence, and the rover's insides powered up, with the internal and external lights blazing to life. Everyone squinted, wincing in the glare, most instinctively holding up their hands to block the intense shocking light.

"Whoa," someone breathed on the open frequency.

"Right?" someone else whispered back.

For the first time, they got a decent look at the entire carved-out space. Huge boring machines, massive equipment, vacuum pumps, and more vehicles, mostly scrapped, filled this huge carved-out space next to the long tunnel. The open sky was a hundred meters further.

Small trembles in the ground. Dust settling down from above. A few small pebbles bounced down around them.

"We've gotta get Ares inside, and get outside, stat." Stein said firmly.

"Which one should we take?" Sitara asked.

"Tank treads might have better traction going down the Mountain," Andie offered.

"But the rover truck thing is more agile," Ric said. "You know — if we need to dodge something or drive around. It probably has a higher top speed too."

The group paused a moment, each making up his or her mind.

Aiyana's voice came through, quietly. "Why don't we take both?"

"What?" someone said.

"Both? But we should stick together . . . " came Reillee's voice.

"No, she's right," said Andie, changing gears logically. "If one of them loses power, or whatever, we can all cram in the other and keep going. Aiya's right. We should take both."

"Sounds good," Stein said, and it became final. "I'll grab the Endurance and take the lead. Who's going to follow me, driving the tank?"

No one spoke. This was all happening a little too fast, feeling a little too real.

"I'll try," Aiyana said. "I got my skimmer's license four months ago."

"All right," Stein said, starting towards the Endurance. "Two with me, two with Aiya then. I'll keep Ares."

Stein hit the buttons to open the door, noticing that Ric and Sitara had closed in behind him. He lifted Ares carefully into the back of the Endurance and waited for his two companions to squeeze in with him. He sealed up and pressurized the airlock.

Aiya, climbing up into the tank, started switching systems on inside the airlock. Reillee and Andie joined her inside, and Andie pulled the outer door shut.

"Remember, the vehicle's stored air is probably stale, so be prepared to go right back on your suit's air supply." Stein told the group. They opened both vehicle cockpit doors, and stepped in to take their places.

Aiyana sat in the left seat of the tank. She looked over and gave Stein a thumbs up through the windows where he sat, in the left seat of the rover.

Both vehicles showed *ATM 1.0* on their status panels.

Stein, still on suit radio, said, "once we open our faceplates, if it smells rotten or like almonds, it's not breathable."

"We should also watch each other's faces closely," Andie's voice this time. "If anyone's lips turn cherry red, we're breathing contaminated air."

"What's that about cherry lips, Andie? I've never heard that before," Reillee asked, settling into a back seat of the tank's cockpit.

"My dad's a SCUBA diver at Silver Lake; he taught me what to watch for when breathing stored air. Older tanks can deliver bad air if they're rusty on the inside."

"Okay, we're watching each other over here. Faceplates up?" Sitara asked from the Endurance rover.

"Let's do it," Ric said.

Stein twisted his flexible faceplate open and took a cautious breath. Stale, dusty, but not rotten or almond-ey.

"Seems fine over here," Aiyana said.

"No red kissy lips over here so far, and no funky smells either. Just . . . dusty, like everything," Ric said.

"We might be all right," Stein said, nodding through the windows at the tank. The tank people nodded back.

He started flicking switches to power up the drive functions on the rover. Aiyana was already doing the same. Both drivers scanned their digital displays, checking the health of the vehicle, exactly as directed in every skimmer learner's permit training course.

"What about Ares?" Andie asked.

Stein looked back, happy to see Ric had just twisted the pressure release on the Ares Prison Box and opened it. The cat popped his head up, panting.

"Ares, look at you, you are all right," Sitara announced to everyone.

"Yay, kitty." "Way to go fuzzball." and other comments flooded into the suit radios, interrupted by a large clang on the roof of the tank.

"What was that?" Andie asked in shock. A fist-sized rock tumbled past the window after striking the top of the vehicle.

"Let's get moving," the teacher said, getting everyone refocused. "Friends, we may need our suits for a much longer time after we get to . . . wherever we're going. We've got to save air and power. Everybody please make sure your face plates are open, but don't take off your suits. Power them down, and turn off the air supply valve. Since you'll still be wearing your suits as we drive, you'll have to override the automatic air. Please check each other off now."

Stein held his wrist display up for his students behind him to verify. One of them slapped his shoulder in confirmation.

A moment's pause, and both vehicles were humming, everything seemed ready.

He was about to turn on the vehicle radio when the Endurance speakers crackled above the driver's seat. "The tank's radio defaulted to channel 8,

Mr. Stein," Andie said. It's like Andie was inside his head—insightful little genius. If he ever had a kiddo of his own, he hoped for one like Andie.

"Okay, let's switch over to channel 9, Andie. That's the channel they used to use for emergencies, if I remember my retro TV correctly . . . I think this qualifies."

"If anybody's even listening," Ric put in.

"All set over there, Aiya?"

"Ooooone seeecond . . . okay, all set." Aiyana responded, putting the venerable tank in gear and test touching the foot controls. The treaded tank's headlights blazed to full brightness. Aiyana sounded more confident by the minute. Releasing the vehicle's radio comm button, Aiyana turned toward Andie, now seated beside her.

"Andie, remember you once asked me what I'd do with a tank? I'll tell you what I'm gonna freaking do with a tank."

"Hrm?" Andie asked.

"Get us the hell out of here." Aiyana smiled with confidence Andie had never seen in Aiyana before, not once.

"Um, Mister Stein?" Sitara's voice came over the radio, though she was right next to him.

"Yeah, Sitara?"

"I just want to tell you . . . thanks. We would still be trapped inside the Pocket or lost in those tunnels if it wasn't for you getting us out of there. Thanks for not abandoning us."

Stein paused, looking at her.

"I love all you guys, ridiculously. Never doubt this—you are all my kids. But don't call me dad, that's weird," Stein said hastily.

Choked-up releases and sighs over the radio.

"Let's roll," Stein said, wiping his cheek.

Two vehicles that hadn't been driven for twenty-five standard Martian years pulled smoothly out of their berths, turned right, and headed toward the end of the cave and the Martian night beyond. Dust continued to rain down occasionally, pebbles rattling the vehicle rooftops.

Aiyana, following the rover, eased the tank out of the large vehicle tunnel and under the open, starry sky. Here was a large, flat plateau, big as any football field. Snugged up against the Mountain slope, two dozen concrete parking spots had been built, but surprisingly, no vehicles were there. The place looked deserted.

The control panel chronometer display in both vehicles suddenly lit up, red digits reading 20:17. Map displays flashed to life on the above-window screens in both vehicles. GPS status on both showed 5-6 satellites overhead and a strong nav signal.

Andie leaned over Aiyana's shoulder. "Whoa, check out that view."

Over the open channel, Stein's voice. "Ares, will you watch for anything rolling toward down at us from above?"

"Mew," came the cat's reply.

"That still blows my freaking mind," Sitara's voice over the radio.

"He can see movement in low light extremely well. Here, let me darken our cabin lights even more . . . and there," Stein said. Aiyana instinctively did the same for the tank.

"Mew," said Ares again.

Reillee asked, "What did he say?"

Stein replied. "He said *mew*. Now please everyone keep your head on a swivel, we're going to have rockslides and crevasses to deal with. Everyone be a spotter for your driver, please. There's no telling how long it's been since this road was maintained. Long drive ahead."

"Are you guys seeing this?" Aiyana asked. "Sitara, what does that look like ahead of us, on the road?"

Sitara said, "are those vehicle tracks, in the dust?"

"Lots of them, maybe a dozen or more."

"But that makes no sense," Aiyana said. "There's no one else here, I mean, we didn't see anyone else, and wouldn't they have grabbed these two rides before leaving?"

"Unless they left years ago," Andie offered.

"Nnooooo, these tracks are sharp, even a gentle breeze would have fuzzed them a little. These are fresh. Besides, they're all identical. These were rovers, and they all left at the same time, very recently."

"Ooooh, look down there." Andie basically shouted across the radio.

Kilometers below them, down on the plains, two . . . no, three MagLev trains rocketed away across the plains in divergent directions, one clearly bound for Port Mons or New Marrakech to the North, the other two tearing across the plains to the right toward Jupiter's Crossing or Nerus. Much slower-moving white headlights and yellow taillights of hundreds of ground vehicles were just now becoming visible, illuminating the dark fields of solar panels as they fled.

Stein only spared a brief sideways glance, and then laser-focused on the dirt and pebble-covered road ahead. Where there were straightaways, a wider road, and no debris, he pushed the vehicle up to 55-60 kph. Where there were boulders, questionable patches, sharp turns, or steep drop-offs, he slowed to jogging speed. They made turn after turn, winding back and forth down the side of Olympus Mons. Left, then right, then sharp left followed by hairpin right. More lights could be seen far below, those slow-moving lines, fanning out in several well-defined directions.

The radio channel fell silent for long moments as everyone took in a spellbinding view.

Chapter Four

Was Hope Alive?

"I wonder if my folks are all right," Aiya said, without preamble.

"Hey, we may still be in range of a tower or two," Sitara said excitedly. "Let's 'ping' our families, so they know we're all right. They should ping us back if they can, correct?"

Everyone got busy pulling out tablets or handy phones.

"Andie, will you do Aiya's ping for her?" Stein said, while holding up his own tablet for Sitara or Ric to grab. "because texting and driving is just ... stupid." A pause, as screens tapped and hopeful pings were pulsed out, in the blind.

Aiyana did not hand a tablet over to Andie.

"Hey, want me to ping your folks?"

Aiyana switched off her radio. "Nope," Aiyana said simply, staying focused ahead as she steered the turns.

"What? Why not?"

"Same deal as before—they won't ping me or look for me. You won't see me begging for their approval—I'm done." Aiyana said, with finality.

Andie looked at her. Then she nodded. Aiyana looked ahead.

"Everything all right back there?" Stein asked from the lead vehicle.

Aiyana cued the radio once more. "Yep, we're all good here."

"Anybody have a response yet? Any return pings?" The comm channel was silent. Nothing. "Okay, that's a good thing—it just means we're outside tower range. Suggest setting pings to repeat every ten until one of us gets a reply," Stein said.

More silence followed as they drove, following dozens of fresh wheel-tracks down, down, down the curving mountainside road.

After another ten minutes of driving, they started dropping in elevation faster as the true steep slopes of the mountainside plunged. Around a new bend, forward floodlights confirmed: a rockslide of huge boulders had fallen loose from a cliff face far above. The road ahead was completely covered in rock piles taller than either vehicle. Stein brought his rover to a stop.

"Well . . . crap," Stein muttered, after looking upslope and downslope. The way forward simply did not exist. The slope below them was too steep to drive down. The roadsides looked tumble-down-like-an-action-flick steep. The largest boulders, jumbled with smaller boulders, piled in a long line of rockfall that stretched above and below the road.

"How do we get past this?" someone asked, barely heard on the radio.

"What if we loop a cable over the boulder and use the tank to tug it free of its resting place?"

"That seems like a bad idea. What if it rolls off the edge, and drags us down with it?"

"Maybe the cable has a quick release? We could have someone ready to do that."

A pause in the conversation.

"Look at the manifest, see what we're hauling. Or maybe our rover has some kind of winch on it?" Sitara asked.

"Or explosives!" Reillee said enthusiastically.

Ric rifled around and pulled out a whiteboard manifest, complete with dry-erase marker, long dried out. "Well, there is a cargo cable winch, but no, nothing I can see . . . our cargo looks like . . . ugh."

"What? What are we hauling?" Stein asked.

"Looks like a shipment of long-expired protein packs, pro-digestive enzymes, you know, that helpful gut bacteria stuff."

"Great, let's dump it out there and it can digest the boulders."

No one spoke for a moment.

"I've got it," Aiyana said over the radio. "Mr. Stein, can you please back up a bit?"

"Uh, sure, Aiya, what do you have in mind?"

"I'm driving a tank," Aiyana said, as if that explained everything. The radio was silent for a moment. "Just trust me."

"Oookay," Stein said.

"Tank people — let's do up our suits, just in case," Aiyana said. Another pause.

Then she nudged the tank forward, pulling past the Endurance, and Stein backed off to make way. The Endurance crew watched as the tank rolled forward, centered on the road, and stopped.

The left tread tracked forward while the right tracked backward. In a matter of seconds, Aiyana had turned the tank around backwards.

Drivers, now face to face, smiled in greeting to one another.

Once she was lined up straight with the road, Aiyana used the back-up camera to ease gently right up against the rockslide. Concentrating intently, and not looking up from the camera screen, she rolled the tank back one little bit at a time. The back end made very gentle contact with a large, round-ish boulder that looked higher on the pile than the others. She pressed the accelerator very gently. The tank bumped to a stop when it touched the boulder.

She pressed the accelerator down a bit more. Still no movement.

Pushing the pedal nearly to the floor, she heard the engine groan with the increased burden. Watching through the front, vehicles face to face, the Endurance crew saw the boulder begin to shift, rolling awkwardly back, up onto the rockslide.

The tank pushed on, one centimeter at a time. Then the speed picked up to walking pace. The boulder spilled aside when it jostled against another, and rolled away downhill. Aiyana kept going, pushing up against an unstable pile of rocks, now visible. She made contact with the pile, and smaller rocks slipped and fell away.

Some metal-rock groaning came over the radio channel.

A larger boulder behind the pile moved, sliding at first, then also rolling away under its own weight. The rock pile was likewise shifting as the upper rocks fell free. From inside the tank, a metal crumpling sound made Andie and Reillee wince and turn to look backward over their shoulders.

"That's just the cargo cage up on the back, nothing critical," Aiyana said. A few ominous thumps and loud bangs sounded inside the tank's thick metal shell. "I hope," she whispered.

The back-up camera view now showed a split image, the left half of the image showing the stars above, the right side almost kissing another large rock inside its protective wire frame. Aiyana squinted and leaned in closer to the image, accelerator pedal still pressed down. The largest of the boulders had rolled free, sliding down the far side of the rock pile, and others were still shifting.

A mass of smaller boulders uphill, half the height of the tank, were no longer supported by the larger ones that had fallen free. They started to move downhill. From the rover, the cat hissed.

"Watch out!" someone shouted on the radio.

"Got this!" shouted Aiyana. Aiyana floored the tank accelerator. Boulders above fell into the gap she had created, but with the speed they had suddenly acquired, continued to roll, tumbling downhill instead of coming to rest in the empty space.

She continued to press onward, instead of retreating, pushed the last of the boulder pile aside, creating a neat, oversized speed bump in the road, as tall as a man, and a roughly-rounded twenty meters from one end to the other.

Aiyana pressed the tank on further, still driving backward, until she was fifty meters beyond the rockslide and back on flat roadway. Stein shook his head in wonder. "Wow," he breathed. "Okay, our turn."

He put the Endurance into low gear and eased it forward. He only scraped the shielded metal underbelly twice, following Aiyana's example of keeping some momentum going.

The rover's large wheels, on independent suspension from each other, rose and fell separately as they pushed over different rocky obstacles. Still, its four occupants were jostled around. The walking pace kept the rover from getting hung up on the protruding rocks underneath. Stein only had to stop and back up once to clear a taller rock jutting up.

"Yessss," someone whispered on the radio after both vehicles were clear of the rockslide. Aiyana stopped the tank on the right side of the roadway. A collective sigh of relief washed over the radio.

The rover pulled up next to the tank and stopped.

"How did you know that would work, Aiya?" Sitara asked.

"I didn't. Desperate times." Aiyana winked through the window, catching Stein's eye.

He gave a hearty smiling thumbs-up in return.

"Aiyana, you the boss." Ric exclaimed.

"And way to go, most excellent tank!" Sitara said.

"Your tank needs a name," Ric said.

"We should call it 'George,'" Reillee suggested.

"You can't call a tank George . . . that's like calling a planet George,"

Sitara said back.

"Still, give it a strong, tough, manly name," Reillee said.

"As long as you don't call it George," Sitara said.

"Okay, you're so smart, you come up with something."

"Um . . ."

Another pause.

"Lauryna," Aiyana said simply.

"Laur-ee-na?" someone asked on the radio.

"Yes, because she's going to save me, she's going to save us all—get us away from danger." Aiyana explained.

A pause while the others mulled it over.

"Lauryna." Ric smiled. "It's a good, strong name."

Stein spoke up. "Before we drive on, let's find a wider spot to do a quick visual check of both vehicles, cool?" Stein said on the radio.

Aiyana turned back to facing forward, and Stein passed the tank to head for a much wider stretch of road, something resembling a side pullout. He drove a full loop around the tank then said, "you picked up a few bowling-ball-sized rocks as fresh cargo, and the cage is crumpled. Looks like something black and slimy burst from a box in the cargo cage. Just oozed down over the back end then froze."

"Spare synthetic oil maybe," Andie said.

Stein continued. "Your left-side tread guards look bent on the back end, but nothing's touching the treads. So, looks okay."

Aiyana did a careful circle of the Rover next and reported all looked in perfect condition.

"Your vehicle could use a power wash, sir," she playfully called over the radio.

Stein smiled at her through the screen. Making eye contact through the windows, he replied, "And yours could use a few love-taps with a ball-peen hammer."

"A ball-p . . . what?"

"It's a . . . forget it. Ask Mr. Chuumock next time you see him," he smiled again. "Yes, I just gave you a homework assignment."

Andie, by reflex, pulled out their tablet, paused, then put it away, blushing slightly.

A pause, then Ric spoke up, "How's our pressure? Any scary lights or leaky sounds?" The radio was quiet while both vehicles did look, listen, and feel checks.

"All quiet and green lights here," Aiyana said, easing out of her helmet seal, letting it fall backwards, and shutting down her suit. Her two passengers did the same.

"We're good over here too," Stein responded. Endurance and Lauryna continued onward, downward, on a long curving ramp for the next half hour. No other rockslides or crevasses stopped their progress. The previous vehicle tracks still stretched out ahead, as if leading on to safer places.

The road ahead led under a high, slender metal bridge. It was clear they were well past halfway down the long winding road, and flat plains stretched out a few kilometers below to the horizon in several directions. A low ridge, far across the solar fields, blocked starlight above the flat horizon.

Soundlessly, a large metal blur whooshed right above them, stirring up dust all around. A fast-passing stream of bright lights lit up the mountainside as both vehicles jolted to a stop in the shock of the moment.

Then the overhead traffic was gone, continuing down the tracks below.

"Whoa." several people gasped simultaneously.

"Was that a MagLev train?"

"Man, that was cool."

Intermittently, the taillights of the train winked into view, then vanished behind some rocks. Then they reappeared on the plains below, curving away gracefully to the left.

"So, that one is heading for Port Mons?" Reillee asked.

Sitara spoke up on the channel. "But think how quickly Port Mons would fill up with people—the welcome center can hold, what, a thousand maybe? Two thousand? They'll probably have to go to the Westdown settlement, or the domed markets of New Marrakech or something."

Both vehicles started back up and rolled on. Moments later, another MagLev train blasted past, behind them and down the tracks in a blur of red and silver. Ten minutes later, on tracks now far behind, a train climbed upwards in a blur of white and silver, heading back into the city.

Both vehicles pressed on for another twenty minutes.

Then an "uh oh" came in like a murmur over the radio. Andie broke the silence. "Uh, Mister Steinheiser? We may have a little problem here. One of our three lights on the cabin's main atmo panel just flipped green to amber."

"Which one? What's the label?"

"It's the CO_2 gauge. I think it's building up, inside here. The lights for both O_2 and overall pressure are both still green."

"If the indicators are the same for all vehicles, that means we have . . . "

"Roughly an hour before it flips red," Aiyana answered. From his driver's seat in the Endurance, Stein nodded.

Reillee looked sideways at Aiyana. Aiyana saw him staring. "What? It was one of the questions on my Skimmer's Permit Test," Aiyana explained.

"Well, we've got our suits. And what about extra filters?" Stein asked, imagining where they might find a fresh CO_2 filter.

"Already checking Mr. Stein–" a long pause, while a search was conducted.

"No, there aren't any extra filters back here in the overhead bins, just an empty drawer labeled 'CO_2 Filters.' Ugh. Are there any extras over in the rover?"

"I'll take a look," Sitara said, climbing out of the front passenger seat to go look. Ric searched around as well. After they both searched around,

Sitara shook her head.

"Found one." Ric answered at length on the radio from the rover.

"Ok, cool, but are they compatible?" Andie asked.

"Looks like this one is labeled Type III, Short, Round. What kind does the tank need, Andie?"

"One sec."

"Which kind?" Reillee was getting anxious.

"Hold on to your potatoes, all right? I have to look it up." A pause. "You guys aren't gonna believe this. Type V, Tall, Hex."

"Great. Shouldn't we have figured this out by now?"

"Right? Ya got any duct tape over there?"

Six humans, and maybe one cat, paused to appreciate the irony.

"Let's press on — we'll just have to find a filter somewhere, or eventually we can all crowd into the Endurance when the time comes."

"I can't believe they didn't stock extras, just in case," Reillee said. "It's so . . . wrong." He looked worried.

Aiyana looked down at the display, the amber light silently urging them to drive faster. She patted the dashboard of the tank. "Come on, baby," she whispered.

As an afterthought, Aiyana set a timer for one hour in red digits, started the countdown, and swiped it up to the display above the passenger seat.

Endurance, with Lauryna faithfully following, finally reached a level patch of ground that felt like the end of the winding mountain road. The road widened to at least three or four lanes, but without any striped lines.

Stein pressed the accelerator, bringing the rover up to its top speed.

"Can you keep up Aiya?" Stein asked.

"Race ya, if you dare," Aiyana replied, grinning. She steered to a different 'lane,' staying with the rover and matching its speed, cruising behind and to the left.

Wide as it was, the road was barely discernible from the low, dusty dunes. From here, a long line of distant taillights, those vehicle convoys far ahead, were visible. "Those lights over there . . . is it an evacuation convoy?" Sitara asked softly from the passenger seat next to Stein.

"Duh," Ric said, leaning forward from the seat behind Sitara.

Sitara bopped Ric on the head. "Bloody Kho-taa," she said.

The stars shined steadily down. The vehicles made steady, speedy progress along the flat, dust-covered road. For a half kilometer, the road curved gently right, and far ahead, a lone, stationary light hovered above the road. They saw a moment later it was a shed, of sorts, with a bright light on top. At the shed, several roads met in an intersection.

As they approached the intersection and the small structure, Stein spoke up. "All the vehicle treads turn back to the right, heading to the Mountain, not to safety."

"That's weird . . . should we go as well? Maybe rescue some folks?"

"I get the feeling none of those vehicles had drivers," Stein mused, his voice trailing off. "All the tread lines are too perfectly straight."

"So they were on auto drive? Or something?"

"Same protocols as the Founder's Stones, probably." Stein said.

"Wait, what? Founder's Stones?" Reillee asked.

"That's right, you guys were all in the Ghosts' Hideout when it happened. Seems like every Founder's stone in the city popped open simultaneously. Escape hatches . . . with ladders, can you believe that?"

"So our families might have made it out already?"

"I sure hope so, all these ground cars, skimmers, and . . . wow, there must be thousands, or maybe tens of thousands of vehicles running in and out of the Mountain to evacuate people. Remember that all the skimmers used to drive the 'roads' of the desert, say thirty or forty standard years ago? It was how people got from city to city before the trains."

Andie's brain, in overdrive as usual, beat the others to a deeper thought. "So . . . all those empty parking spots up where we exited? They just auto-drove to where they were needed."

"But the rockslide: wouldn't that have stopped them completely?"

"No, the tracks went neatly under the rocks. I remember from the back-up camera," Aiyana said. "They prolly got past before it happened."

"And they're still self-driving, probably filled up with people by now," Stein added.

"But how in the world? A million people in a few thousand ground cars?" Andie asked.

"Don't forget rocket shuttles . . . and all the MagLev trains we've been seeing," Ric added.

"Man, those things must be packed." Reillee shook his head.

Andie did some mental gymnastics. "Even if they packed two thousand people on board every train, the evacuation doesn't add up. Even if they had an entire day . . . like 90% would be abandoned to whatever happens to the city."

"Okay . . . now bring in every planetary shuttle, I think there are eighty or a hundred of those, right? They land, people climb aboard in Exo-Suits—and bam. All three running day and night; they just need time," Ric reasoned.

Both vehicles slowed as they approached the building. A single high-watt LED bulb, dusty but burning bright, was perched on its highest point with a few antennas. Without the light bulb, they might have run right into it in the dark.

"I got a ping back! I got a ping, here on my tablet." Sitara said with a thrill. Everyone instinctively checked their own screens. Aiyana looked ahead at the small building, imagining where to park. Sitara immediately got to recording a voice message in the back of the vehicle.

"Ooh, my dad sent me one too," Andie said.

"Anyone else? Parents or family contacts?" Reillee said, shaking his tablet and tapping the screen.

"I've got one," Stein said. "My Tanya is in some huge waiting area, about to load on a massive people mover with eight wheels. She says it has Space-Xcursion Adventures Tour Bus written on the side. What the heck is a tour bus?"

Ric received a ping at almost the same time. "Yep, my sister Merilee . . . um, looks like she's up on the top of the Mountain, in the greenhouses waiting for a rocket shuttle to Port Nerus. That's so crazy."

"At least she's all right," Sitara offered.

They reached the building. Stein drew the Endurance to a halt a dozen meters from the structure, and Aiyana brought Lauryna up alongside. Then she grabbed her own tablet, refreshed it, and checked again.

Andie was at her side. "Anything?"

"Nope," she said simply. She drew in a long, deep breath, and let it out slowly through puffed cheeks. She stared out the window ahead, not really focusing on anything.

Stein glanced over at the tank as he spoke, making eye contact with both Andie and Aiya through the windows. "Looks like it may have some maintenance gear, or other essentials. Maybe the right kind of filter for that amber situation. Shall we check it out?"

"Sure thing, Stein. Who do you want to go, and who will stay here?" Andie asked.

"Well, who's good at fixing things? Anyone can join me," Stein said.

Andie said, "I'm more of a puzzle-solver, not really much of a . . . wrench-turner."

"My aunt is practically screaming for details," Ric said, adding "I need to compose a lengthy text here."

Sitara kept her head down, recording a second message, this one for little Sundeep.

"I'm free to help," Aiyana said. Andie squeezed her shoulder.

Stein furrowed his brow, but kept looking at her. "Sounds good, thank you." He set the brake on the rover and eased out of the driver's position. Over the radio, Andie and Aiyana heard him add "Okay, little buddy, we don't have an ExoSuit for you, so please just stay with the students here in the cab, all right?"

"Mew," came a faint reply over the radio.

"Do you need a litter box? I might be able to bring something back from inside that could work."

"Mrrrr..Meeeew?" Ares said, with an expectant look.

"What did he say? Uh, what did that mean?" Ric asked.

"I haven't figured that out yet," Stein admitted.

Andie spoke up over the radio. "He says he's hungry."

"Is that it? Are you hungry?" Stein asked.

"Mew," Ares said.

"Sucks not having decent vocal cords, huh buddy?" Ric asked the cat.

"Mew," Ares said, looking up at Ric. The teen shook his head, smiling broadly. He scratched the cat's head behind the ears, then turned back to his tablet. Ares hopped back up on the dashboard, looking ahead at the shack with the light on top.

Stein sealed up his suit, powered it on, and checked the vitals. He traded places in the cab with his two students and sealed the airlock compartment door. He could see Aiyana doing similar actions in the other vehicle.

"All set over there, Aiya?" Stein asked on the suit radio.

"I got you loud and clear, Mr. Stein. Why did I volunteer for this . . . ? Okay, turning on cooler air, and my suit air is at . . . 88% or so."

"We've got this—maybe something inside can help us. Bring a tablet in your suit pocket, just in case. Oh, and Aiya?"

"Yeah?"

"Have one person in the tan—Lauryna—listen in to our suit channel. . . but leave their suit air turned off. Can you arrange that?"

"Sure thing."

Andie did a comm check a moment later. From the Endurance, Ric also connected with the suit radio channel, doing a voice check of his own then muting his mike to compose and send important messages.

Stein and Aiyana stepped down from their vehicles and walked to the front. Vehicle headlights cast long, tall human shadows up against the building's white and tan walls. The structure, small enough at first, felt dark and foreboding as they approached.

Above the closed door, a stencil-sprayed sign showed

LOGISTICS SHED #332 (RED TRAILS)

Shed 332 looked to be in decent enough shape. This building was barely wide enough to hold a rover, but had no vehicle airlock. It seemed to be a supply shed for individual or small-group teams with its one walk-through airlock.

"Red Trails, that sounds ominous . . . " Aiyana said, gesturing up at the sign.

"Weren't these solar panel farms originally laid out in colored zones?" Stein asked no one in particular. Aiyana shrugged.

Stein tried to activate the airlock panel with its console power button. No response.

He brushed at it with his gloved fingertips and stabbed a few different buttons. No lights, no activity. Zip. Glancing in through the small airlock window, he could see the inner airlock door stood wide open. Debris was clearly scattered about inside.

"Not good," Stein said.

"What?" Aiyana asked.

"See for yourself," he said, stepping out of her way.

She leaned up, standing tiptoe to look down, inside, and up in all directions. Her hands clenched and released. "Should we still go in?"

Stein nodded. "It should be safe in our suits. I don't imagine there's been any air pressure inside for a very long time," Stein answered. "Hope no one's in there."

Andie spoke up. "I'm surprised the shack didn't implode."

"Yikes. I forgot you were on the channel," Aiyana said.

"Uh, you got this?" Andie said, adding, "Sorry for the jump scare."

"Yeah, Samhain's over, so save it for Halloween, will ya? Eleven months away."

Andie smiled, leaning forward in the tank's driver seat, squinting for a better look. The lone light shone down quietly. Stein reached for the door's bright red handle.

"You might wanna stand aside . . . no, the other side . . . so if anything does come blasting out, you're not in the line of fire."

Stein braced his feet wide, twisting one boot in the dusty ground for better traction. He looked once to make eye contact with Aiyana, then screwed his eyes shut. He pulled down on the handle.

At first, there was nothing. Then a small jolt, as the handle popped free of the dust and grime of ages and swung all the way down. The door popped open slightly, the action disturbing the tiniest bit of dust. Nothing flew out.

Stein opened his eyes. "All right. Still here," he breathed a sigh. Pushing the door, it opened, eventually wide open enough for them to step inside. Aiyana stepped over the threshold first, suit lights shining inside. Stein looked over her shoulder as best he could. He could hear her breathing faster in his ear. She stepped through the second doorway.

The place was a mess, but not a total war zone of clutter. A few papers were scattered, some dark substance had spilled and splattered the entryway floor, long dried out. The walls were lined with cabinets, tool crates, and utility drawers. Small food-pack boxes, empty, filled up an overflowing waste bin in a corner, next to the entrance to a single bathroom stall, open and dark inside.

An early-model Exo-Suit hung on its storage hook on the far wall. The dark faceplate stared back at them. In the middle of the room stretched a long table with a handful of chairs pushed under—no food items were there, but a couple hot/cold beverage canisters had been set down before the last people here left.

Stein licked his dry lips, and suddenly realized he was extremely thirsty. "Incredible," he said.

"What's that?" Aiyana asked.

"This place, 332, is all shot up, yet it's still doing the job. Still standing strong, still holds its integrity."

On the far side, a chair was knocked over and behind it, a small sealed blue plastic barrel lay on its side. Here and there, other clutter and detritus had been apparently kicked out of the way. Two other small blue kegs stood against the wall next to the ghostly Exo-Suit.

Stein walked straight, while Aiyana walked left, around the table on the other side. A dead rat, desiccated and shrunken, lay in a corner. Aiyana drew in her breath sharply but didn't scream. She exhaled slowly, willing herself to calm.

"Where's Ares when you need him?" Aiyana said.

Stein nodded, looking at her and smiling. "Right?"

"Let's check these cabinets . . . oh, and open every drawer you can find. We need filters, anything that looks edible, and any full air canisters."

"Ooo, look up, there," Aiyana pointed.

Above the racks and cabinets was a huge mounted map of color zones. Three-digit numbers, interconnected by red lines, blue lines, green lines, and brown lines, covered the map in a chaotic spiderweb. The center of the map showed wide fields of solar panels, interspersed with more of the three-digit markers.

"Now that's helpful. Well done."

They both leaned back as best they could so their headlamps could illuminate the map, then snapped enhanced images on their tablet cameras. Then they swiped the digital pics to the rest of the group, and to both vehicles' computer screens.

Stein thumped the blue plastic canisters with his boot. It skittered away, the fallen one, but both standing containers resisted his kick. He gripped each from a top handle and hefted it; heavy and sloshing slightly.

The label on each read "WATER, POTABLE, 10L."

"Yes. At least we have some water now, looks like we are now the proud owners of two . . . yep, ten-liter canisters. Plenty to last us all until we get to where we're headed. The rest of the day, maybe longer."

"Looks like there's another one over there," Aiyana said, pointing over in the far corner.

"Hmm, we've got enough for ourselves and this drive with just two." He paused, thinking. "Could you set that other full one up on the table, and leave it there?"

"Um . . . can do?" Aiyana said, lifting the heavy water canister and thumping it onto the table. " . . . in case others need a rescue from the three-thirty-second?"

"In case others need a rescue from the three-thirty-second." Stein nodded, smiling.

No filters, no air tanks—but drinkable water, that they needed. After opening the last few drawers and seeing nothing else worth salvaging, Aiyana stood before a large white board, still bearing the faded writings of the last logistic-ey things done in this room. She tried some of the dry-erase markers; all were dried out. She looked at the tray, and pried up a red grease pencil instead, and wrote on the side of the board that still had empty space.

Aiya was here
Olympians forever!

Stein watched her do this and nodded. Aiyana turned to Stein, blushing in her helmet slightly, and smiled back. As they stepped toward the exit, Stein took an old tool tray, dumped out a handful of battered screwdrivers and wrenches onto the table, and thumped the back of it with a gloved hand. Some dust fell out, but otherwise it was now empty. He tucked the tray under one arm.

He hefted one water canister, and Aiyana grabbed the other. As an afterthought, she grabbed the largest crescent wrench Stein had dumped out and slipped it in a belt loop on her hip. "Is this water safe to drink straight from the canister?" Aiyana asked.

They stepped outside, and she closed the outer door.

"Probably not. We should filter it through both vehicles . . . or use those Emergency FilterStraws, even. Those things last forever; I've used them on skimmer rides with my buddy Nikos, down through the *Noctis*."

"That sounds epic," Aiyana said. Stein murmured in response. He scanned the distant horizons to the east. The first hints of dawn glowed above the mountain tops.

As they rounded the vehicles to climb back inside, Aiyana let out a shout. "Hey! Hey, look at this." Stein set his water canister down and joined Aiyana at the back of the tank.

"What is it?" Ric chimed in over the radio.

"Check it out . . . supply boxes strapped to the outside."

Aiyana thumbed open an unpressurized case beneath the twisted cargo cage. Here different parts and consumables rested in a jumble inside. Flipping past a few innocuous things, she lifted and tossed aside a burst food pack, some empty water bottles, and proudly hefted a CO_2 cartridge, still in its silver shrink-wrap. On the side, in plain letters, was printed Carbon Dioxide Scrubber, Filter Type V, Tall, Hexagon.

"Oh yeah!" Stein called out. "Way to go Aiya. Let's do the swap-out now and use the amber one as an emergency backup." Both drivers climbed back inside their vehicles, each hefting a water jug. Filters were switched out, and the Lauryna's amber light turned green after a few moments. Aiyana patted the dashboard again, a huge grin on her face.

Both vehicles backed up from the building, and turned to the right to continue on across the plains.

First light crept across the skies above; the stars began to fade. The highest slopes of the Mountain were, naturally, the very first touched by direct sunlight—something none of them had ever seen before. With one glance back at the shack that probably had saved their lives, Stein led his little convoy toward the much longer convoy, far ahead across the plains.

As they approached the line, they could see hundreds of vehicles moving in perfect precision, all at the same stately pace . . . auto-drive for certain. The long line of cars, reminiscent of some ant colony in an old-Earth biology video, drove from the far right toward the far left, heading North. Endurance and Lauryna slowed.

"Can we cut into this line?"

"I'm not sure we would want to try."

Aiyana pulled the tank to a full stop alongside the rover, with the line of steadily advancing vehicles moving across their path, directly ahead no more than 30 meters.

The occupants of both vehicles stared across at each other, considering.

"Look over there, left side," Ric said. "Is that the end of some other convoy?"

"Might be our best bet," Stein said, "we just slide in behind, go wherever they're going."

Stein paused, just looking in the windows of the convoy ahead of him, occasionally seeing faces pressed up to windows, group after ragged group, looking out.

"Any objections? Thoughts?" There were none. "Right then, follow me, Aiya, but let's not automatically assume we're going exactly where that convoy is headed. Let's keep our distance, but don't look like we're trying to keep our distance."

Andie spoke up. "I'm betting that longer convoy is heading for Port Mons or New Marrakech, but where is . . ." She paused, then zoomed in to the map photo taken from Shed 332. "Hey, check the map you took pictures of—that blue dot is where the shorter convoy is headed, I think? It's written small, kind of fuzzy." They zoomed in to the picture in both vehicles.

"Blue Edge?" Ric asked, "or Blue Bridge?" They drove on, and in ten minutes had caught up to the end of the shorter convoy. Both vehicles matched the 60 kph speed of their chosen convoy. The longer convoy continued uninterrupted on the right, with a child waving every so often at the tank and the rover. Andie waved back.

As they approached a cluster of low hills, the two convoys diverged. The right-side line of vehicles peeled away, following a road that led down a canyon. The left-side convoy, the one they had joined, climbed up a steep ramp, avoiding the canyon completely.

Signposts at the fork in the road showed bold white letters on a black background. Two signs pointed right, and a smaller sign pointed left. "Blue Ridge," Stein clarified, seeing the signposts ahead, adding " . . . according to that sign, it's just fifteen clicks away," Stein said, grinning heartily. "Ladies and gents, we'll be back in civilization in less than 30."

A flood of relief washed over them. Stein heard giggling over the radio, and he looked sideways at Sitara and saw tears welling up in her eyes. Ric just hugged on her from behind the passenger seat where she sat. Someone let up a "whoop" across the vehicle radios.

As the tank approached and passed the road signs, Andie called out the distances. "Wow, so it's 15 to Blue Ridge, 75 kilometers to Port Mons, and 840 to New Marrakech? Yikes."

"Right? I wouldn't want to be stuck in those people movers for ten hours. That's a painful long haul."

"Maybe they'll stop somewhere to rest a while? There must be some rest stops."

"We'll figure it out when we get to Blue Ridge, whatever that is." Stein said. They drove onward and climbed up a single-lane road for twenty minutes. When the road leveled out, it widened significantly. Here, a long line of empty vehicles waited their turn to head back down the Blue Ridge road.

Now it was bright enough to see all around — they turned their vehicle headlights off. It became clear the road was about to end, heading straight for a tall-standing cliff that climbed straight up to a sharp ridgeline above. Right before meeting the rock face, the road turned sharply left and ran straight along the rock wall. The vehicle line ahead slowed and stopped, all lined up in some odd, perfectly straight traffic jam. After a few moments, the vehicles before them moved forward a hundred meters, then they stopped again.

As they waited to go forward, everyone peered out their nearest windows.

"Check out the Mountain," someone on the radio exclaimed. They all turned to look left. None had ever seen it from this perspective before. Even from a few kilometers above the plains and some thirty kilometers away, it was still too large to be completely viewed from this angle.

"So majestic . . ." someone whispered.

Stein and Aiyana eased their vehicles forward whenever they could.

Roll, stop. Roll, stop.

Andie looked up through the front window. "Huh. There's a row of windows up there, like ten stories above us. Some kind of bunker maybe?"

"Or a VIP lounge for us, with fine dining and fancy drinks?" Reillee said, energized.

"Yeah, I'm sure that's exactly what it is," Sitara said. The convoy moved forward again.

They eased under a long, unbroken awning over the road, leaving them feeling like they were in a traffic tunnel, but with the left side wide open.

Continuing forward, alcoves and caves appeared on the right side, cut right into the cliff wall. They could see abandoned maintenance spaces, some construction gear, and what looked like several wide garages. Most stood empty, but a few had machine parts and empty shells of abandoned vehicles. The last few people-movers in front of them had stopped to line up with a row of large vehicular airlock doors extending out from the rock face. Clearly, this was where people exited their vehicles to go inside.

Ahead, the recently-emptied buses rolled away around a cluster of rocks and out of sight. Stein squinted, then keyed his radio mike.

"Aiya?"

"I'm here."

"Let's not try to dock here, we need to park in those alcoves behind us. Can you reverse, then back in? Pick a garage big enough for us both?"

"We just passed one that might fit both. Okay, backing up." She threw the gears into reverse and neatly backed the Lauryna into a large, empty bay. Stein backed the Endurance in beside her a moment later. They put both vehicles in park.

"Weird, no signal in here," Reillee said, tapping his phone screen.

"So, let's power down, seal up our Exo-Suits, and see if we can find an airlock," Stein instructed the others. They all re-sealed suits and did the usual checks, eager to get inside and find out what this Blue Ridge place was all about.

Stein hefted a cat-in-the-box, and a moment later they all stood in the large, multi-bay garage. They walked to the back, climbed up steps onto a raised metal walkway, and found an airlock entry point.

"Civilization," someone whispered over the radio.

"A ladies' room," someone else whispered, eliciting a chuckle.

The group stepped inside.

Chapter Three

Oh, For A Muse Of Fire!

O nce through the airlock, they found themselves in a break room. Quickly shrugging out of the suits they had worn for ten hours, they flopped the suits down across couches and chairs, in case they were needed later. Ares wandered to an empty plant box in the corner.

"Now that is a thing of beauty," Reillee said, noticing a WC sign over a nearby door. He ran for the door, but Ric beat him to it. "Heyyyy!" Reillee protested as Ric shut the door in his face.

Sitara shook her head, rolling her eyes. "Boys." She looked around a corner and found a second bathroom, a larger one. She beckoned to Aiyana and Andie, who gratefully followed.

Ten minutes later, when everyone was done, they met up in a small, adjoining recreation room. The hallways here looked empty, but they led to abandoned closets, a small bunk room, a kitchen, and an open dormitory. The living space here had a maintenance focus, a serious purpose.

"I'm guessing there's more to this place since we haven't seen anyone else yet. Let's go find out what's really going on." The group started down what looked like the main hallway.

Aiyana held Stein back for a moment while the others wandered ahead. She spoke in a low tone.

"Mister Stein, if they do some kind of roll call thing . . . don't mention me," Aiyana said hastily.

"Why not? Your folks will be worried sick, I'm sure," Stein protested.

"I'm pretty sure they aren't worried . . . sick or otherwise. I'm letting it ride, to see if they reach out at all."

"I can't talk you out of this?"

"Please, I'm not asking you to decide if what I'm doing is right or legal. I'm asking you to trust me." She looked into his eyes, expression intense.

Stein looked back, his face betraying a difficult inner struggle. "Aiya, I have to report that you made it out in one piece."

Aiyana reached into her oversized pocked and held up her tablet. "Look, no ping. Nothing at all. If my folks ping me, which they won't, or . . . even if they reach out to you to see if I'm okay, then I'll message them and do what I must. But if they never do, I'll have my answer. Does that make sense?"

"No, it doesn't." He kept eye contact. Aiyana said nothing.

He sighed, then his voice softened. "But I'm not living your life, am I? You are. That, I can trust in." He made up his mind. "You have my silence."

"Thank you. Really." She exhaled, giving him a big hug. She spoke into his shoulder. "I reach adult status in just a few months if that helps." He smiled, nodding.

Stein let the hug go, and they caught up with the others, Ares too. A few turns later, the group reached another door, bearing a 'No Access" sign, but the sound of a crowd came in from the other side. Opening the door, they found themselves facing in a huge surge of humanity, hundreds of people, all shuffling down a large hallway, heading to the right.

They stepped through as a group and nonchalantly joined the throng.

Andie looked back, making a note of the door and its location. Stein noticed Andie doing this and did the same as he adjusted Ares in his arms. The cat looked all around, unnerved by the crowd.

The refugee processing center seemed to be barely-controlled chaos. Small children cried fussily, miserable from their own individual ordeals, while parents and teenagers stood bedraggled. Some munched on energy bars or drank water bottles handed out by badge-wearing volunteers.

The first station ahead, a podium, seemed to have the purpose of getting groups sorted into lines for in-processing. A lady looked down from a small, raised lectern as Stein and his students approached. She made eye contact with Stein, still carrying Ares in his arms.

"How many in your party?"

"Uh, six, ma'am. Seven if you count this guy."

"And are you their parent? Are you parent to any of these minors?"

"No, I'm their science teacher. We were separated from our families, but we suspect they're being sent somewhere else."

"That's very common, I'm afraid. Unaccom—"

"I'm sorry, Ma'am, but what's through those doors ahead? Are we under lock-down?"

"No, this is just an evacuee site that's never been used before today. After you pass through the next set of stations, accountability first, then medical, you will have free run of the facility. Inside there are dining halls, individual rooms, showers, and a small recreation area. We are all in this together until the crisis is over, I'm afraid."

"I understand. Will I be able to remain with my students? We've been through a lot together."

The officer looked from one student to the next. The teens nodded their agreement, intently listening for the verdict on their immediate future.

"Once through the next station, your status will be updated on the MarsNet from MISSING/UNKNOWN to PRESENT/ACCOUNTED FOR

(BLUE RIDGE). You are free to regroup after you are assigned your CHU unit. Now, unaccompanied minors — "

Again, Stein interrupted. "Sorry, what's a chew?"

"Consolidated Housing Unit, C-H-U, your CHU is your shelter, your personal sleeping space while you're a guest of this facility. So, unaccompanied minors, please go stand in line number six for accountability. Sir, you can go to line one, it's the fastest.

Stein pointed at Ares, held in his arms. "Can my — "

"Yes, your cat can remain with you, and if you have her shot records, that will help get you through medical. Thank you for getting your students out safely, that's . . . pretty commendable. You can all meet up on the far end. Next, please."

They shuffled past the podium into a larger room, where one line split into six. Stein thanked the lady as he passed, and she nodded back.

As the teens peeled off to join line #6, Aiyana grabbed Andie by the arm. She whispered in Andie's ear, who nodded a few seconds later. Aiyana returned to stand with Stein, watching the other four teens leave. Andie gathered up Sitara, Ric and Reillee, quietly telling them not to ask any questions. They gave Andie quizzical looks but kept quiet. Stein noticed Aiyana by his side.

"Aiya?" Stein started to ask.

Aiyana's voice dropped, barely above a whisper. She kept her eyes ahead while leaning into him, saying "Mister Stein, all I need you to do is not call me out. Can you do that?"

"Uh, maybe. What are you planning?"

"To not be accounted for."

"How do you think you'll make it through the next four stations without being noticed?" He motioned ahead, pointing out several blue-uniformed personnel actively scanning the crowd.

"I'm working on it."

"I better work on it with you."

Groups shuffled forward in their six lines. A few uniformed MERF technicians and guards eyed the crowd, presumably keeping order. None were armed. Many looked bored or tired.

As Aiyana and Stein reached third in line to have their identity scanned, Aiyana made deliberate eye contact with Andie through the crowd. Andie gave the barest of nods.

Andie screamed.

Through an impressive blood-curdling shriek, they started jumping around, bumping into both friends and strangers. People in the nearby lines jolted in surprise. Ares snapped his head around toward Andie and hooked his claws into Stein's shoulder. All faces in the processing center turned to look, except Stein, who watched Aiyana slip away. Even the MERF uniforms stepped toward the scream, trying to crane their necks over the crowd to see what the problem was.

Aiyana stepped lightly behind the distracted guards, or whatever their title was, to the far side of the first station. She put on a look of mild curiosity, acting interested in whoever had screamed. She now stood in section two at the back of the next line.

Andie's scream faded into shouts of, "get it out, get it out!" while dancing in place like a maniac. "A spider, down the back of my shirt—I can feel its legs." They shook off their jacket, a collared shirt, and plucked at their white tank-top, for effect. Ric brushed down Andie's back, assuring them no such bug was there.

Andie apologized profusely to strangers nearby when nothing creepy-crawly could be found, breathing heavily. They picked up and shook out their dropped items in a desperate attempt to find the critter, though of course, nothing crawled out.

A moment later, guards and MERF personnel stepped back to their spots, and got the lines moving again.

"Are you really that freaked out about spiders?" Sitara asked Andie.

"Nah, I kind of got used to them. Our first apartment was below street level, and I found them in my room all the time. They're kinda cool." Andie smiled, pulling on the jacket.

Sitara laughed out loud, then stopped herself.

Back in line #1, Stein had his palm scanned and Ares had his neck microchip scanned. He caught up to Aiyana, who had waited for him.

"Clever girl," Stein said to her.

"After all we've been through? Not as clever as I'd like—I still have three more distractions to come up with. Care to help with the next one?"

"Well . . . you don't need a distraction if you work here. See that volunteer, over there?"

"Yeah, the brunette with the huge chest, handing out waters?"

"That's her. See anything missing?"

"No, I . . . . oh, wait." She turned back to Stein, who let the Volunteer badge peek out from under Ares in his arms.

"After Andie's little performance, she walked up to me. She really liked Ares and asked to hold him." Stein shrugged. "So I let her. She doesn't know it, but she gave me this badge. And no, I didn't touch her."

"Interplanetary man of mystery," Aiyana said, smiling up at her teacher.

"Right? Okay, all you need to do now . . . is follow some other volunteer back through to wherever the food and water is, and then stay on the far side and wait for us."

"You make it sound simple," Aiyana said.

"Remember, you're on a mission to pick up water and snacks—see the work they're doing? Just don't look around, like you need anyone's permission. In fact . . . I have an idea," Stein said, hastily clipping the 'MERF Volunteer' badge to the lapel of Aiyana's collar.

Stein raised his voice, slightly louder than necessary. "Miss, I have a splitting headache." He rubbed his forehead with his free hand and looked at Aiyana. "Can you please go see if they have some pain meds on the other side? My head is killing me."

Aiyana caught on quickly, responding with a wink, "I don't know if they'll let me, but I can sure go and ask."

"Thank you. The sooner the better, being stuck in this line," he called after her as she walked away. He managed a weak smile though his 'pain.'

Aiyana walked behind another volunteer, a man carrying an empty protein-bar containers, and stayed in step with him right past all remaining stations. None of the uniforms paid her the slightest attention.

At the next station, medical, Stein answered routine questions about personal illness, any injuries sustained while evacuating the city, and so forth. He kept his responses truthful but vague, then messaged his students briefly not to mention that they had their own transport. *Don't lie, but just don't bring it up.* Then came two more stations, Interwebs CityNet connectivity and basic Blue Ridge digital info-packs.

After the last station, Aiyana caught up with the group as they were being herded into a small theater with a large screen down front. The words "Situation Update" dominated the screen, bland dark letters on a white background. Aiyana walked beside Andie.

"Hey, there you are." Reillee said, smiling broadly.

Everyone looked at Aiyana, and a few hugs were shared.

"Hey miss, where's my Ibuprofen?" Stein asked in mock indignation.

Aiyana bopped him lightly on the arm. "For your . . . headache? Suck it up, sir, and have a nice day." She smiled.

Stein burst out laughing. The others grinned as they walked to the middle of the theater to find their seats. Ares stood on Stein's lap, stretched, and walked across several laps to get to Andie.

Then Ric spoke up. "Yeah, Aiya, we were all a little hungry over in queue #6 . . . I mean, I thought you'd bring us a candy bar or something, o keeper of the backstage pass. You had free run of the place, right?"

"I wanted to do that, sure, but did you get a look at the badges?"

Ric frowned, trying to remember what they looked like.

Aiyana continued, saying "they're numbered. That means that Miss Wellendowed would eventually notice her missing badge — getting others to help her search. They would have found it on me."

"So what did you do, ya ninja?" Reillee asked.

"I . . . uh, dropped it in this small break room, the one for volunteers, and joined a crowd of people heading for the cafeteria . . . 'scuse me, the Dining Hall, they're picky about names, and I did a little exploring too. By the way, nice scream, Andie. Made me jump, and I was expecting it."

"Thank you very much," Andie said, cheeks rosy. "I expect payment for my amazing performance." They scratched Ares, who was now purring contentedly and leaning in to the scratches.

"Give you all my pocket money, if it wasn't so useless in this place," Aiyana replied.

The lights dimmed. The briefing was about to begin. A MERF spokesman stood at the front.

"Ladies and gentlemen, I'm Technician Parsons, and I'm here to give you the latest update on our situation, evacuating the city. I'm sure you have a thousand questions, but I ask you to please let me get through my part, which will explain much. Then I'll try to answer your questions. Let's jump straight in."

The slide changed to a map of the surface of Mars, complete with the seven cities, smaller outposts, rail routes, and roads connecting them.

"Right now, we're in a facility designed by the original Builders more than a hundred standard years ago — they named it Blue Ridge. It has a fifteen-thousand-person capacity, citizens and MERF people combined, because that's how many were living in the city at the time this place was carved out. They didn't anticipate we would eventually number a million souls or that the Mountain would come alive in our lifetimes."

The audience paid rapt attention; the screen changed to a cutaway of the Mountain. A star up near the top-right edge of the plateau showed the Mons Megaplex city, with dozens of rock layers going down to the flat plains and deeper into Mars' crust. Well below the plains, a red line went across the lowest rock layers.

"The magma is rising, but verrry slowly. We may have five more days before it reaches the city, or we may have two weeks. Unfortunately, it seems to surge then pause, making estimates difficult. Regardless, we must treat this as an immediate emergency. No one is taking this lightly, and many of us haven't slept for more than twenty-four hours, much like yourselves." A few yawns around the room confirmed this.

"The majority of MERF personnel, however, are still inside the Mountain, working evacuations in three different ways. The main staging area is under the city, using ground vehicles, rovers and buses, like the ones we all arrived in.

"They're also using MagLev trains to speed people westward to Jupiter's Crossing and Nerus, and north toward New Marrakech. Those trains are in surge mode, running double-capacity, at top speed, around the clock.

"The rocket fleet has been launching from atop the Mountain, in all three directions toward the other three space ports, and then still other trains carry the people to the more distant cities. The entire planet's resources are on full support through the crisis.

"I know you are more concerned about your family and friends, so let's discuss that part next. If you have an electronic device, please grab it out now and let's connect you to your Accountability App.

"Please find the icon on your MarsNet with this logo," Parsons said, changing the slide. "See that white calligraphy, the letter "A" with the circle, on the blue background?"

He looked down to the front row; a lady had raised her handy phone.

"Yes, ma'am, that's the one. Once you open the App, please first check your own status by entering your name, first and last in their blanks. If it says 'PRESENT/ACCOUNTED FOR (BLUE RIDGE)' then you have been correctly in-processed and the system is up to date for you. Before we do any searches for others, which I know you are all eager to do, is anyone not showing 'present and accounted for?'"

He paused. Aiyana ignored his question while she typed in a search for her own folks. No one raised a hand.

"Very good then. Soon enough, you'll learn that all entertainment streaming and video streaming apps have been disabled, to avoid crashing our Blue Ridge CityNet. You will be able to text your loved ones any time you wish, and we advise you to 'ping' them to make first contact if you haven't already.

"Please keep in mind those convoys and trains, many of them, will be underway for hours, and many citizens are still waiting their turn to evacuate. This will take days. So a 'status unknown' does not mean anything except that they haven't arrived at their first stop yet. So please do not jump to conclusions, and keep checking every so often. This will take time.

"Your loved ones, as soon as they reach a location with a reliable signal, should receive your ping, and be able to ping you back. The important thing here is you are safe. Reflect on that please, and I ask you as a personal favor, reach out to as many people here as you can, your CHU neighbors, the MERF technicians stationed here, who miss their families every bit as much as you do. Get to know them. Volunteer if you can and keep as busy as possible."

"Now, what are your questions?"

Several hands went up, and he started calling on different people in the audience in turn.

"When will we be able to return to the Mons-Plex?"

"If it fills up with magma, which is possible, we will not be returning. But we don't know that for certain — the rising magma may slow down and not fill up the city. I'm no geologist, and even if I were, I wouldn't want to make dire predictions any more than I would want to give false hope. We will just have to wait and see. We can only monitor things, from up in the AEOC."

"The what?" someone else asked, down front.

"Up at the top of Blue Ridge, MERF's Alternate Emergency Ops Center, is keeping a close eye on the Mountain and the evacuation. The primary facility back in the city is still running everything from the business district, though we expect they will transfer control here in a day or two."

"How is our evacuation progress?" someone in the back called out.

"It's slow, we will need every hour the Mountain gives us to get everyone out. I don't have exact numbers, but progress is slow. It takes time to evac a million people."

Murmurs erupted all around the room at hearing this.

Another hand was raised. "How long will we be able to survive in here? Is there enough food? Air?"

"Yes, we have enough for all our needs for the time being. We are bringing in food shipments from multiple ports, including automated supply convoys in cargo trucks. Shipments are arriving constantly, as well as being sent to other cities as well. So please, get your three squares a day — it is far easier to keep us all healthy than try to heal someone who falls sick from malnourishment or dehydration.

"Let's also consider the air for a moment. You might have noticed there are no trees here at all. The Builders chose this place when they discovered hot springs feeding the tunnels far below, and we are growing huge vats of blue-green algae to constantly produce our oxygen. Our MERF biologists are growing these vats at the fastest rate possible, and they will be able to stay ahead of the demand, as long as we don't take in any more evacuees.

I suggest avoiding the algae life support sections though, it stinks down there." A few chuckles around the room.

"So, unless you really need to clear your sinuses, or you are a trained biologist and feel like lending a hand, I'd stay up here in the residential and recreation areas.

"On that subject, let me bring up a list of jobs for you to consider. You probably noticed the volunteers who kept you hydrated and fed during your in-processing."

He changed the slide, and a list of volunteer opportunities came up. Most were housekeeping roles: refuse, laundry, cook staff, janitorial, personnel processing, and similar duties.

Reillee leaned over to Aiyana. "You should volunteer for in-processing, I hear you're excellent at that," he whispered, grinning broadly.

"And I can keep people from falling asleep." Andie said.

Parsons the Briefing Officer continued.

"The need for volunteers could not be greater. Our thanks in advance for all who are willing to help. With that, let me have you all go and get a meal, and find your CHU. Volunteers are standing behind the back row, and they are happy to assist you. If you have other questions, please join me down in the front. Thank you all, I wish you well."

Walking in the direction of the canteen and mess hall, five teens, a teacher, and a cat looked forward to soothing rumbling bellies, and then grab a much-needed rest inside their CHUs, whatever those might be. Aiyana spoke up as they walked out of the briefing hall. "The food doesn't look half bad."

Aiyana led on, straight ahead through a meeting point of three tunnels.

"Down that way, on the right, that's where our CHUs are, our dorm rooms. But I don't have one assigned, so maybe someone will share with me? Anyways, back that other way is a second CHU residences area, mainly the MERF people, plus the larger of the washroom facilities. Behind us, up that elevator, is the AEOC thingy, where officials come and go through security. They won't let us through without some major authorization."

"This way to the Mess Hall." Aiyana led on, straight ahead. Volunteers came and went, working the food service lines, hauling away kitchen waste, restocking trays and utensils, and doing every other necessary thing.

Meal choices were limited, but the first meal, chicken a la king over brown rice was surprisingly tasty. They washed it down with what tasted like grape Kool-Aid. Apparently desserts were at the evening meal only, giving everyone something sweet to look forward to. After eating, the group set trays on a conveyor belt leading to the back and they exited the dining hall to find their CHU residences.

In the residential cavern, where rough-carved walls stood least five stories tall, they found thousands of stacked small-cubicle residences, the Consolidated Housing Units. Metal staircases and walkways climbed up four flights, all supported by girders and I-beams anchored into cavern walls and the ceiling above. The rooms themselves were smaller than the SmartHotel rooms where visiting students were housed in ACSA — closer to sleep lockers than hotel rooms.

Stein and his students were housed in completely different areas. Stein peeled off, walking with the cat once more in his arms in what he hoped was the right direction. Ares scanned around, taking it all in, sniffing the air. He wiggled down out of Stein's arms and walked alongside the man.

Andie and Aiyana headed together up to Andie's assigned unit, and the others found their rooms on the same level, a few doors down. They were up on the highest level, four stories up the metal stairs, and down the walkway to the far end.

They entered their dwelling, a simple, old-fashioned key-and-lock system with a brass disc engraved with the cluster number, floor, and door number. Inside furnishings were simple, but functional. The bed looked to be a full-size, enough for two to sleep side by side maybe, with a metal clothing closet that, when opened, had simple shelves on one side and a space to hang up clothes on the other. Both spaces stood empty.

By the door was a simple flip-down table and single aluminum chair. At the back of the unit, a slotted, fan had been fitted into the back wall, with a simple chrome switch to increase the airflow through the unit.

There was room enough for the two teens to move past each other as they explored their new home. No plumbing was evident, but next to the flip-down table, a single power outlet with two plugs stood ready.

The bed had a mattress, but no sheets, no pillows. Andie slipped off their jacket, rolled it in a ball, and flopped down on the mattress, coughing in the small dust cloud. Using the jacket as a rolled-up pillow under their head, Andie looked up at the ceiling, eyes closed.

Aiyana smiled at this simple act. "Never thought I'd describe our furniture back in The Pocket as luxurious," she said to her roommate.

"Mm hmm," Andie replied, letting out a deep sigh they had been holding in for ten hours or longer. "I miss the big Afghan carpet . . . whoever brought it in for us."

"Think about it, I bet we have Stein to thank for that. Oh, hey, check this," Aiyana said, sitting down in the aluminum chair, "there's an info-card stuck on the mirror . . . hmm, looks like linens are at the supply station by the mess hall, and we can charge our devices on this pad built into the pop-down table, right . . . um . . . here."

She released the catch on the table, and when it clicked into its 'open' position, a dark charging pad in the tabletop became obvious. She went on. "The card also describes consolidated shower units, toilet trailers, water conservation tips, off-limits areas and food services."

"So, let's go grab some linens, I guess?" Andie suggested.

Andie and Aiyana headed back toward the mess hall and the supply windows. As they passed by, the large projection in the common area showed news coverage of the evacuation and how excruciatingly slow things were going. Estimates put the evacuation at under ten percent complete.

Stein and Ares, however, were assigned a CHU unit on a different block and level. After getting himself and Ares settled in, he pinged Aiyana and Andie to invite them both to come chat with him in person in the place he and Ares now called home. Then he connected with the CityNet. It was high time he made an important call to his dear Tanya.

* * *

The teens put their linen run on hold.

A short time later, the two knocked at Stein's door. Andie could hear voices inside, and heard Stein complain about Ares stepping in front of the camera as he chatted with his bride. After a few more murmured phrases, the call ended and Stein opened the door.

"Yikes, students in my home, this is so awwwkwaaaard . . . " he said with a sideways grin. He waved them in.

Andie rolled their eyes, and said, "Because your home is sooo much grander than ours," with a smile. Andie walked over to scratch Ares behind the ears where he sat on the bed.

"Was that your wife?" Aiyana asked. "How did you even get video to work?"

"I cheated. I logged in to my Mons High School faculty portal—they haven't shut down the classroom connections yet. So basically, I tricked the CityNet into thinking I was vid-chatting with her from F-105," Stein said.

"Clever," Andie commented.

Stein smiled at the compliment. "Check it out—I can also watch the teacher cam in the classroom, and pan it out the window, the blinds were left open. Maybe we can get a glimpse of how things are going back home. You know, if the school gets flooded with . . ." Stein looked grim, then shook off his dark thoughts. "Anyhow, I've been thinking about our vehicles. We should keep them for future use, so that means we need to do a few things."

"I'm not giving up the Lauryna," Aiyana said firmly. "So whatever you're thinking, I already agree."

"And I have no intention of abandoning the Endurance," Stein said back. "Your tank is ancient, and the rover is a small-capacity vehicle, so they won't be needed for the evacuation. We need to do a few things—stock them up, as if we're about to drive clear to Nooma Outpost, or wherever. Then, figure out how to permanently block them from being remotely commandeered into some convoy."

"Where we parked them . . . there was no signal, right? And we disabled the auto-drive. So in our chosen parking spots—I don't think they can be taken away," Andie said.

"Still, better safe than sorry. Want to go do that now?"

"Absolutely," Aiyana responded firmly.

Andie shrugged. "Okay, and while you two are doing all that technical stuff, I can use that time to continue looking into Eli Ellis."

"You're doing that now?" Aiyana looked confused.

"Yes, there's things he wanted us to find, and I haven't finished going through all his video journals. I'd rather not wait until the burial chambers are filled up with magma, to learn whatever he left us to discover."

Stein just stood there, confused. "Um . . . burial chambers?"

"Let's walk and talk, if that's all right," Aiyana said. "I can tell you on the way."

"Um . . . okay, let me see if I have everything," Stein patted front and back pockets on his trousers and his vest then looked down at Ares. The cat squinted his eyes.

"What? You have water, food, and a makeshift litter box. What more can a cat ask for?"

Ares just looked at him.

"I'll take him with me," Andie said suddenly. "Would you like that, you furr-ocious beast?"

"Mew," Ares mewed, hopping down to stand next to Andie.

"It's settled then," Andie stood, and brushed right past their friend and teacher, with Ares following. Aiyana shrugged and exited as well, saying nothing further. Stein locked the CHU door behind him, pocketed his key, and they all filed down the nearest metal staircase.

A moment later, and after goodbye hugs, Andie and Ares peeled off to walk through the common area back to Andie's room. A few people milled about the common areas, but not too many. Andie was surprised to notice another cat, a beautiful gray long-hair wearing a kitty harness, relaxing on a table where two older ladies conversed.

"Hey look, you may have a friend or two here after all," Andie mused. Ares did not comment but looked at the other cat, sniffing the air, his tail twitching back and forth.

* * *

Stein and Aiyana left the residential cavern and turned past the theater toward the in-processing stations. The huge space was completely deserted now, its tables and chairs folded up and carried back to the residential common areas.

Aiyana paused by the break room. "Hang on, should we grab some food from the volunteer break room? You know, stock up the vehicles."

"Solid," Stein said, looking around the break room for whatever it offered. They each grabbed a case of 48 protein energy bars before heading onward. They passed through the other in-processing zones and the raised podium, all vacated. Not a soul was around.

"Any contact from your parents yet?"

"Nope."

"And you'd like to keep it that way?"

Aiyana shrugged. "It's in their hands."

"And what of Reillee's parents? Any word?"

Andie spoke up. "They're still 'unknown-missing' in the system. No pings, no DMs. I'm worried about him."

They walked the entryway hall toward the vehicle airlocks, finding the correct *No Admittance* door they had entered through before. As they slipped through and headed into the abandoned maintenance dorms, Aiyana brought her teacher up to speed on their earlier adventures in the lower tunnels.

She described how she and Andie had discovered the white-tile airlock below the wrecked skimmer site, the vast burial chamber, the blue door, weird round room, and the other tunnels they had discovered.

He listened intently as they reached their stashed Exo-suits and suited up. Stein asked the occasional question, then, after they had sealed up and cross-checked, the two continued their discussion on their private suit radio channel.

They passed through the maintenance bay airlocks and were relieved to find both vehicles right where they left them.

Using dust brooms and pry bars, they cleaned the rocks off the back of the tank. Aiyana used her recently acquired crescent wrench to un-bolt and remove the mangled cargo cage and whatever remained of its damaged, spoiled cargo canisters. After the external work, they entered both vehicles and disabled every remote-access link they could think of in the on-board computers. Power and air in both vehicles looked good.

Then the two searched the maintenance bay and scrounged extra filter cartridges for both vehicles, along with simple tools and anything else they could think of. After an hour of effort, all that remained was the water.

Hefting both 10-L bottles, they re-entered the complex, still suited, and found the closest working spigot to refill tanks with fresh water. A quick swig revealed the water tasted flat but refreshing enough.

After securing these inside both vehicles, Stein stretched his aching back and looked outside at the dimming light. Night was falling; their eyes were sore from being up for nearly 30 hours.

It was time to get back inside and get some much-needed sleep.

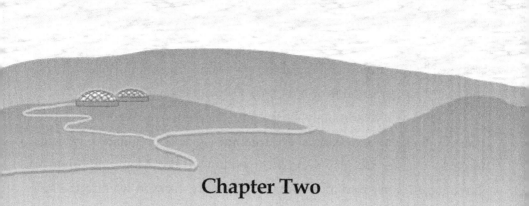

Chapter Two

No Place For A Human

B ruce Jackson's team did its best work right in the path of danger.
The time had come to relocate his emergency response team to the
safety of Blue Ridge: thirty-seven hours had passed since the evacuation
first sounded across the city.

He toured the room for the very last time, pausing to review the three
evac routes: maglev trains, ground vehicles, and the rocket fleet.

First, the trains. Trains arrived empty and were quickly filled to
double-capacity before being sent shooting down the mountainside to
safety. Families sat in groups, with children on laps or nestled in sleeper
compartments, two or three strapped into every bunk bed. After leaving
the MonsPlex station, train conductors informed passengers whether
they were headed East to Jupiter's Crossing or North to Port Mons. After
arriving, they would transfer to trains and only the luck of the draw
determined which of the seven cities they ended up at. A lucky few found
themselves riding the rails as far East as Nooma Outpost, and others, as far
North as New Skye. Jackson nodded in satisfaction at the status screens—

with nearly fifty trains running at top speed cris-crossing the face of Mars, this was their fastest outflow of people. He walked on.

Ground vehicles, mainly buses and people-movers, poured out of the Mountain controlled by AI swarm logic. Several long lines of vehicles fanned out across the plains and diverged toward Port Mons and Jupiter's Crossing. All appeared to be running smoothly. Jackson went to the last station, the rocket shuttles.

He frowned at the Shuttle statistics—these made the smallest impact on the overall effort, with each rocket taking just a hundred passengers at a time. He listened in as the local officer, seated here, updated his counterpart at Blue Ridge.

" . . . but what if a shuttle departs the Watney greenhouse launch pads but can't land because the previous rocket is late in clearing the pad?" the face on the screen asked.

"Then . . . they execute a second burn and do a go-around."

"A go-around of the whole planet?" The Blue Ridge face asked.

"That's correct. The shuttles are designed for orbital flight . . . even if they haven't routinely been used that way. Our pilots are more than capable—most do a straight-in, unload, and under thirty minutes later, fly back to pick up more."

"Imagine being a passenger on a go-around—that's a trip they'll talk about forever," the Blue Ridge officer said.

"Okay, let's skip the chatter," Jackson interjected. "I want handovers complete in ten minutes."

"Yes sir," both controllers said together. The controller seated next to Jackson continued. "Okay, Blue Ridge, the mobile Space Traffic Control and Landing Systems we set up has all nine greenhouse pads running smoothly, three from each greenhouse. Exo-Suit supply is good. This leaves only one major problem, and that is straight-up out of our hands."

The Blue Ridge counterpart listened, but did not guess what the problem might be.

Jackson thought about it. "The fuel," he murmured to himself.

The primary controller switched screens. "It's the fuel reserves," he confirmed. "We're going to run out of rocket fuel in one more day, maybe two if we slow the surge. We've never pushed all our rockets to this level, ever. Maglev trains only need electricity from the reactors and solar farms. Ground cars just need fresh power cells while the drained ones recharge. Our rocket fuel reserves, however, will dry up very soon."

"So what you're saying is in a day or two, trains and ground cars are all we have left."

"That's correct."

Jackson nodded, thanked the briefers, and walked away. He sat and looked up at the volcano's ground-penetrating radar display — the magma was steadily rising and had reached the 30-kilometer line under the city. Shaking off dark thoughts, he stood and cued up the microphone.

"Your attention please? All controllers, please complete handover to your Blue Ridge counterparts at this time. Relief crews remaining here, you evac in twelve hours, at which time this facility will be abandoned. Primaries, when your handover is complete, go immediately to the departure rally point and suit up; our shuttle will arrive in ten minutes. You have two minutes to wrap it up — move with a purpose."

Briefings concluded; the final relief controllers took their seats. Blue Ridge action officers assumed control from their remote location. Outgoing controllers stood and left, exiting down a side hallway toward the suit-up rally and a small elevator they had never used before. Jackson picked up a copy of the latest city-by-city totals and waited for his last departing controller to exit the room. All stations showed green; handoffs complete. Standing at the room's exit, he looked back one last time.

The large central screen showed:

CITY EVACUATION IN PROGRESS

Status: 12% Evacuated

Then he turned on his heel and left the room, reading the paper in his hand as he walked.

SITE	EVAC CAP.	EVAC CURRENT	FILL RATE
Blue Ridge	15,000	15,436	103%
Jupiter's Crossing	25,000	3,400	14%
Westdown	9,000	4,200	47%
Port Nerus	5,000	4,500–5,500	(transit only)
Port Mons	5,000	4,500–5,500	(transit only)
Port Marrakech	7,000	6,500–7,500	(transit only)
Nerus City	200,000	32,500	16%
New Marrakech	700,000	42,000	6%
Libertas	50,000	12,000	24%
Hathorton	11,000	6,400	58%
Skye City	15,000	3,750	25%
Phobos Station	2,000	1,250	(No Evac)
Deimos Station	500	450	(No Evac)
New Kyiv	2,000	1950	98%
Nooma Outpost	300	320	107%

At the end of the hall, a suit-up room had several alcoves of Exo-Suits hanging on racks. To the side of the elevator, Jackson saw a familiar bright red door with a sign "Authorized Access Only." As he and the other stragglers grabbed their suits, he shook his head in wonder — why had he never taken the effort to find what was beyond the red door? Too late now.

On a whim, he pressed his hand to the ident plate to see if it would open. A red laser line scanner ran swept quickly across the room, scanning all who stood nearby.

Beep-beep. Nope.

As far as he knew, the red door had never been opened by anyone.

An admin assistant approached, handing Jackson the shuttle mission profile. He accepted it, finished suiting up, and joined his departing controllers inside the elevator. The doors slid closed behind him. As he and the last few on his primary team rode upward, he read the message.

Skipping past the other details, he focused on one entry. Pilot-in-Command: *Eliza Griffin.* Good. If anyone could deliver them safely from one bare, undeveloped site to another, it was her.

Jackson had been briefed earlier that Eliza and her crew had made several risky flights to various bare-rock landings as volunteers — several hundred stranded evacuees owed Eliza and her flight crew their lives.

The elevator doors opened, and he stepped into an open room with a single airlock on the far side, opposite the elevator. The entire outgoing team had gathered here, four dozen officers and senior leaders, performing final suit checks. A technician standing by the external airlock announced in a loud voice their shuttle had just landed outside.

The first group to finish their suit checks lined up at the airlock — small groups took turns transiting the chamber and stepping onto the dusty plateau outside.

With the last group to clear the airlock, Jackson made his way to the ten-story-tall rocket, watching a previous group ride up the rocket's side elevator to an open hatchway halfway up. As he waited his turn, his earpiece beeped, indicating a high priority flash message had just been sent to him.

He swiped it open on his wrist digital display.

His head fell he read the message.

MERF Director Victor Dunne had been found dead in his residence. Jackson shook his head in disbelief; he had liked and respected his boss. Now he was gone.

Early reports indicated he had suffered a stress-induced heart attack before attempting to leave the city. There was no suspicion of foul play. Without ceremony, Jackson immediately became the MERF Director. His turn came to step onto the rocket's elevator.

He rode to the top, deep in thought.

* * *

A short time later, the rocket blasted off smoothly, following a graceful curving arc up to an altitude of seven thousand meters. At the apex, the brief weightlessness made everyone's stomach lurch like the first drop of a roller coaster. When the thrusters kicked in to slow the rocket's fall, the gravity inside increased to an extreme level—slightly more than Earth's 1 gee. It descended neatly until landing six minutes later, with Eliza nursing the thrusters through to touchdown, gentle as a leaf landing on the surface of Silver Lake. Jackson saw out his window that Eliza had nailed their landing site perfectly.

During the short flight, word spread quickly about the Director, and as the team collectively un-strapped to disembark, conversations about Dr. Dunne continued in low tones. He would be *sorely* missed.

Out the window, they could see two ground vehicles kicking up dust trails toward the rocket: one, a large people-mover and the other, a small staff car. The flight crew secured the ship and extended the rocket's side passenger elevator. One by one, passengers descended the steps to the elevator level beneath them, then loaded up in small groups to ride down to the ground.

Jackson went up the staircase instead, toward the cockpit. He summoned Eliza Griffin to a private meeting in an electronic control room just beneath the cockpit deck. She stepped in a moment later, wearing her navy-blue flight suit, black wavy hair pulled back in a bun at her collar. "Mr. Jackson," she said by way of greeting.

"Eliza." He nodded. "This will come as a shock, but I'm relieving you of your flight duties," he said, noting the surprise on her face.

"Landing wasn't that rough," she joked. He smiled back.

"You set us down light as a feather. This has absolutely nothing to do with your competence as a pilot. In fact, you're the best we've got. That's why I need you to assume your new duties immediately."

He paused. She listened.

"You may have heard Director Dunne is no longer with us," he said.

"Yes, I did hear that," Eliza confirmed.

"That means I am the de facto Director, and I find myself in immediate need of a competent Deputy."

Her eyes popped wide open.

"There is no one on my senior staff who can be spared in the midst of this crisis." He paused. "You are the new Deputy Director."

Eliza stood shock-still, confusion all over her face. She stammered something, but at that moment, Jackson looked away, tapping his earpiece. He looked out the window at the two ground vehicles below.

"This is Jackson, say again, over? . . . no, send them all now to get checked in, but hold that staff car please, seats for two." Then, whatever Jackson heard in reply, he nodded and closed the channel. He turned back to Eliza.

"Look, you're already in the mindset of taking action and you've handled who knows how many IFEs in your career. You keep your cool under the worst pressure, and you've saved hundreds in the last 24 hours

325

alone. You're creative and most importantly, decisive. That's exactly what this situation calls for."

She looked at him for a moment, mind furiously tearing through swaths of ideas.

"I have a couple conditions," she said simply.

"Those will have to wait. For the time being, I simply need you to say yes, and come down that lift with me, right now."

Without further protest, she said, "I accept."

"Good. Let's get you to your new station."

He gestured up, toward the cockpit above. "How's your copilot?"

"Best I've flown with," she said without hesitating. Jackson nodded.

"Tell him to launch immediately, and get back into the rotation. His flight engineer can take the right seat, and he can pick up a standby pilot wherever they send him."

"On it," she said, crossed to the stairs, and climbed up to gather her gear and give the crew their instructions. Jackson tapped a few directives on his tablet, informing HQ Shuttle Control of the personnel change and waiving the two-pilot requirement for the next flight. By the time he finished all this, his new Deputy had returned, Exo-Suit on and ready to head down the lift. They powered up, did a radio cross-check, and descended together.

As soon as their ground car cleared the blast zone, the massive *Raptor Five* engines ignited behind them. The ten-story vessel lifted off in silence to rejoin the rescue efforts for as long as fuel held out.

Half an hour later, Eliza Griffin was sworn in and given her Director's Level all-access credentials—the biggest field promotion the planet had ever seen.

* * *

Aiyana looked at Andie. "I know that look."

"We need a cat's Exo-Suit, if we're going to take him back to the Mountain with us," Andie said, looking down at Ares.

"Great, I'll just pick one up from the supply window," Aiyana said with a sneer.

"Ooo that's a good idea," Andie said.

"Um, hello, sarcasm?"

"Well, check anyway, would you? Like I said, we need him when we go back."

"There's no way they'll let us," Aiyana said, exasperated. "Even Stein wouldn't let you go."

"That's it! We convince Stein, so he can convince the people in charge. Aiya, you're a genius!" Andie stood and dashed away. Ares followed.

"Wait, that's not what I . . ." But Andie was gone.

Aiyana fumed a little bit, shook her head, and walked off toward the supply service window.

Andie found Stein quickly, alone at a picnic-bench table in the common area, where several hundred had gathered to watch the latest news on a large screen. Ares hopped up on the table and looked pointedly at Stein. The cat did not blink.

Andie also sat without speaking.

"Hello, what's up?"

"We need your help."

"Sure thing, is everything all right?"

"Not really."

"Ooookay." He waited for Andie to continue.

"There's a place, under the city that's not far from the crypts. We absolutely need to get in there before it's lost forever."

"You're saying you want to go back."

"Yes."

"No. Absolutely not."

"Stein, it leads to something . . . important. Elias Ellis tried to—"

"Oh, him? What did he say is there?"

"He was convinced that under the city, like deep in an unexplored magma tube, there's something waiting to be discovered that could affect all of humanity on Mars. And just the entryway we found . . . predates the builders. It predates the first settlers."

"What makes you say that? Is this about that weird round room?"

"Yes? Oh, Aiya told you, okay. Here, it's easier if I just show you."

Andie brought up clips of the weird round room, Ares' reckless leap, and the strange grooves cut into the weird round room's floor.

"I think this place is a plug of some kind, to protect whatever they put on the other side. I mean, magma tubes don't just end, do they?"

"No, not generally. But protect it? From what?"

"I don't know. But something worth protecting is something worth looking into, isn't it?"

"You're making a lot of assumptions."

"Yeah, I guess I am. But Elias did as well. Take a look."

Andie shared Uncle Eli's notes about the blue door and showed footage of the door. Elias was very clear in his original video journals—he felt that whatever was there was critical to humanity's future on Mars.

"So you see . . . if we do have enough time, say, just a day or two, then there's time to at least try and see what's beyond the weird round room," Andie said.

"You've convinced me—but they're not going to let us go," he said.

"Mister Stein, all the estimates say the city won't be breached by the magma for at least two or three more days at the earliest, so it seems we have enough time. One thing is certain, though: after a week, those tunnels and the round cryptic chamber . . . won't even exist."

"I think the best they'll agree to is diverting some MERF patrol in the city to go searching."

"You know that won't work—they don't know where anything is, and we do. We can get in, get past the weird round room, and get out."

"I understand. But all we can do is ask."

"Okay . . . just take me with you then, you know, to plead our case?" Andie said. "Because I'm not abandoning this quest left by my ancestor so that some MERF stranger or stuffy . . . cubicle person . . . messes it up."

"Cubicle person? You mean a bureaucrat? Okay, maybe they'll listen to reason."

Andie nodded. "Oh, tell him you're a geologist, he might take you more seriously."

"Good idea." Stein reached for his tablet and accessed the Blue Ridge home directory. He tapped out a brief note to the new MERF Director, one Bruce Jackson, and tagged it 'high importance.' He clicked 'send.'

"Now all we can do is wait, and hope."

They were both surprised when a response came through just ten minutes later—an admin assistant's reply made it clear that Stein's time with the Director would be very brief, to share his perspective as a geologist. The reply stressed that right now, mid-shift, was convenient, if he could enter through the EOC security station immediately.

Stein turned the screen so Andie could read it.

"Um, wow," Andie said. "So . . . let's go, I guess?"

They stood and headed directly to the security checkpoint. Ares followed, all curiosity and zero hesitation. Within moments of arriving at the counter, security personnel slapped a visitor badge on Stein and Andie and escorted them both to a small lift. The security guard raised an eye at the cat but said nothing. Authorization had come from the very top; the cat must be part of it.

The elevator doors opened, they rode to the top. Here, they passed through another security point, and were admitted to a small conference room overlooking the operations floor. Below, dozens of duty stations had been arranged in the standard horseshoe configuration, facing a swarm of flatscreens displaying all kinds of information. Beyond were broad windows, through which the mountain itself and the plains below could be clearly seen.

They waited, but only for a moment. The door opened, and the tall, barrel-chested Director entered. Stein stood and extended his hand. Jackson shook it without ceremony, and then nodded and shook hands with Andie.

"Thanks for seeing us, Mr. Director," Stein said.

"Don't mention it," Jackson replied, adding, "what can you tell me about our situation, Mister . . . Steinheiser?"

Stein was prepared for this. "The magma rising, it will probably move in fits and starts. But I bet your in-house experts already told you that—how long do they think it will take for full evacuation?"

"My experts have been telling me it's rising steadily and will continue to do so, but as far as evacuations so far, it's excruciatingly slow. Thankfully the magma is filtering upward from thirty clicks deep. Once it hits the vehicle evacuation tunnels . . . I don't like to imagine that if we have folks still trying to get out."

Jackson gestured through the windows at the central screen:

CITY EVACUATION
IN PROGRESS

Status: 15% Evacuated

Stein and Jackson watched the display for a moment.

Stein spoke up. "Still, a hundred fifty thousand people in under two days, that's impressive."

Jackson shook his head before answering. "Like I said, slow going. So, what were you saying about fits and starts?"

"Yes, sir. Imagine the mountain is like a water barrel filling up from a hose, but inside there are blocks, internal tubes, and a mix of empty containers. The barrel would fill quickly until it reaches some of those empty spaces inside the barrel, then the overall rising water might seem like it's slowing down. But once those open spaces inside the barrel fill up, the overall rising water would seem like it's rising much faster."

Jackson nodded. "So what do you advise?"

"I think you're already doing it. But if you have scans of where any other empty magma chambers might be under the mountain, that might give you more insight into those fits and starts. What other challenges are you facing?"

"Some looting has started, but thankfully crimes against people are rare. Distributing food and water is another challenge."

As if on cue, a Cargo Mobility officer slipped into the room and handed Jackson an urgent please-sign-this-now tablet. Jackson quickly scanned it, pressed his thumb to a sensor, and passed it back. The officer slipped out without a word.

"I heard you and a handful of students didn't follow evac protocols either, but still made it out in good order."

"They were trapped in a side tunnel, it's a long story. We left through that city side tunnel and found a separate airlock that led outside."

"The side tunnel that you left the city through—is it still open?"

"The pocket? No, it was buried in a collapse. No one else is getting out that w—"

"No, I mean the exit from the side tunnel itself—it's like 2 meters tall, right? Did you guys leave it open? It can't be left open . . . "

"What has that got to do with anything?"

"Was-the-tunnel-door-left-open-or-not?" The question came out as one long word.

"Oh, goodness, I wish I . . . wait, lemme think."

Stein paused, trying to remember. He glanced down at Ares, who was making a disturbing amount of eye contact. Stein held a hand over his mouth and murmured something downward. Ares muttered "mew," still looking at Stein, eyes wide.

Andie just watched the exchange, saying nothing.

Stein turned back to Jackson. "I remember now. It made a loud thud after we exited, and almost clipped his tail off," he said, indicating Ares.

Ares squinted at Stein's comment. Stein shrugged back at Ares.

"Well, I sure hope so," Jackson said.

"Why does it even matter, the tunnel door, whether it's open or shut?"

"Never mind. We've got bigger problems. Many citizens ignored the instruction to go down into the escape tunnels and instead headed for the train station; it's practically overrun."

"Sounds like choke points evacuating Naples in 2183, or even Vesuvius destroying the Roman city Pompeii. Thousands of years later, and we've hardly learned a thing."

"Maybe we got it right this time around. Look, I've really got to get back to—" he said, turning to leave. Stein walked with him, and Andie and Ares followed through the door.

"Gotcha—I need just one thing."

Jackson stopped at the top of a small staircase to listen.

"I need you to let us go back." Stein said flatly.

Jackson rolled his eyes and headed down the steps. "Not happening."

Andie spoke up for the first time. "Sir, the magma is rising, right?"

"Yes, pushing up through deep fissures, right now at . . . " he glanced at a screen, " . . . twenty-nine clicks deep. It's only a matter of time before the entire flow bursts out the side of the Mountain like some big . . . lava balloon." He looked out the command center windows, across the plains toward the Mountain.

Andie finally spoke up. "Sir, please, we found something in one of the lower caverns no one has ever seen, and my research tells me it might change our entire future on Mars. But whatever is down there—it's about to be lost forever."

"What are you talking about, young lady? I know all about what's under the city."

Stein looked hard at Jackson. "You don't know this."

Jackson turned to look at Stein, eye to eye.

Stein pressed on. "Just think of the potential—it could be some lost secret, or a way of taking our next steps on Mars. Think of—"

Jackson leaned in. "Look, I don't know what you think you found under the city, but my answer is no. That mountain is no place for a human to be headed back to, not now. Plus we need every able-bodied person working recovery."

He gestured back, pointing over Stein's shoulder and continued. "You're a professional, you're a geologist. What you have told me was insightful, and I need that here and now, not—" he swept a hand toward the doomed mountain. "So please, just go report to mobile ops and they'll tell you where to get set up."

"But . . ." Stein's turn to step forward, the two men almost nose to nose.

Stein held the urge to stand on tiptoe. Jackson was tall. Really tall.

"Dammit, I know I can help in better ways, just let me try."

"You're not going back into that mountain!" Jackson shouted, pointing an arm sideways out the observing windows. "Report to mobile ops now, that's an order."

A pause. Stein blinked, stepped back, and wiped his cheek. "Come on, Andie . . . it's time for us to go," their teacher said softly.

Jackson looked at Andie, seeing the shock all over their face. His angry expression softened. He nodded, then turned away to get back to his tremendous burden of leadership.

* * *

Andie pinged Aiyana as they rode the lift down. A few moments later the teens met back in their shared dorm room. Stein went to walk it off.

"How'd it go?" Aiyana asked as Andie and Ares walked in and shut the door. Stein had gone somewhere else.

Andie flopped down on the bed and let out a long sigh. "Uggggg . . ."

Aiyana sat in the aluminum chair. "That good, huh?"

"Stein tried, but he totally crashed and burned. I tried to explain what we had found, but by then it was two strong men standing toe-to-toe. I just wish Stein would help us sneak out on our own, but now he's all checked in and working some big science job here in Blue Ridge."

Aiyana nodded but did not respond.

Andie exhaled again, frustrated. "Mmm, how'd it go with a cat suit?"

"The supply section politely told me get lost," Aiyana said. "Nothing like that here. But they did give me a few meters of line and some hooks to hang up laundry, so yaaaaay, laundry. Plus, I have this mesh bag for hauling dirty clothes." She patted a sealed packet on the desk next to her.

"Oh wow, they're the best. Ugh, so where are we supposed to find you a suit, Ares?" Andie asked the cat.

Ares jumped down and walked to the door, mewing insistently. He put a paw on the door and mewed some more.

"Wait, you have an idea?"

"Mew," the cat said.

"Mew means yes," both teens said together. They both smiled and stood to follow the cat. Andie grabbed the packet on the way past.

Ares bolted out the open door and was off like a shot down the metal walkway. Slamming the door, both ran after the cat in bounding strides.

At the bottom of the stairs, they followed him past latrines and shower

334

units, all cold water and low pressure. They followed him toward a different stack of CHU dorms.

Up one staircase, down the row halfway to the far end, and up another staircase, Ares paused, sniffing the air. The cat looked left, then right, then left again, then up. He ascended the stairs. Within minutes, Ares had led them up another level and halfway down the row of doors on the third level. He stopped at a door that looked no different than the rest.

"This one, are you sure?"

"Mew," said Ares. Pausing, they heard a low murmur of conversation inside. Aiyana knocked softly at the door.

An older lady opened the door and looked at the two teenagers.

"Uh, hi," Andie said as she stood in the doorway, which led into a double-wide room, twin bunks against both walls. "I'm Andie."

The lady's friend, seated further inside the space, looked up and smiled.

"I'm Lee," the standing lady said, smiling gently. "And that's Susie. What can we do for you?" She looked tired, as they all were.

"I heard you have a cat . . . oh, there he is, and might even have a pet Exo-Suit you could let us borrow?" Andie gestured down at Ares, standing at their feet.

Lee seemed taken aback. She glanced at the left bunk, where a fuzzy, gray, long-haired Norwegian Forest Cat lounged, staring back with bright green eyes.

"That's a bold request, young lady," she said, not unkindly. "But I'm afraid I can't let it go. What if my Thor needs it himself?"

Andie did not give up. "Bold may be what helps us save humanity on Mars, ma'am. I'm trying to get back to the Mountain at all costs, to find something under the city before it is lost forever, and I need to take this fellow with me," Andie said, gesturing at Ares, who had locked eyes with Thor. Thor stared intensely back.

Lee still looked skeptical. "What do you think you'll find?"

Aiyana spoke up. "We found the builders, well, we found their burial chamber. They left us knowledge and insights into their explorations of the planet . . . and it's about to be lost forever."

Andie turned the camera's viewscreen around, to show Lee some images of the burial chamber.

"Wow, that's amazing. And you need your cat to get you there? I don't follow what you mean."

"He is as smart as you and me," Andie said simply. "And he knows the way."

"Nooo, that couldn't be possible."

"Ares, I'm going to turn my back and cover my eyes. Will you count the number of fingers Lee holds up, and speak that many times please?"

Ares mewed several times.

"Six."

"Uhhh," Lee said, taken aback.

Andie turned back around. Aiyana said, "The cat is extremely smart. And even if you think this was just some trick, the pet Exo-Suit has an emergency beacon in it, which we could use to call for help if something bad happens. You might just be saving our lives."

Lee nodded. "I was an archaeologist in my younger years back on Earth, before coming here with Susie when we both retired. But can you even get there and back in time?"

"We have our own safe way back into the Mountain and out again, to chase down those important answers."

"Well, I'm still not sure . . ."

"Ma'am, MERF has its hands completely full—they can't spare anyone to chase after these answers. The voices of our ancestors are about to be silenced, forever."

Lee smiled. "You certainly have enthusiasm. What do you think, Susie? Can we trust these nice young ladies to bring Thor's suit back to us?"

Susie addressed both teens. "What are you really after, girls? What do you hope to find by going back to the city?"

"There's cryptic writings down there, maybe even artifacts of the builders themselves? We won't know for sure until we get back in."

Susie made up her mind. "Oh, give them what they want—they look trustworthy enough," she said, shuffling up a deck of cards at a small table between the beds.

Lee looked at Andie, tilting her head and saying with a coy smile, "all right. You can borrow the suit," holding up her pointer finger and adding, "but don't forget where you got it." She turned and opened a locker, pulled out the small suit and passed it over, along with two spare air canisters.

"You may have just saved us all, ma'am." Andie said, then awkwardly held out their arms and leaned into Lee, who stepped closer to share a warm embrace.

"Something about you reminds me of my granddaughter, Paige," Lee said, smiling a grandmother's smile.

"Then I hope I get to meet her someday," Andie replied, stepping back and letting the hug go.

Lee nodded. "See what you can find . . . go learn some things," Lee said.

Andie looked at her quizzically, then nodded and turned away, cat suit over her shoulder.

* * *

Aiyana triple-checked Lauryna's controls and ensured the nav-computer had been disabled. Now, the tank's computer would only take its positioning data from the GPS satellites, not from the towers scattered across the valley floor. She didn't want someone assuming control—they were about to violate direct orders from the big boss.

Andie bit into a protein energy bar and passed one across to Aiyana, adding, "thanks for not grabbing the mango soybean chicken kind. That's just . . . wrong."

"Combinations nature had never intended," Aiyana said as she flicked a few more buttons on the dashboard and switched on the overhead viewscreens. She ran final checks of power, pressure, and O2 — everything was in the green.

Nestled in the back was a case of four Compact-80 air tanks, and half a dozen Compact 40s as a backup. Tucked inside the rear storage lockers were four new CO_2 filter cartridges — yes, Carbon Dioxide Scrubber Filter, Type V, Tall, Hex. Aiyana had re-filled and tied down the 10-L blue water canister from the '332 shed' behind the driver's seat, next to the borrowed cat Exo-Suit. Their retrieved Exo-Suits, folded in the back seat, each had its multi-tool, a short utility knife, and full power charge. Even the laundry line and its mesh sack sat in the pile of supplies.

Andie strapped themselves into the right seat. Aiyana looked around and took a moment to try to think of anything forgotten or left to chance. Ares hopped up on the dashboard, looking forward.

On one of the overhead displays, Aiyana swiped up the map she had photographed back at Shed 332. She set that image side-by-side with the GoogleMars map app, where a blinking orange arrow appeared, pointing West, on top of a black dot labeled Blue Ridge. She zoomed-in the map.

"This is so much easier in daylight," Aiyana said, patting Ares and slipping on a pair of dark sunglasses she had scrounged. Andie linked their phone to the Redtooth sound system and found a Tartarus tune with a sick beat. She started head-nodding to the beat.

Aiyana put the vehicle in gear and pulled straight out of the hidden garage alcove into the mid-morning sunshine. Ares squinted in the bright light but stayed at his post.

The tank turned left, following the winding road down the ridgeline; for the first few moments they were hidden from above by the overhang of rock. She drove slowly, cautiously. She leaned forward and looked up, imagining the row of windows somewhere high above.

"See any vehicles for us to slide in behind?" Andie asked, calling out over the loud music.

Aiyana shook her head. "I think the convoys ended when we arrived." She checked the rear camera feed. The cracked screen still showed half-sky, half-ground behind them. "I'll have to MyTube on how to fix that," she mused, and Andie nodded.

"Oh, and let's add a little luck to our situation." Aiyana reached in a pocket and pulled out the *Subaru* emblem recovered from the wreck, and clicked it into a handy phone holder up on the dashboard.

"And cross your fingers we don't get noticed," Andie said to Ares. The cat squinted back, then looked ahead, down the desert road. He curled up and rested his chin on crossed orange paws.

* * *

High above, in the EOC bunker, the vehicle control officer pinged Director Jackson with a routine notification. Jackson stepped down and approached the man's station. They both eyed a blinking red line of text on the screen.

"VCO, what've you got?"

The VCO pointed at a camera view on a different flatscreen, where a lone vehicle, a tank, kicked up the barest of dust clouds as it rolled away. "Sir, it looks to be an old Type VII, treaded cargo vehicle under its own power, no auto-signature. Someone's driving that thing."

Jackson squinted, as if he could see inside the rover's cockpit.

The VCO spoke. "I . . . could break in through its transponder and lock out the controls . . . then it would automatically return, whoever they are, to the motor pool."

Jackson said nothing as he looked at the camera view. The tank kicked up more dust now.

"Shall I hold them?"

"No . . . leave them to me. I'll deal with them myself."

"As you wish, sir," the VCO confirmed.

"Carry on," said Jackson, patting the controller once on the shoulder.

Jackson smiled to himself, snorted, shook his head, and headed back to his Director's post. A supply technician was waiting for him, holding another priority request.

Moments later, the VCO looked at the same screen again, where he thought he had glimpsed a second dust trail. He panned the camera around, but saw only the original tank, still on course for Olympus Mons.

He ran a transponder sweep, searching the desert floor. The scan showed only one vehicle, which he had basically been told to ignore.

He rubbed his eyes, exhaustion setting in. 'Carry on,' the boss had told him. He zoomed the camera back up to its extreme-wide-angle, then zoomed in on the long vehicle convoys still crawling out of the Mountain, in their neat, orderly lines.

* * *

"You're kicking up dust, I think," Andie said.

"It's on purpose," she responded. "Remember this windy road down is like a one-lane choke point; I want to get clear of it so we don't get blocked in. When we hit the plains, I'll take her up to top speed. Top speed, toward the erupting volcano. Remind me again why we're doing this?"

"Because I don't have my license yet."

"All right . . . I wanted to hide Lauryna in a better spot regardless."

"Wait, hang on just a second . . . you're planning to keep it as your own?" Andie asked.

"Smartest one in the room," Aiyana said, smirking sideways.

"They're not gonna let you keep it," Andie said.

"Yeah, we'll see. How can they take her if she's not on any inventory, and she emits no signals?"

"Okay, we've established you're a whiz with vehicles. Just how are we going to find our way when we hit all those twisty-turney ramps going up the mountainside?"

"We still have our GPS. She's just listening to those satellites above, and interpreting it all onto our map screen. Plus, our escape drive down the Mountain is still listed under *recent destinations*. See?"

"You're really not worried, are you?"

"Well, yeah, I'm worried, but not about getting lost. Plus, in another half hour, we'll be too far away for them to even see our dust trail. We'll look just like some . . . dust devil at that distance, I'll bet."

* * *

Lauryna slowed as they approached Shed 332, finding it right where they had left it. In full daylight, a couple similar sheds could be seen, far off in several directions.

"Should we go inside?"

"I don't think so, I mean, how much time do we have before the lower tunnels and chambers are blocked?"

"Point," Aiyana replied.

Keeping the tank rolling, they passed the 332 building and turned right at a crossroads. She hit the accelerator, and moments later started climbing the same hillside road they had come down the day before.

A short way up the ramp, Ares craned his head up curiously at the MagLev train bridge as they passed under it. The dust was just settling from the last train that passed, already tens of kilometers away and getting smaller by the second.

Both driver and passenger strapped their harnesses down, snug. They continued their climb up the mountain road.

* * *

Back in the EOC, another four hours had passed. Eliza Griffin took a shift at the helm so her boss could get some rest. She looked over the status screens, willing the screen with all her might to tick over to a higher number. The pace was starting to really pick up, finally.

The central screen showed:

CITY EVACUATION IN PROGRESS

Status: 24% Evacuated

* * *

The tank climbed the Mountain much faster now than it did in pitch darkness and they eventually arrived at the rockslide that had nearly blocked their escape before.

Aiyana tapped the brakes as they approached. She snugged down her shoulder straps. The treads crunched over the first few loose pebbles and cobbles. She pushed the accelerator just a little bit harder. The tank groaned as it climbed up the first jumble of loose rocks.

The main weight of the tank reached the top of the rock scrabble. Ares stood on his haunches, balancing himself. His eyes remained fixed ahead.

Under the treads, rocks shifted and rolled. The tank lurched, sideways toward the edge. Aiyana hit the brakes. The tank stopped, then slipped to the side a bit farther. After another second, their sideways sliding also stopped.

Andie shouted, "wooo . . . oah!" Aiyana gritted her teeth.

Ares started to slide sideways, and objects in the back of the tank slid and shifted.

The cat tried to grip the dashboard, but with nothing there to hold onto, he slid right onto Andie's lap, sinking his claws into both legs.

"Owch! Ares!"Andie let go the armrests and wrapped both arms around the cat. He looked out the window, eyes wide open.

Then the tank slid some more. The back right corner dipped down.

Andie gripped Ares tighter. Aiyana squeezed the steering yoke as her adrenaline surged.

The front left corner of the tank lifted up. Andie looked out the passenger-side window on the right, seeing straight down the steep slope outside the windows.

As the back end slid lower, the view out the front windshield was nothing but sky.

Chapter One

Not Yet . . .

Aiyana kicked the tank into low gear and floored it. Both treads spun forward, kicking gravel and smaller rocks out backwards. Rocks rattled the undercarriage, and pellets and dust sprayed out in all directions as the tank slid nearer to the rim.

After a few agonizing heartbeats sliding sideways, the treads kicked enough small rocks out of the way on both sides that they found larger rocks to bite into, and the Lauryna's front end started to nose back down.

They moved forward a few meters, and the front end came down with a loud crunch of rocks and gravel underneath. Aiyana kept the accelerator pressed down as they edged forward, still spitting rocks and gravel.

Both teens were breathing heavily from fear and adrenaline. Ares looked wildly around through the windows, content to be held tightly in Andie's arms. Shoulder straps held them in place, cutting into Andie's shoulders. More rocks slid down the side, dislodged by the vehicle's aggressive passage. A moment later, the tank eased over the last of the rockslide and back onto solid road.

Aiyana pressed on, still at full acceleration, downshifting as they got further from the slide. A hundred meters further, Aiyana slowed, and stopped, looking back at the rock pile. Ares jumped back onto the dashboard, eyes wide and tail twitching wildly.

"Wow," Aiyana said, chest heaving through fast, frightened breaths. "Everybody good?"

"Yeah. Oh boy." Andie reached across to pat Aiyana's arm.

Aiyana got the tank moving again, snaking back and forth . . . up and up . . . back and forth . . . higher and higher as they neared their goal.

"We're headed for the motor pool where we found our vehicles, right?"

"Exactly," Andie said.

"Have you considered entering through the Overlook, at the top of the Needle? You know, from our Star Party?"

"Um, remember what happened last time someone drove that road?

"Oh yeah," Aiyana conceded.

"Plus, anyone could come out the overlook exit and swipe your tank — we'd be stuck."

"An even better point," Aiyana murmured.

"Our best bet is how we came out, and then maybe through the "X" fake alarm door. I just hope the two-wheel H-D we parked is still there."

"What if we get lost in all those lower tunnels?"

"We'll have our wrist maps to follow, remember we had tracking on in those tunnels before? Plus, we have this little guy and his boss-level hunter skills," Andie said, nuzzling Ares. "All I need is that one crossroads intersection, the one with the five tunnels.

"And then the weird round room." Aiyana sighed. "I don't think I can deal with that trap again. There's something about that place, gives me total freaky-freakies."

"If Uncle Eli's messages and those markings on the floor mean what I think they mean, it's our only choice. The two chevrons? I think they're arrows, showing us the way forward."

Aiyana muttered a short curse under her breath, inhaled, and drove on.

As an afterthought, Andie added, "We'll bring that rope too, you know, the laundry line they gave you? But my guess is, we won't need it."

The road continued up to the plateau and the large parking area.

After one final turn, they arrived. Andie thought about the cryptic chamber, the sphere room . . . intelligent design absolutely, for sure was behind it. They had to be telling humanity something. But what?

They crossed the flat-carved parking area, where the open vehicle tunnel had been.

"Um, Youston, we have a problem," Aiyana said.

"Oh."

The vehicle tunnel . . . wasn't there. The way they had driven out was a caved-in wreck, filled with boulders and rubble from upslope.

"Uhhhh," Aiyana murmured, parking the tank just past the edges of the cave-in. "Yeah." She brought the tank to a full stop.

"What do we do now?"

Aiyana slipped off her sunshades.

Ares let out a "Rr-mew," and looked back over his shoulder at Andie. He then looked back up toward the top of the rock pile. Both teens leaned forward, craning upward to see whatever the cat was indicating.

"Ooo, I see it, buddy," Andie said, looking at one upper corner of the rubble pile, where a small gap seemed like it might still be open, up and over the top of this most recent cave-in.

Aiyana wheeled the vehicle around, bringing it to a halt, pointing toward the exit ramp. She set the rover controls and system on 'sleep' mode, instead of powering it down completely, in case they needed to beat a hasty retreat later.

Unbuckling from the front seats, the three suited up. Aiyana grabbed the *Subaru* token and slipped it into a pocket. Andie tapped open auto-

346

tracking to follow once they got inside. The digital camera was in an outer thigh pocket, for surely they would need it.

The two cross-checked their suits for full air tanks, full power, and did their 3-suit radio link. Andie slipped three spare Compact-40 tanks into the laundry sack and slung the cord over one shoulder. Aiyana set Ares' suit to ping a distinctive Pet ExoSuit location 'beep' every five minutes.

"Ready?"

"Ready."

"Mew."

Andie cycled the vehicle airlock; they all hopped down onto the rocky ground and closed the door. "Whoa, see those? It's our tracks from when we evacuated yesterday. Crazy."

They reached the rockslide, and carefully started picking their way up over rocks and boulders, toward the small opening near the top. Ares was the first to the top, being far more nimble in his suit. The teens finally reached the top gap and squinted down into the darkness.

"The light at the portal—I see it! I mean, you know, the Airlock. It hasn't totally collapsed inside," Andie was ecstatic. They picked their paths carefully down through the other side of the rubble and stood, at last, in the shaded tunnel beyond. The motor pool had been buried in a full-on cave-in. Thankfully, the tunnel ahead was smaller, and still intact all the way to the airlock outer door.

They switched on headlamps and grabbed out handheld flashlights from the suit's side pouches. Ares' little suit lamps also turned on at a simple touch. Andie switched the pouch with the three extra tanks to the other shoulder, and Aiyana checked the clothesline was tucked safely into a thigh pocket. They walked to the outer door, its single light shining brightly. Andie popped it open. They stepped inside and pulled the door shut to cycle the airlock.

"Yes, it still works!" Aiyana was relieved.

The ground trembled roughly, whether in welcome or warning—the walls rained down small trickles of dust in the air. Teens and their cat staggered together, stumbling left as the ground shifted. Andie took a knee, but Ares kept his feet. Aiyana gripped the door frame and waited for the trembling to subside. Then she sealed the inner door behind them.

Inside, wrist displays confirmed full pressure, *ATM 1.0*, proper mix, so they flipped open helmets and let them flop back. They let Ares hop out of his suit to save power and air. He trotted along warily beside Andie.

They walked onward, and Ares, whether he intended to or not, matched the teens perfectly, turn for turn. Fifteen minutes later, they stood before the black "X" portal with the phony warnings all over it. Ares climbed back into his suit, all three sealed up, and did one final round of suit checks. Everything was ay-okay.

Andie looked the second door over, glanced down at Ares and then at Aiyana, shrugged, and cycled the small chamber's air. Through the second door, which shut behind them, they were back to *ATM 0.01* on their displays. The H-D skimmer was right where they had left it. Andie took the clothesline and the mesh bag with its compact-40 tanks and nestled it all under the back seat.

Aiyana powered up the motorcycle, got it pointed the right direction, and the three mounted up as before. They sped off down the long, black tunnel, headlamps shining bright. Auto-tracking led them onward.

* * *

Aiyana swung the blue door shut and sealed it behind them; the skimmer was parked just on the other side. Ahead lay the rough, downward-sloping magma tube that ended at the weird round room and the darkness of a dead end. But Andie bounded confidently onward, looped coils of line in one hand and bag with spare tanks in the other. Aiyana gritted her teeth and followed, beads of sweat on her brow despite the suit's cool air.

Ares led the way, a little too eager. His bouncing lights ran on ahead, and sure enough, when the teens glimpsed the darkness of the sphere room ahead of them, Ares had already disappeared over the edge.

"Come on, I think between Uncle Eli's video logs and my own educated guesses, we can open the way forward." The two reached the edge.

Below, Ares walked in small circles, fixated on the strange marks cut into the floor. Aiyana shined a hand-held lamp all around the entire space. It was just like before, a perfectly-curving sphere in every direction.

"See? Nothing. Dead end." Aiyana breathed heavily. "Can we go?"

"Nope. See if there's some place where you can anchor that, will you?" Andie asked, handing over the clothesline. "Look out below, Ares." Andie slid the bag with the compact-40s over the side and sat down to ease over the edge. With a huge breath and an exhale, Andie slid down the curving surface, right past Ares and the bag.

"Okay, I found one of those stone pokey things in caves to wrap the rope around back here.

"Which one? Stalactite?"

"It's the kind that sticks up, not the one hanging down."

"Stalagmite then," Andie said, pulling an air tank from the bag.

"How can you tell the difference?"

"Stalactite, with its letter "t" in it, means 'top.' That's how I remember."

"How is a stala—how can one of those things even be here? Doesn't it take thousands of years of dripping water?"

"Volcanic magma tubes that drain quickly can leave little ones behind," Andie said. "I saw it in a video once, in Stein's class. Was it small?"

"About the size of my thumb, so yeah. Hope it holds."

"If I'm right, we won't need it. Just drop the rope end down here and join me, will you?"

"Wait. I'm not staying up here?"

"I mean, you can if you wish, but if my guess is correct, I'm about to open a door forward. What if your side gets closed up when the way forward opens?"

"Like some kind of weird round airlock?"

"Maybe? This is as far as Uncle Eli got before he abandoned the effort. This is the place he describes as where he 'lost' his son."

"What does that even mean? Didn't his son leave Mars to live on Luna?"

"Yeah. I don't know what he meant, but his suspicions about what lies ahead, and my guesses, I hope, are about to make something happen." Andie and Ares both looked up at Aiyana.

Aiyana looked back, still breathing deeply. Then she shrugged.

"Okay. I'm coming. But if we die, I'm gonna kill you."

Andie smirked and held the one compact-40s down near the floor carvings. Aiyana eased over the edge and slid down, using the rope to slide down slowly.

"For the record, I have a really, really bad feeling about this," Aiyana said, picking up the bag with the other two air tanks inside. The end of the rope trailed along the ground within easy reach.

"There are no buttons to press, no key holes. How do you open a door . . . that isn't there . . . with no buttons or keys?"

"I've got my key right here," Andie said, holding up the air cylinder.

Holding it in one hand and gripping the air valve with the other, Andie said, "Stand back. I don't know how what happens next." Andie twisted the end while pointing the tank valve down into the grooved gaps in the floor. A jet of atmospheric gases blasted out, pushing Andie gently back. Andie reset their footing and leaned into the effort, Aiyana steadying her friend from behind.

A steady stream of gases gushed down into the gaps, with much of it escaping across the floor as a mist before evaporating and vanishing.

A crack of vibration, barely audible, but clearly felt through their boots, rocked the sphere. Ares skittered back as the floor where he was standing suddenly lifted, and a corresponding part on the left, where the end of the rope dangled, dropped down.

Andie twisted off the blast of air and both teens stepped back as far they could to watch as the room changed. Their two flashlights cast around. Ares stood behind Andie's boots and peeked around to watch.

The right side of the room, directly opposite where they entered, was slowly opening up, revealing a new tunnel that continued downward. In the middle of the room, a slab of the curving black stone rotated up and over, as if on a hinge, the left side dipping down as the right side lifted. Andie stepped forward out of curiosity as it turned up and over, Aiyana gripping their arm to stop them getting too close.

The right side rose up, reached the top of its rotation, and started to sink back down on the left. Andie shined their light down into a dark chasm below.

A dozen or more meters below the point of rotation . . . there was something down there, a figure, lying still. "Look!" Andie called out.

Aiyana leaned forward to see what it was—the stone slab continued its rotation; they would lose sight of the chasm below in a few seconds. Before it vanished from view under the rotating slab, Andie's hand lamp briefly shined on a space suit, helmet closed, lying completely still, the face mask frosted over in ice crystals.

"Wha—" Aiyana cut off her own words in complete shock. "Was that what I think it . . . was that a body?"

"Um . . ." Andie stammered. "Oh no . . . I think I know who that was."

"Who?"

"Tell you in a minute. Look, it's stopped."

The rotation locked itself in a new position with a thud, again felt through their boots. Before them, a neat set of steps led back up to the tunnel they had entered from on the left, and a ramp led onward and down to the right, where the rough magma tube continued.

"Did you catch the name on the lapel? I couldn't make it out completely. Looked like Deutsch or Dutch, something like that."

"I don't care, let's get out of here," Aiyana said.

Ares apparently supported this sentiment, as he padded in his little space suit over to the new tunnel opening, glanced down, and walked in.

"Um, yeah, we can talk about it later," Andie murmured, momentarily at a loss for words, thoughts racing.

The tunnel forward started rough, but a few meters in, they found a carved staircase, with perfectly-squared off steps, leading down into inky blackness. A few steps along, Ares looked back up at his humans.

A staircase.

"Oh . . . wow. How far down do you think it goes?"

"The core, I think."

A long, unending stairs disappeared down into darkness, going far beyond the range of their head lamps or flashlights. Andie swept the light over ceiling, walls, and the staircase where the cat waited. All was completely smooth, zero embellishments. Above, the ceiling curved up, across, and down the other side.

Aiyana took the first step. "Odd."

"What's that?"

"The steps are slightly too tall, it's weird. Whoever cut these stairs, maybe they were taller?"

"Or they just had a slightly higher step, maybe?"

"Good thing the staircase isn't that steep, we can skip steps."

"Look, there's a flat part, then more steps." They both stepped down slowly at first, then started taking steps at two or three at a time, making faster progress.

Andie paused to count. "Every twenty-seven steps, there's this flat part. Then another twenty-seven, it looks like."

"I wonder why they chose that number," Aiyana remarked.

"Because they just . . . liked the number 27?"

"What if it's just to stop someone tumbling all the way to the bottom?"

They continued down a while in silence. Andie lost track of how many of these platforms and 27-step sections they had skipped down, three at a time. Ares seemed to be enjoying himself, always one platform ahead.

"How deep does this go? Halfway to the base of the Mons? Or more?"

Their senses gave no sensation, no frame of reference. They descended this way for another 15 minutes before the bottom of the staircase came into view. Ares stopped several steps up from where the steps ended. The teens arrived at the bottom. Here the stairway ended in another flat floor and on through a tall, squared off entryway.

"No door, interesting."

"O_2 check," Andie prompted. The two held their wrists next to each other, and both confirmed they had less than half of their usable air remaining in the compact-80s. Ares was at a comfortable 60% remaining. Aiyana patted the bag with their reserves, and Andie held the partially-empty tank they had used as a key in the weird round room.

"Let's take ten minutes, tops, to explore whatever is inside, then we have to head back."

They faced the doorway together. Ares, for once, stayed put. This entryway was narrower than the staircase, however, just wide enough for a person to walk through with arms lifted slightly to both sides.

They shined their lights inside and stepped across the threshold.

Ares stayed close at their heels.

* * *

"Sir, the magma is rising faster," the geologist reported to both Jackson and Eliza Griffin, looked over his shoulders at the ground radar displays.

"Not clear why it changed speed."

"Probably surging after some other, deeper magma chambers filled up," Jackson guessed, thinking on what Stein had told him before.

The geologist glanced up at his boss, nodding.

"How much time before it hits the city?" Eliza asked.

"It's likely—" but before the man could finish his thought, a new alarm sounded throughout the EOC. The rising magma just breached ten kilometers below the city.

"Mute those alarms please?" Eliza shouted above the blasting tone.

The alarms were muted. The central screen now showed:

CITY EVACUATION IN PROGRESS

Status: 51% Evacuated

* * *

The teens stepped through the doorway. The room was about the size of a high school classroom, but with higher ceilings and no other way in or out. Andie set the spare tank down and slipped the camera out of its pocket to start recording.

Aiyana twisted the top of her hand-held light, to its widest floodlight and set it on the floor to shine up at the ceiling. This cast the entire room in a soft glow.

"The ceiling," Aiyana said. Andie and Ares both looked up. The writings here resembled the weird round room's grooves in the floor. Andie panned the camera up to catch the details, snapping a few stills.

1||i 7ᴙ11. li. |vil 7|ᴙ17ivᴙ||Livᴙ IiLli|ᴙ .|ᴙi 7ᴙ11.

oo ᴙ oo ᴙ OO   OOo ᴙ OoOo

/// \\\   ///

oOo ᴙ oOo   OOO ᴙ oo ᴙ oo

i 7ᴙ11. li. |vil|IiL| 7ᴙ11. 7ᴙ11|7il 7|ᴙ17ivᴙ||Livᴙ IiLli|

"What are you trying to tell us?" Andie breathed, snapping photos.

The room was a perfect rectangle and stood four meters, floor to ceiling. On all the walls, detailed, intricate carvings filled multiple panels. The room's floor was empty, aside from two short pillars, waist-high, casting long, diverging shadows from where the flashlight stood in the entryway.

Atop each pillar sat a bowl, roughly the size and shape of a large popcorn bowl, made of the same pitch-black rocky material as the walls. Andie walked over to the left bowl and looked inside.

"It's half-full with . . . some kind of powder, it looks like," Andie said, looking in the left bowl. Aiyana walked over to peer in as well. Andie gingerly touched the dried powder with a gloved fingertip and held it up to the light.

"Dust? In a bowl . . . this looks just like ordinary desert rust dust."

"Weird," Aiyana said, walking over to look at the other bowl. "Look, this one has some kind of flat seal. Like a dark wax or something."

Andie prodded and sifted the dust around in the left bowl, to see what lay beneath. Nothing. What appeared to be an empty bowl had been half-filled with rust dust, a hand's-width deep, and nothing else.

"This rust dust was put in here on purpose," Andie stated confidently.

"How do you know? It could have collected there like everywhere else."

"No, look at the walls, the floor — no dust at all. So . . . logically, it was poured into this bowl, deliberately."

Aiyana looked around, nodding. "Well, we'd have to break the seal on this other one to find out what's inside." Shining a helmet light straight on it revealed nothing of its contents . . . no light got through the flat top. Andie grabbed out the digital camera and started snapping pictures of all sides of both bowls, leaving them otherwise untouched.

The wall straight opposite the entryway was dominated by two bas-relief carved, perfect circles.

"The one on the left is smaller . . . oooo, it's Mars," Aiyana said. "See? Here's Valles Marineris, there are the Triplets, and yes, that's O-Mons. Looks perfectly accurate."

Andie walked to the other circle. "Well, this one's Earth, but the continents look a little off."

"Looks okay to me," Aiyana said.

Andie shook their head. "It's not. Stein offered extra credit to anyone who hand-drew an accurate map of all the continents . . ."

"So you did."

"So I did. But look, it's close, but not a perfect match of the coastlines. Plus, this one has a few extra islands where there aren't any. See here? Where the Florida archipelago should be — here it's attached, a peninsula. Weird . . ."

"Like Florida used to have a land bridge?"

"Maybe." Andie snapped more photos.

Aiyana walked past the Earth circle carving toward the right wall.

"Look, animals!"

Carved here, on the Earth side, were dozens of animal and plant forms, with some figures above a long, diagonal wavy line, and others below.

"A woolly mammoth — I'm so glad they brought them back to the tundra," Aiyana said. "Such gentle beasts — hey, look at the tusks and the mouth, they look . . . strange."

"There, is that a horse?"

"If it is, those are really strange hooves. They splay like hands."

They scanned other animals they had no names for. One looked like a huge badger, and next to it was a squat, armored creature with a small, low head. Here and there, tall conifers filled the spaces, but no depictions of broad-leaf trees.

"Look, hiding in the trees, leopards or something." Aiyana pointed. One had gigantic, oversized fangs, and the other, with more moderate fangs, both looked to be on the verge of attacking what seemed like a tall, feathered dinosaur missing its forelimbs.

"Hm. No humans, no apes. Lots of birds though."

Below the wavy line were two huge sharks, slightly different from each other, three kinds of whales, with one larger than the sharks. Nearby was carved an even larger octopus-like . . . no, squid-like creature. Andie counted aloud, reaching eight arms and two tentacles trailing behind a streamlined, pointed head. The squid looked to be in a prominent place among the creatures of the oceans. It dwarfed even the whales.

"Strange that some carvings are so correct in the details yet clearly missed the mark in others," Aiyana said.

"What if they're not off at all?" Andie asked, taking picture after picture.

"Hmm," was her reply.

Crossing carefully past the two pillars so as not to disturb them, Aiyana stumbled, and caught herself. "Whoa, careful." Ares jumped back out of the way.

Catching her footing, Aiyana turned to look at what had tripped her. Andie looked down as well. A small square, tilted 45 degrees to a diamond shape, was set into the floor in front of the right pillar. Andie shined a light over, and saw the other pillar had one before it also.

"That looks like a button sticking up from the floor."

"Well, let's not accidentally step on it, right?"

Both teens crossed carefully to the Mars-side wall. Here, a wide cutaway view of Olympus Mons filled the wall in extremely accurate detail. Both sides showed steep cliffs, with gradual slopes above that, rising up to the top, with a few crater-gaps at the peak plateau. Inside the Mountain, clear-cut long straight lines, shafts, had been cut from the top, converging as they descended, but not quite touching at the ends.

"One, two, three . . ." Aiyana counted eleven lines that led from the top surface of the Mountain down into the middle, where they just ended. Each line simply stopped at a certain point, all ending at the same level less than one-quarter the distance down from the top plateau.

"What do you think they are?"

"No idea. Unless we're standing inside one of those points?"

"Hm. I don't see any shafts leading up to the surface above us, just those writings on the ceiling."

"Could the stairwell be the shaft?"

"Maybe, but these shafts look steeper than 45 degrees. So probably these are something we haven't come across."

Both teens turned back to the center of the room. There looked to be little else to see. All that remained were the two pedestals, and their two diamond squares sticking up from the floor.

"Those really look like buttons, meant to be pushed," Andie said. Ares walked over and looked at one, his head down. The cat's lamps lit up a red line in the floor.

"What's this?" Andie looked closer, shining a flashlight on one red line, then toward the other pillar and its own red line. Each was a straight-line groove in the floor, straight to its corresponding pedestal. Each red line each climbed up its pedestal.

Aiyana looked at her side, shaking her head at the raised button.

Andie took pictures of both pedestals, including floor, front, sides, and behind, and stepped back to take in the entire room. Checking how full the camera's memory was, 87%, they flipped over to video mode.

"So . . . what now?"

"Isn't it obvious? These buttons were meant to be pushed, and they're connected to these bowls, somehow. See the red lines?"

"Obvious, like how? We both push these buttons . . . and just . . . hope?"

"They want us to see something. Something that connects Earth and Mars. I bet it's like a hologram show or something."

"You watch too much sci-fi," Aiyana said.

"There's no such thing as too much sci-fi."

Aiyana sneered back, one hand on her hip.

"We're out of time. Are we doing this or not, Aiya?"

"Mew," encouraged Ares.

"What the hell," she said. Each stood behind a button. Andie kept the video capture running.

"One."

"Wait. Are we going on three, or after three?"

"Hm. On three means *on* three."

"Okay, together."

Ares backed up. Teens kept eye contact.

"One."

"Two."

"Three." Two booted feet stomped down.

The cat turned and ran, vanishing through the entryway, barely ahead of a solid black slab as it descended and sealed both teens in the room. They felt the thud through the soles of their boots yet heard nothing at all. Andie walked back to the slab and pressed both hands against it, trying to push. Aiyana tried to push too. Not even a little budge.

They looked at each other. Then . . . a bright light from behind them cast their two shadows on the slab before them as it grew brighter.

They both turned slowly toward it.

Andie had the presence of mind to raise the camera back up, to capture whatever was to happen next.

Both faced the light.

A square piece of the black rock floor, between the two pedestals, had lifted several centimeters out of the floor, and the bright glow shone out in all directions, getting brighter and brighter. The entire room was glowing now, not a bit of the room's extremities was left in shadow.

This . . . luminescence . . . had with it something else, a fuzzy quality to it. It was almost like going out of focus, at first. The room before them rippled strangely, as if water was flowing through it.

Then they both could see a white fog seeping into the room from the same location. From under the square panel, what looked like dry ice or some crazy concert fog effect poured out in all directions, coating the floor until it floated across to the walls and gently rebounded back on itself, moving in eerie, shifting white ripples.

Andie focused the camera on the square and kept recording.

Soon, the entire floor was ankle-deep in foggy, white vapor-gas.

More of the gas settled into the room, filling it up higher and higher, up the walls.

Aiyana looked at the atmo monitor on her wrist display.

Andie panned the camera down to include the data on their own wrist.

"Do you think it's some kind of acid gas? Like, it might eat through our suits?"

"I can't . . . no, that can't be right," Andie replied, shaking their head. Both teens cast around nervously as the white gas continued to rise, now at thigh level.

"Look," Aiyana held her wrist display up closer, which now showed *ATM 0.19*, a mixture of nitrogen and oxygen in nearly equal amounts. "Weird?"

In much smaller partial pressures, CO_2 and H_2O were also reading on the wrist monitor. At the bottom end of the display, traces of Ar, CO and O_3 rounded out the readings. If anything else was in the room, it was too scarce for suit sensors to measure.

The temperature had somehow climbed from -54° up to -22° in under a minute.

"What the — ?" Andie said, not quite believing the suit's instruments.

"Rr-mew?" came over the radio in both teens' ears.

"Ares!" Andie breathed with relief. "Are you all right?

"Mew," came a little cat voice.

"He must be just outside the slab."

The white gas reached their waist level.

"Rr-mew?" came Ares' plaintive cry over the radio once more.

"Just hang on Ares, something is happening in here. The room is filling up with a gas, a vapor . . . like a cloud . . . first impression, it's not going to hurt us. But if you stop hearing our voices, you'll know we're not here anymore. If that happens, I want you to run all the way back the way we came and join the evacuation any way you can. But not yet. All right? Not. Yet."

"Mew," came the cat's voice, then he stayed quiet for the moment.

"Look, the gas. It's turning clear," Aiyana said.

The gas continued to rise, sure, but as it did so, it went from opaque to semi-translucent to perfectly clear.

Andie held one wrist up above the white cloudy layer, hoping the camera view could capture both changing conditions in the room and the changing numbers on the display.

The small screen showed *ATM 0.46*, now with a much higher partial pressure of Nitrogen, compared to the other gases. The temperature kept climbing, and was now nearly the freezing point of water, at -3° . . . then it jumped to -1° . . . then to +2° and kept climbing.

At length, the temperature showed a rise of more than sixty degrees from starting levels, the air in the room now completely clear as the temperature reached a t-shirt comfort level of +20°.

The last of the fog dissipated in trace wisps, leaving just the glow of the central square panel in an otherwise crystal clear room.

Andie looked down at the wrist display and with the camera, captured the last vestiges of white gas vanishing into the warmer air. Panning the camera around, they let it capture the final, stabilized conditions.

Andie paused the recording to read the camera display—its storage showed 98%, flashing red. Andie switched off the power—its little battery, too, was running low. Folding the camera's view panel closed, they slipped the camera back into a thigh pocket.

Both wrist displays showed ATM 0.85.

"Eighty-five percent, how crazy is that?" Aiyana shook her head, taking a couple steps and looking around the brightly-illuminated room.

"That should be enough for me to breathe, for just a short while, right?" Andie asked.

"Um, for you to *what*?"

"See here—the final mix is 70% nitrogen, 29% oxygen, 1% argon, and other gaseous compounds at just a fraction of a percent."

"Anything poisonous—anything toxic?"

"No . . . none of these would actually kill a person, if my AP chem skills are correct."

"Okay, since I know you're gonna do it, I won't try to talk you out of it. Gimme the camera."

Andie dug it out and passed it over. Aiyana switched it back on and had Andie swipe right on their wrist display to show vitals: heart rate and breathing. Aiyana snapped a single photo, then turned off the camera. Inside their faceplate, Andie breathed deeply: in through nose, out through mouth. All was ready.

"My animal survival brain is screaming at me not to do this."

"I'm screaming at you not to do this."

Despite every instinct, and years of routine suit training and survival conditioning, Andie's logical, scientific brain was still firmly in charge.

Aiyana gripped Andie by both shoulders.

Andie reached up, twisted the faceplate dial just below the chin, and swung it open.

Chapter Zero

Again–Not An Earthquake

The air hit their face, making Andie blink in surprise.

"The air, it feels . . . warm."

"You are out of your mind."

Andie took a few cautious sniffs. "Smells dusty, and . . . almonds. Ozone, maybe." From behind the sealed door, the cat murmured into the radio.

Chemistry aside, a deep breath would lead to . . . a fit of coughing . . . or just funky, breathable air. Andie breathed in deeply.

And fell into a fit of coughing.

With nostrils burning a little and eyes tearing up, it was clear this was not quite Earth-normal air.

"Wooo, that's a rush. May be the higher oxygen," with much blinking and slight shake of the head. "The almond smell, and it feels . . . how can I put this . . . like an itching sensation in my lungs." Andie coughed several times and sank to take a knee. Aiyana crouched with her friend.

Taking one more itching lungful of air, then another, Andie cleared their throat and said, "It's kind of like being in an airlock after a severe dust storm, you know, when the air is a little gritty? But without the dusty film buildup on the back of my teeth." Another few coughs.

"Well, your lips aren't turning cherry so there's probably no contaminants. Are you seeing stars? Feeling dizzy?"

"No, just the rush from the extra oxygen. Can you just—" Aiyana snapped one final picture of the wrist display vitals, which had not changed much at all. Heart rate was up, a little. Then, she powered down the camera again, and handed it to Andie to put away.

Ares hissed loudly over the radio. Less than a second later, the ground, the walls, and ceiling began to shake again. Dust sifted down from new cracks in the ceiling.

Andie heard a loud hissing sound, but rapidly dimming like the volume in the room was being turned down. Andie's ears popped. The raised square in the floor stopped glowing. The room quickly fell dark. Eyes widening, with dawning awareness that somehow the air was rapidly escaping the room . . .

They slammed down the faceplate and twisted its seal shut. Aiyana cranked up the airflow in Andie's suit from the wrist controls.

"A quake, a big one!" Aiyana shouted. The display showed suit internal pressure of ATM 1.0 within seconds, next to the external number, which showed *ATM 0.48*, and dropping.

Andie felt a drop of wetness in one nostril, and when it dribbled down onto their lips . . . blood. They shook off a moment of dizziness and both teens watched wrist displays carefully.

The pressure in the room plummeted.

The display showed ATM 0.31 . . . ATM 0.27 . . . ATM 0.22, and eventually stabilized at ATM 0.04.

The glowing square panel had vanished, back to fully-flush with the rest of the stone floor. Even the square edges where it lifted had vanished.

Aiyana turned back to the slab blocking the doorway, staggering one step as the floor trembled. Andie stood shakily, balancing through the tremors, and turned to the door as well. In full silence but with only minor vibration in their feet, the slab slowly rose, seemingly of its own accord.

Ares stood in the middle of the doorway, panting slightly inside his little cat faceplate. The cat did not enter the room but watched expectantly. The room lurched sideways. All three stumbled. Andie almost knocked one of the bowls off its pedestal.

"We're taking these . . . with us," Andie breathed. Taking no time to argue, Aiyana hefted the sealed bowl with Andie. Finding it far lighter than expected, Aiyana nested the sealed one inside the open bowl, right on top of the rust dust. Aiyana lifted both bowls together while Andie grabbed the bag with the extra air tanks, confirming all three were inside.

Aiyana looked up at the slab, feeling like they had just thieved some priceless golden idol. The massive stone doorway . . . stayed open.

The cat skittered back as both teens crossed the threshold together. There wasn't so much as a whisper from the door or the room behind him. Andie reached down to grab Aiyana's flashlight where it rolled around on the floor, and clicked it into a belt loop.

The three turned toward the staircase. Ares began climbing immediately. The ground trembled.

Time to run.

Up the steps.

Up. A thousand. Steps.

* * *

Earlier estimates had finally caught up with the actual evacuee count. Under one hundred-fifty thousand people remained in the rapidly emptying city. One-third of that number had sought refuge in the Watney

Way breezeway and the three greenhouses, as if the last part of a sinking ship, the top mast, might keep them alive a bit longer. Rockets still blasted off every fifteen minutes, visible through the greenhouse domes.

The central screen now showed:

CITY EVACUATION IN PROGRESS

Status: 86% Evacuated

Jackson, now running on bad coffee and good intentions, ordered the vehicle evacuation route to be shut down within the hour. He rubbed his sore eyes.

Controllers knew all the lower tunnels, where people had crowded into their tour buses, would soon be filled with fast-moving, glowing liquid death. No new ground cars were dispatched to Olympus Mons, and those currently loading were directed to expedite boarding and get out of the Mountain, post haste.

Eliza stood watching over the shuttle rockets' progress, still running at surge capacity, with ground-based fuel reserves completely depleted. Most shuttles still had tanks more than half-full, but the first several to go 'bingo fuel' made their final flights and were grounded.

MagLev trains, with their station set well above the subterranean tunnels, were given a window of three more hours to operate, and no more.

Then the Mars Grand Council made an unexpected decision: one special train, a cargo-fit, would be sent among the passenger trains back to the city. Their unique mission: save the herd. The plan: race over from Jupiter's Crossing, climb the Mountain tracks, load up all seventy-four horses, then race back down, turning North toward New Marrakech.

The desperate plea that prompted this decision had started among the citizens themselves—very vocal social media influencers had pointed out that since human evacuations were nearly complete, something had to be done to save the horses.

The chosen train, fitted with open-bay cargo containers and piloted by an all-volunteer crew, departed Jupiter's Crossing. The worlds watched, humanity holding its collective breath as the train pulled into the overcrowded Mons Terminus station.

The horses, skittish to begin with in natural disasters, had been heavily medicated to calm them. The loading, tying down with harnesses, separating males from each other and isolating mares in heat plus two foals . . . had been hastily planned out before the train arrived. The wranglers packed in as many alfalfa bales as the train could carry after the horses were loaded up. A lone mare, a beautiful *First Nation* American Paint, was lost during roundup, having panicked and sprinted away into the forest.

The herd's destination: the sports arena in New Marrakech, the one boasting real grass—that would become the herd's new home, if they could just get safely away from the volcano.

* * *

Both teens' breathing came in ragged, heaving breaths. Quads burned, arms ached. They took turns carrying the two bowls up the staircase. Allowing only momentary breaks as they climbed, the trio bounded up as fast as they could without risking their precious cargo.

"Check . . . your air," Andie panted in heaving breaths as they finally reached the top of the staircase.

"Must . . . be below . . . five percent . . . I don't even have a number," Aiyana panted, holding up a wrist display with a steady red LED glowing next to the words "Air Supply".

"Same." Andie shook their head inside the helmet. Lights popped before their eyes—the tank may have gone empty. Both were re-breathing unfiltered air. Ares' supply was in the amber, hovering just above ten percent, but he showed no signs of distress, yet.

Andie took one last glimpse back down the staircase. In the darkest, farthest edges of their vision: a dim splotch of reddish light.

"What is that?"

"Magma? Let's MOVE."

A moment later, the three had bounded into the weird round room. The door stood open, the steps up to their exit still in place.

Ares led the charge up through the sphere and out the other side.

"Wait." Andie shouted. They skidded to a stop. "Aiya, pull my tank, put the compact-40 in its place."

"What are you doing? Are you out?"

"Yes . . . and I want to try . . . closing the door behind us . . . I hope?"

Aiyana lifted the frame-shell up on its hinge from Andie's air tank and twisted the Compact-80 tank free. She grabbed a full 40 and twisted it down, snug into place. She handed Andie the larger tank and slammed the suit back shut. Andie took a deep breath and shook off a dizzy spell.

Taking careful aim, Andie threw her exhausted tank down into the weird round room, nozzle first. It struck and cracked open, releasing the last of its gas all over the floor. The tank popped up comically, arced, and fell back down.

The stepped ramp they had just climbed up started to cycle, dropping away as the doorway they had just passed through began to close. Andie looked down, trying to catch a glimpse of the figure far in the chasm below the ramp as it rotated, but never got a clear view.

Within a moment, the weird round room was back as they had originally found it—a mysterious, spherical dead-end.

They ran up toward the blue door. Aiyana carried the bowls and Andie looked to make sure Ares was clear of the door. They slammed it shut as an extra barrier behind them.

A violent lurch of the room sent all three flying forwards. The stacked bowls skittered out of Aiyana's grasp and across the dusty floor, sliding up against the bike. Luckily, they did not break.

Andie staggered sideways while trying to stand, but with the next tremors, slipped and stumbled backwards against the stone wall, striking hard with a loud crunch of their helmet.

They stepped around awkwardly, trying to stand up.

An alarm sounded in Andie's helmet, not the decompression alarm, thank all the gods, but an intermittent pinging in groups of three.

Beep-beep-beep. Beep-beep-beep. Beep-beep-beep.

The beeping warbled. Then it went silent.

Andie looked up, seeing Aiyana standing. Ares was out of sight, but he still had to be somewhere nearby.

"That was crazy!" Andie said, brushing their wrist free of dust, tapping the display to wake it up.

Aiyana didn't reply. She just looked at Andie with a puzzled look.

Andie looked down. The wrist display was dark. They tapped repeatedly, trying to wake it up. Nothing. Aiyana pointed down. The top third of the suit pack, the section containing its power cell, radio, and other electronics had broken away, just above the air tank.

Aiyana grabbed Andie by both arms, saying something with clear concern—no, outright terror on her face. All in complete silence. Andie waved their hand up in front of where helmet lights should shine. No light. The suit had suffered a complete power failure.

Aiyana saw Andie's shoulders rise and fall, and saw they were not choking or coughing. Still breathing. She cast around wildly for the bike — there, just a few meters away, by the exit tunnel. Aiyana yanked Andie towards it, losing her footing, catching herself, then stumbling again, right into the vehicle with a bump.

Aiyana gripped the handlebar with one hand and steadied herself on the seat with the other hand. She pointed a finger at her own chest, and made a slashing motion across the neck. Andie knew Aiyana had also just run out of air.

From the bag, Andie grabbed out the second tank, and fumbled open Aiyana's suit back. A few clunks, a mild hiss, then after a moment, a louder hiss. A blast of cool air washed over Aiyana's face. It was the first sound other than heavy breathing Aiyana had heard in several moments. Twisting the tank in as far as it could turn, Andie snapped the Exo-Suit casing back shut. Aiyana touched a few buttons on the wrist display. She held it up for Andie to see. ATM 1.0, Est. Remaining: 20 min. The red LED winked off; the amber one turned on.

Andie started looking wildly around, searching. But without helmet lights they could see little in the darkness. Aiyana spoke into the radio to the only other one who could hear her.

"Ares, can you show yourself to Andie please?"

Ares hopped up on the back seat of the bike. Aiyana pointed. Andie nodded inside the helmet and gave a thumbs-up. Then, they pointed at Aiyana and at the handlebars. She nodded back.

Aiyana mounted first. The bowls were not going to fit under the back seat, so after Ares hopped up to hold the handlebars, Andie held the bowls awkwardly between the two riders after cinching down the lap strap.

Aiyana hit the sequence of commands to bring the skimmer to life. The ground continued to tremble, with dust and pebbles raining down every so often around them. She see-sawed the skimmer back and forth a few times until it was pointed the correct way. She gently applied a twist to the throttle. She felt one hand grip her shoulder, and risking a quick peek under the other arm, saw that Andie held the bowls snugly against their abdomen with the other hand.

The skimmer, loaded down with humans, cat and artifacts, moved slowly at first in the gravel, then, upon reaching the top of the steep slope, accelerated smoothly down the leveled-out tunnel.

Adrenaline surging, Aiyana's mind sharpened to its highest focus, recalling with perfection every turn and landmark along the ride. Through multiple intersections, sharp turns here, straightaways there, landmarks all whizzed past in a frenetic blur. After ten minutes of borderline-reckless driving, the group had reached the phony-warnings airlock. The skimmer came to a reluctant halt, kicking up gravel on both sides as it screeched and skidded to a stop.

Ares hopped down and stopped in his tracks. He looked up at the air pressure light on the portal door, the one that should have showed green. It showed bright red—zero pressure on the other side. They took turns looking through the small window, seeing cave-ins had blocked the way ahead. No light shined through from the other side of the door.

If cave-ins had ruined this route, then the motor pool areas, the evacuation routes, those might be impassible as well. This . . . was not the way out.

Andie mentally cast through all the possibilities. The Pocket, the Needle? The Overlook? No, the way to get there was on the other side of this door. The evac routes below, the ones leading to the buses and ground vehicles? Nope, they would be filling up with magma soon, if that glow in the long staircase hadn't been in their imagination. And, the only way to get there was on the other side of this door.

What was left? Aiyana thought hard. Nothing came to mind.

Andie grabbed her arm, and knelt to write in the dust: BURIAL ROOM

The crypt! And past that, the white-tiled exit—that way might still be clear. The airlock they had stumbled across while searching for that ridiculous laser pointer—it was all they had left.

Turning the skimmer around before loading it up made startup go quicker. Andie slapped Aiyana on the shoulder, noticing a quiver in their hand. It was starting to get chilly inside the suit.

They shot back down the tunnel. After making a couple wrong turns, Andie eventually pointed at a landmark that seemed familiar. Aiyana nodded and powered on ahead. In her mind, a flow of rising magma was right behind them.

And there it was again—the crossroads! Here, they had originally found the massive burial chamber—and several other divergent paths they hadn't had the time to explore. Aiyana drew the skimmer to a stop and looked at the gloom of the burial chamber.

In the dust there, two sets of shuffling boot prints, and one set of little cat boot prints, stood testament to an earlier adventure, a more innocent time. Andie got a little choked up, knowing the fate that awaited this place, what would happen in a very short time.

The Mountain was about to claim them. Now Andie understood.

Aiyana glanced back at Andie, now shivering inside the suit. To Aiyana, it looked as though Andie whispered something while staring into the chamber, but they did not dismount. Andie slapped Aiyana's shoulder.

Ares hunched down, front paws curled over the handlebars. Aiyana shook off the moment, exhaled, and turned the skimmer, sacred burial space now on their left. The white-tiled exit should be straight ahead now if she remembered correctly. It had to be.

One last look. Then an obvious nod. Another slap on the shoulder, and a tight grip.

Aiyana twisted the accelerator grip handle. The vehicle's power level had turned amber, but she knew what remained was more than enough to take them the rest of the way. On her wrist, seven minutes of air remained.

White tiles ahead. Quick stop. Dismounting, Ares leapt straight over the handlebars and stood by the door. Andie unclipped and stood, carrying the bowls as Aiyana opened the first door. The three stepped through; Aiyana pulled the door shut and sealed it. The outer door opened at her gentlest touch, and they practically leapt out of the airlock into bright sunlight, Ares staying close by in the occasional tremors. Aiyana tugged the outer door shut, not really knowing why she bothered to. Habit, perhaps.

All three squinted in the bright afternoon sunshine, after hours of exertion in near-total darkness. The cliff's edge before them left only a small balcony for them to stand. A sheer drop-off below — no, that wouldn't work. A climb, then? They probably couldn't strap Ares to one of their suits and juggle two bowls then climb . . . not a chance of that. Were their two cables still here? They looked and saw no sign where they had been stuck in the rock-gap weeks before.

Andie set the bowls down. Checking their pockets in desperation, they searched for . . . they did not know what. There was nothing left, not even the green woven bracelet.

Ares perked up, suddenly looked off to the left, searching around for something. Aiyana looked in the same direction. Andie didn't see this — they kept sifting through whatever they might still have. There was just one Compact-40 remaining to split between the three of them, but Andie doubted all three would last that long. There was nowhere left to take refuge from magma flood, undoubtedly filling the lower passages nearby. It would come bursting out the side of where they stood in just moments, maybe. Half an hour at most.

Then Ares bounded away over some rocks, stumbling occasionally on pebbles as he ran. Aiyana watched after him, confused expression on her face. The cat rounded a boulder at the edge of the drop-off and disappeared to one side. By now Andie, shaking like a leaf and teeth chattering, had noticed Ares was gone. They stood and followed Aiyana.

Aiyana stepped up around the boulder where she had seen Ares disappear.

On the far side of a six or seven-meter gap, and several meters below, a lone vehicle had parked right near the end of a narrow, carved-out mountain road. A rover. A rover named Endurance. Their dorky science teacher, in his glasses and trimmed reddish beard, was just unbuckling himself from the driver's seat to seal up his helmet.

He looked up, noticed them watching him from above, and waved enthusiastically. Within moments, he had begun to reel out a cable from the winch attached to the rear cargo section of the rover.

* * *

In the four hours that followed, many things had changed.

Endurance and Lauryna picked their way back down the mountainside using creative navigation and satellite pictures to discover the un-blocked roads down. When they hit the level plains, the two made a beeline for Blue Ridge at top speed. Crossing the gap, power in both vehicles running dangerously low, both approached the Blue Ridge garages unchallenged.

Maybe they were expected; maybe they were irrelevant.

After its upward surge, the magma flow slowed nearly to a stop for a few hours, giving them precious time to cross the open plains. After a brief rejoicing among the evacuees, and no small amount of false hope, the magma started rising again, but this time at its fastest rate recorded.

Mars, great god of war, and his blacksmith Vulcan were determined, with hammer and heat, to wage violence no matter how many reprieves the humans had enjoyed.

All ground vehicles had cleared the plains — there was just no knowing where any lava might burst free. The last stragglers fleeing the foot of the Mountain hastily skittered away to the North and to the East, as fast as their wheels could take them. Their dust trails settled and the valley floor fell still.

Inside the city's original EOC, the last 24 action officers were ordered to abandon their stations, leaving all terminals on and permanently awake. Every camera, computer, and AI assistant was similarly left powered-on, in full-awake mode. The last person out turned off the lights and locked the EOC outer doors. The last orbital starship, dangerously low on fuel, loaded them up and blasted off for the Blue Ridge landing pad. After landing, the rocket was secured — the brave flight crew joined the other evacuees inside for a rest and a well-earned meal.

The cargo train carrying the herd had rocketed down and away, making the broad, sweeping left turn across the plains, followed carefully by the best zoom cameras at Blue Ridge until the train passed out of sight in canyons leading to New Marrakech. A few last few passenger-filled trains hit the plains at their usual breakneck speed, heading toward the closer Jupiter's Crossing settlement. When the last train cleared the plains, all eyes turned toward the Mountain.

Every external airlock and tunnel bulkhead leading out of the city was locked down and sealed by Blue Ridge controllers.

The last group of two thousand crowded into the train station were left with one option: cross the city and ride up the Big 'Vater to the Greenhouses and await their fate.

Darkness crept across the Martian sky. The sunset glowed with its usual blue fire. A final tally showed seventeen thousand citizens would have to ride it out in the greenhouses. MERF technicians, many of them, had given away their seats on the last few rocket flights without hesitation. Free French Fries were handed out without prejudice, and light music played throughout the three greenhouses.

Families strolled among the towering forests; the last available tents were pitched in clearings, and a vigil was set up around the Janaki Tree. Pen lights and luminarias, still on display from the recent Samhain harvest festival, winked on one by one as the light levels outside dropped. They huddled. They held each other close, praying to the deities of their forefathers for deliverance. Despair started to set in.

* * *

Ground radars kept the updates pouring in—the magma was beneath the evacuation tunnels, surging up through the twisting magma tunnels.

One final, blasting announcement reverberated throughout the empty city, notifying any who had foolishly remained behind that this was their last, their very final call to catch the elevator up to the greenhouses. Half an hour later, under full darkness, the elevator was brought to the top, and turned off.

Dozens of camera feeds, carefully monitored, showed no movement throughout the city—no final stragglers desperately seeking a way out. Aside from the occasional fish breaking the surface of Silver Lake, the city was still.

The Blue Ridge big central screen showed

CITY EVACUATION IN PROGRESS

Status: 98.5% Evacuated

From his director's station, Jackson pulled a small brass key from his pocket, inserted it in its designated receptacle, and turned it. One second later, the remote command spread across the whole Mons-Plex CityNet, and every last Founders Stone swung neatly shut on its hinges, falling perfectly flush as if never opened. Every dwelling and business sliding entry doors followed—every doorway to a home, shop, skyscraper, and business. Jackson slipped the key back into an inner jacket pocket.

Thousands of camera feeds watched the Mons-MegaPlex carefully.

Just before midnight, the magma breached the evacuation tunnels.

One by one, cameras in those tunnels beneath the city locked in freeze-frame or flipped to static as they were overcome by the heat.

The next hit was ACSA. Cameras across the ACSA cavern showed magma rising between buildings, trees catching fire, first individually, then whole hillsides of trees, like torches, blazed with light until everything in the arboretum was consumed. Magma poured through multiple points, rushing through the empty spaces and flooding them.

Blue Ridge controllers hastily turned off the air handlers to slow the spread of smoke and cinders. The broad ACSA Crossroads door was slammed shut and sealed — the tunnel connecting the Crossroads with the city was deliberately collapsed using explosives. The West Tunnel, with its elevated walk and historical displays, was also detonated and collapsed, with the strong doors at both ends sealing it up tight.

Camera feeds inside the Mons Megaplex itself showed the serene city. Temperatures held steady and sprinklers were left on wherever city water pressure allowed.

At his Director's station, Jackson leaned forward, hands gripping the upper shelf. He held his breath in anticipation. Eliza Griffin stood by his side, tears welling up, but still she looked determined.

"Come on . . . come on . . . work, dammit . . . work." Jackson muttered. Tension hung in the air.

Far below the EOC, the briefing theater and common areas were filled with the refugees, thousands gathering around the huge screens on the cavern walls. No one breathed, eyes stayed glued on screens. Stein stood close to his five students and classroom cat, looking down at his tablet's TeacherCam view of room F-105 and then back up at the big screens before him. Reillee stood on his left, and Ric stood on his right, holding Sitara as tears streamed down her face unchecked. Andie and Aiyana stood just in front of Stein. Andie trembled as she held Ares. Choked sobs could be heard throughout the crowd.

Stein watched his tablet, horror growing inside him. The temperature showed a slight tick upward, but the hallway hadn't filled up with magma yet. The cat stared ahead, occasionally twitching his eyes in annoyance.

Now, a rumbling rippled the ground under their feet. The magma engulfed the Mons High School tram station and lapped against the sealed doors of the school's main entrance. The school camera there succumbed to the heat; the image froze.

Then . . . it happened.

On all the external camera feeds, a single, bright yellow lava flow burst right through the side of the Mountain at the city level.

Then several more gushers burst through the rock face alongside the first one.

A collective intake of breath, and simultaneous shouts of "No!" and a few screams echoed around the common area.

* * *

Up in the EOC, Jackson pumped his fist.

"I knew it," he muttered so low only Eliza could hear.

No one looked his way at first. He let out the breath he had been holding. He dropped his fist and slumped heavily into his seat, still watching the display. An admin troop, a Technician Decker, glanced over, stood, and approached to see if Jackson was all right. Eliza also looked at him, blinking through tears streaming down her face.

Jackson was openly sobbing now, but he was smiling. "My friends," Jackson said, "everything's gonna be all right."

"No, sir, it isn't. Didn't you see what just happened?" Decker asked.

Jackson smiled and nodded. "Keep your eyes on those screens, Mister

Decker. Don't lose hope . . . see for yourself."

Admin officer Decker returned to his post. Jackson rubbed his eyes, and more tears came pouring down his cheeks. He laughed out loud. He exhaled, laughed, and cried some more. Eliza looked back up at the camera feeds, thinking her new boss might have lost his mind.

* * *

Stein looked up from the tablet at the camera views. Every channel, every news broadcast, had switched to the external views of the Mountain, watching the tragedy unfold. Cameras zoomed in to the glowing yellow gushers pouring down the side of the Mountain, a bright flow where none had existed before during Mars' two and a half billion standard years.

At first, the lava fountains blasted straight sideways in a bizarre fan-shape, through multiple fractures in the rock. These fell, cascaded down, and collected in parallel valleys. They ran in fast rivulets and joined each other, racing down toward the plains below. Ultimately, one mighty glowing river poured down the Northeast face of the Mountain.

The empty MagLev train lines and roads at the foot of the Mountain were overrun. When the lava river hit the plains, it slowed, the bright glow turning orange then red as it fanned out toward the solar fields. Within moments, hundreds of little flash-puffs flared up and quickly snuffed out.

Still no lava burst through the school hallways, but Stein knew it was just a matter of time. He kept the feed of his classroom going, and next to him, Ric glanced down at it, sniffing.

"It must be a frozen image after the cameras melted?" the teen asked. Ares wriggled over Andie's shoulder and peered down at the screen. Stein held it up for the cat to see more closely. He put a paw up at the corner, where a blinking pair of dots showed the time on the camera and the SchoolNet.

Stein looked at him—how could he know about the clock?

00:12 ticked over to 00:13. He was still watching a live camera feed. Surely the whole city was filled up by now? Lava flows continued blasting forth, silently racing down the steep slopes.

His classroom showed some dust particles drifting down across the camera's view, but the room, strangely, was still intact. The news had ceased all ACSA feeds; the cameras in that cavern had melted away completely. Feeds across the city showed skyscrapers, fields, forests, and so on, still standing there, with a several-degree rise in temperature.

Word spread quickly: the city was saved, out of danger.

After much confusion, the joy that followed echoed across the whole Solar System.

* * *

The evacuees trapped atop the Mountain, the "Forest People," as the news media called them, settled in for an extended camping excursion that lasted half a Martian year. In the plus column, they wouldn't be running out of food, fresh air, or water anytime soon. Upslope from the greenhouses, sprawling solar fields still fed power to the greenhouses, as well as to the empty city below. The abandoned capital was put on power rationing, with only the environmental controls kept at full to preserve the parks, the forests, and Silver Lake.

After several requests, Stein was eventually allowed back into the EOC, to meet once more with the director.

"I see you're safely back," Jackson said, eying Stein and Andie as they entered the room bearing strange burdens. The director seemed much more at ease, even smiling.

Andie and Stein each set down a bowl on the table before him, one still encapsulated under its smooth black seal, the other still holding four centimeters of rust dust.

Ares jumped up on the table and sat between the two bowls, taking credit for his fine work.

"Never in human history has so much been owed by so many to one so fuzzy," Andie said, scratching Ares behind his ears.

"Huh? Now what's that supposed to mean?" Jackson asked.

Ares licked his shoulder, exactly as cats do.

Andie set down the hand-held camera on the table before Jackson, along with a few folded, ruffed-up papers with photos and sketches on them. Andie pointed at the camera.

"The things we captured in those images probably no longer exist. So please try not to lose them," Andie responded, now smiling and turning to leave. Ares hopped down to follow them out. Stein nodded to the Director and turned away as well.

Jackson didn't say anything, but he watched them carefully, wondering what exactly had just been dropped in his lap.

Stein paused in the doorway, looking back to the MERF Director. "And I wouldn't break the seal on that other bowl in here," he said, looking around the room. "I don't know exactly what's inside, but I'll bet you credits to cruisers it's organic. Non-Earth . . . ancient . . . organic."

Jackson's eyebrows raised and he watched the teacher leave the room.

Around the corner, Stein paused at a small office, letting Andie walk on ahead. He looked through the open doorway, where the room's sole occupant looked up at him with shock on her face.

"Mister Stein!" Eliza said. He trotted over to her and embraced his former student where she stood—the same lady he had last seen at Dr. Holm's lecture . . . the same one who had just two days ago been field-promoted to MERF Deputy Director.

Andie, with Ares at their feet, pressed the elevator button and stepped back to await its arrival.

"Are you hungry?" They asked the cat. "I'm starving."

"Mrrrr..Meeeew?" Ares requested.

"I don't know, let's see if we can find some," Andie said back.

"Mew," Ares said. The elevator doors opened.

The two stepped in and Andie thumbed the button for the ground floor. They were all too eager to catch up some more with Aiyana and the rest of their circle of friends, but first . . . Andie owed dad a phone call, and owed a nice lady her pet Exo-Suit back.

* * *

In the deserted capital, from the upper storehouse window overlooking Silver Lake, a lone figure scanned the waters. He looked up across the utterly silent, empty city, his eyes reflecting a row of floodlights along the shore line.

"So . . . it seems I'll no' be meetin' ma' maker today after all," he murmured, proud Scottish accent bold in every word. Resting both hands on the windowsill, he tapped two fingers, skeletal finger bone tattoos just visible in the dim light.

He stopped tapping and looked up. The CityGlow™ lights above flickered and danced, then went dark. A moment later, the starry sky returned.

"And what's yer game, I wonder?" he asked the stars above.

His fingers resumed their thrumming, like a heartbeat . . . and Daemon bided his time.

Epilogue

Three months had passed since the evacuation. The people of Nerus had opened their city, but nerves were getting frayed. The Mons-Plex refugees wanted to know if returning to their city would ever be possible, but magma still dribbled down the flanks of the Mountain. None of the routes back was deemed remotely safe. It might be months, or a hundred years — no one knew for sure. The city stayed empty.

The Herd was now settled in at their pasture in New Marrakech — the oversized futbol arena had become a new tourist attraction. The lost mare was mourned and memorialized.

Sitara, Ric, Reillee, and Andie started classes at Nerus High School, home of the "Fighting Legionnaires," or *The Legion* as they were known by students. Classes were filled to bursting, but they made do. Trace made an excellent tour guide — suddenly he was no longer the new kid. They had about 400 days until graduation, just over thirteen months on Earth.

Several names stayed on the MISSING/STATUS UNKNOWN list, including Aiyana, Reillee's parents, and about 1,750 others lost in accidents, cave-ins, vehicle breakdowns, or decompression mishaps while fleeing the capital city.

Only one person knew where Aiyana had gone—the tank named Lauryna had vanished from its last parking spot. Stein had hoped to see Aiyana off, having pulled all the extra money he could onto a pocket money card—but he was too late. When he stepped into the alcove parking garage to leave his gift, all he found was a set of fresh tank treads leading away through the dust, a few discarded filters, and a handful of Twinkie wrappers in the waste bins. The group of friends, including Stein, knew Andie would speak up if a dire need arose. Under the new name Aiyana had chosen—Andie also kept that to themselves—she would soon register as an adult in a different city, solidify her new persona, and start a new life.

Aiyana's 'folks' simply never looked for her. No ping, no message. And so, Aiyana Laughingwater's name remained among the missing.

Stein and his bride Tanya had been assigned to a studio apartment in an allergen-free apartment complex . . . so to Andie's surprise and delight, Ares moved in. Shaw barely resisted the idea, declaring his intent to study the cat's obvious intellect, for science. Not because he had grown to like Ares a lot, but . . . for science.

Andie was in for another surprise. The new MERF Deputy Director asked Andie to a meeting at MERF's new headquarters the following Friday morning. Shaw phoned Eliza Griffin to ask what it was all about, and after a perplexing yet reassuring chat with her, he had left it up to his kiddo to decide. Andie opted to go alone.

That Friday finally arrived. Andie fed Ares, then left the apartment to head uptown. Distracted and lost in thought, Andie hadn't noticed a small, fuzzy companion shadowing them the entire way.

At the MERF building, Andie climbed the steps and reached for the double doors. Ares mewed to be let in. After recovering from the jump-scare, Andie held the door open for the cat, giving him a small bow like a doorman from some golden-age mystery novel. Eliza was already there, smiling and walking over to greet Andie.

Shaking hands firmly, Ms. Griffin passed Andie a clip-on access badge, with 'WELCOME GUEST (Escort Required)' printed in large, friendly letters on the front. A geo-dot and tracker button were stuck to the back.

"Hello, Andie. I'm Eliza. How are you?"

Andie stuttered, in awe of her bold presence. Eliza wore a crisp business suit, pencil skirt tapering down just past her knees and just looked sharp. Her long black tresses were pulled back into a bun, with two delicate ringlets at her temples.

"Um, overwhelmed. And confused. Why am I here?"

"I'll explain everything upstairs. Let's chat as we go, shall we?" Eliza gestured toward security. Andie fell in step beside Eliza, who swiped an access card on a row of simple turnstiles and invited Andie to swipe the visitor badge and follow her through.

Andie made as if to follow, then glanced back. It was then Eliza noticed the cat, lingering behind the turnstiles.

Andie spoke up. "Oh him? I never go anywhere without him anymore. He needs to come along."

Eliza cocked an eyebrow, looking skeptical. She considered the cat.

"Is he your comfort animal?"

Andie shook their head. "Hm, no . . . Ares is more like my boss."

"Well, we all have one of those. He'll have to be scanned, same as the rest of us."

"Okay." Andie gave the cat a look and shrugged. Ares squinted one eye slightly.

"Come on through, my guy," Andie said.

Ares looked left, then right. He chose a completely different turn-style, two spots to the right, and trotted through, head high but still passing cleanly under the bars. He fell in at Andie's heels, carefully avoiding the other MERF people walking here and there.

At the security scanning tubes, Andie scooped up the cat and held him high overhead, like some offering to the mechanical gods. The machine whirled around them.

"I feel ridiculous," Andie muttered.

"Yeah, I bet that's a first for security too," Eliza said, smiling a sideways grin. "This way to the 'vators." They stepped in, and Eliza pressed the top floor button, swiping her badge in the same motion. The doors closed.

"You know, that video footage you shot inside the small Reaction Chamber is a real game changer. It showed basic combinations of chemical reactions, most of which we already know. What we think the upper and lower tracks of characters show . . . is how to use the steady heat of the volcano and normal rust dust to produce Carbon Monoxide and metallic iron. Then, electrolysis and combustion reduce into other useful things like water, breathable air, and rocket fuel."

"No kidding? So, whoever inscribed that writing must have known O-Mons would eventually . . . "

"Erupt, exactly," Eliza said. "The Mountain becomes the factory for just one step of a multi-part process. Its deep magma chamber and conduit—"

"Excellent use of terms," Andie said.

"Yeah, that's Stein's fault. The Vesuvius lesson and that stupid cutaway diagram he made us hand-draw a dozen times. I assume he still teaches that lesson?"

"Wait. You had Mister Steinheiser as a teacher too?"

"Indeed, I did. So . . . the volcano. Mons is a shield, making the eruptions steadier, less sporadic and less violent. It simmers rather than exploding, that's why we think . . . 'they' put the room there for you to find. Anyways, the conduit is where the heat is harnessed, and as long as the temps exceed 1400 or 1500 Kelvins, it's enough for us to add carbon to the iron oxide, with the organic compound in the bowl, and burn it. The ultimate result, we think, will be an abundance of greenhouse gases."

Andie looked down, processing this information. "So, Mars rust dust, combined with the carbon we provide, somehow, in the volcano's high heat . . . helps us thicken the atmosphere. Terraforming."

Eliza nodded enthusiastically. "It's not the whole solution — it's just one of many ways. But it will shorten terraforming from four or five hundred standard years down to . . . well, maybe within our lifetime, if we can melt both polar ice caps and crank out even more greenhouse gases from all our industrial sites."

"Earth could help — they still have too much carbon in the air for another couple hundred years at least."

"True." The elevator dinged and the doors opened. Exiting the top floor, Eliza strode out purposefully. Andie rushed to keep up, and Ares stayed close. They stepped out into a mass of individual offices in one huge common space, modular furniture as far as the eye could see.

"Yikes, cube city."

"Not a fan?"

"No way . . . no way. This is crazy," Andie said, occasionally seeing a head pop up over a cubicle wall. This was not in any future Andie wanted. Eliza led onward and reached an office with her name in brass letters. Under the name, the title "Deputy Director" stood neatly in smaller letters.

"Are you okay?" Eliza asked.

Andie followed her into the room, and the cat followed Andie.

"I'm good, just not sure what you wanted me here for. Don't get me wrong, it's . . . impressive."

"And worth it, trust me. I got my digital paws on something . . . well, better for you if you see it for yourself."

Eliza dimmed the lights and shut the door, setting the electronic lock.

"What you're about to see doesn't leave this office, agreed?"

"Ms. Eliza, I don't . . . "

"Agreed, Andie Ellis, great-times-seven grandchild of Elias?" She said the words carefully, deliberately, eyebrows raised.

Andie looked at her, shocked. She was serious. This, whatever it was about . . . was serious. Andie nodded, then looked at the cat. "What do you say, Ares, can we keep a secret?"

"Mew."

"Yes, ma'am, we agree."

Eliza shook her head, smiling at the exchange. She activated security protocols and set a sound dampener to prevent eavesdropping. The cat jumped lightly up on the desk.

"So, has Stein taken you on any crazy field trips?" Eliza asked as she clicked buttons.

"Yes, we went up to the overlook and actually got to go outside."

"Bet that was memorable," Eliza said, clicking more links.

"Good times," Andie said without embellishment.

"For today, you take the big chair. There's a clip I'd like you to watch."

"Uh, all right," Andie said, easing into the tall chair, which squeaked when sat upon.

Eliza leaned over Andie's shoulder, popped open a few more hidden folders, and entered an encryption key too quickly for Andie to follow. A lone file sat in that well-hidden folder. Eliza tapped the file open, and a few scientist faces appeared on the screen.

The date stamp read 04-12-2032 — numbers never used on Mars. The video was clearly . . . ancient. Four scientists, in stereotypical lab coats, sat around a small table.

Eliza said, "this working group back on Earth, during the earliest Mars explorations, designed our capital city after its magma chamber cavern was found. They weren't even technically part of NASA yet."

"Wow, that's . . . pretty cool." Andie said, eager to learn something new. It also didn't hurt that this was some super top secret thing as well.

"I have your word, never to repeat what you've seen here?"

"Yes. I'll do my best to brain dump it, soon as I leave," Andie said, the curious scientist within, now fully activated.

"You'll find forgetting will be difficult."

"Then why show me?"

"I'll explain after, just trust me for a moment."

She tapped the triangle 'play' button.

"All our simulations show that the magma will bind up and turn solid in the smallest capillary tunnels, so our idea to protect the city . . . might work."

"How small are we talking? What diameter?"

"Large enough to admit a person, but not a vehicle or even one of those treaded motorcycle thingies."

"We've got to come up with a better name, they aren't exactly motorcycles, they're made to . . . skim . . . over sand dunes."

"Save it for another time. Today, it's about protecting the city from a slow eruption."

"Right. So in the smaller tunnels, if the magma hits an obstacle, it might cool enough to seal off that tunnel. Like blood clotting a . . . small cut, for instance."

"Correct. That's why the Braille cave probes never found a tube smaller than three feet wide. They had already cooled and sealed themselves off a billion years ago."

"Exactly. So, just a small bit of cooling is needed, when the magma hits a door that can withstand the heat."

"But won't it just melt through? Burst into our city through the thousand weak points we create for people to evacuate?"

"Not if the hatchways are sealed after everyone is safely out."

"But that's maybe . . . a hundred thousand people, or more? Could they all get out in time?"

"That's up to them, and how fast the magma rises. They may have hours, or weeks."

"And a ton of unknowns."

"That's why our portals need to use Steel 147, coated in high-grade ceramic. Its melting point only needs to withstand a thousand degrees for a few seconds for the magma to form a hard shell against the door. That stops the flow. If that happens, the closed door did its job.

"But how are we going to make sure they never carve tunnels bigger than 3 feet wide?

"If they do it would have to be made of a substance that can withstand much higher heat for a longer time. The bigger the door, the higher the melting point needs to be."

"There are so many problems with this plan. The next magma surge may be in a hundred years, or a hundred thousand, or never. How can we design an evac system that will last indefinitely?"

They paused, then one spoke up. "We don't have to. Terraforming should have the planet well on its way within a few hundred years of the cities reaching capacity."

"Point is, eventually cities won't be in caverns anymore; they'll be up on the surface."

"But after it erupts—wouldn't people permanently avoid cities built in or around volcanoes?"

"Not unless human nature changes a whole lot. The people of Naples, Italy put a gift shop atop the Vesuvius vent. A freaking gift shop, on the rim of an active volcano.

The other three just looked at him.

"What? I took my family there when we were studying volcanoes for this project. My five-year-old son tried to climb down into the crater vent and he almost succeeded. You see I don't have any hair left because of that boy . . . "

The room was quiet for a few ticks.

"Okay, but that's the thing: we don't need the city to last thousands of years, just hundreds of years.

"So we go with the escape hatches option, with thousands of ground cars that are already in common use until better transportation comes along . . . like that crazy MagLev train thing Tom Watkins is developing."

"Right. Once the trains are built, all the cars and buses, ten or twenty thousand, get parked in the Undercity, as a way to drive the people down these evacuation ramps, out the side of the Mountain."

"Will people even part with their cars to start using MagLev trains? I know I'm never giving up my Corvette."

"Maybe they'll surprise us. The younger generation is far better than we give them credit for. Our parents created the problem, so they started things like the E.P.A. 'Give a hoot, don't pollute' was a thing. Then our generation started fixing the problem, but we are still handing our kids a broken planet. It's them, today's young people, who will be remembered for saving the world."

"Okay, we're divided on what they will do, but that's the point, right? It's in their hands. Let's do the best we can with what we have now."

"Agreed. So what other concerns?"

"I've got one. The magma rises up, we get the people out. So, what happens when the magma reaches the city?"

"We have to assume it's a lost cause."

"Not necessarily—in these scans, right here, see how under the city cavern, there are these miles of twisting, turning magma tubes? Can we use those somehow?"

"What if we drill out deliberate weak points to divert the magma out of the mountain before it floods the city?"

"Like the spillway on a dam. But where ... ?"

The four pored over the scans.

"Have geodynamics find the right spot, somewhere that will release the flow of magma in a safe way down the volcano's slopes but in a way that doesn't make the city collapse above it."

"Any other concerns?" The room was silent for a moment.

"One. How do we keep curious people from exploring the escape tunnels? Prying open these things in their homes and offices ... what are they? Like ... heat-resistant manhole covers?"

"We'll have to think about it. Hide their true purpose in plain sight. Put them everywhere. Present them as something else entirely, something innocuous."

"Or something special, a fixed object. Something the people can respect, or ... or revere."

"Then we wipe all record of the tunnels from the plans and publicly release that they're sacred markers, or some such."

"And we should distract them from looking down all the time. . . with some tunnels that go upward, we should make those part of the plans, give the people a sense of adventure. Anything to keep them looking up. 'Keep looking up,' that's what we should tell folks."

"We can have the great astrophysicists, astronauts, celebrities, even teachers ... start using that phrase now, make it an ... adventurer's mantra, of sorts. Keep looking up."

"Oh, and we already have plans to cut in a huge freight elevator to the Mons rooftop, where the greenhouses will go. We could outfit those elevators to carry large groups of passengers. Another escape route?"

"I like it. But how would we make that interesting enough for people to go up top?"

"Some kind of lure, maybe? We'll have to think on it."

One thumped the table with a free hand. "Offer them free food."

A laugh rippled around the table.

"Speaking of food, I don't think well on an empty ... "

The video ended. The screen showed the words:

END OF LINE.

Andie blinked, a thousand thoughts cris-crossing that brilliant mind. The room was quiet as Eliza gave Andie a moment to digest. She turned up the lights.

"That was . . . wow, yeah."

"Right? Answers a lot of our questions. But still, secrecy makes sense."

Andie nodded. "So, about that secrecy . . . "

"Why all the cloak and dagger here and now?" Eliza offered.

"Yeah, why go to so much trouble to share this with me? Couldn't we just broadcast it on tonight's news?"

"You're idealistic. These things are best guided by realists, or . . . even pessimists."

"What does that mean?"

"People would quickly start to question what other projects have been going on right under their noses." Eliza made a dramatic flair with a sweep of both hands.

"So . . . what you're telling me is that one set of escape tunnels wasn't the only thing the builders made that isn't common knowledge."

"Now you're getting a broader perspective. The boring companies never stopped working; they still have a hundred years of work ahead of them. The mountain's ongoing tremors are mistaken for ripples in the mantle, but most often, it's us." Eliza paused, then went on.

"So when you gave us your footage of the *Reaction Chamber*, it changed everything. Even now, and going clear back to the first settlements . . . we protect whatever the public isn't ready for. We have to anticipate human nature, good and bad. So our legacy here will continue for . . ."

"Always."

"I couldn't have said it better. Always."

"I'm thinking big, Ms. Eliza," Andie said with a laugh. "Isn't that what Stein always challenged us to do?"

"Smartest one in the room," Eliza said with a knowing smile.

"I don't think I can claim that title, not today," Andie said. "Is there anything else you want to tell me?"

"I think that's enough for one day, don't you?" she said.

Andie gave a little head shake, shaking loose another cobweb in their brain. Eliza watched Andie process more high-speed thoughts.

"How did you get them to let me watch the video in the first place?"

"Being me . . . has advantages." Eliza said back. "I made it a condition of taking a desk job that I could build a five-member brain trust, my team, who would have access to certain . . . truths . . . as we determine what's best for humanity on our fair world."

Andie and Ares watched Eliza, waiting for her to continue.

"You are one of the five. You thrive on challenges, and your passion for science? Well, I trust in that."

"Who are the others?"

"I think you've only met one of the other four. The rest, maybe you'll meet them someday . . . or maybe never."

"So who's the one I know? Can you tell me that?"

Eliza shook her head. "My little secret . . . for now," she said, leaning over Andie's shoulder.

Eliza brought up a command prompt and swiftly deleted the file from the network. A hard delete. Unrecoverable, irreversible. Before Andie could react, the file was gone.

"But what did you . . . ? Wha . . . ?"

"Secrets, Andie. The world isn't ready to know some things. And now, you and I and Jackson are the only ones who have that little piece of the puzzle. I imagine the real reason I got permission to show you that video, is that Jackson trusts you."

"Trusts me? Well, he's a complete jerk for not trusting Mister Stein. You can tell him I said that."

"Tell him yourself," she said, gesturing at a ceiling-mounted camera. "He's watching that camera feed, I'm sure."

Andie's jaw dropped, cheeks flushed bright red. "I'm sorry, I didn't—" then they straightened up and exhaled, getting composed.

Eliza chuckled. "You don't have to be someone's bestie in order to work well together, right?"

"That . . . is for sure. I had a gut feel he knew what he was doing, telling us we couldn't go back into the Mountain. Made me want to go even more."

Eliza shrugged. "You'd have to ask him. I think he didn't want you running back into the burning building, so to speak. But I also think he knew he couldn't stop you, not with the Lauryna in your pocket."

"You know about the Lauryna? Wow. Uh . . . I guess it's a good thing we turned it in during the reclama—"

"No, you didn't. You parked it at one of the vehicle repair alcoves on the north flank of Pavonis Mons, alongside Endurance. The rover is still there, safe and sound. Don't worry, your secret is safe with me. Well, with us." She gestured at the camera. "I think we have trust, don't we?"

"Yes," Andie said at length, wondering just how many bugs and trackers were scattered across the seven cities for Eliza to remain this well-informed all the time.

"By the way, your friend, the one in that tank . . . she's much better at covering her tracks than Stein—we have no clue where her treads have taken her. East, is it?"

"No idea what you're talking about."

"Uh huh," Eliza said. "Speaking of trust . . . deleting that file was the price I had to pay for Jackson to let you see it in the first place."

Eliza turned toward the small glass bubble in the ceiling and gave a big, obvious thumbs-up.

Andie considered the camera. "How can you work like that? Camera in your face all the time?"

"Oh, that? Just you watch." She crossed the room, dragging a chair behind her.

Eliza stepped up, slipped out of one high heel, and swung it like a dirk in some medieval action movie. Both the glass dome and camera shattered nicely and sprinkled down in small pieces.

She slipped her foot back into her high-heeled shoe, brushed a few bits of glass from her suit jacket, and stepped down. Sighing in satisfaction, she slid the chair neatly back in place.

The cat looked up at the busted camera.

"Won't he just have another one installed?"

"Well, I'll probably destroy that one too. We'll see who rusts first."

Andie blurted out a laugh. They grinned heartily at each other.

"Besides, I'm certain he thinks I'm a jerk too," Eliza continued, "but that's what he needs–competence, not kiss-ups. Since we don't know when we'll be able to head home, being amazing every day is our only option."

"Yeah . . ." Andie had a surprising surge of sadness, thinking about the Mons-Plex, Mons High School, the pocket, her home, Chucklehead . . . so far beyond reach. Her eyes clouded up as she thought about the hamster.

Eliza was still smiling. "So what's next for you?"

Andie shrugged, wiping a tear away. "Back to school next week—Nerus High, so I'm a Legionnaire now, I guess. Dr. Kumar is still my AP chemistry teacher somehow, but I worry about Mister Stein—he hasn't been picked up at any schools yet. He's finishing a book, giving tons of interviews, and is starting work on some screenplay thing, I think. But you probably know that's not his thing."

"Mm hm. I have a hunch everything is gonna work itself out," Eliza said in a low tone.

Andie nodded, stuck out a hand, not wanting to seem too casual. Eliza clapped hands and gave a smile with a knowing nod. They held on a moment longer, making solid eye contact, then let go.

The cat jumped down from the table.

* * *

Moments later, Andie and Ares stepped out into the CityGlow™ sunshine and crossed the open plaza toward the *Caesar's Terrazzo* hotel and casino resort.

A 'ping' grabbed Andie's attention, a message invite to sign up for new science elective offerings at Nerus High.

"No way!" Andie blurted out loudly, seeing Steinheiser's name next to the course titles. A random couple stopped mid-sentence and looked up.

"Ares, check it out." Andie held the tablet down for the cat to see. "Oh yeah, your eyes are for finding prey in the dark. Sorry."

The cat mewed something Andie didn't understand.

The man and woman glanced at each other, then shuffled quickly away.

"Mister Stein is teaching at Nerus High now, can you believe it? Oooo, I can't wait to tell Ric and Sitara. And Reillee, and . . ." Andie paused, then nodded. "Everything is gonna work itself out."

Andie paused. Wait a second . . .

Andie turned and looked back up at the building they had just left. The top three floors were mirrored; Andie saw nothing moving inside. No former student of Stein's was visible there either, looking sharp in her black, pinstriped business suit, helping humanity thrive across the Seven Cities . . . all day, every day.

Andie gave a knowing nod . . . just in case someone was watching.

The cat looked up. Was that a little grin at the corners of his mouth?

Nah . . .

Andie re-read the message, then looked down at their furry friend. "He's only teaching electives, total class size is twelve students—so, I'm guessing it's a small room? You might be lounging without any sunlight."

The cat considered this.

"Mrrrr..Meeeew?" he said.

"I know. You're always hungry."

Then the two set off toward home.

A classroom for a dozen students . . . it could work. They would adapt, regardless of the room's look or feel.

A teacher and his students just needed a little space.

----- THE END -----

Acknowledgments

Prof. Donald Anderson, Editor Emeritus, *War, Literature & the Arts*. Though I do too much *telling* in my work (his admonition: don't tell us; *show* us), he taught us the two most important things in storytelling. First, write from your *gut*. Not your heart, not your mind; they'll be all over the place—the true story comes from your gut. Second, set up your characters, put them in a situation, and *tell the truth*. That's all. Whatever your characters are destined for, whatever trials they must face and how they stumble or grow along the way, the absolute best any storyteller can hope to do is enunciate truth.

Nathan Lowell. Author of the "Trader's Tale from the Golden Age of the Solar Clipper" series (Quarter Share, Half Share, Full Share, et al.), Mr. Lowell showed us that you don't need an interplanetary war, alien invasion, or superhuman abilities to craft a compelling story. Those other art forms are compelling, but in retrospect, sometimes all it takes is a good man who knows how to brew an excellent urn of coffee to get things rolling right. Nerus City honors Mr. Lowell's work celebrating the common man, with every flaw and insignificant-seeming contribution. These are the people whose tales are most worth sharing.

Bob Gallo, PADI Master Instructor Extraordinaire, for teaching my dive buddy Mark and me how to not die, as we earned our Open Water SCUBA certifications in the sparkling waters of Guam. Also, credit to him for teaching us the importance of the compact-80 and knowing where your dive buddy is at all times. Future variants of these basic teachings will be critical to humanity for generations.

Douglas Adams. Author of the five books in the Hitchhiker's Guide to the Galaxy trilogy, and his other excellent titles. Shamelessly quoted, referenced, and thieved by so many through decades of science fiction as an art form, and rightly so! I hope you, dear reader, can appreciate the Easter eggs stashed here among these chapters--it's all done with love and great respect for Mr. Adams' fine works. Fine works indeed.

Dr. Neil DeGrasse Tyson: from this high school Astronomy teacher to the man many of us regard as *the* Astronomy teacher to our modern world, thank you! Dr. Tyson, who has reached the whole planet through his many works, I ask his forgiveness as I take liberties and used his name in vain after a lifetime of inspiration . . . may we all 'keep looking up.'

Chersti Nieveen, editor on this project. She showed me the way to take a 'day in the life' *episodic* approach and turn it into a smooth-flowing story. She helped me with both characters and storytelling; I'm grateful!

All members of the **332nd Air Expeditionary Wing**, the "Red Tails," past and present: since its inception, such a proud legacy! Starting with the *Tuskegee Airmen*, the top-tier World War II bomber escorts, down through the wing's expeditionary mission in our modern age—my fellow Red Tails—brothers, sisters, there is always a seat for you at my table.

To the real Andie, Trace, Aiyana, Ric, Reillee, Chuumock, Tanya, and Ares: these amazing individuals each deserve a story of their own, whether here and now on Earth . . . or in the 2350s on Mars. You inspire! You are valued, you are appreciated. I see you! Each of these amazing individuals will continue to inspire us in Mars High School, Book Two: *The Legionnaires*, with a special focus on Aiyana's journey.

And finally, the **Diné**. I mean nothing but respect as I share a future world partially viewed through the noble eyes of the Navajo. Aiyana is one of your daughters; her inner peace, acceptance of others, and celebration of traditions are my homage to you. If I have given any offense or committed any error, I ask your pardon. You are the people.

About the Author

J. Sandrock grew up traveling the world in an Air Force family, graduating from the American Embassy School in Delhi, India. Sandrock lives in Salt Lake City, Utah with his beloved bride Mindi. His three kiddos Jacob, Rachel, and Paige are his forever pride and joy.

Following in his father's and grandfather's footsteps, he served 24 years wearing Air Force Blue, with assignments in Germany, Italy, Guam, several U.S. states, and deployments to the Middle East. Upon retirement in 2014, he taught high school science for seven years (Earth Science & Astronomy) in one of Utah's largest high schools, where he expanded the Astro program to become one of the finest in the state.

Graduates of Granger High Astronomy are reminded of their two remaining homework assignments: the first is due when humanity sets foot on Mars, and the second, when Comet Halley returns in 2061.

To all who wonder what awaits us beyond the horizon . . . may you live long, and prosper.